Praise for *Ge.* o

Also available from Elle Kennedy

Out of Uniform
Hot & Bothered
Hot & Heavy
Feeling Hot
Getting Hotter

Off-Campus
The Deal
The Mistake
The Score
The Goal

Outlaws
Claimed
Addicted
Ruled

***

A full list of Elle's print titles is available on her website
www.ellekennedy.com

Getting Hotter

Out of Uniform

Elle Kennedy

Author's Note

I am SO excited to be re-releasing the *Out of Uniform* series! For those of you who haven't read it before, this was one of my earlier series. It also happens to be one of my favorites, probably because this is when I realized how much I love writing bromances!

Seriously. The boy banter in these books still cracks me up to this day. You see more and more of it as the series progresses, and by the later books there are entire chapters of crazy conversations between my sexy, silly SEALs.

For new readers, you should know that a) you don't have to read the stories in order, though characters from previous books do show up in every installment. And b) the first six stories are novellas (20-35,000 words), while the last four are full-length novels (85,000+ words).

I decided to release the novellas as two books featuring three stories each (*Hot & Bothered, Hot & Heavy*) making the total books in the series SIX rather than the original ten.

Getting Hotter is the second of the full-length novels.

***PLEASE NOTE: This book has NOT changed, except for some minor editing and proofreading. There are grammatical differences and some (minor) deleted/added lines here and there, but for the most part, there is *no new content*. If you've previously purchased and read *Getting Hotter*, then you won't be getting anything new, aside from a gorgeous new cover!

So, I hope you enjoy the new cover, the better grammar, and the hot, dirty-talking SEALs who to this day hold such a big place in my heart!

Love,

Elle

Chapter One

"C'MON, GIRL, DON'T BE HATIN'. JUST GIMME YOUR DIGITS. I PROMISE you won't regret it."

Miranda Breslin slammed a bottle of Coors on the counter and flashed a polite smile at the very young, very cocky guy who'd been hitting on her for the past twenty minutes. "Sorry, not interested," she shouted over the techno beat blaring out of the club's speakers.

Her persistent suitor rested his elbows on the counter and leaned in close. "Aw, don't be like that, girl."

Thanks to the seizure-inducing strobe lights zigging and zagging from every direction, she could only make out bits and pieces of the guy's appearance—shaved head, impressive body. But great abs aside, the guy couldn't have been a day older than twenty-one, and his vocabulary was abysmal. Her six-year-old twins spoke more eloquently than this dude.

"Enjoy the rest of your night," she said. And then she promptly extricated herself from the situation, untying her short black apron as she moved away.

She was due for a break, but when she saw the crowd gathered at the other end of the counter, she stifled a groan. Alex, the other bartender on duty, clearly had his hands full with a group of inebriated women decked out in shiny clubbing outfits.

When he noticed her retying her apron, he gave a firm shake of the head. "I've got this, hon!" he yelled over the deafening music. "Take your break!"

Sidling up to him, she moved her lips close to his ear. "You sure you can handle this rush?"

Alex gestured for her to go, his unruffled expression telling her he'd be fine. No surprise—absolutely nothing fazed the guy. She'd only been working at OMG for four months, not long enough to get overly chummy with any of the other bartenders, but she did have a soft spot for Alex, with his spiky blond hair and perpetual laughter.

Rounding the counter, she stepped into the throng of bodies filling every square inch of the dark nightclub. There was a small employee break room past the restrooms, but getting there required some effort. Since it was Friday night, the club was packed, and she had to push and wiggle her way through the crowd like she was playing an annoying game of Twister. By the time she made it to the back, she was sweaty, annoyed and reeking of the awful cologne one of the men out there must have bathed in.

She'd just neared the break room when someone grabbed her from behind.

"Where you rushing off to, girl? I thought we were connecting."

Miranda's shoulders stiffened. She slapped the intrusive hand off her arm and turned to scowl at the guy from the bar. "I told you, I'm not interested."

"But I am," he protested, the glazed look in his eyes leaving nothing ambiguous about his level of sobriety.

His gaze rested on the cleavage spilling from her low-cut red tank, then traveled down the length of her legs, bare beneath her black miniskirt. The tank-skirt combo was her "uniform", and as the guy leered at her, she mentally composed a letter to the club's owner stating all the reasons why female employees should not be asked to dress like ho-bags.

"C'mon, just gimme your digits," he pleaded.

Jeez, again with the digits? This kid was relentless. Might be time to dust off the old Erin Brockovich speech.

"Look," she said through clenched teeth, "I'm not—"

A raspy male voice cut in. "Beat it, buddy."

One second the flirty kid was in front of her, the next he was gone, scurrying away like he was being chased by the cops.

Miranda didn't need to turn around to know who was standing behind her. While other women might have been overflowing with gratitude, she was just mildly irritated.

"I'm not going to say thank you," she grumbled. "I already told you I can take care of myself."

Seth Masterson stepped into view, his metallic gray eyes filled with the mocking glint she'd come to expect. "I know you can."

She arched her brows. "Yeah? So then why'd you interfere?"

He shrugged. "My way got rid of that moron quicker."

Despite herself, Miranda found it hard not to laugh. Yep, Seth's "way" was extremely efficient. All he had to do was level some poor dude with that lethal stare of his, and—*poof*—the unwanted admirer disappeared. Seth had been pulling this same magician's act for more than three months now, scaring off any man who dared to flirt with her. What started out as a quick stop-by a couple times a week, just to "check how she was doing", had become almost a nightly routine.

Now when she worked a shift, she was surprised if Seth *didn't* show up.

Any other woman might have swooned from all the attention, but Miranda wasn't one of them. Having her own personal bouncer was more aggravating than comforting. Nope, Seth Masterson didn't provide her with even an ounce of *comfort*. If anything, he achieved the opposite effect, unsettling her with his commanding presence. He had *bad boy* radiating from every sexy, muscular inch of him, from the perpetual beard growth on his face, to his scruffy dark hair, to the piercing gray eyes that were forever undressing her.

"Like I said, I could've handled it. Now if you'll excuse me, it's time for my dinner break." She brushed past him and strode into the break room.

Seth, of course, followed her right in. One thing she'd discovered about him? He didn't play by any rules, a trait she found ironic considering he was in the military, where rules were a way of life.

Sighing, she walked over to the small fridge across the room. She grabbed a bottle of water, uncapped it, and chugged half as she headed for the ratty plaid couch that had seen better days.

Seth lingered near the door, watching her with disapproval. "Dinner is a bottle of water?"

"Dinner was fish sticks and French fries three hours ago. I won't be hungry for a couple more hours." She stretched out her legs and stared up at the cracked plaster ceiling, letting out an aggravated breath. "Why do you keep coming by, Seth? You don't need to check up on me every frickin' night."

"I'm not here to check up on you."

"Oh really? So Missy called off her guard dog?"

"Nope. Mom's still insisting I keep an eye on you."

She held back a groan. She loved her former boss to death, but Missy Masterson, God bless her soul, had no idea what she'd unleashed when she'd asked her son to keep tabs on Miranda.

At first, she'd appreciated the gesture—the move from Vegas to San Diego had been jarring, and it was always difficult to adapt to a new city, especially when you didn't know a single person there. But now that she was more settled, she no longer needed Seth Masterson to hold her hand.

In fact, that was the last thing she wanted. Because another discovery she'd made about the man? When he touched her, she turned into a pile of hot, gooey mush.

"Well, tell Missy that while I appreciate everything she's done, I'm doing just fine."

Miranda took another sip of water, then set the bottle on the table by the couch and bent down to unlace her black sneakers. The club owner might demand the female staff display whatever T&A they could, but he didn't begrudge them comfortable footwear. Still, she'd only been tending bar for three hours and already her feet were killing her.

As she kicked off her shoes and began to massage her right foot, she saw Seth's gray eyes following the movements of her hands. His expression took on that smoldering gleam, and then he left his perch by the door and approached the couch. His strides were long, predatory.

"Not doing as fine as you claim, huh?" he taunted.

She rolled her eyes. "My feet hurt. My life, on the other hand, is *just fine*."

The couch cushions bounced as he flopped down beside her. Instantly, the familiar scent of him wafted in her direction. Aftershave, a hint of pine and the faint traces of smoke. Of course he was a smoker. A bad boy had to have his vices, after all.

She dug her thumbs into the arch of her foot, knowing the ache in her feet didn't bode well for the rest of the night. She had four hours left in her shift. Four hours of running up and down that bar catering to the Friday-night crowds. And tomorrow she'd be in the dance studio from morning until late afternoon. Her poor feet were definitely going to revolt if she kept this up.

"What's wrong?"

Seth's voice interrupted her thoughts. She glanced over, frowning. "Nothing's wrong."

"You just groaned. A weary, life-sucks-ass type of groan."

She blinked. "I did?" When he nodded in confirmation, she let out a sigh. "I was just thinking how I have to be at the studio at ten in the morning tomorrow and how much my feet are going to hate me for it. Tending bar all night and then standing en pointe all day is no piece of cake."

"No, I imagine it isn't."

He sounded genuine, not a hint of condescension in his voice, and Miranda's eyebrows rose. "Really? You're not going to roll your eyes and tell me I know nothing about real pain? You know, 'cause I'm not a badass SEAL like you?"

"Trust me, babe, I've got nothing but the utmost admiration for dancers. Once when I was a kid, I sat there watching my mom soak her feet after three back-to-back performances." Seth blanched. "The way her feet looked is comparable to any battle wound I've come across."

Miranda burst out laughing. She didn't doubt it. People often had an idealistic view of dancers as beautiful, magical creatures, but one look at a dancer's feet and that bubble of perfection was liable to burst. Calluses, blisters, cracked toenails, red, flaking skin…frankly, it was just plain gross.

For a moment it surprised her that Seth knew what actually lay behind the curtain, until she remembered that he'd pretty much grown up backstage at the iconic Paradise Theater on the Vegas Strip. His mother had been the star of the show for twenty years before retiring, and now worked as the head choreographer. Missy also happened to be Miranda's mentor and staunchest supporter; for a girl who'd grown up without a mom, Miranda had been utterly grateful to have someone like Missy in her life. After Miranda's grandmother died and left her a small inheritance, Missy was the one who encouraged her to buy the dance school in San Diego, and it was the best decision she'd ever made.

"I should get back to work." She leaned forward to slip into her sneakers, only to jump when she felt Seth's hand on her arm.

Her breath caught. She found herself going still. It had been so very easy to shrug out of that young guy's grip in the hall, but here, with Seth, she couldn't bring herself to push him away.

"How long are we going to fight it, Miranda?" His voice was rough, his expression darkening with what she could only describe as sinful challenge.

She gulped. Ignored the flashes of heat rippling over her flesh. "Fight what?" she asked, feigning ignorance.

He laughed, slow and deep. "You're really gonna pretend it's not there? The chemistry between us?"

"We don't have chemistry."

And yep, she was a filthy liar. She and Seth had so much chemistry they could open their own laboratory. Or teach a college science seminar. Or—

He cut into her thoughts once more. "I've been very patient up until now. Pretending not to notice the way your nipples get hard whenever I'm around. And how your cheeks get all flushed and sexy. And don't get me started on the way you look at me." His voice grew even raspier. "Those big hazel eyes of yours eat me up like I'm a big, juicy steak, baby."

Nipples hardening? Check.

Cheeks scorching? Check.

Eating Seth Masterson up with her eyes? Well, she couldn't tear her gaze from the sensual curve of his mouth or the strong line of his jaw, so yeah, might as well check that off too.

Even though Seth must have noticed all three responses, Miranda decided to keep playing dumb. It was the only way to maintain some semblance of control over a conversation that had swiftly and unexpectedly gotten out of hand.

"Big, juicy steak?" she echoed dryly. "Someone thinks highly of himself."

He just laughed. "We both know you're attracted to me."

"Oh, we both know that, do we?"

"And I'm attracted to you," he said with a shrug. "But unlike you, I'm not gonna bat my eyelashes like a Disney princess and act like I don't want to get you naked."

She swallowed again. Harder this time. Her mouth was so dry she felt like she was swallowing sand, but she didn't dare reach for her water bottle because she knew Seth would comment and attribute her sudden thirst to the effect he had on her.

"I have to get back to work." Wiggling out of his grasp, she stumbled to her feet.

But he was equally quick. He stood up and caught her around the waist with one muscular arm. He didn't yank her against him, just rested one hand on the small of her back and used the other to tip her chin up so she had no choice but to look at him.

"Say the word, Miranda."

Her heart was beating so fast she could barely hear her own voice over the frantic hammering. "What word?"

"Yes."

"Yes what?" she stammered.

He gave that mocking chuckle of his. "That's the word—*yes*. And I want you to say it. I want you to give me the green light so I can finally put my hands all over you the way I've been fantasizing about for months now."

"Seth…" It was meant to be a warning, but his name slipped out on a breathy whisper, sounding very much like an invitation.

"Come on, baby, I've been such a good boy." His gray eyes gleamed with sex and danger. "Put us both out of our misery."

She stared into those stormy-silver depths, feeling her resolve crumbling. Losing herself in his seductive spell. God, it had been so long since she'd had sex. *So* long.

He aimlessly stroked her lower back. "Miranda…" He trailed off, moistening his bottom lip with the sexy drag of his tongue, and then he leaned in close so that his lips hovered over her ear. "I want to fuck you."

A shiver ran through her. Oh crap. Oh no, no, no. She was *not* allowed to get turned on.

Too late.

Okay, she was beyond turned on. The pressure between her legs was unbearable, her nipples so hard they could cut glass, her breathing completely off-kilter.

Enough. She couldn't keep letting herself respond to this man. Seth was a bad boy to the core. He did what he wanted, when he wanted. He had no sense of decency, no filter that monitored the sarcastic or overtly sexual remarks that came out of his mouth. He wore all black and smoked cigarettes and never shaved. In other words—he was trouble.

And sure, that air of danger he radiated would have turned her on when she was a teenager, but guess what, it was the last thing she wanted nowadays. She'd already thrown her life away for one dangerous bad boy—and she'd gotten knocked up at eighteen as a reward.

The memory of Trent was all it took to banish her rising desire.

Squaring her shoulders, she pushed his hand off her waist and took a step backward. "What you want makes no difference," she said quietly. "I won't get involved with you."

Resignation fluttered across his face. "What's your reason this time?"

She set her jaw defiantly. "Same one it always is. I'm a mom."

When he blanched slightly at the M-word, she let out a wry laugh. Oh, for Pete's sake, why hadn't she just led with that instead of letting this conversation drag on for far longer than necessary?

In the four months she'd known Seth, he hadn't shown the slightest interest in her kids, and if the subject did happen to come up, he usually donned a blank look and acted indifferent to everything she said. She didn't know why, but for Seth, children seemed to be on par with root canals and canine fashion shows, both of which he'd expressed extreme dislike for.

"I don't have time to fool around with you," she went on. "Or anyone, for that matter. Between raising two six-year-olds, working five days a week at the studio and part-time here at the bar, I barely have time to read the paper, let alone have sex."

To her aggravation, Seth grinned. "That just proves how much you need me."

"Oh really?"

"If reading a newspaper takes priority over having sex, then clearly you've never had your world rocked."

"I don't need any rocking in my world. I get motion sickness." She laced up her sneakers, then headed for the door.

He trailed after her. "Fine, I'll let this go. If that's what you want."

"It is." A rush of relief flooded her belly. Thank God. Fighting off Seth's advances the past few months had been much harder than she'd ever admit.

"Don't look so happy." He smirked. "I meant I'd let it go for *tonight*."

Crap. She should've known it wouldn't be that easy.

Seth blocked her path before she could open the door, running a hand through his messy hair. His hair was short, but definitely not the military cut every man in San Diego seemed to have. Black locks often fell onto his forehead and curled behind his ears, and she couldn't count the number of times her fingers had tingled with the urge to smooth back those unruly strands.

"When's your next shift?" he asked.

"Monday."

"Eight to close?"

It didn't surprise her that he knew the exact time of her shift. God knew he came to the club often enough.

"Hey, I have an idea," she said with a big fake smile. "Maybe you can go somewhere else on Monday. The Tavern or the Sand Bar, maybe Hot Zone—ooh, there's this new club on 4th that you might like. I heard it attracts a lot of young women looking for a good time…"

When she flashed him a *how-awesome-is-that* look, he simply laughed it off. "I'm not looking for a random lay. Trust me, if I wanted to get laid?" He lowered his voice to a smoky pitch and snapped his fingers. "I could get laid just like that. But see, that's not what I'm after."

A sigh lodged in her chest. "What are you after, Seth?"

"You."

Equal parts arousal and irritation pleaded for her attention. Ignoring both, she released her breath and crossed her arms over her chest. Seth's gaze immediately rested on her cleavage, more pronounced now that her pose was pushing her breasts up. She promptly let her arms dangle to her sides.

"I don't have time to play games with you," she muttered. "I have too much on my plate at the moment, and even if I wasn't busy, I still wouldn't say yes. I'm a mother, first and foremost. My kids are my life."

He rolled his eyes. "I'm not asking you to put the rugrats up for adoption."

"No, you're just asking me to pretend they don't exist and launch myself into some whirlwind sexual affair with you. How will that even work? You're going to sneak into my apartment after I tuck Sophie and Jason in and ravish me while they're sleeping next door? You'll pay for a babysitter while you and I go to some sleazy motel?" She shook her head. "For the millionth time, I'm not interested."

He rewarded her speech with his trademark smirk. "Has anyone ever told you that you look sexy when you lie?"

"What does that even mean?" she mumbled. "Whatever. Don't answer. In fact, don't say another word."

She brushed past him and yanked on the door handle. Out in the hall, the drum and bass bounced off the walls and vibrated beneath her feet. Perching her hands on her hips, she turned to scowl at Seth.

"I'm serious. Quit coming here every night. Quit hitting on me. Quit acting like being my former boss's son gives you some kind of say in my life."

As usual, he seemed unfazed by the rejection. Stepping closer, he brought those tempting lips to her ear again, his hot breath fanning over her skin. "See you Monday night, Miranda."

"Seth—"

Holy crap, had he just licked the shell of her ear? He *had*. And now his lips were closing over her earlobe.

A jolt of pure desire hit her hard and fast. Before she could lay into him for his sheer presumption, he was moving away.

"You've got my cell number," he reminded her. "Call me when you're ready."

When. Not *if*.

Presumptuous jerk.

As her heart pounded up a storm in her chest, she watched Seth stride off, angry with herself for noticing how incredible his ass looked in his black jeans. Angry at him for walking away without once looking back, while she was standing there like a slack-jawed moron, unable to take her eyes off him.

"Who was *that*?" The breathy female voice came from the long line in front of the ladies' room.

Miranda met the eyes of a young blonde in a gold micromini and black halter top. "That was our resident troublemaker."

The blonde grinned. "My kind of trouble. I'd trade my firstborn for even ten minutes with that hottie."

A few of the other women in line overheard the remark and laughed, but Miranda only managed a weak smile. Being around Seth Masterson was utterly exhausting. She was forever on guard, waiting for his next seductive ambush, steeling herself against the sexual magnetism he possessed in spades.

You have a problem, Miranda Rose Breslin.

She totally did, didn't she? Why was she always attracted to bad boys? Those kinds of men were all well and good in the movies, but in real life you had a better chance of teaching a dog to send an email than taming a bad boy.

She needed to do something about this silly schoolgirl attraction, pronto. Maybe she ought to lock herself in her bedroom tonight and put her vibrator to good use. A few orgasms and she'd be thinking, *Seth who?*

Seth Masterson, that's who, and you're an idiot if you think your battery-operated boyfriend will make you forget it.

Oh for the love of…was that Seth's voice in her head?

Wonderful. The man was already shadowing her at work. Haunting her dreams. Starring in her fantasies. And now he was narrating her damn thoughts.

How on earth was she supposed to vanquish this attraction when even her own subconscious was against her?

With another sigh, Miranda headed back to the main floor of the club. And prayed that the deafening dance beat would pound all thoughts of Seth right out of her head.

Chapter Two

SETH HAD NEVER FELT MORE ON EDGE AS HE STALKED INTO THE DARK townhouse he shared with Dylan Wade. Seeing Miranda on a nightly basis was absolute torture, and tonight had been particularly brutal. Probably because it was the closest he'd ever come to battering through her defenses. He'd seen her pulse jumping in her throat when he'd told her he wanted her. Heard her intake of breath. Witnessed the haze of arousal in her eyes.

She could deny it all she wanted, but Seth knew when a woman was hot for him. And this one was. Big-time.

Which was a damn good thing, because he was hot for her too. He'd wanted Miranda Breslin from the second he'd laid eyes on her. They may have officially met four months ago when he helped her move into her new apartment, but he'd already been lusting over the woman for more than a year by then.

First time he'd seen her was backstage at the Paradise, which he pretty much considered his second home. Miranda had been sitting at a vanity table while a makeup artist hovered over her. She'd worn an elaborate costume studded with blue jewels and adorned with peacock feathers. The leotard-like outfit had offered a lot of cleavage and emphasized her long, shapely legs, made even longer and shapelier thanks to her sheer silver stockings and high-heeled dance shoes. She'd yet to put on her feathered headdress, so her long sable-brown hair had been slicked back in a tight bun, drawing his attention to her high cheekbones and intriguing features.

In that moment, Seth had never encountered a more appetizing sight. And yeah, maybe coming off a six-month-long deployment had intensified the punch of lust he'd experienced, but here he was, a year and a half later, and he still hadn't come close to meeting a woman who turned him on as much as Miranda did.

"You struck out, huh?"

He nearly jumped out of his own skin when the deep male voice cut through the silence of the house. He flicked the light switch in the kitchen to find his roommate leaning against the L-shaped counter.

As Seth's heartbeat steadied, Dylan nonchalantly sipped his glass of water like he had no care in the world.

He also had no stitch of clothing on.

Dylan's naked body was neither new nor off-putting—Seth had seen enough of it after three years of living with the guy, not to mention all those times they'd tag-teamed chicks. Without batting an eye, he stalked past the blond SEAL and opened the fridge door.

"Judging by the silence, you struck out hard," Dylan remarked, unconcealed amusement in his voice. "Don't you think it might be time to give up?"

"Never." He grabbed a bottle of water and twisted off the cap.

"What is it about that woman that gets your panties in a knot, man?"

He wasn't in the mood to be harassed, not when his cock ached so badly he could barely stay upright, but just as he was about to offer a sarcastic response, he noticed the genuine curiosity in Dylan's green eyes. Huh. Weird.

Instead of snapping, Seth simply shrugged. "She yells at me a lot. I kinda dig it."

Dylan burst out laughing. "I'm not sure what to do with that."

"Plus, she's hot as hell. Smart as a whip. Tough as nails. Doesn't take crap from anyone, especially me."

And apparently capable of turning him into a sappy loser who stood around at two in the fucking morning, listing his favorite qualities about a woman.

Dylan set his empty glass in the sink. "Is this a mommy complex thing?"

"What the fuck are you talking about?"

"I was watching that new talk show today, the one with those two dorky therapists who wear matching glasses. They did a whole segment about men having this subconscious need to marry their mothers. Well, not their mothers, but, you know, chicks who *remind* them of their moms."

Seth grinned. "I thought we decided you weren't gonna watch that crap anymore."

"I know, but ever since Oprah went off the air, there's shit-all on TV during the day. I was bored as fuck today."

"You poor thing."

"Anyway, it was interesting. And it totally applies to you. Mom's a showgirl, your new crush is a showgirl…"

He rolled his eyes. "It's not a crush. It's lust. I want to get her into bed. End of story."

"Whatever you say." Dylan strode toward the oak cabinets over the sink, opened one and started rummaging around.

"Besides, Miranda is nothing like my mother. They're both dancers, but their personalities couldn't be more different."

Hell, if Miranda had Missy Masterson's personality, Seth would run in the opposite direction. He loved his mom to death, but the woman was loud, flighty, and had no tact. She belonged on one of those reality shows where the women got very noisy and said things like "talk to the hand, bee-otch".

But despite her scatterbrained nature and garish sense of style, Missy was a good mother, a ferocious lioness when it came to her cub, and that loyalty and maternal pride extended to the dancers she now trained, Miranda included.

When his mom phoned and demanded he keep an eye on Miranda, Seth's first thought had been *hell yeah*. Moving to a new city was tough, and he'd been more than ready to show Miranda some Southern California hospitality. Helping her unpack some boxes, taking her out to a dinner or two, and then, if they happened to wind up in bed…well, he sure wouldn't be complaining. Except there was one thing he hadn't banked on—her stubborn determination to resist his advances.

And he also hadn't anticipated the baggage she came with.

Kids.

Two of them.

Christ. Like one wasn't bad enough.

As he sipped his water, he watched Dylan assemble a baffling collection of items. A box of crackers from the cabinet. A block of cheddar cheese from the fridge. Chocolate syrup. A knife, presumably for the cheese.

"Anyway, if you do have a thing for Miranda because she reminds you of Missy, that's perfectly healthy."

Seth sighed. "Do you realize you have absolutely no credibility right now?"

"Why not?" Dylan added a box of sugar cubes to the growing pile in his hands.

"Because you're walking around the kitchen with your cock flapping in the wind like the American flag."

"What can I say? My dick's a patriot."

Seth snorted. "Yeah, I'm sure you—okay, seriously, what the *fuck* are you gonna do with all that stuff?" he demanded as Dylan grabbed a pack of toothpicks and a saltshaker from the cupboard.

His roommate strode toward the kitchen doorway. "Some of this is for eating, the rest is props."

"Please tell me you have a girl in your room."

"Duh."

"Thank God, because I just pictured you drizzling chocolate syrup over your own balls, and almost threw up."

"Quit fantasizing about my balls. Pervert." Dylan tossed one final grin over his shoulder before disappearing.

Seth chugged the rest of his water. He left the kitchen, peeling off his black T-shirt as he made his way to the bathroom. Considering the relentless throbbing down below, he really ought to be taking a cold shower, but when he yanked his jeans off, the erection that popped up and slapped his abs was impossible to ignore.

Screw it. One way or another, he was getting some relief tonight.

Two minutes later, he dunked his head under the shower spray, letting the hot water slide down his face and neck. Rivulets coursed down his chest and dripped onto his hard cock, making it ache even more.

With a strangled groan, he leaned forward and rested his right forearm on the tiled wall. Then he brought his left hand to his groin and encircled his stiff shaft. At that first stroke, a shudder of anticipation racked his body.

Christ. He needed this. He hadn't been with a woman in two months, not since he'd picked up that cute tattooed redhead at a bar after another one of Miranda's rejections. He'd brought the woman home and screwed her all night long—and yet the encounter had left him entirely unsatisfied. He'd tried again a week later, cozying up to one of the ladies Dylan had come home with, but try as he might, he hadn't been able to muster up any enthusiasm. Or an erection.

Miranda, damn her, had ruined him for all other women. He needed to fuck her, ASAP, before he completely lost his mojo.

Every muscle in his body tightened as he worked his cock, jacking it in a fast, furious rhythm, moving his hips to match the frantic pace he'd set. Steam filled the shower stall. His breath came out in harsh pants.

An image of Miranda's tight ass flashed across his mind. Shit, she had a great ass. Looked particularly juicy in a pair of black tights. And her tits… His hand moved faster, mouth filling with saliva as he pictured those round, perky breasts bouncing beneath her tank top each time she walked up and down the bar counter.

The base of his spine began to tingle, all the blood in his body migrating south to pulse between his legs.

"Fuck," he mumbled. "Fuck, fuck, *fuck*."

He came with a ragged grunt that bounced off the walls. A rush of pleasure flew through him, and his hand went still as hot jets shot out of his dick and landed on the tub floor.

After he caught his breath, he uncurled his fist and let his hand fall to his side. Damn it. Not enough. He didn't feel an ounce of relief. The climax had been good, but his erection refused to subside. Stiff shaft, tight balls and, holy shit, but the anticipation was building again. The pressure that had just been blown to smithereens began to re-form into a knot of sexual desperation that throbbed in his groin.

"Son of a bitch," he mumbled.

Smothering a groan, he brought his hand back to his dick and got ready for a repeat performance.

Cursing Miranda Breslin the entire time.

"Sorry, honey. I was chatting with my roommate." Dylan entered his bedroom and flashed his trademark ladies'-man smile at the naked girl in his bed.

The blonde giggled as she studied the various food items in his hands. "You weren't kidding about the chocolate syrup."

"I never kid about chocolate syrup."

He sank on the edge of the bed and dropped the supplies on the patterned bedspread. Next to him, Kelly scooted closer and reached for the plastic Hershey's bottle. She popped the lid with her red-manicured fingers. "So what do you say, sailor? Feel like getting dirty?"

"Me? Uh-uh, baby doll, you're the one getting dirty."

He swiped the bottle from her hand and had her flat on her back in the blink of an eye, eliciting a delighted shriek from her pouty lips. He wrapped his fingers around the bottle, turned it upside down, and squeezed. Chocolate sauce trickled onto Kelly's bare breasts.

"And you'll be getting sticky," he rasped, dipping his head and letting his mouth hover over her delectable double-Ds. The girl was built like a Playboy Bunny, all tits and ass and long golden limbs.

Dylan licked a drop of syrup off the tip of one pearly-pink nipple. "And wet," he murmured. Another lick. "I think you'll get pretty wet too."

With a moan, she grabbed his hand and shoved it between her legs. "Already am," she said breathlessly.

He trailed his finger along her slick folds, then pushed it into her pussy. He groaned. Yep, she was wet. Very, very wet. He'd been so damn bored all damn day, but this, right now, totally made up for it. No-strings sex with a cute girl who didn't mind getting a little kinky? Could anyone say *living the dream*?

Kelly squealed as he grabbed hold of her thighs and shoved them apart. He lowered his head and brought his mouth to her core, flicking his tongue over her clit, the taste of chocolate and sex infusing his taste buds.

"Mmmm, tastes good," he murmured, working her tight channel with two fingers while he latched his mouth on that swollen nub and sucked.

Moaning, she rested her hands on his head to keep him in place. Right. Like he was going anywhere.

"More," she pleaded, rocking her hips faster.

He fingered her harder and rode out the resulting orgasm, his own arousal heightening at the sexy sounds she made and the way she moaned his name, over and over. When she grew still, a sleepy smile stretching across her face, he reached for the condom on the bedside table and tore open the package.

He'd just rolled the latex onto his erection when his cell phone rang.

"Shit," he said with a sigh. He grabbed the phone and studied the screen, his irritation transforming into a knot of worry. His brother's number was flashing on the display. And since it was three in the morning, he couldn't think of any reason Chris would be calling other than to deliver bad news.

With growing alarm, he signaled to Kelly that he needed to take the call, ignored her disappointed look, and pressed the Talk button.

"What's wrong?" he demanded in lieu of a greeting.

His brother's answering laughter brought a rush of relief. Chris wouldn't be laughing if he was calling with bad news.

"Nothing's wrong," Chris replied. "In fact, everything is very, very *right*, little brother!"

Loud music and muffled voices in the background made it difficult to hear what Chris was saying, but the guy was slurring, that was for sure.

"Are you drunk?" Dylan asked warily.

Next to him, Kelly slid off the bed and slipped into the white button-down he'd tossed on the chair. "I'm going to use the loo," she whispered before darting toward the bathroom.

"I might be a little drunk," Chris admitted. "But a man's gotta bust out the champagne when the woman he loves agrees to marry him!"

Dylan's heart sank to the pit of his stomach like a body chained to a cement block. Oh shit. Had he misheard, or had Chris really just said—

"I'm engaged!"

Yep, he'd heard right.

"To...uh, Claire?" he had to ask.

More laughter filled his eardrums. "Of course to Claire! Who the hell else would I propose to?"

Um, anyone other than that bitch?

Dylan kept the nasty thought to himself. His older brother didn't have a clue that he despised—absolutely *despised*—Chris's latest girlfriend. Fuck. Make that *fiancée*. Chris was actually marrying the woman. That snooty, judgmental, prissy, materialistic woman.

Lord, he'd hated Claire McKinley from the moment he'd met her.

Chris had brought her along on his last business trip to San Diego, and the three of them had gone to Dylan's favorite diner for lunch. Everything about Claire had rubbed him the wrong way—the self-righteous glint in her brown eyes, how she'd turned her nose up at the menu as if diner food was utterly beneath her, the way she'd tapped her French-manicured nails on the table like she was dying of boredom. By the time lunch was over, he'd felt like strangling her, and the next two visits hadn't gone any better.

He had no idea what his brother saw in that woman. She was attractive, sure, but good looks didn't make up for the whole being-a-total-bitch part.

Show your future sister-in-law some respect...

He blanched as the thought registered. Oh shit. She would be part of the *family* now.

"So that's it? Silence? No congratulations?"

Chris sounded so upset that Dylan gulped down a lump of guilt. "Sorry, I was just in shock." He injected a note of excitement into his tone. "Congrats, man. I can't believe my big brother is getting married. When's the big day?"

"We're thinking December."

Relief trickled through him. Eight months away. Hopefully Chris would change his mind long before then.

"So I don't care if you have to beg or bribe every naval officer on the base—you're getting leave to attend my wedding," Chris declared. "Can't have a wedding without the best man, right?"

"You sure you want me standing up there with you? I don't want to steal your thunder, you know, what with me being so good-looking and all."

Chris barked out a laugh. "I'm not worried. My future bride only has eyes for me."

Another blast of music rippled over the extension. It sounded Latin... salsa music?

"Where exactly are you?" Dylan demanded. "Don't tell me you proposed at a salsa club."

"No, I proposed at LeBlanc's," Chris answered, naming one of the fanciest restaurants in San Francisco. "But Claire wanted to celebrate, so she dragged me here. We're at that club you and I went to last time you came home."

Dylan's eyebrows shot up, even though Chris couldn't see him. He remembered that particular nightclub catering to a more rowdy crowd, like *Dirty Dancing*-style shit. Claire had chosen to go there? Seemed like the last place a goody-two-shoes snob like her would pick to celebrate an engagement.

"Anyway, I couldn't keep the news to myself, and I knew you'd be up, night owl that you are. We're going over to Mom's tomorrow morning to tell her."

He suppressed a sigh. And ten minutes after Chris and Claire left Shanna Wade's house, she'd be on the phone with her younger son, demanding to know when *he* was getting married. Dylan adored his mother, and the two of them had always been close, but no matter how many times he told her he wasn't ready to settle down, she never seemed to hear him.

"Well, at least this will give Mom something to do, planning the wedding," he told his brother. "She's been kind of bored and cranky ever since she quit her job."

There was a beat. "She was bored and cranky even when she had a job."

"True."

"Okay, well, it's late and I'm ready to forcibly remove Claire from the dance floor and take her home," Chris said with a touch of exasperation. "Just wanted to share the good news with my baby bro."

He rolled his eyes. Only a two-year age difference between him and Chris, yet his brother never failed to act the part of the perpetually wiser older sibling.

"Congratulations again," he said with fake enthusiasm. "Pass that along to Claire, too."

"I will. Talk soon."

After they hung up, Dylan turned his head in time to see Kelly saunter out of the bathroom.

"Everything okay?" The mattress bounced as she hopped back on the bed.

"My older brother's getting married."

She smiled, tucking a strand of blonde hair behind her ear. "An impending marriage is typically *good* news, sailor. You look like someone just died."

"Something did die," he grumbled. "My brother's manhood. Trust me, this chick he's about to saddle himself with for the rest of his life? She's god-awful."

"Speaking of manhood…" Kelly shot a pointed look at his cock, which had gone soft, the condom sagging off the tip.

Great. Now Claire McKinley was destroying his sex life. The way she would destroy Chris's future.

Okay, that was extreme. Chris's future wasn't destroyed. And to be fair, Chris had the tendency to be a goody-two-shoes snob himself. There was a reason Dylan didn't talk to his brother about his sex life. Some of the shit he was into, Chris would *never* understand, not in a million years.

"How about you put your womanly charms to use and get me nice and ready again?" Dylan drawled, licking his bottom lip as he met Kelly's blue eyes.

She licked her own lips, already peeling the unused condom off his shaft as she scrambled into position between his legs. She wrapped her lips around the blunt head of his cock, summoning a groan from deep in his chest. He closed his eyes, but not before he saw her reaching for the discarded Hershey's bottle.

All thoughts of his brother and Claire McKinley flew out of his head. Let Chris make the mistake of his life. Dylan would help the guy pick up the pieces later, when it all fell apart.

For now, the only thing he needed to concentrate on was the hot suction of Kelly's mouth as she sucked chocolate syrup off his dick.

Chapter Three

"In other news," the Channel 8 news anchor chirped, "the San Diego Zoo welcomed some new residents this morning. Piggy the Lioness gave birth to four healthy cubs. Mother and babies are resting comfortably, and zoo officials hope to reveal the new additions to the public in the next few weeks..."

Miranda tuned out the news report as she stood by the stove, flipping pancakes. Why on earth would anyone name a lioness *Piggy*? Shaking her head in bafflement, she slid a pancake onto the empty plate on the granite counter.

"Did you hear that, Mom? Piggy had *babies*!"

She glanced over her shoulder to smile at her daughter, who was sitting at the kitchen table braiding the hair of her favorite doll. "I did hear it," Miranda confirmed. "What do you say, should we go meet Piggy's babies?"

"Yeah! Let's go today!"

"We can't. Didn't you hear what the lady on the TV said? Piggy and her cubs are resting right now. We have to wait until the zoo says we can see them."

Sophie's bottom lip dropped out in a pout. "Fine."

Turning off the burners, Miranda carried two plates to the table and placed one in front of Sophie, the other by the empty chair. She headed back to the counter to grab her own plate, then joined Sophie at the table.

"Jase!" she called. "Breakfast!"

When her son didn't come skidding through the doorway, Miranda frowned. "What's he up to?" she asked her daughter.

Sophie's expression was too angelic to be trusted. "I dunno."

She narrowed her eyes. "Spill, missy. You know I don't like it when you two keep secrets."

"But, Mommy, I really don't know." Sophie had the nerve to bat her eyelashes, all liquid brown eyes and innocence.

Miranda was used to it. Her twins loved only one other person more than they loved their mom: each other.

Whatever bond they'd formed in utero had followed them right out of the womb—they always had each other's backs, no matter what, and Miranda could swear they possessed the ability to read each other's minds. Maybe even communicate telepathically. As toddlers, they could be in the same room for hours without saying a single word. They conducted entire conversations with their eyes, and if anyone tried to hurt one of them? The other came running to the rescue.

Normally, she loved the idea that her kids were so intrinsically connected, but at times like these, when one of them was up to no good, it was impossible to get them to turn on each other.

"Soph, if you don't tell me what Jason is doing, I might have to reconsider giving you a solo in the summer recital…"

Sophie tilted her head pensively, looking far too mature for her six years. "You wouldn't." Her voice was matter-of-fact. "Everyone gets a solo in the summer recital and I know you wanna see me do the solo 'cause I heard you tell Ginny that." She beamed. "*And* you told Ginny you loved my enfoozeeazim."

"Enthusiasm," Miranda corrected, choking down laughter. It figured that Sophie would see through the empty threat. The girl was way too smart for her own good.

"Here I am! Sorry! I was doin' stuff!"

Jason flew into the room with the same level of intense *enfoozeeazim* he threw into everything he did. The kid was a bundle of energy and always had been, unlike Sophie, who was more laid-back. Sophie was also capable of extreme focus, which she displayed during ballet class, while Jason's head was all over the place, bouncing from subject to subject in a whirlwind pace that made Miranda dizzy. Fortunately, his short attention span wasn't hurting him in school; the twins' kindergarten teacher assured her both kids were doing well. In fact, their reading and writing levels could even be considered advanced for their age.

"And what kind of *stuff* were you doing?" Miranda asked as she popped open the cap of the maple syrup bottle. She drew her trademark syrup happy face on Sophie's pancakes, which made her daughter grin, then did the same for her son, who was doing his damnedest to avoid her gaze.

"Kid stuff, Mom. You wouldn't understand."

She bit back another laugh. "Okay, let's go through the list. Will this *stuff* make me mad?"

"No," both twins said immediately.

"Is it dangerous?"

"No."

"Illegal?"

"No."

"Will it require me to clean up a huge mess?"

Hesitation.

Miranda sighed. "Come on, guys, you know how much I hate cleaning."

Sophie giggled. "Cleaning sucks."

"*Sucks*," Jason agreed, reaching for the glass of orange juice by his plate. He chugged the entire thing, then said, "Juice me."

A laugh flew out of her mouth. "Yes, sir."

As she poured him another cup of juice, she watched her daughter from the corner of her eye, making sure Sophie was actually eating her food instead of pushing it around on her plate the way she was sometimes prone to do.

"So this mysterious project of yours will only cost me a couple hours of cleaning?"

"We can try 'n clean first," Sophie offered, oh so gracious. "But if we do a pooey job, you can help."

"Sounds fair." She gave her son a pointed look. "If you pour any more syrup on that, you'll be eating pancake soup. Not to mention guaranteeing a visit to the dentist."

He hastily put down the syrup bottle. It was the D-word. Worked every time.

"…making its way northward. Hurricane Nora is not expected to hit the West Coast, but there is a chance it will reach California in the form of a tropical storm."

Miranda turned her attention to the small TV on the far end of the kitchen. The screen revealed a complicated-looking weather map with a bunch of squiggly lines that made no sense to her. But the weatherman standing to the side of the map seemed pretty damn excited, animatedly pointing to it as he continued to dole out information.

"Now, most Eastern Pacific hurricanes lose steam as they travel north and their winds are weakened, but this one is expected to have a larger impact than we're used to, folks. Starting tomorrow afternoon, we can expect powerful winds, torrential rain and extensive coastal, as well as inland, flooding…"

Sophie's head swiveled to the screen, her fork poised halfway to her mouth. "Oh no! What if we get washed away?"

"We won't get washed away," she assured her daughter.

Jason gasped. "What if there's a big tide wave—"

"Tidal wave," she corrected.

"—tidal wave, and it whooshes over here and then everything is *underwater*? How cool would that be?"

"That would *not* be cool at all," Miranda replied.

"But we would live under the sea!"

"Like *The Little Mermaid*," Sophie piped up. "*So* cool."

She decided not to point out that if a tidal wave hit the coast and wiped out Imperial Beach, they'd all be dead, but it was too early in the morning to get all morbid around six-year-olds. Instead, she quickly finished her pancakes, then tidied up the kitchen while the twins ate.

She wasn't too worried about this impending storm. Everyone kept making such a big deal about this hurricane, but Ms. Nora had been spinning her wheels for days now without dishing out any of the destruction she was supposed to. Miranda had stocked up on supplies the day after the weather network announced the storm was moving north, but she doubted San Diego or its surrounding areas would be affected. You always had to take what the weatherman said with a hundred grains of salt.

After breakfast, she helped the twins get ready, then left them to their own devices while she darted into her room to shower and change. She slipped into a pair of leggings, a sports bra and a tank top, tied her hair in a ponytail and shoved her feet into a pair of pink flip-flops. She hadn't put any effort into her appearance, but it wasn't like she needed to impress the wannabe ballerinas she'd be spending the day with.

Five minutes later, she and the kids reconvened in the hall—Jason wearing his blue-and-white Little League uniform, Sophie in a cute yellow sundress with her ballet bag slung over her shoulder.

"You guys ready?" Miranda asked with a smile.

"Yeah," they said in unison.

She cocked her head. "You both used the bathroom like I asked?"

Hesitation.

She sighed and pointed at Jason. "You. Pee. Now."

The kids broke out into laughter. Jason darted into the washroom, then Sophie took her turn.

As they left their small ground-floor apartment, Miranda fixed Jason's blue baseball cap, then tweaked one of Sophie's long brown braids. Outside, she ushered them into the older-model, secondhand sedan that had miraculously gotten them here from Vegas without once overheating.

She started the engine while they buckled up. Jason's baseball practices coincided perfectly with Miranda's Saturday schedule, and since he was best friends with the coach's son, he usually went over to their house after practice while Miranda kept Sophie with her at the dance studio. In the evenings, she picked Jason up from his friend's, and the three of them went to the twins' favorite pizza place for dinner.

She loved the routine, loved spending time with her kids. She might not have planned to have a baby at eighteen, certainly hadn't expected to end up with *two*, but she didn't regret her decision to keep her babies and raise them alone. Sophie and Jason were her entire life, and they were such good kids.

Come on, baby, I've been such a good boy...

Out of nowhere, Seth Masterson's raspy voice floated into her mind, bringing a shiver to her body.

No. No, no, no.

She *had* to quit thinking about the man. He had no place in her life, for Pete's sake.

Her gaze strayed to the rearview mirror, and she spent a few seconds watching the twins chatter to each other in the backseat. For a moment, she tried to imagine Seth sitting next to her. His big, muscular body crammed in the passenger seat, his arm hanging out the open window as he held a cigarette between his fingers.

A sigh got stuck in her throat. No, he didn't belong in her life. As sexy as he was, and as tempted as she was to remove her Mommy hat for a few hours and enjoy what would undoubtedly be some amazing sex, she couldn't.

Men like Seth were nothing but trouble. They blew into your life like a hurricane. Lured you in with their bad-boy charm and got you out of your panties. Then they disappeared, leaving a big mess in their wake.

Well, she didn't need the headache, thank you very much. There was already one storm barreling its way into her life, and it went by the name Nora.

Though she got the feeling that Hurricane Nora didn't have half the destruction potential that Hurricane Seth was capable of.

SETH AND DYLAN HOPPED OUT OF SETH'S JEEP AT EIGHT THIRTY ON Sunday morning, striding toward the beach. They were bare-chested, wearing shorts, sneakers, and sunglasses that were proving to be unnecessary. The sun had already risen, but the sky was overcast, making Seth wonder if that tropical storm the weather reports kept stressing about would actually make an appearance. He hoped not. He'd been looking forward to a long workout, the more strenuous the better.

When he and Dylan had moved in together three years ago, they'd started working out on the beach every morning, usually with fellow SEALs Cash McCoy and Jackson Ramsey, who rounded out Seth's circle of friends. Not that he wasn't buddies with the other men on the team— he was. But letting down his guard and sharing his feelings and all that shit? He only did that around Dylan, Cash and Jackson, which was pretty fucking weird because he'd never really done the whole friendship thing before.

Truth was, he hadn't had a single male friend growing up. He'd been the loner bad boy who smoked weed and cigarettes and wandered the Strip looking for a fuck or a fight. Raised in a dressing room filled with half-naked women, constantly surrounded by females who, once he got older and grew into his looks, were dying to jump his bones. Needless to say, it had been seriously jarring when he'd enlisted in the navy— suddenly he'd gone from a room inhabited by gorgeous showgirls to a dormitory full of tired, cranky and hungry males forever being screamed at by their commanding officers.

But somehow, he'd grown close to not one, not two, but *three* of his fellow recruits. And for some messed-up reason, those three put up with his bullshit and actually gave a damn about him.

"They're late," Dylan remarked, glancing up and down the deserted stretch of sand.

Seth shrugged. "McCoy probably couldn't bear to drag himself out of Jen's bed. Dude's whipped, that's for sure."

"Yeah, but he's whipped by the sexiest woman on the planet. That's not really much of a hardship."

He couldn't deny that Jen, Cash's girlfriend, was stunning, but Seth wasn't into those perfect California-girl good looks. He was drawn to women with interesting faces rather than classically beautiful ones. Like Miranda, with her big hazel eyes, tilted at the corners to give her an exotic feel. The slightly crooked mouth, a bit too wide for her angular jaw. The unusual combination of olive skin and a sprinkle of freckles. To him, Miranda was more appealing than any cover model.

"Whipped is whipped," he answered with a shrug.

Dylan grinned. "Cut McCoy a break. And you know what? I'm happy for him. He's in love."

"Poor bastard."

"You know, one of these days you'll fall just as hard, and I'll be right there, laughing and pointing."

Seth swallowed a laugh. Yeah, whatever. He didn't do pansy-ass shit like *love*. He wasn't a believer in love at first sight or the idea of "falling" in love, which implied not having a say in the matter. As far as he was concerned, love was a choice. You chose to open yourself up to it, chose to feel something for the other person, chose to let those emotions develop and grow.

Well, he was choosing not to do any of that crap.

A loud whistle captured their attention, and they turned around to see Cash and Jackson stalking across the sand.

"Sorry we're late," Cash apologized as he bumped fists with Seth, then Dylan. "I, uh, got delayed."

Seth rolled his eyes. "I bet you did."

Jackson spoke up in his Texan drawl. "With all the sexercise McCoy's been gettin', there's really no reason for him to even be here."

"I don't know, he's looking kinda flabby," Dylan countered, his green eyes focusing on Cash's bare chest. "Someone should send the CO an anonymous letter informing him that McCoy is slacking on his training."

"Flabby? Uh-uh, I'm in peak physical condition." Cash smirked. "And it's okay to be jealous of my intensive sexercise regimen. I won't think less of you for it."

That earned him incredulous looks from both Dylan and Jackson, who gave him the finger and proceeded to defend their sexual prowess by listing all the chicks they'd hooked up with over the past month. Seth tuned the boys out. He couldn't contribute much to the convo, anyway. He hadn't gotten laid in eons, thanks to one very stubborn former showgirl.

It drove him fucking nuts that she refused to give in to the attraction sizzling between them. So what if she had a pair of rugrats at home? It wasn't like parenthood equaled mandatory celibacy. Surely she could set aside some time for a few rounds of hot, sweaty fucking.

And bad idea, thinking about hot, sweaty fucking while surrounded by three other men. As his cock stiffened to half-mast, he pushed all thoughts of Miranda from his head and focused on the tail end of his friends' dispute.

"After a certain amount of times, sex with the same person becomes that ratty shirt you've washed a hundred times," Dylan was arguing. "Suddenly it's not so colorful and it doesn't fit the way it used to and you're not sure you even like it anymore."

"Whoa, that's deep," Cash said dryly.

"All I'm saying is, quantity eventually kills the quality. So be warned, a few more months and this super-duper sex you're bragging about? It'll be nothing but the old Metallica shirt you don't wear anymore."

"Jen will *never* become an old shirt." Cash's voice oozed with confidence. "I guarantee it."

Seth kept his mouth shut, but he was totally with Dylan on this one. Regular sex with the same chick was bound to get dull. At least in his experience.

"Anyway, let's do this thing." Cash glanced up at the sky, wary. "I don't like the look of those clouds."

They'd trained on this beach for years, so the workout was one Seth could do in his sleep. The sky remained overcast during the four-mile run, but once they hit the water, a light rain began to fall and the water grew choppier. Although the waves were nothing to freak out about, when Cash called out and suggested they head back, nobody protested.

They were a mile out, making their way to shore when all hell broke loose. A crack of thunder exploded in the air. The sky grew darker and darker in a matter of seconds, an onslaught of rain blasting out of the black clouds like water from a broken dam.

Gritting his teeth, Seth concentrated on swimming in a straight line, a damn-near impossible feat when the wind was determined to blow his body right back into the middle of the ocean. He was gasping for air by the time he reached the shore, thoroughly exhausted as he staggered out of the water, Cash hot on his heels.

He heaved himself onto the sand, rain and seawater dripping down his bare chest. Squinting, he studied the angry waves, experiencing a spark of relief when he spotted Dylan's blond head bobbing in the water, powerful arms slicing through the current.

After Dylan and Jackson made it to shore, the foursome stared at each other for a long moment, then tipped their gazes upward while the rain soaked them to the bone.

"Holy shit balls," Dylan exclaimed. "It's the fucking Apocalypse."

"Let's get outta here," Cash shouted over the wind.

Getting back to their cars proved to be a whole other workout. The rain fell harder and the wind blew faster, providing a wall of resistance each time Seth took a step. The thunder was so loud he couldn't hear his own thoughts, and each time a bolt of lightning sizzled over the furious ocean, it was easy to see that the waves were gathering in size and speed.

When he finally stumbled up to his Jeep, he let out a breath heavy with relief.

Cash and Jackson raced to the SUV in the neighboring space. Cash unlocked the driver's door and glanced over at Seth. "Text when you get home so I know you made it there alive," he called.

"Same goes for you two," Seth called back.

He and Dylan practically dove into the Jeep. Fortunately, the top was up, so they were spared having to drive home in a torrential downpour.

Still, they were both soaking wet and cursing up a blue streak as Seth started the engine.

"That came out of nowhere," he said, shaking his head in amazement.

"Looks like that annoying weatherman was actually right for the first time in his life." Dylan paused. "He's probably at the studio, gloating up a storm...ha. Get it? Gloating up a storm..."

Seth stared at his friend. "Yeah, I got it the first time you said it, and it wasn't funny then either."

He reversed out of the parking space and turned onto the main road, the windshield wipers working so furiously he was surprised they didn't fly away. Raindrops battered the roof of the car, so loud it was like the Jeep was being hit with an unending stream of golf balls. Luckily, he and Dylan only lived five minutes away. Visibility was totally shot, and the vehicle must have hydroplaned half a dozen times on the short trip home, but Seth got them there in one piece.

He parked in the driveway and killed the engine, then gazed at the scary black chaos beyond the windshield before shooting Dylan a sidelong look. "Ready?"

Dylan sighed. "Yup."

He reached for the door handle. "See you on the other side, brother."

The second he was out in the open, Seth was hit by a gust of wind that almost knocked him right off his feet—and for a man who stood at six-three and boasted two hundred pounds of solid muscle, that spoke volumes about the intensity of the wind.

By the time he and Dylan made it through the front door of the house, he was exhausted again. When he took a step, water spilled out of his sneakers and formed a huge puddle on the hardwood floor.

"You think we should board up the windows?" Dylan winced as the wall behind him rattled from the storm's assault.

"Nah, I think we'll be fine." He kicked off his wet shoes. "I'm hopping in the shower."

He headed for the bathroom, where he stripped off his trunks and turned on the faucet. His shower was quick, just a few minutes under the spray to warm up and wash the saltwater off, and then he toweled off and headed to his bedroom. He threw on a pair of gray sweatpants and a black wifebeater, listening to the whine of the wind and the pounding of the rain. Outside his window, the sky had grown even darker, nearly black now. And it was only ten thirty in the morning.

As he stared at the rain streaking the windowpane, a pang of worry tugged on his gut. Shit. It was Sunday. That meant Miranda was teaching at the dance school today. Hopefully she'd looked out the window when she'd woken up this morning and had the sense to cancel the day's classes.

Maybe he ought to check in, though. Just in case.

Without allowing himself to question his actions, he grabbed his cell phone and dialed Miranda's number.

He immediately got bumped over to voice mail.

"Miranda, it's Seth," he said gruffly. "The weather's shitty. Call me back."

Not the most articulate message, but it got the job done. Too bad it didn't guarantee a speedy response—it took three hours for her to get back to him, and when her voice came over the line, she sounded harried and annoyed.

"I saw your number on my phone," she snapped. "What do you want, Seth?"

"Wow, remind me never to be concerned about you," he said sarcastically. "I just wanted to make sure you're okay."

She had the decency to sound ashamed. "I'm sorry. I shouldn't have snapped like that. Things are ridiculously crazy here."

"Where are you?"

"The school."

Another wave of worry washed over him. "Have you taken a look outside, Miranda? There's a fucking tropical storm out there. Go home."

"Trust me, I'm trying," she said irritably. "I already cancelled the afternoon lessons, but a lot of the kids that were here for the morning classes can't get in touch with their parents, so I'm trying to organize a carpool."

"You need help?" He was already marching to the door. "I can be there in fifteen."

"No, it's fine. Really, Seth, don't come here. The other teachers and I can handle it. We just need to bundle up the kids, pack up their stuff, and then we're getting everyone home. I just can't leave until Jase gets here."

"Who's Jase?"

Her tone took on a bit of an edge. "Jason. My son."

Right. Her kid. Why did he keep forgetting she had one? Wait, make that two.

Probably because you don't want *to remember.*

He ignored the internal taunt. Fine, so he wasn't particularly thrilled that Miranda had two children, but that slice of misfortune wouldn't stop him from doing his damnedest to get her in bed. He'd already made it clear he wasn't applying for the position of her baby-daddy, and he also wasn't going to pretend to like kids just to sleep with the woman. Still, acknowledging the rugrats' existence couldn't hurt his cause.

"Your son's not with you?"

She sounded upset. "No, he was at a friend's house. The parents are dropping him at the school. They just called to say they're ten minutes away."

"Good. Once they arrive, get everyone home. The roads aren't too bad yet, but the weather reports are saying there's some risk of flooding." He paused. "Might be some power outages too. You got candles and flashlights at home?"

"Yes, Seth. I also have canned food and bottled water and something called common sense and basic survival knowledge." Her sarcasm reverberated through the line.

"Good," he said again. "Call or text when you get home."

"If I remember."

"Don't fucking give me that. If I don't hear from you in an hour, I'll get in my car and—"

"Fine," she interjected. "I'll call you."

With that, she hung up, leaving him staring at the phone in frustration. That woman drove him absolutely insane. So fucking independent, determined to do everything on her own, even when she desperately needed help.

He could see why his mother had worried about Miranda moving out here. The women who danced at the Paradise were like a close-knit family, always looking out for one another. They'd mothered Seth to the point of exasperation when he was a kid, and he knew Miranda had experienced that same maternal attention and sisterly devotion. He also knew she hadn't once asked any of them for help in the four years she'd worked there.

Now that she'd left the Strip, she was completely on her own, raising two kids alone, and Seth worried that she'd never be able to swallow her pride and seek him out if she was truly in trouble.

Or at least that's what he thought before the doorbell rang nearly an hour later.

Dylan, who'd been watching the storm coverage in the living room, glanced at Seth in bewilderment. "Expecting anyone?"

He shook his head, getting a sinking feeling that he wasn't going to like what he found on his doorstep.

Setting his beer bottle on the pine coffee table, he rose from the couch and headed to the front hall. He'd only intended to open the door a crack, but a gust of wind blew it open, almost smashing him in the face. He stopped it just in time, then took a second to gape at the three bedraggled creatures huddled on the front stoop.

Miranda's dark hair was drenched, wet strands glued to her forehead and whipping around in the wind. In her leggings and T-shirt, which were also soaked, she wasn't dressed for the weather, but the children plastered to her were. Two of them, wearing matching yellow raincoats with the hoods up, clinging to Miranda's legs and wobbling each time they got blasted by a rainy gust.

"You just going to stand there or are you going to let us in?" Miranda yelled, her voice tinny amidst the persistent drumbeat of the rain.

Seth blinked, recovering fast. He ushered her and the children inside, then struggled to shut the door. He was yet again drenched, and new puddles were forming on the hardwood.

He focused on Miranda, whose eyes looked a tad wild as she pushed hair off her face.

"You okay?" he demanded. "What happened?"

She blinked a few times. Glanced around the small entrance, as if she couldn't comprehend what she was doing there. Then she opened her mouth and said, "My apartment is…"

Seth waited. When she didn't finish the sentence, he prompted, "Your apartment is what?"

Miranda wasn't the one to respond. Rather, it was one of the dark-haired imps by her side, a little girl with pigtails and big brown eyes peeking out of her yellow hood.

"Underwater," the girl announced.

He furrowed his brows. "What?"

"We live underwater now."

Chapter Four

"LIKE *THE LITTLE MERMAID*, 'CEPT IT WASN'T LIKE *THE LITTLE MERMAID* AT all," Sophie explained in dismay. "It was cold and wet and icky and—"

Miranda snapped out of her trance and placed a hand on her daughter's shoulder. "Hush, Soph. I can explain it to Mr. Masterson—"

Seth snorted.

"To Seth," she amended, meeting his amused eyes. "I'm so sorry to just show up like this. I had your address in my phone and I didn't want to drive all the way back to the school when your house was so much closer. Imperial Beach is closer to Coronado than it is to the city—" Wonderful, now she was giving him a geography lesson. "And I couldn't call because there was no signal and—" she gulped, trying to collect her composure, "—Ginny and Elsa live in studio apartments and I didn't want to put them out, but I remember you saying you had a spare room and…"

She was too mortified to keep going, so she stopped talking altogether.

Seth's voice was oddly gentle. "It's okay. Tell me what happened when you got home."

"Our place flooded. I opened the front door to find three feet of water in our hallway." She gestured to her soaking-wet leggings and ballet flats. "I waded in there to assess the damage…" Her throat closed up, making it hard to continue. "I guess a few sewers overflowed, and there was also something wrong with my building's gutters—my landlord said something about downspouts draining too close to the foundation."

His expression turned grim. "How bad was it?"

"Bad. All four ground-floor apartments flooded, and with the rain not easing up out there, it's bound to get worse."

A wave of panic suddenly hit her. Oh God. Their entire life was in that apartment. What the hell was she supposed to do now?

Her landlord, a sweet Italian man named Marco, was already at the building when Miranda and the kids got home. One of the other tenants whose apartment flooded had called him, and although Marco had assured the affected residents that insurance would cover their lost belongings and no one would have to pay for the renovations, that didn't solve the dilemma of where she and her children were supposed to live for the next week or so. The only people she knew in town were the teachers who worked for her at the dance school, and she didn't feel comfortable asking any of them for a place to stay.

And she certainly couldn't stay with Seth. It was bad enough that she was about to ask him to spend the night. But a whole week, maybe more? No way.

Miranda forced herself to gain some control over the panic swirling in her belly and focused on Seth, who was watching her with concern. Funny, he hadn't made a single smartass remark since she'd shown up. He also hadn't paid a lick of attention to her kids, who were beginning to whine.

"Mom, my shoes are wet," Jason said miserably.

"And I want Belinda!" Sophie whimpered.

Miranda stifled a sigh. She wasn't looking forward to telling Sophie that her favorite doll had been floating in the murky lake that used to be their home.

Rather than answer the twins, she looked imploringly at Seth. "I hate to ask this, but can we…do you mind if we stay here tonight? With you?"

"Mommy, I want Belinda!"

"My feet are cold!"

What could only be described as terror flared in Seth's normally unfazed expression. She didn't blame him. The stress of the day was finally taking its toll on the twins, whose voices were increasing in volume.

"I. Want. Belinda." A sob slipped from Sophie's trembling lips.

"Seth?" Miranda asked quietly, studying his face.

"Of course you can crash here tonight," a male voice announced.

A tall, blond man in his late twenties appeared in the hallway, his handsome features creased with displeasure as he glanced at Seth. Then his face relaxed and he squatted down, shooting a big smile at Sophie, who made loud hiccupping sounds as she cried and clutched Miranda's hand. Even Jason's eyes were shining with tears, and her son was normally *way* too macho to cry in public.

"Hey there, squirts," the blond guy said cheerfully. "Why you all wet? Is it raining out there or something?"

Neither child said a word for a moment, and then Sophie giggled.

"Duh," Jason said, his tears all but forgotten.

"Weird. I hadn't noticed. I'm Dylan, by the way. But you can call me Mr. Awesome."

Sophie giggled again.

Miranda gawked at the gorgeous man—Seth's roommate, she deduced—grateful for his successful defusing of the tears-and-tantrum bomb that had almost detonated.

"I'm Miranda," she said, extending her hand in his direction. "And this is Sophie and Jason."

"Pleasure to meet you, honey." Dylan leaned in for the handshake. His grip was strong, his palm warm, and his green eyes twinkled with genuine delight as he graciously shook her kids' hands too, eliciting yet another high-pitched laugh from Sophie.

"Did you see, Mom? We shaked hands! Like *grown-ups*," Sophie bubbled.

"Shook hands," Miranda corrected. "And now how about we get you out of those rain slickers and see if Seth and Dylan would be willing to feed us?"

She was probably being presumptuous, especially since Seth hadn't said a single word in the past five minutes, but clearly his roommate was okay with her and the twins being here, so technically she didn't need the green light from Seth. Besides, wasn't he the one who kept checking up on her and offering to help her out?

Well, he finally got his wish—she needed his help, even though it killed her to admit it. If there was one thing she hated doing, it was relying on other people. For *anything*. Her friends in Vegas used to tease her about her inability to accept outside assistance. They accused her of being stubborn and proud, but the reason she preferred doing things on her own wasn't because she didn't want to feel like a charity case. It was because she didn't trust anyone but herself to get shit done. She'd placed her faith in far too many people who had let her down, and she refused to be the one left holding the bag ever again.

But at the moment, she had no choice. Her apartment had turned into Atlantis and all of her belongings were most likely destroyed. Her only possessions in the world were the clothes on her back, her purse and the Ford sedan parked in Seth's driveway, provided it didn't float away.

"I think we can scrounge up something for us to eat," Dylan replied, flashing another one of those endearing smiles.

Jeez, the man ought to open up his own charm school. Miranda had never met a more pleasant, likable person, and she'd only known the dude five minutes.

Seth, on the other hand, was the furthest thing from *pleasant* and *likable*. He was leaning against the wall, his sweatpants and tank top wet and plastered to his strong body, his expression as turbulent as the wind shrieking beyond the door. And yet, rather than cower under that harsh gaze, she was inexplicably drawn to it.

Their eyes locked, and for a moment, Miranda's surroundings faded. She forgot all about how cold she was, how wet and tired and hungry. This was not the time to feel even the slightest bit aroused, yet Seth's presence coaxed the response from her. He was the sexiest man she'd ever met—tall, muscular, imposing. So blatantly masculine with his scruffy beard and unruly hair, his roped forearms and corded biceps radiating strength.

She'd be lying if she said she hadn't fantasized about having sex with him. Because she had. Many, many times.

"Mo-om," Sophie said in a plaintive voice.

Flustered, she wrenched her gaze away and knelt down to help the twins out of their rain gear. She felt more than saw Seth leave the hallway, and a strange sense of disappointment rippled through her. Along with a jolt of disapproval.

He didn't want her children here.

That was the only explanation for his distant behavior, and it seriously grated that he hadn't even taken the time to introduce himself to her kids.

Leaving their wet shoes and coats in the hall to dry, Miranda took Sophie and Jason by the hand, and the three of them followed Dylan down the corridor toward the kitchen.

As a peal of children's laughter drifted into the hallway, Seth cringed and ducked back into his bedroom. It was the third time he'd left his room intending to join everyone in the kitchen, only to change his mind and retreat.

Christ. You'd think he was about to face a pack of rabid dogs rather than two harmless six-year-olds.

Though come to think of it, he'd prefer hanging out with rabid dogs.

Grow a pair, buddy.

But he didn't like kids. As politically incorrect as it might be, it was common knowledge to all who knew him, which was why no one expected him to make an appearance at Lieutenant Commander Becker's house for any Baby Sadie-related events, or asked him to babysit John Garrett or Will Charleston's kids.

He'd never thought he'd say it, but thank God for Dylan. Mr. Awesome had come to the rescue like Mary fucking Poppins flying in with her umbrella, promptly turning a couple of frowns upside down and saving the day.

Seth had seen the gratitude shining on Miranda's face, and for a second he'd experienced a burst of envy. No way could he have made those kids laugh like that. If you wanted him to save the day, put an MP5 in his hands and point him in the direction of a terrorist. He wasn't the kind of man who brought smiles to children's faces.

A soft knock on the door jarred him from a train of thought that was growing more and more unsettling by the second.

"Yeah?" he called brusquely.

The door opened and Miranda poked her head in. Her expression reflected both concern and irritation. "Dylan said you might have some clothes you can loan me. He's going to throw our stuff in the dryer."

"Yeah, I do." His voice sounded gravelly, so he cleared his throat, adding, "You need something for the rugrats too?"

She stepped into the room, shaking her head. "No, they changed into a couple of Dylan's T-shirts." Her lips quirked. "They're practically drowning in them. Your roommate's a big guy."

Seth's jaw tensed. The note of appreciation in her voice raised his hackles and made him take back every nice thought he'd had about Dylan in the past few minutes.

"The big guy couldn't spare something for you to wear?" Seth said with a bite to his tone.

"He made a cryptic comment about how it wouldn't be appropriate." She rolled her eyes. "I get the feeling he thinks it would be treading on your territory if he lets me wear his clothes."

Damn it. Now he had no choice but to think good thoughts about Dylan again. He even mentally awarded his roommate a gold star for knowing that Seth would absolutely murder him if a single item of Dylan's clothing so much as touched Miranda's skin.

"Which is ridiculous," she went on, "because you don't own me, and therefore I can wear whatever I want, regardless of whom it belongs to."

"Maybe," he agreed. "But tonight?" He strode over to his closet. "Tonight you're wearing *my* shirt, babe."

"I hate it when you call me babe."

He shot her a grin over his shoulder. "No, you don't."

"So now you're an expert on what I like?"

"Yep." He tugged a flannel button-down off one of the hangers and handed it to her.

Miranda reluctantly accepted the garment. She ran her fingers over the well-worn material before looking at him in surprise. "This is soft. And it looks worn." She lifted one eyebrow. "I thought you were only allowed to wear black. You know, because you're *so* cool."

"I can make anything look cool, even flannel. And I don't only wear black." To illustrate, he gestured to the fresh pair of gray sweats and white wifebeater he'd changed into.

The way Miranda's hazel eyes rested on his chest a little too long didn't go unnoticed.

Neither did the fact that his confidence had returned with full force the second Miranda's kids were out of sight.

He walked over to the wooden dresser under his window and grabbed a pair of black track pants from the bottom drawer, along with thick wool socks. "The pants will be baggy, but there's a drawstring so at least they won't fall off." He paused. "You want some boxers too?"

Her cheeks took on a pinkish hue. "No, it's okay. Just the pants will do."

His groin tightened as he wondered whether she planned on going commando. From there, the most mouthwatering image flashed in his mind, one involving Miranda's bare pussy, his track pants, and a whole lotta friction.

"What's wrong?"

He met her concerned eyes. "Why do you ask?"

"You got this look on your face, like you were in pain. Are you all right?"

A choked laugh slipped out. "I'm fine."

"What's so funny?" Suspicion colored her tone.

"You're completely oblivious to the effect you have on me, aren't you?"

She let out a startled breath. "What?"

Releasing a breath of his own, he eliminated the distance between them, lifting one arm over her shoulder so he could close the bedroom door. Her eyes widened at his nearness, and her cheeks turned redder.

"What are you doing?" she demanded.

"Giving us some privacy."

Her slender throat dipped as she swallowed. "*We* don't need privacy. *I* wouldn't mind some, though, so I can change out of these damp clothes."

"That can wait a few minutes." He locked his gaze with hers. "You asked if I was in pain. Well, I am."

She blinked in surprise. "But you just said—"

Before she could finish, he grabbed her hand and placed it directly over the bulge in his sweatpants.

Miranda gasped, her mouth falling open. "What are you...oh my God. Jesus, Seth!"

And yet for all the lady's protests, she didn't make a single move to yank her hand away.

His pulse kicked up a notch, his cock growing even harder beneath Miranda's palm. She didn't stroke him. Didn't cup or caress or move her fingers in the slightest. She just kept her hand over the erection straining against his sweats, her lips parted, her pupils dilated.

"Feel that?" he murmured.

Her gaze slowly met his. She looked almost mesmerized as she nodded.

"That's what I've been walking around with since the moment you moved to town, baby."

"Seth..." Reluctance crept into her voice. "Stop. Just...stop."

And then her palm moved. A fraction of an inch. A torturous glide over the hard ridge of his cock.

He groaned softly. "Do that again."

Her fingers froze. Her expression conveyed shock, as if she truly hadn't realized what she was doing.

"This is insane," she mumbled, and then, to his extreme disappointment, she withdrew her hand.

But the sexual awareness zipping back and forth between them refused to dissipate. It thickened the air and made his skin burn with anticipation. Christ, he wanted this woman so badly he couldn't think straight anymore. Every time he saw her he turned into a sex-crazed caveman whose sole purpose in life was to claim his female.

His gaze focused on her mouth, that sexy mouth he'd been fantasizing about for so long.

"One taste." The words slipped out before he could stop them, his voice full of gravel.

"W-what?" she stammered.

"Let me have one taste. One kiss." He brought his hand to her mouth and swept his thumb over her plump bottom lip. The breath she hissed out warmed his fingers. "Please, Miranda."

Oh Christ, he was actually begging.

Begging to kiss a woman.

If his entire body wasn't overcome with pure agony, he might have been disgusted with himself, but at the moment, he couldn't focus on anything other than Miranda. The intoxicating scent of her, vanilla and roses and something soft and feminine. The way her long, damp hair curled at the ends. The fullness of her tits beneath her T-shirt.

He stroked her lip again, then let out another groan when her tongue came out to taste the pad of his thumb. She looked as surprised as he was by her actions.

But he wasn't complaining. Hell no. He just capitalized on that tiny sign of surrender by cupping her chin and lowering his head to take possession of her mouth.

The kiss rivaled the storm that raged outside the house—powerful and all-consuming. Her lips were soft, warm, and he could feel them trembling as he rubbed his mouth over hers in a fleeting caress. There it was, his one taste, and it wasn't enough, not by a long shot. Miranda must have agreed, because she didn't pull away, didn't protest when he coaxed her lips open with his tongue and licked his way inside.

She gave the sexiest little moan he'd ever heard when their tongues met. He swallowed the sound and angled his head to deepen the kiss.

The only contact between them was their fused mouths and his hand resting lightly on her jaw. Her arms didn't come around his neck. His other hand didn't explore her sweet curves. Their lower bodies didn't collide.

And yet it was the most erotic kiss of his entire life.

Disappointment slammed into him when Miranda abruptly tore her mouth away. Her eyes shone with arousal and uncertainty, and she was breathing hard, her chest heaving.

"There," she said. "You got your taste."

He knew she was trying to sound casual, but her wobbly voice betrayed her.

"And you got yours," he answered, lifting his eyebrows in challenge. "So let's hear it."

To her credit, she met his gaze head-on. "Hear what?"

"Your speech about how you didn't feel anything, the kiss was no big deal, it doesn't change your mind about going to bed with me, et cetera, et cetera."

She sighed. "I'm many things, Seth, but I'm not a liar. I *did* feel something, and trust me that kiss *was* a big deal. It was a huge deal, actually."

She might as well have pulled out a two-by-four and smashed him in the gut, that was how shocked he was by her frank admission. Pure triumph soared through him—only to fizzle out like a wet candle when Miranda kept going.

"But you're right. It doesn't change my mind about going to bed with you." Before he could respond, she spun around and grabbed hold of the doorknob.

"Miranda."

She went still. "What?" she asked without turning.

"What the hell is it going to take for you to give in to this?" The echo of defeat in his voice surprised him as much as the next question he posed. "What do I have to do to win you over?"

Her back relaxed. Slightly. There was no mistaking her ironic tone as she glanced over her shoulder and said, "For starters? Be nicer to my kids." Then she slid out the door.

Seth listened to the sound of her footsteps, heard the door of the hall bathroom open and close. He scrubbed both hands through his hair, still feeling winded from that explosive kiss, and now apprehensive, thanks to Miranda's parting words.

Be nicer to my kids.

Fuck, he should've known it would come down to that. He couldn't blame her, either. Whether he liked it or not, Miranda was a mother. Age-wise, she was young—only twenty-four, if he recalled correctly—but in terms of maturity, she was light-years ahead of other women her age. She took her responsibilities seriously, and he was beginning to understand that she was the kind of woman who didn't do a single thing without thinking it through first.

Which was damn frustrating, because, really, who needed to put this much thought into a casual fling? It wasn't that difficult—chemistry, sex, good-bye.

In this case, he'd probably need to add "and let's stay friends" to that list, just in case his mother ever found out. Missy would kick his ass if she discovered he'd pulled his usual love-'em-and-leave-'em act on one of her former dancers. But he had no problem remaining friends with Miranda. He liked her, and they got along. Well, when she wasn't rejecting him left and right.

So yeah, he could do the whole friendship thing—*after* he'd had his fill of her in bed.

Be nicer to my kids.

Fine. If it meant finally satisfying his craving for Miranda Breslin, he could totally manage a few cordial words when he was around her children.

Setting his jaw in determination, he left the bedroom and marched into the kitchen, where he found Miranda's twins sitting at the table. There was a tall glass of milk in front of each child, and a plate of chocolate-chip cookies between them.

Dylan, who was grabbing a beer from the fridge, glanced up at Seth's arrival. "Want one?" he asked.

Seth nodded and accepted the bottle of Bud. As he twisted the cap and took a sip, he felt two pairs of eyes watching him. After a second, he shifted his gaze to the table and returned the stare.

No denying that Miranda's kids were cute. They were carbon copies of their mother, hair the same shade of brown, skin the same olive tone, except their eyes were chocolate-brown rather than hazel. The girl exuded a shrewd sort of perceptiveness, her expression more shuttered than her twin's, whose face was very easy to read.

"What's on your arm?" the boy asked curiously, his gaze glued to the Polynesian design covering Seth's upper arm.

"It's a tattoo, dummy," the girl told her brother in a know-it-all voice.

"I *know* that," he retorted. "I wanna know what it means."

"It doesn't mean anything, kid," Seth said, then took another gulp of beer. "It's just a random design."

"He thinks it makes him look cool," Dylan explained with a grin. He sat down next to Jason, leaving one empty chair at the table—the one beside Sophie.

Seth stared at the chair.

So did Miranda's daughter, before turning to look at him again. He could have sworn he saw a gleam of challenge in her eyes, as if she was daring him to come closer.

Rather than sit down, he leaned against the counter. Call him a coward, but he wasn't going near that table.

A short silence fell, broken by a boom of thunder that made both children shriek.

"It's just thunder, guys," Miranda said from the doorway.

Seth's mouth turned to sawdust as he watched her enter the kitchen. She was wearing the clothes he'd loaned her—the pants were baggy, as he'd predicted, but he hadn't expected the shirt to be so big too. With the top two buttons undone, the flannel neckline kept sliding off one of her shoulders, revealing her supple, tanned skin. But it was the no-bra-strap part that transformed his mouth into a sand dune.

She wasn't wearing anything underneath that shirt. Or the pants. Jesus. She was totally naked under there.

Their eyes met briefly, and Seth knew she'd read his dirty thoughts because she blushed before casting her gaze downward.

"I can't believe how hard it's raining." She sank into the unoccupied chair next to her daughter's. "Let's just hope the flooding over at our place doesn't get worse."

"Did your landlord say how he planned to handle the damage?" Dylan asked, reaching for a chocolate-chip cookie.

"He's trying to get a professional crew to come in this evening, if possible. If not, then it'll happen tomorrow morning. They'll have to pump out the water and shop-vac the place." Her expression turned grim. "I think the biggest concern is sewage contamination and mold forming."

She moved her gaze to the sliding door that led to the small backyard. Rivulets of rain streamed down the glass. In the distance, the sky was a dark, ominous gray.

Miranda's face took on a faraway expression as she started mumbling under her breath. "Who knows what might be damaged. Insulation, drywall, ceilings, floors...definitely the floors. God, and the furniture and appliances, the carpets and bedding, and our clothes and..."

She was beginning to look green, and Dylan quickly interjected. "No point in worrying about things beyond your control," he said gently. "Tomorrow you'll assess the damage and figure out what needs to be done. Tonight, there's nothing you can do about it."

"You're right," she agreed, albeit grudgingly.

"Mom, Sef has a ta-ttoo," Jason blurted out.

"Seth," she corrected with a smile. "Remember we were going to try and practice our *t-h* sounds?"

"Seth," Jason said slowly. Then he nodded, looking pleased with himself.

"And yes, he does have a tattoo." She shot Seth a quick look. "Is there a story behind it?"

He shrugged. "Not really."

"Sure there is," Dylan said with a grin. "It's just not kid-appropriate."

"What's kid-*appoeperit*?" Sophie asked.

"Appropriate. And it means that Seth's story is for grown-ups," Miranda said firmly.

Sophie twisted around in her chair and stared at Seth with a hint of contempt, as if she blamed him for not being able to hear the story. Jason, on the other hand, merely shrugged it off and reached for another cookie.

Okay then. Clearly the girl was the dominant of the two, and the one he needed to watch out for. Good to know. A SEAL always needed to be aware of his enemies, after all.

"So…" Miranda studied the clock on the microwave display. "Huh, it's only three o'clock. Feels much later. What should we do now?"

Dylan spoke up sheepishly. "Well, I kinda promised the squirts we would watch a movie on Netflix. As long as the power's still on and the Internet works, we might as well take advantage of it. If that's okay with you, of course."

"It's fine by me." She turned to her kids. "Any movie ideas?"

As the twins began shouting out film titles Seth had never heard of, he fought the urge to sneak out of the kitchen and hide out in his room again. Sitting around eating cookies and discussing the options for kiddie movie night was *not* his scene. At all.

But he forced his feet to stay rooted to the tiled floor. If he was going to succeed in finally getting Miranda naked, he needed to prove that he could be around her kids.

Jeez, is she even worth it, bro?

The thought gave him pause. He couldn't deny that this was getting pretty fucking complicated. He was going to great lengths to get this woman in bed, even willingly spending time with an age demographic he usually avoided like the plague.

So…was she worth it?

He discreetly watched as she got up, laughing at something Sophie had said. As she helped her daughter up to her feet, Miranda's brown hair, now dry and wavy, fell forward, revealing that bare shoulder he'd been admiring earlier.

A rush of heat coursed through his blood, and his cock stirred beneath his sweatpants.

Fuck.

Of course she was worth it.

She was absolutely worth it.

Chapter Five

"KIDS ASLEEP?"

Seth's low voice startled her as she shut the guest room door and stepped into the corridor. Miranda's pulse sped up when she spotted him at the end of the hall. His magnetic gray eyes were focused on her with such intensity she felt rattled.

"Yeah." She reluctantly walked toward him, wishing she'd decided to turn in herself. But it was barely eight forty-five and she wasn't tired. If anything, she was wide awake and would probably stay that way for hours. The more it continued to rain, the higher her stress levels soared.

What would she find when she went home tomorrow? How much of their belongings could she actually salvage? How long would the renovations take? The floors would definitely have to be replaced, but what else?

"Okay, clearly you need this more than I do."

She snapped out of her thoughts to see Seth holding out a beer bottle.

"Here," he said gruffly. "It might make you feel better. I can see your brain working overtime. Thinking about the apartment, huh?"

She nodded. After a second, she accepted the bottle and brought it to her lips. As the cold liquid slid down her throat, she suddenly realized that Seth's mouth had been on the lip of this bottle just seconds ago. Her heart beat a little bit faster. And faster still when the memory of their kiss flew into her head.

Oh God.

The kiss.

She'd tried blocking it from her mind all evening. She'd curled up with the twins on the comfy leather couch in Seth and Dylan's living room. Laughed at the crazy antics of Shrek and the gang. Munched on the popcorn Dylan brought out.

She'd hoped that if she pretended the kiss hadn't happened, she might be able to erase it from her memory, but no such luck. She'd been excruciatingly aware of Seth's presence all night, even though he'd barely said a word. He'd isolated himself on the sole recliner in the living room and spoke only when spoken to, but she'd felt his gaze burning into the side of her face for the entirety of both movies they'd ended up watching.

Now, that silvery gaze was glued to her again. Knowing, mocking, a tad contemplative.

"You hungry?" he asked after the silence between them had dragged on.

She shook her head. "I'm still full from all that spaghetti we had for dinner. Did I even thank Dylan for cooking? I can't remember if—"

"You thanked him," Seth cut in. "Twice."

"Right. Okay. Well."

She fidgeted with the label of the bottle. The condensation had softened the paper, and she found herself slicing her fingernail underneath it and peeling away the corners. For some reason, she felt incredibly unsettled in Seth's presence.

"Where's Dylan?" she blurted out.

"In the shower."

"Oh."

"Should we sit in the living room?" Seth suggested.

"Um. Sure."

Shit, she had to pull herself together. So what if she could still taste him on her lips? So what if his woodsy, masculine scent drugged her senses every time she inhaled?

So what if his powerful arms looked incredible in that wifebeater?

She trailed after him, clutching the beer bottle so tightly it was a miracle the glass didn't shatter. Why was she so nervous all of a sudden? She'd been around Seth a hundred times over the past few months and never had a problem before. She'd been perfectly capable of talking to him, interacting with him, sparring with him, shooting down his seductive propositions and resisting the attraction between them.

What had changed? Why did she suddenly feel tongue-tied around him? *The kiss, you idiot. It was the kiss.*

"Have a seat. I'll just grab another beer," Seth said when they reached the living room.

Miranda settled on the far end of the couch and brought both legs up, resting the bottle on one knee. She looked around the room, slightly bothered by its lack of…warmth. Judging by this room and the others she'd already seen, Seth and Dylan weren't concerned with personalizing their surroundings. The furniture in the house was sparse, the white walls devoid of artwork or decoration. Everything served a purpose—couch, flat screen, kitchen table, chairs. It kind of bummed her out, especially when she thought of the painstaking effort she'd gone to in order to make her apartment a cozy place she and the kids could call home. And now it was probably all gone—the furniture and knickknacks and personal touches she'd tried to infuse the place with.

Sighing, she leaned her head against the arm of the sofa. When her shirt slid off her shoulder, she blushed, hoping Seth wouldn't comment on the fact that she still wore his flannel shirt and track pants even though her clothing had come out of the dryer hours ago. Call her pathetic, but the clothes smelled like him and she liked being surrounded by his heady scent.

But when he walked back into the room a few minutes later, the scent she loved so much held the unmistakable hint of smoke.

"Sorry for taking so long," he apologized, crossing the hardwood floor with an unopened beer in his hand. "I needed a nicotine fix."

She raised her eyebrows. "You went outside in the storm?"

"Nah, just opened the sliding door and stood in the kitchen. The rain's letting up, by the way. And it's not as windy as it was earlier."

Rather than sit at the other end of the couch, he plopped his big body on the center cushion, his muscular thigh mere inches from Miranda's socked feet.

Her heart skipped a beat. Crap. Why the heck did he have to sit so close?

She decided to focus on the one thing guaranteed *not* to turn her on—his smoking habit.

"So, how long have you been trying to give yourself cancer?" she asked politely.

Seth laughed, the husky sound sending a shiver up her spine. "Oh no, gee, please don't hold back."

She couldn't help but laugh. "Sorry."

"Don't be." He shrugged. "You're right. It's a terrible habit. And to answer your question—since I was fourteen."

"Ah, you rebelled young." She slanted her head. "I'm surprised Missy let you get away with it."

"The one thing my mom hates to be called is a hypocrite. Seeing as she's a chain-smoker herself, she's not one to lecture her son for doing the same. After she caught me with a cigarette that first time, she yelled at me for all of two minutes, then bummed a smoke off me and lit up."

He grinned, and Miranda's heart did a juvenile little flip. He was so much more attractive when he smiled, so much…safer. Those angular features of his softened, the dangerous glint in his eyes dimmed, and he lost that predatory air.

But she wasn't foolish enough to believe that beneath Seth's menacing exterior was a man with an endless supply of smiles and good cheer. Make no mistake—Seth Masterson was not a teddy bear. He was the big bad wolf, and damned if she was going to let him make her his next meal.

"What about you?" Seth asked. "Did you do any rebelling of your own?"

"I got pregnant at eighteen—what do *you* think?"

He chuckled. "So how did it go down? Strict parents, curfew, a million rules that you eventually decided to break?"

"Not exactly. I lived with my father and grandmother. Neither was strict. Neither acknowledged my existence." Even so many years later, she couldn't control the bitterness that rushed to the surface.

He furrowed his brows. "What about your mother?"

"She died three months after giving birth to me. Drunk-driving accident—she was the drunk driver, by the way, and the only casualty in the huge pileup she caused." Miranda offered a grim smile. "Dad got stuck raising a baby. I have no idea why he didn't just put me up for adoption."

"Maybe because he loved you?" Seth said in a surprisingly gentle voice.

"He doesn't love anyone but himself," she retorted. "He was hardly home during my entire childhood. Sometimes I wouldn't see him for weeks."

Seth frowned. "What does he do for a living?"

"Gamble." She barked out a laugh. "I have no idea what he does now—I haven't seen him since I left home—but back then he worked odd jobs, manual labor, landscaping, whatever he could find. Then he'd take his paycheck and cash it at the casino. And then he'd lose every penny, come crawling home and beg my grandmother for money."

"Is your grandmother still alive?"

"She died a year after the twins were born. Stroke."

"Shit. I'm sorry. What was she like?" The cushions shifted as he leaned forward to put his beer on the simple pine coffee table.

After a second, Miranda did the same, then brought her knees up to her chest and wrapped her arms around them. "She was…tired. She worked as a cleaning lady up until the day she died. She made sure I had clothes on my back and food in my belly, but she didn't show me much affection. My dad was a huge disappointment to her, and I'm the spitting image of him." Sorrow rippled in her belly. "I think she gave up on me without ever even giving me a chance."

"I'm sorry," Seth said gruffly.

"The one thing she did do was pay for my dance lessons. To this day, I'm still baffled by it. Maybe she wanted me out of her hair four evenings a week. And she left me some money when she died, which I also don't understand."

"Maybe she cared about you and that was the only way she knew how to show it," he countered.

"Maybe."

"Is it that hard to believe that the woman who fed and clothed you and paid for your dance lessons might have actually loved you?" he teased, reaching out to tweak one of her knees.

Miranda jumped the moment he made contact. "Sorry," she murmured. "I'm just…"

"Determined to keep me at arm's length," he finished darkly.

"Don't look at me like that."

"Like what?"

"Like I'm committing some horrendous crime by not agreeing to sleep with you. You're a good-looking guy, Seth. You can have any woman you want—so go pick one and let this go."

As usual, he didn't acknowledge her latest rejection. "Why was it a huge deal?"

She ran a frustrated hand through her hair, tucking the long strands behind her ear. "What are you talking about?"

"That's what you said after I kissed you, that the kiss was a huge deal." His eyes narrowed. "Why?"

"I don't know why I said that," she answered, starting to feel flustered. "It wasn't really a big deal at all. I mean…I guess…whatever. Can we not talk about this anymore?"

Ha, fat chance. Like Seth would ever drop the subject now. That stupid stammering fest would only succeed in heightening his curiosity, not eliminating it.

Sure enough, his expression took on that familiar mocking light. "So are you going to tell me or should I start guessing?"

She gritted her teeth.

"Guessing, it is. All right…the kiss was a big thing because…you're in love with me?"

Her jaw dropped. "What? *No.*"

"Huh. Not sure if I should be insulted by how fast you shot that down." He shrugged. "Okay, then it must be 'cause you've never been kissed like that before. It was *that* amazing, huh?"

Aggravation climbed up her throat. "You're really not going to drop this, are you?"

"Nope."

She leaned forward and grabbed her beer. A few sips later, she didn't feel any less embarrassed about the conversation or the confession sitting on the tip of her tongue.

"Come on, baby, spit it out."

She met his inquisitive gaze. "It was a big thing because it's the first time I've kissed a man since the twins were born."

Silence.

And then some more silence.

Seth was staring at her like she'd grown horns and a tail, as if the fact that she hadn't been making out with men left and right was truly astounding. The longer he stayed quiet, the more uncomfortable she became, and the discomfort only skyrocketed when understanding dawned on his face and she saw him grasp what she *hadn't* said.

"Shit, you haven't had sex in *six years?*" he blurted out, each word dripping with incredulity.

She managed a quick nod. Her cheeks were so hot she knew she must look like a tomato.

"*Six* years."

She finally found her voice. "Seven, if we're going for accuracy here."

"*Seven* years?"

"Yes, and stop looking at me like that."

"*Seven years!*"

She heaved a sigh, wishing he would quit acting like her admission was incomprehensible. Lots of people went without sex.

Right?

"Wow. Just...wow." Seth shook his head in amazement. "I guess parenthood does equal celibacy."

"What?"

"Nothing." He took the beer from her hand and promptly dropped it back on the coffee table, his movements quick and decisive. "You just blew my mind, you know that?"

She clenched her jaw, a little tempted to clock him one. An impulse that deepened when he opened that smart mouth of his and said, "Oh, baby, you need this just as much as I do, don't you?"

"Need what?" she grumbled.

"Me. You. Naked." His smile was beyond cocky. "You need to be fucked. And badly, from the sound of it."

Even while her skin prickled with offense, her lower body tingled and pulsated in response to his lewd assessment of her situation. "I don't need anything from you."

"You haven't been with a man in seven years." He still sounded downright flabbergasted. "How have you not gone insane yet? What happens when you're struck with that basic carnal urge to come?"

"I'm perfectly capable of taking care of my own urges," she said stiffly.

"So you get yourself off?"

A fresh dose of humiliation heated her face. "Yes, Seth, I get myself off. Happy?"

"Not in the slightest." His silvery gaze burned molten hot. "I won't be happy until *I'm* the one getting you off."

As her thighs quivered and her clit throbbed like she'd just placed a vibrator on it, Miranda averted her eyes and tried to compose herself. She suddenly wished she'd gone somewhere else for refuge, *anywhere* else. Why had she thought coming to Seth's house could possibly be a good idea? Why had she willingly placed herself in the path of temptation?

"Miranda."

Ugh. Why did he have such a sexy voice? Why did he have such a sexy *everything*? She kept her gaze on anything but Seth, but that didn't deter him from sliding closer.

She squeaked out a protest when he lifted her legs into his lap. "What are…"

Her voice died. So did her common sense, because when she shifted her head and saw that Seth's lips were closing in on hers, she made no effort to stop him.

The kiss was as hot and explosive as the one in his bedroom. Flames licked at her skin, spreading to every erogenous zone in her body. Her breasts. Her nipples. The hollow of her throat. Behind her ear. Between her legs. When he nipped her bottom lip with his teeth, her core clenched, the pressure becoming unbearable.

God, he knew how to kiss. She would have expected him to be rougher, greedier, but he took his time, stoking the fire building inside her with the fleeting brushes of his mouth and teasing exploration of his tongue.

She was helpless to resist. She sank into him, wrapping her arms around his broad shoulders and clinging to him as if she were hanging off the edge of a cliff and he was her lifeline. Except a lifeline was supposed to make you feel safe, and Seth…he made her feel anything but.

As he thrust his tongue inside her mouth and deepened the kiss to an even hotter, even more terrifying level, Miranda experienced something akin to free-falling. Her sense of equilibrium was gone, her heart pounding, her breath lodging in her lungs.

And that was *before* he touched her chest. Once his large, warm hand covered one aching breast, all bets were off. Her body went haywire on her—nerve endings crackled, head fogged, pulse raced. Not even the hint of smoke on his tongue could spoil the mood. If anything, the evidence of his bad habit only reminded her of how dangerous he was, and though she wasn't proud of it, a thrill shot through her. Why did bad boys excite her so much, dammit?

"You're not wearing anything beneath that shirt," he muttered against her lips.

"No." Her voice was a shaky whisper.

Seth cupped both her breasts possessively, growling as he gave them a not-so-gentle squeeze. When he lightly pinched her nipples through the shirt, she felt it between her legs and whimpered. With no bra acting as a barrier, the flannel abraded her nipples, and they puckered and tingled and pleaded for more attention.

Dipping his head, he nuzzled the crook of her neck. "You smell like heaven." He nibbled on her feverish flesh. "Taste like heaven too."

His facial scruff scratched her in the most delicious way, but there was nothing more delicious than the way he continued to fondle her boobs. Squeezing, pushing them together, teasing her nipples into two hard peaks.

"See, you need this," he rasped, his breath hot on her neck. "You *want* this."

Arousal had tightened her throat and rendered her vocal cords useless. He had her at a complete disadvantage—here he was, sure of himself, confident that his touch was having the desired effect, and here *she* was, struck mute, hardly able to remember what sex even felt like, so desperate for release she couldn't even make her hands work so she could touch him in return.

"Ahem."

At the sound of someone clearing his throat, Miranda flew off Seth's lap as if her life depended on it. She swiveled her gaze and found Dylan in the doorway, his short blond hair damp from the shower, lime-green eyes twinkling with amusement.

"Am I interrupting?" he asked casually.

"Yes," Seth grumbled, at the same time Miranda blurted out, "No, not at all."

Dylan smiled faintly. "Uh-huh. I see. Anyway," he glanced at Seth "Cash called. He spoke to the LT, who says everything's a go for tomorrow, rain or shine."

"Shit. They're gonna drop us in the middle of the ocean for that training op even if the storm's still raging?" Seth sounded anything but excited.

"Yesiree."

"Well, ain't that gonna suck."

As the men hammered out a few more details, Miranda was grateful for the opportunity to collect herself. She discreetly fixed the neckline of her shirt, then ran her fingers through her hair. Were her lips red and swollen from those blistering kisses? And could Dylan see how hard her nipples were?

Oh God. This had been a much-needed interruption. If Dylan hadn't walked in…shit, what would have happened?

You would have let Seth Masterson fuck you.

She gulped. Wow. That matter-of-fact voice didn't hold back any punches, did it?

But the voice was wrong. She wouldn't have slept with Seth just now. Her good judgment would have reared its head and stopped her before she did something so stupid, right?

"I'm turning in," she burst out, cutting Dylan off midsentence.

Seth was off the couch in a nanosecond, his expression darkening. "It's only nine thirty."

"And I have to be up at six. Besides, I'm super exhausted," she lied.

"Miranda…" She heard the note of warning.

"You two keep chatting," she said in an overly cheerful voice. She edged toward the doorway. "And thanks again for letting us stay here tonight. I really appreciate it." Two more steps and she reached the door. "So, um, yeah, g'nite, guys."

She darted out of the living room before either man could respond. A moment later, she walked into the dark guest room and released a breath of relief. Disaster averted. She'd gotten out of there, and now there was no chance she'd be having sex with Seth tonight.

Her gazed moved to the double bed, the only piece of furniture in the room other than the tall chest of drawers against the adjacent wall. Seth and Dylan took the word *minimalist* to new extremes, though she suspected it had a lot to do with their military status. She didn't imagine there to be much clutter or waste in the navy.

Sophie and Jason were sleeping soundly beneath the patterned comforter, lying on their sides on opposite ends of the bed. She smiled in the darkness, then undid the drawstring of the pants Seth had lent her and let the material pool at her feet. Seth's shirt hung all the way down to her knees so technically she didn't need to worry about modesty, but she still went to the dresser to rummage through the neatly folded pile of clothes Dylan had left there. She found her black bikini panties and slipped them on, then climbed onto the bed, doing her best not to wake the twins.

Sophie stirred in her sleep and made a soft sniffling sound, prompting Miranda to lie still. She needed both her kids to get a good night's sleep.

Because at this point, who knew what chaos tomorrow would bring.

Chapter Six

OH, THIS WAS BAD. IT WAS SO VERY BAD MIRANDA ACTUALLY FELT LIKE throwing up. Choking back the rising nausea, she met the sympathetic eyes of her landlord and said, "How long will the cleanup take?"

"To pump it all out and remove the floors, two days," he replied in perfect, albeit heavily accented, English. "The crew will discard any contaminated items. Everything will be documented for the purposes of insurance."

"What about all our personal belongings? When can I come in and catalog everything?"

Marco didn't answer for a moment, signaling to a passing member of the cleanup crew and calling out something in Italian. The men moving to and from the vans parked at the curb wore an array of protective gear—green hip waders, rubber boots, gloves, masks. You'd think there was a hazardous waste spill in there instead of a few feet of rainwater.

Then again, even one foot of water would have been an utter disaster. Miranda's heart had dropped to the pit of her stomach when she'd followed Marco into the apartment to survey the damage. Most of the water had been drained, so she'd been able to walk around in her yellow rain boots with no trouble.

No, the real trouble was the fact that anything with the misfortune of touching the floor was soaking wet and most likely unsalvageable. Luckily, most of her clothing was dry—everything in the top dresser drawers had escaped the flood, as did the hanging items in the closet. Even better—her important documents had come out unscathed, since she stored them all in a portable file folder at the top of her closet. And the twins' room had barely been affected, which was the biggest miracle of all because now she wouldn't have to replace any of their gazillion toys.

"I'll have the men working around the clock so we can get you and your family back here as soon as possible," Marco said kindly. He was only in his midthirties, but when he squeezed her arm in reassurance, his touch was oddly paternal. "Tomorrow morning you can come back to go through your things. The crew we hired is full-service, so they will assist with the cleaning and drying."

"That's a relief," she said gratefully.

Marco lightly patted her arm. "I promise you, Ms. Breslin, everything will be taken care of. I apologize again for the inconvenience. I was not informed that the gutters were built improperly."

She believed him. Marco had been genuinely horrified yesterday when he'd discovered the state of the ground-floor apartments. He'd already insisted she didn't have to pay next month's rent and had refused to budge when she'd protested.

"Don't worry, you'll be able to come home in three days, four days maximum," Marco added before moving away.

Miranda loitered on the tidy front lawn for a moment, staring at the two-story building she'd been calling home for the past four months. White stucco made up the exterior, the tiled clay roof a pale shade of pink. There was no lobby, just an open walkway and two sets of stairs at each side of the building leading to the second-floor apartments.

The place was nothing to brag about, but it was pretty and clean, and even though the backyard was small, it was big enough that she could plant a garden back there. And at least she had a yard—the upstairs apartments got balconies, which was why Miranda had been ecstatic to land a ground-floor one.

Well, she wasn't feeling too ecstatic anymore.

With a weary exhalation she headed to the curb where she'd parked the sedan. It was nine thirty in the morning, the sun was shining and the sky was a cloudless blue. The only hints that a storm had ravaged the area yesterday were the leftover puddles on the asphalt.

Since morning had brought with it nothing but good weather, most schools were open today, including the twins', and she didn't have to pick them up until three. She'd been hoping to spend the day at the apartment cleaning up, but now that Marco had sent her away, she had no idea where to go.

Back to Seth's? Both he and Dylan had been gone when Miranda and the twins wandered into the kitchen this morning. She knew they were at the navy base doing some kind of training operation, and she kind of hoped it lasted until the wee hours of the night because she couldn't face Seth right now. She'd barely slept last night. Rather, she'd lain there sandwiched between her kids, tossing and turning, thinking about how incredible Seth's kisses had felt and how badly she wanted to kiss him again.

Until she figured out how to get a handle on this attraction, she needed to keep her distance from him.

She finally decided to drive into the city. She'd seen on the news that most of the inland flooding had occurred in her neighborhood, Imperial Beach, along with several of the other coastal towns in the area, but San Diego hadn't experienced much water damage. Still, it wouldn't hurt to check on the dance school.

To her relief, the building that housed All That Dance was in perfect condition. When she wandered through the various studios, she found nothing but glossy wood floors and sparkling mirrors.

She changed into a leotard and dance shoes, deciding to get a workout in as long as she was here. Popping her iPod into the dock near the door, she queued up her favorite playlist, the one she turned to in times of stress. At the school she taught ballet and modern lyrical, but today she decompressed with straight-up hip-hop moves that left her sweaty and breathless by the time she called it quits an hour later.

That little dose of dance medicine was all she'd needed to brighten her spirits, and when she got back to Seth's place a short while later, she was even whistling to herself as she let herself in with the key he'd given her.

The whistling died in a sharp wheeze when she entered the kitchen and found Seth at the counter. He wore black basketball shorts that hung low on his hips, a gray T-shirt, and his feet were bare.

"What are you doing home?" she asked in surprise.

The coffeemaker clicked, and Seth grabbed the pot by the handle and poured himself a cup. "We're done for the day. Want some coffee?"

After a beat, she nodded, then accepted the mug he handed her. She blew on the hot liquid and said, "How are you done for the day? It's barely noon."

"Baby, I was up at four o'clock this morning and in the ocean at five for some heavy-duty underwater demolition. I've earned the right to call it a day." He sipped his coffee and headed for the sliding door, an unlit cigarette in his hand. "Join me outside?"

She hesitated again.

"Jesus, Miranda. I don't bite."

An unwitting laugh burst out. "Yes, you do."

His lips twitched. "Yeah, you're right. I *do* bite. But only the good kind of biting."

He looked like he was waiting for her to ask "and what's the good kind?" but no way was she opening *that* door.

Holding her mug with both hands, she followed him out to the concrete patio, which housed a small round table and two plastic chairs. Although the surrounding grass was mowed, the yard was as barren as most of the house's interior. No garden or flowers or bird feeders or any of the fun things she and the twins had put in their own yard.

"You and Dylan really don't care much for decorating, do you?" she said wryly.

"Not really," he replied, his cigarette dangling from the corner of his mouth. He shoved a hand in his pocket and extracted a black Bic lighter. The lighter hissed as he flicked it, the tip of his cigarette glowing as he brought it to the flame.

Miranda didn't lecture him. She wasn't a smoker herself, but she believed in letting other people make their own mistakes. Besides, who was she to reprimand anyone about bad choices? She'd made quite a few of those in her own life.

"So what did your landlord say?" Seth sat down, exhaling a cloud of smoke in the direction opposite her.

She joined him at the table and quickly filled him in, finishing with a glum, "He said it'll be three or four days before we can move back in."

"You'll stay here until then," Seth said without delay.

She suppressed a sigh. "Thanks for the offer, but I think we'll check into a hotel. Probably after I pick up the twins from school."

"Why would you pay money to stay in a hotel when I have a perfectly good room you can use for free?" He sounded incredibly annoyed.

"Because...I don't want to put you out," she said feebly.

"Bullshit."

She lifted her chin in defiance. "Fine, you want to know the real reason? I'm tired of the way you keep trying to get me into bed when I'm clearly not interested."

A low laugh rumbled out of his chest. "You seemed pretty interested last night when we were making out on the couch."

"It was a moment of weakness," she admitted. "But it can't happen again. There's too much on my plate right now to get involved with anyone, even if it's just a casual fling. I'm getting this dance school off the ground, getting used to a new city, trying to make a new life for me and my kids. And now our apartment got flooded and my stress levels are even higher." She shook her head. "So if you're offering us a place to stay in exchange for me going to bed with—"

"The offer isn't conditional, for chrissake. I'm not asking you to screw me in exchange for room and board." Seth's eyes flashed. "Fuck, Miranda, what kind of asshole do you think I am?"

Guilt splashed around in her belly when she realized the wounded look on his face was genuine. God, she'd actually hurt him.

"Seth…dammit, I'm sorry." She suddenly wished she'd just kept her mouth shut. "I don't think you're an asshole, and I appreciate the offer, okay? But if my kids and I are going to stay, we need to set a few ground rules."

His hard expression relaxed, but she noticed he took an extra-long drag on his cigarette. "Let's hear it."

"No sex." When he didn't respond, she hurried on. "I mean it. An affair between us is a bad idea."

"Whatever you say."

His noncommittal tone brought a spark of irritation. "It is," she insisted. "And not just because I don't have the time or energy for it at the moment. I'm not cut out for casual flings. I can't separate emotions from sex, no matter how hard I try, and I don't want to get hurt."

He grimaced. "Why must women always complicate the simplest things?"

She burst out laughing. "Sex is not simple. It's the biggest complication of all, and if you don't believe me, just look at my kids. They're living proof of exactly how complicated sex can be."

Seth didn't answer.

"I won't deny that I'm attracted to you—you know I am. But I can't act on it. I don't want a fling, and if you can't promise to be a gentleman and stop trying to seduce me every other minute, I'm staying in a hotel."

He took another pull off his cigarette, then leaned forward to snuff it out in the glass ashtray on the table. His mouth was set in a tired line as he rose from his chair, the muscles of his broad chest rippling beneath his T-shirt. The bottom of his tattoo poked out from beneath his sleeve, and the intriguing black design distracted her for a moment. She'd have pegged him as the skull-and-bones type, but she much preferred the ink he had.

Forcing herself to focus on the topic at hand, she shot him a firm look. "Can you promise me, Seth?"

Dragging a hand through his hair, he locked his gaze with hers and said, "For as long as you're here, I'll be a perfect gentleman. Now if you'll excuse me, I'm going to lie down for a while." He took a step to the door, then halted. "Help yourself to anything in the fridge if you get hungry. Dylan's out shopping for groceries, so don't worry, you and the rugrats will be well fed."

As she watched him go, a tornado of conflicting emotions swirled through her body, making her feel exhausted. It drove her nuts that she could never quite get a handle on him. One minute he was the consummate badass, trying to lure her to the dark side with his mocking words and wicked kisses. The next, he was making sure there was enough food in the fridge to feed her and her children.

Who was he, really? Was his whole rebel thing an act? No, she doubted that—Seth was too rough around the edges to be faking it. But he must have a softer side, right? He couldn't be all thorn and no rose, could he?

Biting her bottom lip, she fixed her gaze on the tall fence separating Seth's yard from his neighbor's. Did it even matter whether Seth possessed a warm and gooey center beneath his crunchy exterior? She'd made it clear that she wouldn't be getting involved with him, so there was no point in searching for the "real" Seth or prying into his psyche.

What she really ought to be figuring out was how on earth she'd be able to spend the next three or four days in close proximity with the man—without forgetting everything she'd just told him and ripping his clothes off.

To Seth's annoyance, Miranda's rugrats didn't take the news well—once she informed them that they were staying with Seth for a few more days, both kids promptly burst into tears and clung to their mother like they were scared she'd be abducted by aliens if they let her out of their sight.

It made for a rather stressful dinner, this time prepared by Seth, which had earned him an amazed look from Miranda. She kept shaking her head each time she glanced at the grilled chicken and roasted potatoes on her plate, as if she couldn't fathom that someone like him could create such a meal.

It was actually kind of insulting, evoking a prickly and defensive reaction that only got worse when Miranda swallowed her last bite of chicken and said, "Wow. That was great. I still can't believe you cooked dinner."

All the shit he'd gone through today was finally beginning to get to him, weighing down on his chest and bringing a bite to his tone. "I'm not some helpless case who can't take care of himself, Miranda. I'm fully capable of cooking my own food. I also know how to do laundry and mop the floor and sew a button back on."

Silence descended over the table.

In the seat across from him, Dylan shot him a WTF look that Seth ignored.

"I'm sorry," Miranda said awkwardly. "I guess I shouldn't make assumptions."

More silence. The rugrats were sitting on either side of Miranda. Their tears had dried up, but both kids looked miserable, which stumped him because they'd known about the flood in the apartment since yesterday, so why the delayed reaction?

"Where'd you learn to cook?" Miranda prompted as she reached for the water glass on the table. She took a small sip, eyeing him over the rim.

"Not from my mom, that's for sure," he said gruffly. "Usually she'd already left for the theater when I got home from school, so I learned to fend for myself. Sometimes I'd watch some cheesy cooking channel to figure out what to make."

Dylan snickered. "Oh, that's pure gold. I can't wait to tell the guys that you wore aprons as a kid and pretended to be Julia Child."

He scowled at his roommate. "Do it and you won't live to see your next birthday."

Both of Miranda's kids began to cry again.

Just like that. No warning, no provocation. One second they were sitting there quietly, the next they'd unleashed the waterworks.

Looking concerned, Miranda wrapped an arm around each child. "Guys, what is going *on* today? I know you're upset that we can't go home for a few days, but we'll have fun here, I promise."

Dylan voiced his agreement. "You'll get to watch movies and stuff yourselves on cookies and popcorn, and you can tell everyone in your class that you're having an extended sleepover. Think of how jealous they'll be."

Neither Miranda nor Dylan succeeded in calming down the twins, whose faces were red and splotchy and covered with tears and snot.

Seth resisted a groan. Christ, how was this happening? In *his* house? How could he have possibly thought letting Miranda and the rugrats stay here was a good idea?

Miranda murmured words of comfort, but eventually she excused herself and ushered the kids out of the room, leaving the men alone to clean up.

"I can see why you like her," Dylan confessed, gathering everyone's dirty plates.

"Yeah?"

"Or rather, why anyone would like her. She's gorgeous, smart, amazing with those kids. The thing is, I don't get why *you* like her."

"What's that supposed to mean?"

He followed his roommate to the sink. Together, they began scraping leftover food into the garbage, while Dylan took his sweet-ass time responding.

"You don't go for chicks like Miranda," Dylan finally said. "You only do temporary, and I hate to break it to you, bro, but that woman has permanent written all over her."

His jaw tensed. "I know."

"Do you? Because it doesn't seem like you do. Let me spell it out for you. That gorgeous, smart woman out there?" Dylan gestured beyond the kitchen doorway. "She's a mom, and she loves those kids something fierce, in case you haven't noticed."

"Oh, I've noticed," he said grimly.

"And you, for some unexplained reason, have an aversion to anyone under the age of eighteen."

"Why does everyone act like I'm auditioning for the role of those kids' father? I'm attracted to Miranda, plain and simple. I want to sleep with her, not marry her."

Dylan started running the plates under the tap before shoving them in the dishwasher. "Well, she ain't gonna sleep with you," he said bluntly. "She's not the type for a casual fuck. Anyone can see that."

Seth couldn't even argue, because he knew Dylan was one-hundred percent, categorically *right*. Miranda herself had made that loud and clear only hours ago.

So why the hell couldn't he bring himself to abandon the cause? Why was he chasing after a woman who didn't want a fling? And even if he *did* succeed in wearing down her defenses, she'd said so herself—she didn't do casual. She would want more from him.

He wasn't ready to give anyone that *more*. The only commitment he wanted in his life was the one he'd made to the SEALs. He was a soldier first and foremost, and he had plenty of solid ass-kicking, world-saving years left in him.

Truth was, no matter how many successful ops his squad had carried out, he still didn't feel he'd scraped even the tip of the iceberg in terms of making a difference in this sorry world. Not that he was some tree-hugging do-gooder, but he did feel the need to be doing something worthwhile. Something that had value. Something that gave *him* value.

"Ugh," Miranda's voice came from the doorway. "I calmed them down, but they still won't tell me what's freaking them out so bad." She headed for the table and began clearing the remaining items.

"You don't have to do that," Dylan called from the sink.

"Yes, I do." She handed him the empty glasses, then grabbed some paper towels from the dispenser on the counter. As she wiped the table, she let out a sigh and said, "Hopefully Soph and Jase don't cause too much trouble when I'm at work tonight. They're acting so damn weird."

Both men froze, exchanging panicked looks.

Seth attempted to sound casual. "You're bartending tonight?"

As in, leaving the rugrats here with him and Dylan? The mere thought of it sent a jolt of terror through him.

"It's Monday. I told you I'm working at the club tonight." Her eyes narrowed in understanding. "Oh, for the love of God, you two. I'm not forcing you to babysit my kids. I have a regular babysitter who watches them on club nights. Monday, Wednesday, Friday and Saturday—though I doubt I have to tell *you* that, do I? You have my schedule memorized."

Seth ignored the sarcastic jab she lobbed his way and dried his hands with a dishtowel. Next to him, Dylan looked equally relieved. On the entire drive home from the base earlier, Dylan had been moaning about how the only thing that would ease his aching muscles was lying on his back while a hot chick rode him like a cowgirl, so no doubt the guy had been horrified to think he might have to spend the night babysitting instead.

"What time do you start?" Dylan asked.

"Nine," she replied. "Why?"

"Maybe I'll catch a ride with you. I'm meeting a few guys downtown tonight, right near your club. I'd take the Jeep, but I plan on getting hammered."

"Sure, no problem. Oh, and if you're interested, all domestic beers are half-price tonight, between ten and midnight."

Dylan looked incredibly intrigued by that. "We might have to stop by then."

Miranda walked over to throw out the paper towels. Seth was only standing two feet from the sink, and when she got near, her scent filled his nostrils and sent a dizzying rush of lust through him.

To make matters worse, all she ever wore was leggings. Super tight ones that clung to the contours of her shapely legs. She had a dancer's legs—long and lean, not heavily muscled, but radiating strength. And grace. Damn, the woman was graceful. Sometimes when he watched her work the bar, it was like witnessing a ballet in progress.

"I'll be at the club tonight too, so you might as well ride with me," Seth told Dylan as he moved away from the counter to place some much-needed distance between himself and Miranda's sexy body.

Her expression displayed sheer frustration. "No, Seth, you promised you wouldn't bug me at work anymore."

He had to laugh. "I made no such promise, babe. Wishful thinking on your part, maybe?"

She grumbled something under her breath.

"What was that?" he asked sweetly.

"Nothing." With a frown, she drifted to the doorway. "I'm going to hang out with my kids until the sitter gets here."

Both men watched her go, and then Dylan turned to him with a perplexed look. "What are you hoping to get out of this, bro?"

The question gave him legitimate pause. He took a moment to consider it, to ask himself, what *did* he want from Miranda?

Her body?

Her submission?

Her…approval?

No, the latter was so preposterous he fought a laugh. He didn't need Miranda's approval. So what if she viewed him as nothing more than a sexed-up bad boy with all the depth of a birdbath?

He *was* a sexed-up bad boy. Though he did have more depth and substance than anyone suspected. He just kept it to himself. He had nothing to prove to anyone, anyway, seeing as how he'd stopped caring a long time ago what people thought of him.

But you do care what she thinks. You care a lot.

"Fuck," he muttered, turning away from his roommate's inquisitive stare. "To tell you the truth, I have no idea what I'm hoping to get out of it. No fucking idea."

Chapter Seven

SOMETHING WAS GOING ON WITH SETH. DYLAN COULDN'T FIGURE OUT what, and he knew there was no chance in hell his smartass jerk of a roommate would shed any light on the matter. But it was easy to see that Miranda had gotten under the guy's skin. Like *really* under the skin, burrowed deep like a tick.

He'd never seen Seth so rattled before, and he had no idea what to make of it. Out of all his teammates, Seth Masterson was by far the toughest. Not necessarily the biggest—at six-five Jackson had him in height, and Becker definitely outmuscled him—but Seth was unquestionably the most lethal. He possessed an eerie sense of calm in the face of danger, always the first one to enter a hot zone and the last one to leave.

Nothing scared Seth Masterson.

Except, apparently, two cute little six-year-olds and their sexy-as-sin mother.

Sighing, Dylan turned away from Seth's stiff, gloomy profile and focused on the storefronts whizzing past the Jeep's passenger side. It was getting dark out, and most of the shops were closing up for the night. Good. That meant all the cute salesgirls would be done with work and heading to the city's bars and clubs to unwind.

He definitely needed to get laid tonight. Earlier this morning during the training op, a wave had slammed him into the side of the boat, and now his shoulder ached like a motherfucker. He could hardly be considered injured, but the CO had ordered him to take a day to rest the shoulder, so there was nothing stopping him from getting drunk tonight. And laid. Yup, he had the green light for that too.

"Who exactly are we meeting?" Seth asked, his hands moving over the steering wheel to make a left turn.

"O'Connor, Rhodes and a few ensigns from the base."

Seth slowed down as they reached the heart of downtown and scanned the street for parking. "What about Cash and Texas?"

"Cash is chilling at Jen's place. Jackson pled exhaustion."

And although he wouldn't say it out loud, Dylan was much more troubled by the former than the latter. Up until six months ago, Cash had been his wingman, but nowadays he was in a relationship with a woman he adored. Dylan couldn't even fault the guy—he adored Jen too, and why wouldn't he? She was not only beautiful, but funny, sweet and way too kindhearted for her own good. She kept trying to find ways to "include" him, whether it was dinner invites or movie nights or swimming over at Cash's place. He totally appreciated the effort she was making to ensure he and McCoy didn't drift apart—bromances were common casualties of committed relationships—but the thing of it was, Dylan wasn't worried about losing Cash.

The reason he was allowing this distance between them to grow was because seeing Cash and Jen together made him...yearn.

For what, he had no clue. A relationship of his own? A woman who loved him?

Whatever it was, it freaked him out, because that strange craving was always accompanied by a vise of self-doubt that squeezed the living shit out of his chest. Because he didn't want to face the fact that maybe he wasn't cut out for what Cash had. And because he hated hearing that nagging voice in his head, the one that reminded him of everything he was.

And everything he wasn't.

"Somebody's pissed off."

Seth's voice, half-taunting, half-amused, jolted him from his disturbing thoughts. "I'm not pissed off. I just spaced out."

"Oh really, so you're not sulking about McCoy blowing you off again?"

"Like I said yesterday, I'm happy for him." He paused. "Hey, did I tell you my brother's getting married?"

"Seriously? Mr. Boring's getting hitched?"

Dylan didn't bother being offended on Chris's behalf. It was true—Chris definitely had the tendency to be boring, but then again, didn't that go with the territory when you chose to be a lawyer? Fortunately,

Chris *was* capable of letting loose every now and then, usually after a few beers and some extra convincing on Dylan's part.

"He proposed to Claire a couple of nights ago."

Seth parked the Jeep and killed the engine. "The shrew?"

"Yep," he said glumly. "Ms. Snooty is gonna be my sister-in-law. Fun."

His phone buzzed as he and Seth got out of the car. An incoming text from O'Connor—*Already inside. Come find us.*

"The guys are inside," he told Seth.

They approached the front door, which was painted black and manned by a bored-looking bouncer in a muscle tee. There was no line out front, one of the upsides of showing up on a weeknight.

Inside the club, the music was blasting and the strobe lights were flashing. The place wasn't packed, but Dylan glimpsed several promising candidates for what he had in store for tonight, including a cute blonde who openly eye-fucked him as he passed her. He made a mental note to find her again and led the way to the bar counter, Seth on his heels.

Miranda was already on duty, looking damn sexy in a low-cut red top. He couldn't judge the length of her skirt because the counter shielded her lower body from view, but he suspected it was indecently short.

Yup, indecent—confirmation came as Miranda stepped toward the mirrored wall that housed shelves of liquor bottles in all shapes and sizes. When she stood on her tiptoes to reach for some Jägermeister, her skirt rode up, revealing the backs of her firm, tanned thighs and the underside of her curvy ass.

"Check her out again and I'll rip your balls off." Seth's voice was deceptively calm as he came up beside him.

Dylan just grinned. "Meow."

"I'm serious, asshole."

"Double meow."

Miranda greeted them with a resigned smile, which was mostly directed at Seth. "What'll it be, guys?"

They ordered Bud Lights, paid Miranda, then moved away from the counter to let a group of scantily clad chicks place their orders. Dylan scanned the dance floor for their buddies but didn't see them. OMG had a cool layout—the dance floor was like a sunken room, sectioned off by a railing that wrapped around it. Low sets of steps on each side of the space led to curtained-off, darkened alcoves—which Dylan had made use of on more than one occasion—as well as seating areas with high tables and stools that overlooked the dance floor.

"Wade!"

Hearing his name over the pounding bass line, Dylan searched the crowd, finally spotting Matt O'Connor and Aidan Rhodes. He gestured for Seth to follow, but the other man just shook his head and edged back in the direction of the counter.

With a shrug, Dylan left his roommate and wandered up the stairs toward his buddies. O'Connor, who boasted a shaved head and a southern drawl, served on his squad, and they exchanged a quick side hug when Dylan approached. He didn't know Aidan that well, but the dark-haired intelligence officer was a good friend of Matt's, and he greeted Dylan with a friendly nod.

"Where's Masterson?" Matt asked.

"Playing guard dog. He's got a thing for the bartender."

The other two men laughed.

Matt sipped his beer, then set the bottle on the wide railing. "How's the shoulder?"

"Hurts like a bitch," Dylan admitted.

Aidan's dark brows furrowed. "What happened?"

"Banged it up during a training demo this morning. And I'm pretty sure our medic was unnecessarily rough when he examined it to make sure it wasn't broken."

Matt laughed. "Yeah, wouldn't surprise me. Texas didn't look too happy when you kept riding his ass about not setting the charges fast enough."

"'S'all good." Dylan smirked. "I got a day's medical leave outta it, and Texas gets to report to the base at oh-dark-hundred hours for underwater demolition part two."

"Way to rub it in. I'm in Jackson's boat. Literally." Grinning, Matt picked up his beer and drained it. "One more," he decided. "After that, you boys need to cut me off, deal? 'Cause Becker will kick my ass if I show up hungover tomorrow."

"Deal." Dylan tipped his head and consumed half his beer in one gulp. "Don't worry. I plan on drinking enough for the both of us."

THE UNNATURALLY MUSCULAR MEATHEAD IN THE CHEESY MESH TANK top had been hanging around the counter way too long for Seth's liking. Leaning against the wall just off the dance floor, Seth tuned out the blaring house beat and waited for the next flash of strobe lighting to illuminate Miranda's face so he could gauge her expression.

She had to be annoyed with Mr. Steroids as much he was, right? The last time Seth had walked past, he'd heard the meathead bragging about how many reps he did at the gym. The fucking gym. Ha. Idiot wouldn't survive a day of SEAL training. In fact, Seth would just love to see Mr. Steroids spend hours on the hot asphalt doing mass calisthenics. Or get hosed down with frigid water while being ordered to jump on and off a pier over and over again.

The *gym*.

Scowling to himself, Seth finally got a good look at Miranda, who was smiling at something Mr. Steroids had said. What the hell? How was she even remotely amused by anything that came out of that jerk's mouth?

No, wait. That wasn't a genuine Miranda smile. This one was tight, didn't quite reach her eyes.

He finished his beer, then ditched the bottle on the little ledge behind him. He was dying for a smoke, but he didn't want to go outside while that meathead was still drooling over Miranda.

When Mr. Steroids leaned in closer and said something that made her frown, only the memory of how angry she'd been last time he'd interfered stopped Seth from marching over there. She claimed she could handle herself? Fine. He was willing to give her the chance.

Three minutes later, when a visibly disappointed Mr. Steroids stalked away from the counter, Seth had to give credit where credit was due. Whatever she'd said had successfully gotten rid of her admirer. Now she was at the other end of the bar, preparing a complicated-looking fruity drink that Seth wouldn't be caught dead drinking.

He waited a few more minutes, just to make sure Mr. Steroids didn't return, then left his perch in the shadows. He fished his Marlboro pack from one of the pockets of his black cargo pants and shoved an unlit cigarette in the corner of his mouth. A glance at his military-issue tactical watch showed it was past midnight. Shit, he had to be up in five hours. But he didn't want to leave yet. He hated not being here for last call. That was when the creeps and a-holes came out to play.

For a moment, he considered asking Dylan to stick around in his stead—dude had tomorrow off, after all—but a quick inspection of the dance floor shot down that idea. Dylan and some blonde were wrapped all over each other like a pair of eels, grinding to the beat of a sultry hip-hop track. The lights zigzagged directly over the couple, and…yep, Seth's roommate had one hand under the chick's shirt, the other tangled in her long hair.

No way would he be able to pry those two apart tonight.

Fine then. One quick smoke, and then he'd say good night to Miranda, and trust that she could take care of herself.

The club offered a small smoking area at the back of the building, and when he exited through the rear doors, he was surprised to find Aidan Rhodes out there with a cigarette. A stocky bouncer stood by the door, nodding at Seth before going expressionless.

"Hey, man." Seth nodded at Aidan in greeting. "Didn't know you smoked."

"Only when I'm drinking." The tip of the cigarette glowed in the darkness as the naval officer took a deep drag. "You heading out?"

"Soon." He lit up, inhaled, and blew a gray plume into the night air. "Just need to figure out how my very drunk, very horny roommate plans on getting home."

Aidan opened his mouth to reply, only to get cut off by the creak of the door as it opened to let a few newcomers onto the patio.

Seth's shoulders stiffened when he recognized Mr. Steroids. And look at that, the meathead had friends, two of them, both of whom clearly belonged to the same pansy-ass gym.

"Hate it when bitches act like they're better than me," Mr. Steroids was grumbling.

Seth noted that all three men were smokers, which kinda contradicted the whole health-fanatic vibe they were trying to give off.

"Dude, I hear ya. Those high-and-mighty types are grade-A cunts," the second meathead declared.

Dropping the C-word? So these losers didn't just dress like douchebags—they acted like it too. Shocking.

"Whatever, dude," the third douche piped up. "Her tits weren't even that nice."

Seth and Aidan exchanged a look. Neither of them said a word, but Seth could tell Aidan was annoyed by the vulgar convo happening next to them. As Aidan's shoulders tensed beneath his white polo shirt, Seth realized just how ripped the other man was. He tended to forget it, since Aidan was only five-eleven or so and therefore dwarfed by guys like O'Connor, who stood well over six feet.

"And at least come up with an excuse I could buy." Mr. Steroids exhaled a cloud of smoke, then guffawed. "You're busy running a dance school? Yeah right, sweetie. You're busy working the pole at the D-Cup Lounge, more like it."

Now Seth's shoulders were stiffer than a fence post. He'd figured the douches were talking about Miranda, but now that he had verification, it was difficult to control the anger simmering in his gut.

Slowly and methodically, he turned to face the three gym rats and cleared his throat to get their attention. "Quick question," he said.

Mr. Steroids looked annoyed by the interruption. He flicked the ash from his cigarette onto the pavement instead of using the bucket of sand at his feet. "What is it?" the guy snapped.

"The girl you're talking about—you mean the bartender, right?"

"Yeah. What's it to you?"

Seth purposefully dropped his cigarette in the ashtray bucket and met Mr. Steroids' impatient blue eyes. "She's my girlfriend," he replied coldly.

Cue: apology.

Or maybe even a mumbled "whatever".

What he didn't expect?

"Well, sorry to break it to you, dude, but your girlfriend's a cunt."

Chapter Eight

HEAVEN. DYLAN WAS IN HEAVEN. HIDDEN AWAY IN ONE OF THE SHADOWY alcoves of the club, he had his back against the wall, an eager girl on her knees before him, and a warm mouth surrounding his dick. Groaning, he pushed his hips forward, threading both hands through the blonde's silky hair as he thrust deeper.

"That's it, honey. Nice and slow."

She moaned in approval, then teased the hard length of him with the tip of her tongue, torturing him with featherlight licks that drove him fucking crazy. He was dying to get inside her, but she wasn't ready to leave the club yet, so they'd ended up striking a bargain—she'd help him take the edge off with a quick BJ, he'd stick around and dance with her until last call, and then they'd head back to her place for a night of fun. Win-win-win.

Another low groan slid out as she wrapped her succulent lips around his engorged head and sucked. Gentle and sweet.

"Ah, that's good, honey."

Suddenly that incredible suction was gone. He glanced down to see a pair of shrewd blue eyes looking up at him.

"Something wrong?" he murmured.

"What's my name?"

A smile tugged on his lips. "You think I don't remember your name?"

She shrugged. "You keep calling me honey. Call me old-fashioned, but I like it when the guy I'm blowing knows who's blowing him."

"Trust me, I know. *Rachel.*" His smile widened. "Last name is…Carver? Yeah, Carver. And you're in college for fashion merchandising."

She looked mollified. "Wow. Okay. You were actually listening."

"I always do, honey."

With a little laugh, she encircled his cock with her delicate fingers and gave it a sharp pump. Despite the brief hiatus, he was still harder than concrete and so very ready to come. Rachel took him in her mouth again, her head bobbing up and down as she sucked him with fervor. His own head lolled to the side, eyes closing and hips moving, balls tight and tingling.

Just as he got close, a familiar voice called out his name.

Dylan cursed under his breath. The black velvet curtain separating the alcove from the public rustled but didn't open.

"Seriously, Dylan, I know you're in there," Aidan called, his voice muffled by the pounding techno beat. "I need you out here pretty bad. Normally I wouldn't interrupt you when you're…yeah…but O'Connor took off a while ago and Zack and Fletch just left, so I need you."

He stifled another expletive. "What's up?" he called back.

"Masterson's about to beat up some guys."

Aw shit.

Shaking his head in disbelief, Dylan gently reclaimed his cock from Rachel's mouth and tucked it into his khaki cargo pants.

"I'm sorry," he told the confused blonde, helping her to her feet. "I have to go. My buddy's in trouble."

Disappointment flickered in her eyes. "Come find me when it's over?"

He nodded, then bent down to brush a kiss on her cheek. "Definitely. And I've got your number, so if for some reason I don't make it back, I'll message you, okay?"

"Okay."

He felt like a total shit as he darted out of the alcove. Aidan was waiting behind the curtain, his dark eyes lined with worry and a hint of aggravation.

"What the hell happened?" Dylan demanded.

"A bunch of morons decided to trash-talk the bartender your boy's panting over."

"Fucking great."

He followed Aidan toward the back of the club, feeling slightly dizzy as the strobe lights assaulted his vision and the deafening music attempted to destroy his eardrums. For a second, he swayed on his feet, growing disoriented and nauseous. Shit, he was drunker than he'd thought. And it was incredibly difficult to match Aidan's breakneck pace when he still had an erection of monstrous proportions.

Fortunately, all signs of arousal drained from his dick the second he and Aidan burst onto the smoking patio.

Unfortunately, the scene they came upon was utter chaos.

Dylan had barely registered it when he became the recipient of an elbow to the groin that made him see stars.

"Son of a bitch," he croaked, doubling over.

A blur of fists and elbows and legs flashed in front of his eyes, heavy male grunts echoing in the night air. He quickly recovered from the accidental nut shot and dove in Seth's direction, though it was clear his roommate didn't need much assistance. Even surrounded by three guys and a bouncer determined to stop the scuffle, Seth was completely holding his own, unleashing left hooks and uppercuts that landed with resounding *thwacks* on their intended targets.

Blood poured out of Seth's nostrils, but he seemed unfazed. The three men he'd decided to take on were bleeding in various places too—mouths, noses, chins. One even had blood dripping from his temple.

"Enough," Dylan snapped as he launched himself into the fold. He nearly caught a blow to the side of the head, but managed to block it at the last second.

"I'm calling the fucking cops!" the bouncer was shouting. The big man succeeded in getting one of the beefheads in a headlock and began dragging his prey away like a lion collecting his carcass.

From the corner of his eye, Dylan saw Aidan grab hold of the other muscleman, leaving Seth to deal with the remaining one until two more bouncers flew onto the patio and put an end to the commotion.

Next thing Dylan knew, he was being thrown backward. A *thud*, then another, as Seth and Aidan landed on the pavement beside him.

"Get the fuck up!" One of the bouncers, an enormous guy with a skull tattoo on his neck, loomed over them, his massive arms crossed over his massive chest.

Dylan staggered to his feet. The adrenaline coursing through his blood, combined with all the alcohol he'd consumed, made him light-headed and more than a little queasy. His stomach churned, prompting him to take a deep breath before he lost his dinner all over the bouncer's feet.

His ears proceeded to ring during the entire altercation that followed, but he understood the gist of what went down. He, Seth and Aidan were being thrown out. So were the muscleheads Seth had decided to pound on. The club manager came out at one point, spewing threats about pressing charges and whatnot, but eventually she lost steam and told them to "get the fuck out of her sight".

The bouncers escorted the men to the curb. Everyone was oddly silent and subdued, and a few minutes later, the three beefheads stumbled into a cab, aiming three death looks in Seth's direction before they disappeared.

Dylan noted that not a single one of those dudes had come after Seth during the wait for the taxi, nor had they offered any parting words along the lines of "this isn't over". And he doubted that had anything to do with the angry bouncers standing four feet away. Judging by the sad, bloodied state those losers had left in, Seth had clearly made an impact.

Dylan's gaze drifted to the two bouncers at the door, who returned his stare with matching menacing scowls. Yeah, there was no way he was getting back in that club tonight. So much for dancing the night away with Rachel.

Hell. He wasn't even in the mood for sex anymore. He'd jarred his shoulder while trying to break up the fight, and it was throbbing again. Damn it. He'd consumed a shit-ton of beer and whiskey shots tonight, specifically to reach the point where the pain faded into that numb sort of nothingness, and now all his hard work was down the drain.

Tightening his lips, he glared at Seth, whose gray eyes displayed sheer boredom. Boredom, for fuck's sake. The guy had just rearranged the faces of three dudes, his nose was a bloody mess, and he was standing there like it was no biggie.

"You couldn't let it go, huh?" Dylan cracked.

His roommate shrugged. "Not really."

Aidan, who hadn't said a word since they'd been tossed out of the club, looked from one SEAL to the other, then chuckled. "Didn't I hear something about you guys getting locked up for brawling a while back?"

"You heard right," Dylan mumbled. "And that last brawl wasn't my fault either. Apparently I hang around cavemen who can't control their tempers."

Rolling his eyes, Seth reached into his pocket for his wallet and dug out a twenty-dollar bill. "I'll spring for a cab for you," he said, handing

Dylan the cash. "I'm gonna hang around here until Miranda gets off."

Dylan barked out an incredulous laugh. "You have to report to the CO in like four hours."

"Which is why there's no point in even going to bed. I'll wait for Miranda to get off, just in case those assholes decide to come back and cause trouble for her."

"Suit yourself. You'll be the one dead-ass tired in the water tomorrow." Dylan pulled out his cell phone and scrolled through the contacts, but his vision kept going in and out of focus. "Shit, I know I have a cab number in here, but everything's starting to spin."

"Forget the cab. I'll take you home," Aidan offered.

"You sure?"

"Yeah, it's not a problem."

Dylan's foggy brain registered a thought. "Aw shit, I can't go home. I don't want the kids to see me drunk."

Aidan's brows shot up. "You've got kids at your place? Since when?"

"Miranda and her children are staying with us," Seth explained. "Their apartment flooded."

"Ah. I see."

"And the rugrats are asleep by now," Seth pointed out.

Dylan stubbornly shook his head. "Don't care. What if they wake up in the middle of the night and find me puking in the bathroom? I refuse to corrupt children."

He'd barely finished his sentence when the world rotated again. He wobbled on his feet, nausea climbing up his throat.

Aidan shot Seth a perplexed look. "How is he able to speak in full, articulate sentences when he's this loaded?"

"No fucking idea, man."

"How about this? Why don't you crash at my place tonight?" Aidan suggested. "I live three blocks from here, and I can drop you home tomorrow before I head to the base."

"That sounds good," he said, blinking rapidly in the hopes that it would help his eyes focus. Then he gave Seth the finger and added, "I'm keeping that twenty, by the way. Reparations for getting in a fight and cock-blocking me. Asshole."

Next to him, Aidan gave a soft chuckle. "Shit. You SEALs really are on constant testosterone overload, aren't you? Fucking or fighting—it's always one or the other, huh?"

Dylan released a breath. "Tell me about it."

MIRANDA WAS DEAD ON HER FEET BY THE TIME TWO A.M. ROLLED AROUND. By midnight, the club had emptied to less than half capacity, so her manager Wendy had sent her to the beer cooler to do inventory, leaving Alex to tend bar alone. Miranda's arms now ached from lifting all those beer cases, she was shivering from being in a freezer for the past two hours, and to top off an already shitty shift, she'd gotten yelled at by Wendy for no good reason. She'd found out later that Wendy's foul mood was the result of a fistfight that had broken out in the alley, but that didn't make her feel any better about being wrongfully screamed at.

All she wanted to do was go home and take a hot bath before collapsing in bed, but that wasn't exactly an option. Her twins could sleep through a tornado, but she didn't want to risk waking Seth or Dylan by rummaging around their bathroom and making noise.

"'Night, Miranda," one of the bouncers called as she left the club through the front doors.

"'Night, Nico."

She rounded the building and made her way to the tiny lot in the rear alley. There were only four parking spaces back there—one was Wendy's, the other three were for employees but on a first-come, first-served basis. Miranda had lucked out and snagged a space tonight, which meant she didn't have to walk to the next block where she normally parked.

"Boo."

The raspy voice came out of nowhere and made her jump two feet in the air. Heart pounding, she spotted Seth sitting on the trunk of her sedan, smoking a cigarette.

"Jesus, Seth! You scared me to death." Her heartbeat steadied, then accelerated again when she noticed the dried blood caked on his nostrils. "Oh brother. Why am I not surprised?"

He tossed his cigarette butt on the pavement and snuffed it out with the toe of his black boot. "What do you mean?"

"I mean, *you're* the one who started that fistfight my manager was bitching about." She unlocked her car. "Forever the troublemaker, aren't you?"

His taunting laughter floated toward her. "Why are you so convinced *I* started the fight?"

She stared at him. "Didn't you?"

After a beat, he broke out in a rueful grin. "Yeah, I did. But you should know that I was defending your honor."

Now she was the one laughing. "Oh really?"

"Really."

Miranda watched as he scraped a hand over his scruffy goatee. Well, if you could even call it that. She actually had no idea how to classify Seth's facial hair. Kind of a beard, kind of a mustache, mostly a whole lot of scruff that made him appear lethal as hell.

"Remember that meathead who was hitting on you earlier?"

She nodded.

"I overheard him saying some very unpleasant things about you. One thing led to another and…" Seth shrugged.

She couldn't help but smile. "I can't decide if that was sweet of you, or incredibly stupid. I'm leaning toward stupid. And whatever that guy said? I'm sure I've been called worse."

"Maybe, but that doesn't make a fuck of a difference to me. If someone disrespects you, I'll damn well step in and make sure it doesn't happen again."

His husky declaration brought a rush of warmth to her chest, which only ticked her off. Jeez. She didn't need Seth Masterson fighting any battles on her behalf. She was perfectly capable of fighting her own battles.

"Anyway, I'll see you at home," he said. "I stuck around to make sure that guy didn't come back to bother you."

Her heart skipped a beat as he leaned in to open the car door for her. His scent surrounded her, made her feel light-headed. Damn pheromones.

He waited while she got into the driver's seat, told her to "drive safe", and then shut the door for her.

Miranda let out a sigh of relief the second he was gone. His presence was so unsettling, and her stupid body responded to him no matter how many times she ordered it not to. Even Trent hadn't evoked such a powerful rush of awareness, and she had no idea how to suppress the constant waves of lust swelling inside her.

It took twenty minutes to get to Seth's house. His Jeep was idling by the curb behind the babysitter's car, and he flashed his headlights when he saw her, gesturing for her to pull into the driveway. Right, he was better off parking behind her since he would be leaving first.

Come to think of it, hadn't he said he needed to report to the base at five? It was nearly three, for Pete's sake.

"Are you pulling an all-nighter or something?" she asked when they met up on the front stoop.

"Pretty much. There's no point in going to sleep now." He unlocked the front door and went in first, which she noticed he did every time they entered a room together. And his sharp-eyed gaze always swept back and forth, as if he was assessing his surroundings for potential danger.

The living room lights were on. Miranda found her regular sitter, Kim, lying on the couch reading a thick biology textbook. The pretty Japanese girl pushed her wire-rim glasses up the bridge of her nose when she spotted Miranda.

"Hey," Kim said, quickly shutting her book and getting to her feet. "The kids are sleeping soundly. I just checked on them ten minutes ago."

"Did they give you any trouble?"

"Not at all. They were great, as usual."

"I'm glad. Come on, let me walk you out."

After saying good-bye to Kim and locking up, Miranda drifted into the kitchen, where Seth was preparing coffee. He didn't offer her a cup, an understandable breach of etiquette seeing as how it was three in the morning and only one of them needed to stay awake.

She poured herself a glass of water before inching toward the doorway. "I should turn in."

"Wait."

His gravelly voice stopped her. Biting her bottom lip, she met his gaze, which flickered with something she couldn't decipher. "What is it?"

"I want you."

She briefly closed her eyes and counted to three. "Seriously, Seth, do we have to do this again? I *know* you want me. You've made that ridiculously clear since the—"

"Just let me finish," he interrupted, sounding so frustrated she stopped talking midsentence.

Wrinkling her forehead, she leaned against the doorframe and waited for him to continue.

"I want you, and it's making me act crazy, all right?" he mumbled. "I've never been rejected before, Miranda."

An unwitting smile tickled her lips. No, she didn't imagine rejection played a large part in his life. The guy was a supersoldier, built like a Greek god, with the face of a bad-boy movie star. Women probably lined up around the block for a shot with him.

"I understand why you don't want to get involved." He met her eyes head-on, his mouth set in a weary line. "And I'm sure I only make it worse with all my flirting and badgering and my attempts to bend you to my will. But I promise you, Miranda, if we do this, there won't be anything complicated about it."

Despite the frantic voice in her head begging her not to open this door, her curiosity won out. "What exactly are you saying?"

"I'm saying I'll take you any way I can get you. I'll take you on *your* terms, not mine."

A laugh popped out. "Yeah, right. It's always on your terms, Seth. That's just the way you operate."

"Not this time." Conviction resonated from his deep voice and gleamed in his sexy gray eyes. "I relinquish control, baby. If we act on this attraction, you'll be the one running the show. When you want it, where you want it, how you want it. The control is yours."

Shock grabbed hold of her and sent her eyebrows soaring. She knew how difficult this must be for him—heck, there was no mistaking the reluctant crease in his forehead or the way he was white-knuckling his coffee mug. Oh no, he was not the kind of man who handed over the reins.

Her lips twitched with unrestrained amusement. "I'll have total control?"

"Within reason," he conceded. "In terms of the when and where, definitely. But the how?" His voice lowered to a smoky pitch vibrating with wicked promise. "I can guarantee that following my lead in the bedroom isn't something you'll find complaint with."

Her core clenched as a stream of dirty images deluged her brain. God. This man was pure temptation. How on earth was she ever going to resist him? When he looked at her with that burning-hot gaze and licked his bottom lip like he wanted to eat her up, she couldn't think of a single reason *not* to sleep with him.

"The flood," she blurted out.

Seth blinked. "What?"

"My apartment is a mess, you know, from the flood. I'm working two jobs, and we've got the summer recital coming up at the end of July, so I need to start thinking about solos and song selection and costumes. My life is a big ball of stress right now," she confessed, though the reminder was more for her sake than his.

"All the more reason to welcome some no-strings, stress-busting sex into your life," he pointed out with a grin.

"No strings," she echoed.

"Not a single one."

She swallowed. "And it's on my terms?"

"That's what I said."

"I...don't know."

She didn't miss the flash of disappointment in his eyes, but it wasn't enough to change her answer—or her mind. She wasn't the kind of woman who jumped into a situation without giving it slow and careful consideration. Once upon a time she would have thrown caution to the wind and dived headfirst into a fling with this guy. These days, she didn't have the luxury of spontaneity. She had her kids, her job, her livelihood to consider.

"I need to think about it," she said quietly. "I won't agree to anything until I've had a chance to think."

After a beat, he released a ragged breath. "Take all the time you need."

"Thank you." She paused. "Good night, Seth."

With that, she left him in the kitchen and hurried down the hall, heart pounding, body throbbing, hormones yelling at her for having the audacity to demand time to *think*.

Sighing, she entered the guest room and resigned herself to the fact that, like Seth, she probably wouldn't get a wink of sleep tonight.

"Yeah, so this is probably a major faux pas, but...dude, how much does naval intelligence pay you?" Dylan called in the direction of the hallway Aidan had disappeared into a few moments ago.

As he waited for the other man to return, he gawked at the floor-to-ceiling windows in the living room and wondered if O'Connor and the others were aware that Aidan was living it up in the land of luxury over here.

Located in downtown's Marina District, Aidan's east-facing condo offered an unparalleled view of the San Diego skyline—that alone was confirmation of how pricey the place must be. The living room was furnished with two black leather couches, a rectangular glass coffee table, and an entertainment system that made Dylan drool. Even in his drunken state, he was able to fully appreciate Aidan's digs and knew the rent must cost the guy a fortune.

"This is actually my dad's place," Aidan explained as he strode into the room wearing nothing but a pair of loose black pants. "His architecture firm opened an East Coast branch last year and he decided to move out there, but he didn't want to sell this place, so I'm subletting it." Aidan grinned. "At a discount."

Dylan shook his head in awe, admiring the electric fireplace and the French doors leading to the outdoor terrace. "Lucky you."

"For real," Aidan agreed with a chuckle. "Hey, did you still want that Advil?"

"That'd be great."

"There should be some in the kitchen. I'll grab you some water too."

Aidan brushed past him and headed for the kitchen, which was separated from the living area by a low wall with a "window" that allowed Dylan to watch the dark-haired man move around. His gaze lingered on Aidan's chest—broad, sculpted with muscle and dusted with dark hair. Dude was in great fucking shape.

He tried to remember if he'd ever seen Aidan shirtless before. He must have—swimming at Matt and Cash's place, on the beach...yeah, he had to have seen Aidan's bare chest before.

So why did his mouth suddenly go dry at the sight of the guy's washboard abs?

Dylan tore his eyes away. Clearly he'd had way too much to drink tonight.

"You sure you don't want the stronger kind? I've got extra strength and the kind for migraines too," Aidan said as he reappeared.

"Nah, I'm good. The pills and a few glasses of water will do the trick. It's what I always do to avoid a hangover after a night of boozing."

When Aidan slapped a pair of ibuprofens in his hand, the guy's fingers lightly brushed over his palm.

His groin tightened, cock jerking against the fly of his cargo pants.

Oh fuck. Not now. And not *this* man.

He gulped down the pills and chugged the water, all the while feeling the other man's dark eyes studying him.

"What?" Dylan said in aggravation.

"You need to fuck, don't you?"

He nearly dropped the glass. "What?"

Aidan grinned, and a pair of dimples appeared. "I cock-blocked you tonight, man. Dragged you out of that alcove before you could finish up with the cute blonde from the dance floor, and I can only imagine how bad your balls are aching right now."

Dylan relaxed. Right, the blonde. At the memory of Rachel—well, Rachel's magical *mouth*—his dick jerked again. Well, at least the little soldier wasn't discriminatory. Blondes, brunettes, girls, guys…didn't take much to keep him happy. Some might even call him fickle.

"You win some, you lose some," he answered with a shrug. But Aidan was right. He was definitely in fucking mode. Muscles tight, body primed for sex.

Another silence fell.

They exchanged a quick look, and Dylan could have sworn Aidan's brown eyes flickered with heat.

Don't even think about it.

"Anyway, I'm sorry I dragged you into the fight. I just wasn't sure how far Masterson would go."

"No, I'm glad you got me. Seth can be a total moron sometimes."

"How long is his girl staying at your place?"

"A few days, I think. Maybe longer."

"How old are her kids?"

"Six."

Aidan chuckled. "Well, if you don't feel like sharing a house with a couple of kids, you're welcome to stay here for a bit. I've got a spare room."

To his extreme disgust, his cock actually twitched again.

For the love of God, buddy, this is not *happening. Chill the fuck out.*

His lower body finally received the memo, much to his relief.

"Thanks, that's good to know," he said. "I'll definitely consider it."

"Cool. Come on, I'll show you to the guest room."

Dylan set off after Aidan, his gaze taking in the smooth expanse of Aidan's sinewy back, the defined muscles that rippled at the guy's every step. It wasn't until he found himself mesmerized by the taut ass flexing beneath Aidan's pants that he realized what he was doing.

Jesus. You'd think he'd been on the receiving end of a blowjob tonight, only to get interrupted right before he could ejaculate, and was now in a state of painful arousal...oh wait—that's *exactly* what happened.

Fuckin' Masterson.

He wrenched his eyes away from Aidan's ass and took a breath, deciding that it had now become imperative for him to jack off tonight.

Otherwise he might do something very, very stupid.

Chapter Nine

Two days. Two whole days, and not one word from Miranda about the conversation they'd had Monday night. Defeat wasn't something that sat right with him, which was probably why Seth was being unnecessarily harsh on the punching bag at the moment.

He was in the garage, trying to distract himself from his continuous state of unfulfilled arousal by using every piece of exercise equipment. He'd already lifted weights, hit the treadmill, and used the chin-up bar, and now he was on the punching bag, sweat running in rivulets between his pecs and down his back.

Thwack, thwack, thwack. He executed a series of jabs that made his knuckles throb, despite the fact that he'd wrapped them up. The soreness was the wake-up call he'd needed, the unspoken warning that it was time to stop. He couldn't bust up his hands, not when he was scheduled to spend the day at the target range tomorrow mastering a new assault rifle the spec ops community was considering utilizing.

Breathing hard, Seth stilled the swinging bag. He unwrapped the white cloth from his hands, grabbed his bottle of water, and chugged it all in one gulp.

He'd just finished drinking when he heard the footsteps. Two sets of footsteps, both far too quiet to be Miranda's, he realized in dismay.

Sure enough, he glanced over in time to see Sophie and Jason pop through the door that led from the kitchen to the garage. They scampered down the short flight of stairs and plopped down on the last step. Two pairs of brown eyes proceeded to watch him. One suspicious. One curious.

"What?" he said irritably.

"Whatcha doing?" Jason asked, his inquisitive gaze moving around the garage.

Seth reached for the towel he'd draped on the weight rack and patted the sweat coating his neck. "What does it look like, kid? I'm working out."

"Why are your arms so much bigger than mine?"

He shrugged. "I'm older. And bigger. And I train."

"Will I get as big as you when I get older?"

"I don't know. Maybe."

Seth had promised Miranda that he'd be nicer to the rugrats, and he'd been trying his hardest to keep his word. For the past two days, he'd made small talk with the kidlets over meals, put forth an effort to answer the billion questions Jason hurled his way, pretended not to notice Sophie's perpetual scowl every time she looked at him.

He'd been polite, cordial, respectful…and had that expedited Miranda's thinking process in any way? Not at all.

He headed for the minifridge and got another bottle of water. He uncapped it, feeling the twins watching his every move. They disturbed him on a whole other level, those two. Especially Sophie, who was currently playing with the end of one of her pigtails and tapping one tiny ballet slipper on the wooden step.

Finally he couldn't take it anymore.

"What?" he grumbled.

She pursed her lips for a moment before answering. "I don't like you."

Her brother looked absolutely horrified. "Soph!"

"Well, it's true! And you don't like him too!"

"But I'm not gonna *tell* him!"

"Why not?"

"Because it's not *nice*."

"*He's* not nice. He doesn't like us."

"Yes he does!"

"No he doesn't!"

Seth observed the verbal ping-pong match without comment. Despite his better judgment, he found himself smiling, a reaction that startled as well as annoyed him. He wasn't supposed to be amused by the rugrats. He was supposed to keep an indifferent air, give them the absolute minimum amount of attention, and high-five himself when they were finally gone.

As the twins continued to argue, he crossed his arms over his chest.

"Why don't you go find your mom? She's leaving for work in a couple of hours. Don't you want to spend some time with her before she goes?"

Their bickering died abruptly.

"She's on the phone," Jason informed him.

"And we don't like you," Sophie added.

"So-phie!"

Seth swiftly held up his hand to silence them, not in the mood for round two. "Listen, kid." He shot Sophie a look that usually made grown men cower—and didn't get so much as a blink from the six-year-old. "I don't care whether you like me or not."

"That's 'cause you don't care 'bout *anything*," she shot back. "Because you're *mean*. And I don't like it here!"

"Soph!" Jason's face was so red he looked like a little dark-haired tomato.

"It's fine," Seth told the boy. "Look, it doesn't matter anyway, because you guys won't be here for much longer. You're going back to your place tomorrow or the day after, remember? And FYI, I'm not mean."

Sophie smirked. "Are too."

"Are not."

"*Are too.*"

Holy sweet baby Jesus, was he actually playing the Are-Not game with a six-year-old?

Gritting his teeth, he fixed both children with a stern glare, pointed to the stairs and said, "Go find your mom. Now."

This time the look did the job. The tone must have helped too, because the kids shot to their feet and hurried up the stairs like they were being chased by bloodhounds.

Once they were gone, Seth let out a breath. Well, *that* had been unpleasant. And now he'd lost all enthusiasm for his workout.

Muttering a string of curses, he headed upstairs and emerged in the kitchen, where he found Dylan at the counter preparing a turkey sandwich.

"Did you really just tell those angel-faced children that you hated them?"

Seth's jaw fell open. "What are you talking about?"

"They just came running through here like bats out of hell. Sophie said you told them you hated them."

Lying little imp.

"I did no such thing," he muttered.

Dylan had the nerve to grin. "I like that kid. She's got sass. Wish she was around all the time, just so I'd get to see that angry, pulsing vein in your forehead more often."

"Well, we might be around a while longer," Miranda spoke up from the doorway.

Seth turned as she walked in with a twin on either side. Visible lines of unhappiness marred her mouth, and her hazel eyes glimmered with frustration.

"I just got off the phone with our landlord," she explained. "There's been a delay, and now he says we can't move back in for another week."

Seth frowned. "What happened?"

"I was too upset to pay attention to the details, but Marco said there was more damage than they thought, and something about ordering more materials. I don't know. Oh, and apparently the living room wall, the one right underneath the gutters? The drywall and insulation need to be torn out and replaced."

"That sucks." Sympathy rang from Dylan's tone.

She made an angry noise. "I *knew* those construction guys were acting weird when I was there earlier today. I kept asking what was wrong, but they wouldn't answer me."

Her misery was written all over her pretty face, which made her appear younger. Actually, no, it made her look her age. Normally, he completely forgot that she was only twenty-four—she carried herself with a maturity that surpassed her years—but when her eyes filled with unshed tears and her lips quivered with frustration, her youth was unmistakable. It made him want to pull her into his arms and hold her close.

"It'll be all right," he said gruffly. "You guys can stay here as long as you need." He glanced at his roommate. "Right?"

"Right." Dylan got a funny look on his face. "I'll even let you have my room, so you're more comfortable."

"Oh no, please, you don't have to do that. I'm fine bunking in the guest room with the twins."

But Dylan was adamant. "That double bed can't be big enough for all three of you. It's all right, honey, I've got a friend with a spare room and he already said I can crash there whenever I need."

"I can't put you out of your own home." Her voice trembled. "I refuse to inconvenience you."

"It's no inconvenience. Besides, I could use a change of scenery."

Seth studied Dylan's features, wondering why he seemed so eager to leave. He must have been talking about Jackson—Texas was the only one Seth knew with an extra room—but why the hurry to move in with the guy?

In all honesty, Seth would prefer it if Dylan stayed home. The dude was amazing with Miranda's kids. He watched movies with them, joked around with them, even gave them piggyback rides on command. Without Dylan there to entertain the kids, Seth would be forced to spend more time with them.

But it was clear Dylan was dead set on jumping ship.

Asshole.

"I'll make up the bed and get the room ready for you," Dylan told Miranda. "And quit arguing. As long as you're staying here, you deserve your own room, okay?"

"Okay," she said weakly.

Seth fought another urge to cross the kitchen and take her in his arms. She'd probably slap him if he tried. Besides, the twins were clinging to her legs like spider monkeys, looking unhappy about this latest turn of events.

"I wanted to go home," Sophie whined.

"Me too! All my toys are at home."

Miranda seemed to snap out of her thoughts. "Actually, most of our things are in Seth's garage. I spent the last two days packing up all the dry clothes and toys and bedding. Remember the boxes I showed you?"

The twins nodded.

"Well, that's our stuff. If you want, why don't we pick out a few items that you can keep in the guest room?"

Sophie's brown eyes lit up. "Like Belinda?"

Miranda's expression grew strained. "I'm sorry, sweetie, Belinda isn't in any of those boxes. She was too wet and dirty. I couldn't save her, hon."

"She's *dead*?" Sophie wailed.

Seth swallowed a groan, knowing the waterworks were about to make an appearance. But although tears clung to Sophie's dark eyelashes, the kid kept her cool, triggering a spark of grudging admiration.

"Will you get me another doll?" Sophie asked in a small voice.

Miranda smiled and tugged on one of her daughter's pigtails. "Of course I will. But not today. For now, why don't you put on your shoes and we'll go to the garage and find you some toys."

Both kids dashed out of the kitchen, leaving Seth alone with Miranda.

She eyed him for a moment, wary, reluctant.

"Why are you looking at me like that?" he said roughly.

"Kim's coming over in an hour to babysit."

He arched a brow. "And?"

"And then I'm going to the club." She hesitated. "I'm only working until midnight."

He refused to acknowledge the tiny spark of hope that hovered in his chest. "Where are you going with this, Miranda?"

Her teeth dug into her lower lip, gnawing, revealing her evident nervousness.

The spark grew bigger.

"Remember how I said my life was a big ball of stress?"

He nodded.

"Well, the ball is bigger now. It's huge, actually. It's ginormous." Her eyes took on a slightly wild glint. "I'm close to freaking out and I don't have time to freak out right now, okay? I need to relax. Just a teeny, tiny bit of relaxation, a few hours where I don't have to think about anything but *me*."

The spark caught flame and burned a path straight to his dick.

"So please, don't come to the club tonight. Stay here, work out, do your hair, I don't care. But when I get home later?" Her chin lifted in fortitude. "You'll be lying in your bed waiting for me. You'll be naked, you'll have protection handy, and you're going to fuck me."

Chapter Ten

THIS WAS A MISTAKE. A BIG FUCKING MISTAKE.

Whatever, man, you need a place to stay, Aidan's got a spare room, end of story.

"Bull-fucking-shit," Dylan muttered.

Wow. He was actually calling bullshit on *himself.* That was beyond messed up. Yet even though he knew his reasons for coming here tonight were bogus as hell, he couldn't seem to talk himself out of it.

So here he was, standing in the expensive, brightly lit lobby of Aidan's condo, waiting to be buzzed up. Miranda had dropped him off on her way to the club, though neither of them said much during the ride over. She'd clearly had something on her mind—something named Seth, no doubt—but Dylan hadn't pushed her to talk. She hadn't tried to force conversation either, which he appreciated.

Comfortable silence was so hard to come by these days, and this one had allowed him to mull over the remark Aidan had made earlier. When Dylan called asking if the offer to crash at his place was still on the table, Aidan had told him to come by whenever. He'd then added, "I'm having a chick over for dinner, but she's always down for some variety, so if you want to join us..."

A three-way? Had Aidan been inviting him to a three-way? But why? The two of them were definitely more than acquaintances, but they weren't quite best buds, either. In fact, the other night was the first time they'd ever been alone.

The other night... Fuck, it had been the alcohol. Had to be the alcohol. And the aborted BJ hadn't helped either.

"Hey, Wade, come on up." Aidan's deep voice emerged from the intercom, and then the glass doors buzzed.

Slinging his duffel over his shoulder, Dylan strode to the elevator bank and punched the Up button. A few moments later, the doors dinged open and he stepped into the car, riding it up to the fifteenth floor. Walking on the clean, cream-colored carpet with his scuffed up shitkickers felt wrong, so he practically sprinted to Aidan's door, which swung open before he could even knock.

Aidan greeted him with a dimpled grin, and Dylan was struck by how damn good-looking he was. Kinda resembled a young Johnny Depp, except with the body of an action star.

"Come in. Lani and I just finished dinner. We were about to have a drink on the terrace." Aidan opened the door wider to let him in.

Dylan toed off his boots and left them on the mat in the front hall, then followed Aidan into the living room, where Aidan's date was waiting. She was a stunning woman, looked to be of Polynesian descent, with smooth luminous skin and long, jet-black hair.

She smiled when she spotted Dylan. "Hello," she said in a soft voice.

"Lani, this is Dylan. He's staying with me this week." Aidan turned to Dylan. "Lani just moved here from Honolulu."

"Hawaiian, huh?" He offered her a warm smile. "How are you liking San Diego?"

"It's beautiful. And the people are so nice." Her dark eyes twinkled in Aidan's direction.

Dylan noticed the remnants of the couple's dinner on the glass table across the room—plates, wine glasses, candlewicks releasing wisps of smoke as if they'd just been put out.

"I should probably get out of your hair," he said ruefully. "I didn't mean to interrupt your date."

But neither Aidan nor Lani acted as if his presence inconvenienced them. In fact, the beautiful Hawaiian just smiled again and said, "You can stay if you want. Have a drink with us."

Indecision flashed through him. Shit. He wanted to stay. He wanted to have a drink with them. But if he did, he knew exactly where this would all lead—straight to the bedroom. And while normally he wouldn't bat an eye at the notion of a threesome, indulging with this particular man probably wasn't the most intelligent move. After his reaction to Aidan the other night, he was a touch worried that he might not be able to control himself if they somehow wound up naked together.

"It's a tempting offer, but I'm gonna have to pass," he told them. "I have to make a few phone calls—my older brother just got engaged. And I need to be up at dawn tomorrow, so I can't stay up late tonight."

Was that a glimmer of disappointment he saw in Aidan's eyes?

Nah, wishful thinking, maybe.

"Well, make yourself at home." Aidan joined Lani on the leather couch and slung one muscular arm over her slender shoulder. "You need a ride tomorrow morning?"

"No, that's cool. Cash is picking me up."

He bid them good night and headed for the guest room, where he dropped his duffel on the hardwood floor and released a long breath. After a beat, he dug his phone from his pocket and sank on the double bed in the middle of the room. The bedframe was a dark oak, the mattress a perfect combination of hard and soft. Dylan made himself comfortable as he dialed his mom's number.

She picked up on the second ring, sounding delighted to hear from him. "Honey! Did you get my message?" Shanna Wade chirped.

An indulgent smile crossed his mouth. "That's why I'm calling. So, you're pretty stoked about this engagement, huh?"

"I'm *thrilled* about it! Claire is going to make your brother such a wonderful wife."

He held back a snort.

"Beautiful, smart, successful. And that girl is so very sweet," Shanna babbled on. "Did I tell you she came by with chicken noodle soup when I was sick last week?"

Yeah, probably because she had an ulterior motive of some sort, Dylan almost replied. He also didn't mention that he suspected Claire had zero respect for his mom, which she'd broadcasted loud and clear during that last visit by scoffing at Dylan's insistence that "homemaker" absolutely counted as a real job. Shanna Wade had been a stay-at-home wife and mother for more than half of Dylan's life, but clearly Claire McKinley didn't think that counted as *work*.

"Claire's a real sweetheart, all right," he said lightly, hoping his mom wouldn't pick up on the distaste in his voice.

"Your brother told me you agreed to be his best man."

"I did. I'm looking forward to it. I've never planned a bachelor party before…"

"Don't you dare get your brother a stripper!" Shanna said in outrage.

He laughed. "Relax, Mom. I won't." Nah, he definitely wouldn't get *a* stripper. More like *many* strippers. But his mother didn't need to know that.

As his mom continued to chat about the upcoming wedding, Dylan got distracted by the sound of muffled footsteps in the hall, followed by a door opening and closing. When he heard soft feminine laughter and a low male murmur, he realized that for all the pomp and circumstance of this condo, the walls were pretty thin.

It wasn't until twenty minutes later, after he'd hung up with his mom and was getting ready to crash, that he realized just how thin those damn walls were.

Thump-thump-thump.

Thump-thump-thump.

Thump-thump-thump.

The unmistakable rhythm of a headboard banging against the wall sent an ambush of raunchy images to his brain. Aidan was probably working Lani over real good—his trim hips pistoning, ass flexing with each deep thrust. Or maybe Lani was doing some riding, impaled on Aidan's cock, her long fingernails digging into his sculpted abdomen.

Saliva pooled in Dylan's mouth. He nearly groaned out loud. Managed to swallow the agonized sound, but controlling the erection that sprang up was impossible. It was official. Coming here had been a bad idea. A really, really bad idea.

But there wasn't a damn thing he could do about it. He'd already given up his room to Miranda; he'd be a total ass if he suddenly demanded it back. And if he went home anyway and tried to sleep on the couch, there was no doubt in his mind that Miranda would drag him back to his room and revert to bunking on that tiny bed with her kids.

So going home was not an option. He supposed he could crash at Jackson's place in Imperial Beach, but hopping from one guest room to another seemed kind of ridiculous. Might as well suck it up and stay here at Aidan's place.

It was only for a week. Surely he could refrain from doing something stupid for the next seven days. Granted, the nonstupid course of action would've been to *not* come here in the first place, but he'd already made his bed, and now he had to lie in it.

Another forbidden image flew into his head.

He quickly shot it down with a mental rifle and banished it from thought.

Alone. He'd be lying in the bed he'd made—*alone*.

WAS SHE REALLY GOING TO DO THIS?

Miranda killed the engine but couldn't bring herself to get out of the car. She stared at the pale light shining through the gauzy white curtains of Seth's living room window. Kim was probably in there, doing homework or watching TV. And Seth…well, he was probably waiting for her in his bedroom.

Naked.

With condoms handy.

Ready to fuck her.

Miranda's cheeks scorched. Gosh, had she actually *said* all that?

She wondered if it was too late to change her mind, but at the same time, she wasn't sure she wanted to. Why couldn't she sleep with Seth? She hadn't had sex in seven years. *Seven* years. Didn't she owe it to herself to get laid? She wasn't a nun, for Pete's sake, and a girl did have urges, after all.

But was Seth Masterson the right man to satisfy those urges? Physically, definitely. She was attracted to him like nobody's business, and there was no challenging his ability to turn her on—she'd almost orgasmed simply from his touching her breasts. But seven years of celibacy was a long time. Shouldn't she ease herself back into the whole sex thing with someone who wasn't so… overwhelming? Dip her toe in the shallow end instead of diving into the deep end right off the bat?

She ran a hand through her hair and released a disgusted breath. Okay. Enough second-guessing. Really, there was only one question of any importance here, one question she always asked herself before she made any life-altering decisions: *Will this hurt my kids?*

She'd posed that same inquiry when deciding whether to leave Vegas, and now she applied it to Seth. To sex with Seth.

Would her sleeping with him hurt Sophie and Jason?

No. How could it? If she was *dating* Seth, that would be a different story. She wasn't an idiot—she saw the way he acted around her kids. Uncomfortable, curt, tense. He'd tried toning down those reactions after she'd asked him to be nicer to the twins, but she still sensed his reluctance to interact with them.

She knew the kids sensed it too, but, ironically, Seth's aloofness only seemed to strengthen her children's determination to win him over. She didn't understand it. Normally Sophie and Jason hated being around folks who didn't want to spend time with them. With Seth, they were on him every second, each trying to earn his approval in their own way—Jason with his endless questions, and Sophie with her smart-aleck remarks.

Unfortunately, neither approach had succeeded in wearing Seth down.

But that wasn't the issue. The question was—would a sexual involvement with Seth hurt her children? As much as she wanted to, she couldn't bring herself to answer yes to that. As long as she and Seth exercised some discretion, the twins wouldn't even have to know they were involved, which meant there was no reason to hold back.

No reason to keep resisting.

Drawing in a deep breath, she slid out of the car and headed for the house.

Five minutes later, after she'd walked Kim out and locked up, Miranda drifted into the guest room to check on the twins. They were sleeping soundly, and neither so much as stirred when she fixed their blanket and planted soft kisses on their foreheads.

Quietly shutting the door behind her, she cast a quick look at Seth's closed bedroom door, then bypassed it on her way to Dylan's room. She still couldn't believe he'd given up his bedroom for her, but it didn't surprise her in the least. Dylan was truly a stand-up guy. Great with kids too—Seth could definitely take a lesson or two from his roommate.

But although it bugged her that he didn't seem to be warming up to the twins, Miranda knew she couldn't be angry with him for it. He wasn't auditioning for the role of Sophie and Jason's father, and she couldn't expect him to love her kids just because *she* happened to think they were awesome.

She entered the master bedroom with purposeful steps, pausing to admire the four-poster, king-sized bed that dominated the large space. Her gaze drifted to the door of the private bath, and she had to wonder if Dylan and Seth had drawn straws to decide which one of them would get this room.

When she stepped into the bathroom, she found it as clean as the rest of the house. Okay, it *had* to be a military thing, because she'd never met a tidier pair of men.

She turned on the shower, stripped and stepped into the tub. The warm water felt like heaven on her sore shoulders and she moaned softly, longing for the day when she could quit her job at the club and just focus on running All That Dance. Soon. Soon the school would do more than break even, and she'd be able to support her kids without spending four nights a week behind a bar counter.

Miranda stayed in the shower for longer than necessary. Washed her hair, shaved her legs, lathered up with the vanilla body wash she'd brought over from the apartment earlier today. Her skin was pink and pruny by the time she stepped onto the fluffy blue bath mat.

In the bedroom, she simply stood there in her towel, chewing on her bottom lip. Should she even bother getting dressed? She'd be naked again soon enough.

The thought sent a shiver dancing up her spine.

What if one of the twins wakes up and needs you?

The mom in her raised a valid point. She quickly rummaged through the duffel bag full of the clothes she'd packed up over at her place. She found an oversized red T-shirt and slipped it over her head, then dug out her hairbrush from her toiletry kit and ran it through her hair a few times. Then, straightening her shoulders, she walked out of the room.

She took several deep breaths and assured herself she was doing the right thing. Urges, dammit. A girl had *urges*.

When she reached Seth's door, she knocked ever so softly. His gruff response came a second later. "Come in."

Swallowing, she turned the doorknob and entered his bedroom.

Oh sweet mother of God.

Her entire body burned as if she'd stepped into a five-alarm fire. The light spilling from the small bedside lamp revealed a very naked Seth lying on the bed. His dark head was cushioned by a couple of pillows, and a hardcover novel whose title she couldn't make out sat on the bedspread next to him.

Her gaze grew frantic, unable to focus on any one detail—there were too many that required her attention. Like his spectacular chest. Lord, that chest. Tight six-pack, perfectly sculpted pecs, a light dusting of hair that arrowed down to his...Oh God, she couldn't even look at it right now, not unless she wanted to self-combust. She focused on his long, muscular legs instead, the intricate design of yet another geometric-looking tattoo on his right shin.

Every inch of her tingled, pulsed, vibrated with pure, raw need. She lifted her gaze to Seth's, unsurprised by the mocking glitter she saw there.

"I'm naked, Miranda." His voice was a sexy, dangerous rasp. "I've got protection." He waved a hand at the end table, where a box of condoms sat innocently, waiting to be opened. "So now give me the word, and..."

She sucked in a wobbly breath. "And what?"

"I'll fulfill the last part of your request."

Oh yes, he would. And she got the feeling *fulfilled* was exactly the right word. After avoiding it for this long, she finally let her gaze rest on the heavy erection between his legs. He was big. Thick, uncut and deliciously hard.

Her breath hitched when he suddenly wrapped his fingers around the cock she'd been admiring and gave it a sharp tug.

She moaned. Out loud. Eliciting a smug smirk from him.

"Everything okay?" he asked casually.

Without answering, she reached for the hem of her shirt, bunched the fabric between her fingers and pulled the garment up and over her head. Leaving her as naked as he was. Leaving her vulnerable. Exposed.

His sharp intake of breath was encouraging. So was the way his eyes smoldered as they roamed her body.

She knew she was in great shape—dancing five days a week guaranteed it—but that didn't mean she didn't feel self-conscious. The last man to see her naked had been Trent, and that was seven long years ago. She'd had an eighteen-year-old's body back then, not nearly as curvy as she was now, and the four-inch Cesarean scar running horizontal to the top of her pubic area hadn't been there before, either.

"Just the way I imagined you," Seth murmured.

She gulped. "What way was that?"

"Beautiful. Fucking beautiful."

Her cheeks heated with pleasure rather than embarrassment. The compliment fueled her confidence and gave her the courage to approach him. Her heart began to pound, legs trembling a little as she reached the side of the bed.

He slid up higher, set his book on the table, and held out his hand. An unspoken question flickered in his expression.

She stared at his outstretched palm.

Now or never, Miranda.

Ignoring the nervous butterflies fluttering around in her belly, she took his hand and allowed him to draw her into his lap. She instinctively straddled him, whimpering when the tip of his cock brushed the top of her mound.

Seth let out a strangled groan. "Yeah, that can't be happening yet. Not if we want this to last."

He quickly rearranged down south so that his erection pressed into her thigh instead. Then he brought his hands to her waist, sweeping his thumbs over her hip bones while his hungry eyes continued to eat her up.

When his gaze rested on her nipples, they hardened in response, her breasts growing hot and achy. Seth didn't say a word as he stared at her. He didn't say a word when he slid his fingers through her damp hair. Didn't say a word as he slowly leaned closer. Or when his other hand traveled up her body, avoiding her breasts and coming up to touch her cheek.

The room was completely silent save for their breathing, hers slightly unsteady, his a soft hiss. Miranda couldn't take her eyes off his mouth. She wanted to kiss him so badly she could taste him.

"Seth," she whispered.

"What is it, baby? What do you want?"

"I…"

His voice was gruff. "I promised you this would be on your terms. Tell me what you want me to do."

"No."

A frown puckered his brow. "No?"

"I don't want to be in control," she confessed. "I'm *always* in control, and I don't like it. So I'm giving you back the control you relinquished. Take it back, okay?"

His mouth quirked in a faint smile. "You sure about that?"

She nodded.

The smile widened, becoming downright predatory. "Okay, then," he said, and then he cradled the back of her head and pulled her mouth down for a hard, reckless kiss.

She gasped, unprepared for the erotic assault, unable to do much more than hold on for the ride. His tongue plunged into her mouth without invitation, so greedy, so dominant, each hungry thrust making her moan with abandon.

The kiss grew hotter and hotter, their tongues dueling and breaths mingling. She laid both palms flat on his chest, steadying herself, feeling the rapid beating of his heart beneath her hands. The evidence of his excitement only heightened her own.

Her eyelids fluttered open when Seth abruptly broke the kiss.

"C'mere, baby, let's show you what you've been missing these past seven years," he drawled.

Before she could blink, he'd flipped her onto her back. He lay next to her on his side, propped up on an elbow, his free hand closing over her breast. A zing of arousal bounced from her chest right down to her core.

"I love these tits," he murmured as he squeezed one, then the other. "I've been fantasizing about them for months."

His seductive touch made her shiver. "You have?"

"Mmm-hmmm. I've jacked off while thinking of them. Several times."

Heat jolted through her. "Really?"

Chuckling, he feathered his thumb over one nipple, toying with the rigid bud. "Why do you sound so surprised? I thought I made it pretty fucking clear how much I wanted you."

"You did. I just...I didn't think you...um, thought about me once you left the club. Out of sight, out of mind, you know?"

He gave a firm shake of the head. "You're always on my mind, Miranda. Always."

Her breath caught, her pulse speeding up. She would've liked to hear more about his fantasies, but apparently he was done talking because he swiftly lowered his head and captured her nipple between his lips.

Miranda jerked as if she'd been electrocuted. Oh *God*. His mouth was so warm, his tongue wet and insistent as he flicked it over her nipple with absolute precision. If she hadn't been lying down, she would've keeled over. Pleasure rippled through her, pulsing in her breasts and vibrating between her legs.

"Feel good?"

She moaned her approval.

"What about this? Does this feel good too?"

He purposefully trailed his hand down her stomach and over her mound, found her clit and drew a lazy figure eight over it with his index finger.

Miranda almost passed out the second he touched that sensitive spot. Her hips lifted, seeking more contact, her thighs parting of their own volition.

Seth idly rubbed her clit, his gaze fixed on her face as if he were assessing her responses. She watched him watch her, but her eyes couldn't stay focused for long. His delicious ministrations were too distracting.

When he pushed one finger inside her, she cried out, stunned by the shockwaves that rocked her body.

Seth immediately stilled, concern crossing his face.

"No, keep going," she pleaded. "Please. It's good. It's so good."

Pure male arrogance lit up up stormy silver eyes. "Not nearly as good as it could be."

Before she could question him, he was gone, his big, muscular body all the way at the foot of the bed. He gripped her thighs, holding them open as he brought his face to her pussy and gave it a soft kiss.

She came.

She honest-to-God came from that one featherlight kiss to her clit, from the feel of his hot breath on her.

Crying out in shocked pleasure, she squeezed her eyes shut while the orgasm ripped through her. Her toes curled, thighs trembled, pulse raced. It didn't last long, just a burst of hot agony and intense bliss, fading as quickly as it arose.

When she opened her eyes, she found Seth looking up at her with unrestrained amusement.

"Can I get started now?" he asked dryly. "Or are you going to spontaneously orgasm again?"

She let out a wheezy laugh, still stunned by the unexpected release that had hit her without warning. "Seven years, *baby*. What did you think would happen?"

His answering laugh, low and husky, made her feel all tingly again. But it was his tongue that transformed the tingling into a wave of excitement that seized her lower body. He licked her slowly, gently, as if he had all the time in the world. Kissed, swirled, teased. Flattened his tongue and swiped it over her clit, then fastened his mouth on the sensitive bundle of nerves and sucked, his happy groan pulsating in her tender flesh.

"I've wanted to do this for so long," he muttered. "I could lick you up for hours."

He rubbed his lips over her clit, back and forth, back and forth, until she couldn't take one more second of torment.

She dug her short fingernails into his shoulders, keeping him in place, bringing him closer. His stubble abraded her inner thighs as he worshipped her. She knew she'd have red marks and beard burn all over her skin by the time this night ended, yet the idea of being marked by this man made her body ache even more.

It wasn't long before the tension began to build again, tightening her muscles, speeding her heartbeat. While he tended to her clit, Seth used the tip of one finger to toy with her. He didn't push that finger inside, no matter how many times she lifted her butt off the bed hoping to deepen the contact. Each time she tried, he just moved the finger away, chuckling even as he continued to lave her clit with his tongue.

"Please," she whimpered.

He laughed again, removing his mouth from her altogether and nuzzling her inner thigh with his stubble-covered cheek.

"Please, Seth. No more teasing."

His lips traveled along her heated flesh, tongue darting out to taste the moisture pooling at her entrance.

Miranda groaned. "Goddammit, Seth. Seven years."

She felt his powerful body shudder with laughter, heard the husky sounds echoing in the bedroom, but she couldn't focus on anything but his hot mouth, so close to where she wanted it to be and yet so far away she wanted to scream.

"I'm sorry, babe. I guess I should show you some mercy, huh?"

And then he slid two long fingers inside her and clamped his lips over her clit, making her explode in an intense rush of pleasure that ripped through her body and sent her mind spinning into oblivion.

When she finally recovered—who knew how long *that* took—Seth was poised over her, his powerful arms on either side of her head, his erection covered with a condom.

A pang of disappointment tugged at her. She'd wanted to do some exploring of her own. Stroke him, suck him, find out what drove him crazy, but one look at his face and she knew he was on the verge of losing every last bit of the control she'd given back to him. His masculine features were pulled taut, gray eyes glittering with need, teeth biting into his bottom lip.

Without a word, she parted her legs wider and met his eyes.

He responded by easing the head of his cock into her, just an inch.

"You good?" he asked hoarsely.

"Mmm-hmmm."

He pushed in another inch. They both groaned.

"More," she breathed.

"I don't want to be too rough. Seven years, remember?"

His thoughtfulness made her heart skip a beat. But he was worrying for nothing—she was so wet and ready for him that slow and easy was completely unnecessary. To prove it, she lifted her hips, hooked her legs around his lean waist, and joined them together fully.

A curse popped out of his mouth. "Holy fuck," he choked out. "God, you're tight."

She mentally thanked all those Kegel exercises she'd done after the twins were born. Maybe it was seven years too late, but hey, better late than never.

Seth withdrew, plunged back in, then swore again. "I'm not going to last."

"I thought SEALs were supposed to have crazy stamina," she teased.

"We do. But not when we haven't had sex in two months." A pained look entered his eyes. "I'm serious, baby, I've got two, maybe three strokes in me."

His honest evaluation of his thrust capacity had her laughing. "Then I guess you'll just have to make it up to me next time."

"Next time," he echoed, more of a question than a statement.

She nodded slowly. "There'll be a next time, Seth."

"Thank God." And he drove his cock so deep she gasped.

He'd been too hard on himself—he lasted *eight* strokes before he slammed into her one last time and grew still, his low groan signaling his release.

Miranda watched his face as he came, floored by the passion she saw there, the naked pleasure and masculine vulnerability. Seeing him so exposed was strangely thrilling. Seth was always so indifferent, quick to taunt and slow to let down his guard.

When he collapsed on top of her, she stroked his back, enjoying the way he nestled his face in the crook of her neck. His facial hair tickled her flesh, his chest hair teasing her nipples. His heart was beating as fast as hers. It felt nice having him lie on top of her, but he didn't stay in the position for long.

"I'm crushing you," he murmured.

They both moaned as his cock slid out. A fresh rush of desire filled Miranda's body. She watched him remove the condom and drop it on the end table, his strong arms flexing with his every move. Her gaze rested on the tattoo covering his left shoulder and most of his upper arm.

"So what's the story behind the tattoo on your arm?" she asked, remembering the comment Dylan had made in the kitchen the other day.

Seth sighed as he lay back down and drew the sheet over their naked bodies. "It's not much of a story. Went to Fiji on my nineteenth birthday with a few other recruits and I met a girl there. She convinced me to get a couple of tattoos. I wanted to get in her pants, so I figured inking up a few body parts was a fair price to pay. So I did my arm and my leg."

"Then there's no special meaning behind the designs?"

"Nope. I got 'em because they looked badass."

She grinned, but she couldn't contradict him. The tats *did* look badass. Funny, how she was always drawn to men with tattoos. Trent had been covered in them too.

As the thought of her ex floated into her mind, she was suddenly struck by another realization.

"That's two," she announced.

Miranda's matter-of-fact declaration made Seth turn his head in curiosity. He was still trying to recover from that mind-shattering climax, so his brain wasn't working at full capacity yet. "What's two?" he asked.

"Lovers. As of right now, I've officially had two lovers."

Surprise filtered into him. "You're serious? I'm only the second man you've slept with?"

His peripheral vision caught her quick nod. Rolling onto his side, he placed his palm on her flat belly and searched her uncomfortable expression. "So there was the father of your kids, a seven-year break, and then…me."

She nodded again, her mouth curving in a smile. "Does that freak you out?"

"Why would it freak me out?"

"I don't know. My lack of experience might be a turnoff."

"Baby, the word *turnoff* doesn't apply to you."

Letting out a soft laugh, she shifted so they were lying face to face. Her hand came up to trace the tattoo on his right side, four rows of small black numbers inked right above his hipbone. "What are those dates?"

The question was expected—it always got asked when women saw him naked—but it still evoked that same twinge of discomfort. "Just milestones," he said, keeping it vague.

"Ah, finally, a tat with meaning. Care to elaborate?"

When he didn't answer, she ran her fingers over the most recent date. "What happened on this day?"

He swallowed the lump that rose in his throat. "That was the first time I saved a life."

Her eyes filled with surprise. "Oh. Wow. Are you allowed to talk about it? I remember Missy saying you can't give any details about your assignments."

"She's right. I can't say much, especially about that particular op. Let's just say we got someone important out of a dangerous place."

"Okay. What about this one?"

"The day I got my SEAL trident." He swiftly rolled over on his back before she could ask about the remaining two dates.

Subject change. Now.

Seth scanned his brain. His solution ended up putting Miranda on the spot. "You never talk about your children's father."

She exhaled slowly. "That's because there's not much to say about him."

Her heavy breath had directed his gaze to her bare breasts, which momentarily distracted him. His cock twitched beneath the sheet covering their lower bodies, but he forced himself to ignore the clench of desire and concentrate on the curiosity her words had inspired.

"Are you still in contact with him?" Even as he asked the question, he knew what her answer would be.

"I haven't spoken to him since the day he signed away his parental rights," she said flatly.

"So you have no idea where he is?" Seth gently rested his hand on her waist, stroking the curve of her hip and upper thigh.

"Oh, I know where he is. Prison. Maximum security." Disapproval rang from each word. "He robbed a liquor store outside of Vegas and accidentally shot and killed the clerk. Trent was convicted of armed robbery, manslaughter and a bunch of other stuff I can't remember. He was sentenced to life, but I think he's eligible for parole at some point. Not sure when."

Rather than pose another question or urge her to continue, Seth waited it out. He'd discovered that people were more likely to share their secrets when they weren't being pressured to spill them, but Miranda was obviously on to him, because she laughed softly and said, "I know you want me to keep talking. Don't pretend otherwise."

He chuckled. Busted.

"You're curious about how I met Trent, right?"

"Yeah, but you don't have to talk about it if you don't want to."

She shrugged. "It's not some big secret or anything. I was eighteen, just graduated from high school, and I was leaving for college at the end of the summer. I landed a dance scholarship at the University of Nevada. Full ride."

"Nice," he said, impressed.

Her voice took on a faraway note. "Yeah, it was nice. I was so excited about it. And then I met Trent. I was working as a waitress at this twenty-four-hour diner on the Strip and one night Trent rode up on his Harley. He was the ultimate bad boy. Leather jacket, arms covered in tattoos, and he was gorgeous. Like drop-dead gorgeous."

With a sad smile, Miranda slid into a cross-legged position, bringing the sheet up with her and tucking it over her breasts. "I was such a goody-goody all throughout high school. I had to be—my dad was wild enough for the both of us, and I didn't want to be anything like him. But when Trent walked into the diner? I wanted to be bad and irresponsible. Just once, I wanted to be the girl who rode on a motorcycle with a hot guy, not the one who saved all her tips in a jar so she could pay for college textbooks."

"So you jumped on the back of his Harley and told your responsibilities to fuck off?"

"Yep." She looked at him in wonder. "I know, right? Very unlike me. I quit my job, which wasn't a huge deal since I already had a ton of money saved up. I packed a bag, left home and spent the whole summer riding across the country with Trent. I lost my virginity at the Grand Canyon, by the way."

"You bad girl, you. You tarnished a national treasure."

"Ha-ha." She rolled her eyes, but the humor didn't last long. "I'm pretty sure that's where the twins were conceived. I was three months pregnant when Trent brought me back to Vegas."

"Wait, you were pregnant that whole time and didn't know it?"

"I was getting periods," she explained. "Or at least I thought I was. And during the second month of traveling, I had morning sickness, but since I didn't realize I was even late, I figured it was the stomach flu. The third month, I didn't get a period, so that's when I finally took a test."

"Was Trent with you?"

She nodded. "We were at a rest-stop bathroom. We waited for the results together, and the second we saw the pink plus sign, Trent tossed the stick in the trash and said it was time for me to go home."

Anger tightened his chest. "Are you serious?"

"Yep. He drove me home to Vegas, handed me some cash and told me to get rid of the baby."

"Fucking asshole."

"Tell me about it."

"But you decided to keep the baby."

"And ended up with two," she said wryly. "Trust me, no one was more shocked than me when Jason popped out after Sophie. He was hiding behind her during every ultrasound. Even her heartbeat overpowered his. Not much has changed since the womb, I guess. Sophie is still the ringleader of whatever shenanigans those two get into."

Seth sat up and reached for the bottle of water on the nightstand. He took a quick sip, then offered the bottle to Miranda, who shook her head.

"So what happened with Trent?" he asked, realizing she'd never concluded that chapter of the story.

"I called him to let him know I was keeping the baby and he told me he wanted no part in the child's life." She shrugged. "I expected that. But what I didn't expect? Seeing Trent's picture on the news a month later and finding out he killed a man during a robbery. That's when I decided that *I* didn't want Trent in my kid's life either. Before, I was open to the idea of letting him visit the child if he ever changed his mind, but after he was arrested, I was all, *hell no*."

"I don't blame you."

"So remember all the tip money I saved up for college? Well, I used it to hire a lawyer instead. He drew up some papers and I went to see Trent in prison. He signed away his rights, and I haven't seen or spoken to him since."

"Do the rugrats ever ask about their dad?"

"Never. I assume as they get older they'll become more curious about him and start asking questions. God, I'm not looking forward to that day." She bit her bottom lip. "What if they want to visit him in prison?"

"They won't." Seth didn't even hesitate. "The rugrats are smart, babe. Smart enough to know that you're the only parent they need."

"You think my kids are smart?" She sounded astounded.

Discomfort squeezed his throat. "Yeah, sure. Of course they are."

Miranda continued to stare at him as if he'd just told her he'd won an Olympic gold medal for synchronized swimming or some shit. "Can I ask you something?" she finally said.

Crap. He knew exactly where this convo was heading, and he needed to derail it. Now. "Uh, yeah, sure."

"Why don't you want children?"

And there it was.

He casually raked a hand through his hair, trying to hide his growing agitation. "Not everyone's meant to have kids."

Her dark eyebrows furrowed. "So you think you're not meant to have kids?"

"Yes. I mean, no." His brain struggled to locate an exit strategy. "I'm just not a kid person, babe. We operate on different wavelengths. They can't talk to me, I can't talk to them. And, uh…" He scrolled through the list of reasons he usually provided when people questioned his no-children stance. "I don't have the patience for them, I guess."

Miranda's expression grew more and more doubtful with each word he said, so he decided to quit talking. Christ, he shouldn't have let this damn pillow talk go on for this long anyway. He didn't do emotional heart-to-hearts after sex. His emotions were locked up tight. Private thoughts, past mistakes, moments of self-doubt—he'd bottled all that shit up a long time ago, and no way would he let Miranda pull the cork.

"I need my nicotine fix." His voice was full of gravel, so he cleared his throat before continuing. "You want to come outside with me?"

Shaking her head, she slowly slid out from beneath the sheet and rose from the bed. "I think I'll head to my room."

Her naked body made him forget every single thing they'd been talking about for the past thirty minutes. Long limbs sculpted with lean muscle tone, dark hair tumbling down her back, curves in all the right places. His mouth grew dry at the sight of her, and all the blood in his body traveled south and settled in his groin.

Miranda didn't miss the thickening of his cock. "Down, boy. You have to wake up early."

As he grabbed his boxers from the chair near the bed and pulled them on, his gaze shifted to the alarm clock on the end table. One fifteen. Fuck. He had to be up in five and a half hours. And if he showed up exhausted again the way he had a few days ago, Becker would rip his head off. So, a quick smoke and then some sleep. Those were the only two items on the agenda for the rest of the night.

Of course, it would be easier to stick to the schedule if Miranda wasn't parading around naked in front of him.

"Oh sweet Jesus," he groaned as she bent over to pick up her discarded shirt.

"What's wrong?" she asked, oblivious.

"You're presenting your ass to me like a mare in heat. For the love of God, put on some clothes before I fuck you again."

Her resounding laughter only succeeded in making his dick harder.

"Next time," he croaked.

She slipped her T-shirt over her head, the fabric falling down to her knees. "Next time what?"

"Just that there'll be one," he reminded her. "Your words, babe."

She visibly swallowed. "I know what I said."

Their gazes locked. The air between them heated, crackling with tension.

"So when?" he asked huskily. "When can I have you again?"

Her voice came out a little husky too. "Whenever you want, Seth."

Hot fucking damn.

He stalked toward her, catching her around the waist with both arms. She gave a rapid intake of breath, then squeaked in delight as he covered her mouth with his and kissed her long and slow.

When he pulled back, he studied her glazed expression, pleased with what he saw. "I'm holding you to that."

Chapter Eleven

ADDICTED. SHE WAS ADDICTED TO SETH MASTERSON. AND AFTER THREE days of hot sex, Miranda was past the point of trying to convince herself this was about combating stress. Granted, the regular orgasms were a fantastic stress-buster, but forgetting the worries of the day was the last thing on her mind when she snuck into Seth's room at every available moment.

She craved him. Craved his kiss and his touch. His wicked tongue and talented hands. His cock buried deep inside her. The pleasure he evoked in her was unbelievable. How was it possible to feel *that* good?

"So you're okay with the track?"

Miranda's head jerked up. "Huh?"

"For the hip-hop number. We good with the song selection?" Andre Howard, one of the instructors, watched her with expectant brown eyes.

"As long as it's the edited radio version," she answered.

"Of course, sweetie. Do I look like I want a bunch of outraged parents on my back?" Andre slung his gym bag over his shoulder and grinned. "By the way, my girls did good today. They'll bring down the house on show night."

They'd better, Miranda thought. The parents of those kids paid a lot of money for these classes, and if she wanted them to enroll their kids for the fall session, she had to give them a good show. Her own group, the girls in beginner ballet, were making progress too, including Sophie, who had a natural talent that made Miranda proud. But she suspected her daughter wouldn't stick with ballet for much longer. Sophie was too smart for her age, too analytical, and she could charm the bees right out of their honey—Miranda wouldn't be surprised if her daughter became a politician someday.

"Oh, and Elsa's in your office. She wanted to talk to you about one of her students," Andre added as they fell into step with each other and headed for the door.

The school housed three large studios, two locker rooms with bathrooms and a shower area, and a small office Miranda hardly ever used. Ginny, one of the other instructors, handled enrollment and payment, and Miranda had hired a business manager to deal with anything else that needed to be dealt with. Although she had a good head for business, she didn't enjoy the business side of running the school. She would much rather focus on the creative aspect of it and let others handle the rest.

Andre, the forever-smiling black guy with a flair for the dramatic, was the first teacher she'd hired. He was a recent Juilliard graduate who'd decided he preferred teaching to performing, and he taught mostly hip-hop, including a coed class that was growing in popularity—he already had a waiting list for the next sessions.

As she and Andre entered the hallway, he flashed his big, dimpled smile. "You tending bar tonight, boss?"

"Unfortunately." She let out a weary sigh. "Weekends are supposed to be lovely and relaxing, aren't they? So why are mine always jam-packed with activity? By Sunday night, I'm ready to collapse."

In fact, she wasn't sure she'd make it through tonight's shift without falling asleep in the middle of pouring a drink. She'd gone to bed at five in the morning, after Seth cajoled her into a quickie when she got home from the club. The resulting orgasm had been delicious—but getting only four hours of sleep, not so delicious. To compound the exhaustion, she'd spent the entire morning and afternoon at the school, teaching three back-to-back classes.

And her day wasn't even close to being over. She still had to take the kids out for their Saturday pizza dinner, drive home, get them bathed and in their PJ's before Kim got there, go to the club, and then tend bar until two in the morning.

Someone kill her. Now.

"I don't know how you do it," Andre remarked. "I swear, you're Superwoman."

"Tell me about it. Anyway, drive safe. I'll see you tomorrow bright and early. I'll be the one asleep at the barre."

Andre laughed. "See you tomorrow, Superwoman."

They parted ways, Andre heading for the front door, Miranda continuing down the hall toward the back office where Elsa Fisher was waiting.

Elsa was in her midforties, a ballerina who'd immigrated to the States after touring the world with a renowned German dance corps. She taught advanced ballet and contemporary dance to the older students, while Miranda worked with the younger ones. Ginny and Andre, who rounded out the teaching staff, worked with all ages.

"Hey, Elsa, what's up?" she asked as she entered the office.

Elsa rose from the desk chair, a frown pinching her thin lips. "The father was here again. He wants to discuss Catherine's future at the school, but he refuses to talk to anyone but you."

Miranda shook her head in annoyance. "But Catherine is *your* student. I already explained to him on the phone that you're the one to talk to in regards to growth and development."

"He insists he must discuss it with you, the owner. He was waiting for you after Catherine's private lesson, but your class ran late so he left. He told me to let you know he'll be phoning you tomorrow."

The billionth sigh of the day shuddered out of her lungs. Okay. No big deal. For some reason, Catherine Porter's father was chomping at the bit for a few minutes of Miranda's time. Clearly he wouldn't take no for an answer, so she'd just suck it up and have a brief conversation with him tomorrow.

"All right. Thanks for letting me know," she told Elsa. "I've got to take off now. You'll lock up after your evening lesson?"

"Of course."

"Then I'll see you tomorrow."

She waved good-bye and left the office, heading for the empty studio where she'd left her daughter. When she poked her head in, she saw Sophie sprawled on a pile of blue mats, playing with the new doll they'd picked out a couple of days ago. Miranda had taken the kids to the mall for the sole purpose of replacing Sophie's beloved Belinda; luckily, Belinda's successor, Emily, was a big hit so far.

"Time to go, Soph," she called. "We have to pick up your brother."

Sophie hopped off the mats, tucking Emily under her arm as she dashed over and threw herself into Miranda's legs with a hefty *whoomp*.

She laughed and stared down at her daughter. "What's this about?"

"Do you still love me, Mommy?" A pair of big brown eyes gazed imploringly at her.

"Why on earth would you ask me that? *Of course* I still love you!"

Relief flooded Sophie's face. "Promise?"

"I promise, Soph, I still love you. I will *always* love you. Always and always and always."

"*Pinky* promise?"

Miranda squatted down to the floor and stuck out her pinkie. After a second, Sophie offered a pinkie in return and they sealed the deal.

"Now," Miranda said, incredibly disturbed by the entire exchange, "can you tell me why you thought I didn't love you anymore?"

"'Cause you ignored me in class today when I tried to show you my plié." Sophie pouted. "And yesterday you only read *one* story after dinner and you usually read *two* and Jase said maybe you were tired 'cause our house is underwater and then he said maybe we would hafta live with Sef *forever* but I said we wouldn't 'cause Sef is mean 'cept sometimes he's not mean, sometimes he's nice, but then he stops being nice when he sees that *we* see he's being nice."

It took a few seconds to make sense of everything her daughter had said. Rising to her feet, she took Sophie's hand, then picked up the two dance bags she'd left by the door. She decided to address one point at a time.

"First of all, if I ignored you today, I didn't mean to. I probably just didn't hear you, sweetie," she assured her daughter, who was clutching her hand so tightly Miranda's bones ached. "And remember we talked about how when there are ten other little girls in the studio, I have to pay attention to all of them instead of just one?"

"I remember."

"I'm sorry if I hurt your feelings, Soph, but I promise I didn't do it on purpose, okay?"

"'Kay."

They exited the building and walked hand in hand to the parking lot behind the school. Miranda tried to remember Sophie's next complaint. Right, the stories.

"And your brother was right. I was very tired yesterday and that's why I only read one story. Hey, know what Andre just called me?"

"What?"

"Superwoman."

Sophie giggled. "That's funny."

"Kind of, but see, it's not true." She lifted her daughter into the backseat and buckled her up, then knelt in front of the open door. "I'm not a superhero, Soph. I can't do everything, and sometimes I get tired and cranky. I know that might not be fair to you and Jase, but sometimes you guys get tired and cranky too, right?"

"Right."

"So what do you say we agree not to get upset with each other at times like those? Deal?"

Sophie smiled. "Deal."

Uneasiness swelled in Miranda's stomach as she reached the final topic of discussion. "And I don't want you to worry. We're not going to live with Seth forever. He's just being a good friend to your mom and giving us a place to stay until our apartment is all fixed up."

Sophie brought her doll up to her chest and began playing with Emily's silky black hair. She avoided Miranda's eyes as she whispered, "Do you like Sef more than you like me and Jase?"

Her heart squeezed. "Oh, sweetie, of course not. I like Seth, he's a good friend of Mommy's, but I could never like him more than you and Jason. I could never like *anyone* more."

"Promise?"

"*Pinky* promise," she replied, sticking out her baby finger.

They shook pinkies again. Miranda teasingly tugged on her daughter's ponytail and got up. "Okay, now we need to pick up your brother before he thinks we abandoned him."

She slid into the driver's seat and started the engine, then pulled out of the lot and merged into the late afternoon traffic. A glance in the rearview mirror revealed Sophie playing with her doll, but suddenly Sophie's head lifted and she locked gazes with her mother.

"I don't wanna go for pizza today," she announced.

Miranda wrinkled her forehead. "But it's our Saturday tradition."

Her daughter stubbornly shook her head. "I don't wanna go. Can you ask the pizza man to bring pizza to Sef's house?"

"Sure, we can get it delivered," she said, baffled. "But why?"

An exaggerated sigh reverberated in the interior of the car. "'Cause you're tired, Mom. Duh!"

With that, Sophie returned her attention to her new doll, leaving Miranda to shake her head in awe and amusement. God, she had great kids. Sweet, perceptive, smart. Just all-around incredible.

The rugrats are smart, babe. Smart enough to know that you're the only parent they need.

Seth's words from the other night buzzed in her brain, immediately followed by the convoluted thought Sophie had voiced minutes ago.

Sometimes he's nice, but then he stops being nice when he sees that we see *he's being nice.*

Out of the mouth of babes.

Was Sophie on to something, though? Was Seth going out of his way to refrain from being nice to the twins? Was he purposely putting distance between himself and her children? Because the other day, when he'd recited his reasons for not wanting or liking kids, something had sounded so...false. And call her crazy, but there might have even been a tremor of panic in his tone.

It suddenly occurred to her that she hardly knew anything about him. He'd grown up in Vegas, he'd been raised by a showgirl, he'd enlisted at eighteen.

But what else? What was his childhood like? What were his hopes and dreams? How did he envision his future?

And did it really matter whether she had the answers to any of those questions? The involvement between her and Seth was purely sexual. Sooner or later it would fizzle out, so why try to forge a deeper connection?

Maybe the less insight she had into Seth's complicated psyche, the better off she'd be.

SETH WAS FEELING EDGY AS HELL AS HE WATCHED MIRANDA WIPE THE corner of her mouth with a napkin, all cute and demure-like. The four of them were sitting on the living room floor around the coffee table, munching on the pizza Miranda had ordered for dinner. The flat screen on the wall was playing an animated movie Jason had picked, but Seth wasn't paying attention to the TV. He was too busy looking at Miranda, same way he'd been looking at her every goddamn second for the past three days.

Everything the woman did turned him on. She made even the most innocuous activities look dirty. Folding laundry, sweeping the kitchen floor—didn't matter what she did, he wanted her. Tonight it was watching her eat pizza that got his blood going. His gaze was glued to her mouth, so focused on it, in fact, that one of the rugrats finally decided to comment. No surprise as to which one, either.

"Why are you staring at my mom?" Sophie demanded.

Seth blinked out of his lust-filled stupor. "Ah, because she had tomato sauce on her cheek."

"I did?" Miranda's dubious look said she saw right through him.

"Yeah, but it's gone now. You wiped it away."

Sophie pursed her lips in disapproval. "It's rude to stare."

"You're right. It is." He met Miranda's eyes. "I'm sorry for staring, Miranda."

"It's quite all right, Seth."

She held his gaze for another second before turning to scold Jason, who was making a huge mess as he dipped his slice into a plastic container of barbecue sauce. Which kinda floored him, because Seth had never met anyone who slathered BBQ sauce on pizza the way he himself did. Neither he nor Miranda's son had remarked on it, but there'd been unmistakable pleasure in Jason's eyes when Seth had called dibs on one of the barbecue sauces. It was obvious the kid liked having something in common with him.

"Anyway, thanks for dinner," Seth said, standing up. "I was dying of hunger when you got home and I couldn't decide what to eat."

Their gazes locked again. Miranda's cheeks turned pink.

You, he told her with his eyes. *I wanted to eat you.*

Still did, too. He wanted to latch his mouth on her sweet pussy and eat her until she screamed his name.

Her tone was nonchalant as she answered, "Well, if you're hungry again later, let me know. I could always stop and grab you something to eat on my way back from the club tonight." *Later* being the operative word in that sentence.

"Actually, I won't be here later. I've gotta be at the base at one a.m. We're doing night dives."

More eye contact. Another unspoken message.

"Whath nithe difes?" Jason demanded through a mouthful of pizza.

"Jase," Miranda chided. "Chew, swallow, talk."

The little boy did as asked, then repeated himself. "What's night dives?"

"It means we're diving in the ocean in the middle of the night," Seth explained brusquely.

"You go in the water in the *dark*?" Jason's eyes widened. "But Mom says it's dangerous to go swimming when it's not sunny."

Miranda smiled at her son. "Dangerous for *you*," she corrected. "But see how big and strong Seth is?"

Jason nodded, visibly awed.

"Well, that means he's allowed to do dangerous things every now and then. He underwent a lot of training, years and years of training, to be able to do what he does."

Seth shifted in discomfort. Each word she said only succeeded in giving Jason a bigger case of hero worship, and he didn't want to be the kid's hero.

"Okay, uh, I'm gonna catch some shut-eye until I have to go," Seth said before she could continue. He gave the rugrats a quick nod, Miranda one final look, and then left the living room.

After he shut and locked his bedroom door, he stripped off his T-shirt, cargo pants and boxer briefs, and made his way to the bed. He hadn't lied—sleep was definitely on the docket. Except he wouldn't get a wink of it unless he remedied the problem down below.

He stretched out on the bed and fisted his erection, disappointed that he and Miranda wouldn't be able to find any private time tonight. But she'd be busy with her kids until the babysitter showed up, and by the time she got home from work, he'd be deep beneath the ocean's surface, engaged in mock amphibious landings.

Closing his eyes, he pumped his cock in quick, even strokes and envisioned Miranda's perky tits. Her dusky nipples, so responsive to his touch. The sexy curve of her ass and baby-soft skin of her inner thighs.

It didn't escape him that he was jerking off to the thought of a woman who was by no means out of his reach. She was right beyond that door, and it drove him nuts that he couldn't just have her whenever he wanted. But Miranda was a mom first—she'd made that abundantly clear—which meant that the twins claimed first priority on her time.

His dick, unfortunately, was of lesser importance.

No sooner had he accepted that grim assessment of his position on the totem pole than a soft knock sounded on the door.

"Can I come in?" came her quiet voice.

His cock twitched with excitement, a drop of fluid seeping from its slit.

He was off the bed in an instant, unlocking the door and tugging her into the room.

"Eleven minutes," Miranda whispered.

He shot her a questioning look.

"There's eleven minutes left in the movie. It's the final battle scene between the aliens and those weird purple monsters. The kids are hypnotized." She was sliding out of her leggings as she spoke. "So we've got eleven minutes to make this happen." Her gaze swept over his naked body. "I see you've already gotten started."

He brought his hand back to his erection and gave it a firm squeeze. "I had no choice. Watching you nibble on that pizza got me hard as a rock."

"Hmmm, I can see that." Her hand replaced his, her graceful fingers curling over his stiff shaft.

When she pumped him nice and slow, he let out a husky moan and reached for her. He slid his hands underneath her shirt and cupped her breasts over her sports bra. Neither of them made a move toward the bed. They simply stood against the door, his hands fondling her tits, hers jacking his cock in a lazy, torturous rhythm that made his vision waver.

He leaned his forehead against hers, his breath coming out in pants as she quickened the pace. "Condom," he ground out.

"In a minute."

Before he could blink, she dropped to her knees, her face level with his cock. Every muscle in his body coiled tight as she gripped the root of him and brought him to her mouth.

Oh Jesus. Wet warmth surrounded him, the suction so unbearably sweet. Miranda pulled the skin taut and delicately licked the exposed head, flicking the underside with her tongue before sucking him deep again. When her hands came into play, one wrapping around his base, the other cupping his tight, achy balls, he hissed out a curse and withdrew from her eager mouth.

"No fair," she complained. "You never let me have fun."

He almost shot his load when he saw her big eyes peering up at him, her lips glossy with moisture. "That's because I'm always in a hurry to get inside you," he grumbled.

"Well, too bad. Today you get to exercise some patience."

"Patience? We only have eleven minutes."

"Eight minutes now," she corrected, her gaze straying to the clock by the bed. "So if you don't want to waste any more time, I suggest you shut up and let me suck your dick."

Hot animalistic lust clamped over him. Well. Who was he to argue with *that?*

Changing positions so that he was the one leaning against the wall, Seth tangled one hand in Miranda's long brown hair and guided her back to his cock. She opened wide, took him deep, and sucked him hard, eliciting a strangled groan from his lips.

For someone who hadn't been with a man in seven years, she knew exactly what to do, exactly how to drive him to new heights of agonizing pleasure. She gripped him with the perfect amount of pressure, pumped with the right amount of force. She tightened her mouth's suction with each downstroke, flicked her tongue over his head on each upstroke. Soon he was pistoning his hips, body straining for deeper contact, desperation building and gathering in his balls.

Miranda let out a muffled moan. He noticed she'd moved one hand between her legs so she could furiously rub her clit. Her excitement fed his own, her enthusiasm bringing forth a rush of male satisfaction. He fucking loved that she enjoyed going down on him, that it turned her on the way going down on *her* did him.

She increased the tempo, her mouth and hand moving up and down his cock, which glistened with saliva and throbbed with anticipation. He was close. Very close. He should pull out. Get a condom. Slide into her tight heat and fuck her hard. Yet he didn't have the strength to leave the warm heaven of Miranda's mouth.

"I'm gonna come," he muttered. "You want it in your mouth?"

Her head bobbed as she nodded, her eyes hazy, shining with passion.

That eager gaze was all it took. He exploded in a boiling rush, one hand entangled in her hair, the other braced on the chest of drawers next to the door. Black dots danced in his vision, his mind losing the capability for thought. A fire of ecstasy burned in his blood, blazing hotter as Miranda's throat worked to swallow.

"Jesus." His erection popped out of her mouth, coated with saliva. "I guess we don't need a condom after all."

Wiping her mouth with the back of her hand, she wobbled to her feet and smiled. A tiny smile boasting of feminine satisfaction, as if she was mighty pleased with herself. "We weren't ever getting to the condom part, *babe*. Wasn't part of my dastardly plan."

"Your plan involved getting on your knees, sucking my cock, and making me come?" When she nodded, he raised a mocking brow. "Then why'd you take off your leggings and panties?"

"So I could get myself off while I was carrying out the aforementioned dastardly plan."

"I see." He slanted his head. "And did you get yourself off?"

A sheepish smiled lifted her lips. "No. I totally got distracted."

Seth checked the clock. "Well, we've still got two minutes left…"

"No way would I be able to come in two minutes."

"Is that a challenge?"

"Seth—"

He dropped to the floor, making her yelp as he grabbed one of her legs and draped it over his shoulder. Her slick folds, pink and perfect, hovered directly over his mouth.

Licking his lips, he tilted his head to meet her eyes and said, "Challenge accepted."

"Are you seriously trying to convince me that the 49ers are a better team than the Bears?" Aidan shook his head in disbelief before taking a long swig of beer. "No way, Wade. You're nuts."

"Me? Look in the mirror, Rhodes. You're living in the past," Dylan retorted. "Newsflash—it's not 1985 anymore. The glory days are over."

Aidan flashed his middle finger.

Dylan's phone buzzed. He glanced at the screen and read the incoming text from Seth, then glanced at Aidan.

"Seth and Jackson are chilling at the Sand Hole tonight. You wanna go?"

Aidan shrugged. "Not really. You?"

"Nah."

They eyed each other for a moment, and something shifted in the night breeze slithering over the terrace. After a beat of silence, they both reached for their respective beers.

Dylan fixed his gaze on the skyline, pretending to be fascinated with the tall skyscrapers and twinkling lights when all he could think about was how good Aidan looked tonight and how awesome the last few days had been.

Despite the awkwardness of that first night, it turned out they made pretty good roommates. Neither of them were slobs, they both liked to cook, they enjoyed watching the same programs on TV. And Aidan subscribed to the NFL network, which meant football twenty-four-seven. Dylan never got to enjoy football talk at home—pansy-ass Seth was all about boxing matches and pay-per-view fights, which was probably a Vegas thing, but annoying nonetheless.

Then again, there was a definite upside to living with Seth: Dylan didn't want to rip the guy's clothes off every time he saw him.

And interestingly enough, Seth, who was intense as hell, was actually *less* intense than Aidan. On the surface Aidan was charming and funny, but every now and then he got quiet, his dark eyes becoming shuttered. And if you looked really hard, you sometimes glimpsed a shadow or two that you couldn't decipher, a hint of the secrets that lurked behind his enigmatic expression. But whatever shadows Aidan harbored, he didn't seem inclined to shed light on them, and Dylan wasn't one to push.

However, when it came to another aspect of Aidan's life, he was far too curious not to bring it up.

"So what's the deal with you and Matt and Savannah?" Dylan asked, leaning back in the cushioned chair.

Aidan grinned. "What do you mean?"

"Those two are in a committed relationship, right?"

"Yes."

"Yet according to Cash, you're frequently over at their place, in Matt's bedroom…" He shrugged. "How does that work exactly?"

Aidan's dimples made an appearance as his grin widened. "You need me to spell out the logistics of a *ménage à trois*, man?"

"Ha-ha. I mean, don't you feel like the third wheel? Matt and Savannah are in love." He paused in afterthought. "Unless…wait, are all *three* of you…?"

"No, the three of us are not in love." Rolling his eyes, Aidan reached for the pack of Newports on the glass table and extracted a cigarette. He lit up, chuckling as he exhaled a cloud of smoke that swiftly got carried away by the breeze. "It's really not that complicated. Matt and Savannah are together and they love each other. Matt's my best friend. Savannah's a good friend."

"Okay, I'm following you so far…"

"Savannah and Matt are also the most sexually adventurous people I've ever met in my life. They like to have fun and experiment, and they also happen to enjoy variety." He flashed those dimples again. "And when they want variety, they call me."

"And it's not awkward?" Dylan wrinkled his forehead. "Aren't they all, I don't know, *intimate* with each other? Lovingly gazing into each other's eyes, whispering *I love you*, all that couple shit?"

Aidan snickered. "If that's how they acted, I wouldn't be there, bro. I have no idea what they're like when they're alone, but trust me, when it's the three of us, it's all about pure, carnal fucking."

A dark thrill traveled up Dylan's spine. When was the last time he'd indulged in some pure, carnal fucking of his own? The kind where you didn't think, didn't question or doubt, didn't stop to consider propriety or pesky emotions.

Cash and Jen.

Shit, that was totally it. The last time he'd experienced that kind of raw, modesty-be-damned sex had been six months ago with Cash and Jen. He'd given his best friend a blowjob that night, slept with his best friend's now-serious girlfriend, and though he'd been with plenty of chicks since then, he couldn't remember any of those encounters leaving him with that same sense of carnal satisfaction.

"Anyway," Aidan was saying, "I'm not sure how much longer the arrangement will last. The three of us haven't hooked up in a few months, actually."

Dylan inspected the other man's face for signs of anger or disappointment and found none. Aidan looked relaxed as hell as he flicked his ashes in the ashtray before bringing his cigarette back to his lips for another drag.

"Maybe they got sick of you," Dylan joked.

"Doubt it. I'm pretty frickin' good in bed."

Aidan's tone rang with humor, but there was nothing humorous about the way their gazes collided again. Or the current of heat that coursed between them.

Breaking the eye contact, Aidan gave a small shrug. "Matt's going to propose to her soon."

"Seriously?"

"I helped him pick out the ring. Nothing too flashy—Savannah hates showy displays of wealth. According to her, only flowers are allowed to be showy." An indulgent smile quirked Aidan's lips. "They're good for each other. They just...*fit*, know what I mean? I think they'll be happy."

Silence descended over the terrace, each man getting lost in his own thoughts. Dylan had to wonder if he'd ever meet that one person who *fit* him. He'd been told he wasn't "relationship material", accused of being too impulsive and fun-loving, qualities which apparently weren't conducive to a serious relationship. Who knew.

"So where are you going to get your ménage fix now?" Dylan asked with a grin.

"No clue. I might have to start inviting myself to the orgies you keep going on about."

"I'm afraid my orgy calendar isn't as lit as it used to be. Cash bowed out when he started dating Jen, and Seth's been panting after Miranda the past few months. Which leaves Jackson, who was always the weak link in my three-way circle. He prefers one-on-one, claims it's the Texas way."

They both laughed. Observed each other again. Reached for their beers.

A groan got stuck in his throat, joining the ball of frustration and lump of unease already taking up residence there. This had never happened to him before, damn it. Lusting over another man? *Just* another man?

With no woman around to balance everything out?

Fuck.

The lack of estrogen on the balcony became glaringly apparent the longer he and Aidan watched each other. Unsettled, Dylan chugged the rest of his beer, but the liquid was lukewarm by now and did nothing to extinguish the fire raging down below.

Enough. He was tired of the strange waves of tension palpitating in the air whenever he and Aidan were alone together. He needed to get laid. It was the only way to purge his body of this tight, antsy feeling, the only way to vanquish this inappropriate craving.

"Shoot, I forgot, I have to return this chick's call." He scraped his chair back and reached for his two empty beers.

Aidan beat him to the bottles. "Make your call out here. I'll take the empties in."

"Oh, thanks, man."

"No problem."

Their fingers brushed as he handed Aidan the bottles. A tiny shockwave coursed through his veins, making him gulp.

With a knowing twinkle in his dark eyes, Aidan headed for the sliding door and quietly moved through the threshold.

Dylan stared at the man's retreating back and resisted a groan. Crap. He was approaching a critical point here. A potential point of no return.

Grabbing his phone, he scrolled through the contacts until he found one entry in particular. Rachel Carver. The blonde he'd met at the club last week.

To his overwhelming relief, she chirped out a hello on the second ring.

"Rachel?" He cleared his throat. "Hey, it's Dylan. Dylan Wade. We met at OMG last week, remember?"

She sounded absolutely delighted to hear from him. "Hi! I'd almost given up on you! I'm so glad you called."

His peripheral vision caught a blur of movement. He turned his head to see Aidan in the living room, one sculpted arm flexing as he pointed the remote at the flat screen before flopping down on the leather couch.

Tearing his gaze away, Dylan forced his attention back on the phone call. "So. Rachel. You feel like hanging out tonight?"

Chapter Twelve

THE FOLLOWING WEEK, MIRANDA MOVED BACK TO HER APARTMENT, leaving Seth feeling oddly dejected and more than a little discouraged. Even with her kids constantly underfoot, he'd liked having her in his house. They may not have slept in the same bed, or even spent all that much time together, thanks to their busy schedules, but he'd drawn comfort from her presence.

And as expected, living with the woman had taught him quite a lot about her. For example, he now knew what a nauseatingly chipper morning person she was, that she cooked the best breakfasts on the planet, and that she sneezed every time she smelled the scent of dish detergent. He'd also discovered that she preferred classic rock to anything contemporary, the History Channel to reality television, and boxing above all sports.

His three favorite fucking things.

The best thing about her, though? She loved sex. Absolutely *loved* it. Maybe it was the seven-year lull, but he'd never been with a more passionate woman. She gave 110 percent in the bedroom—eager, shameless, quick to laugh, open to experiment.

Oh, and the icing on the cake? She was into morning sex.

Very into it, he discovered when he crawled into her bed at ten in the morning, spooned her from behind, and slipped a finger inside her. He groaned at how wet she was. How, even in her sleep, she rocked into his finger and let out a moan.

"Seth?" she murmured.

"Mmm-hmmm." He dropped a kiss on her bare shoulder, pleased that she hadn't bothered with pajamas.

He knew she'd gotten home from the club at two a.m. last night and woke up at seven today to drive the twins to school. After spending another long night in the ocean, he'd turned on his phone to find a text from Miranda, informing him she was going back to bed and to let himself in. She'd signed the text with a winky face, which had brought a smile to his lips.

He'd stopped at his house to shower and change, then managed to drive to Miranda's apartment without falling asleep at the wheel. The team would be doing classroom work for the rest of this week and most of the following one, which meant his sleep schedule would return to normal. For a bit, anyway.

"That feels good," she said sleepily.

He fingered her with lazy thrusts, his cock stiffening and straining against her naked ass. Moisture coated his finger, eliciting a deep growl of approval, and he greedily added a second digit, loving the way her pussy clenched around it. His thumb tended to her clit as his fingers worked her, and it wasn't long before she was gasping and squirming and shaking with orgasm.

While she lay on the bed, warm and boneless and recovering from her climax, he donned a condom, then moved into the spooning position again and eased into her from behind.

"Oh, that's nice," she murmured when his entire length filled her.

"Very nice," he murmured back, planting a soft kiss on the nape of her neck. The fine hairs there tickled his lips.

His cock throbbed, ordering him to go faster, to fuck her harder, but exhaustion and indolence overruled his body's demand. Very deliberately, he pulled out, one inch at a time, but not completely. He kept just the tip inside her, an unbearable tease that resulted in Miranda clenching her inner muscles around him, a hot vise squeezing his engorged head.

Seth let out a curse. "You're evil."

Her choked laughter filled the air. "I didn't do it on purpose. I guess my body wants to trap you in it."

"Baby, I'd happily move in if I could."

He rolled his hips and they both groaned at the tantalizing friction. All talking ceased as he closed his eyes and lost himself in mind-blowing sensation. The iron grip of her on his cock, her silky hair tickling his cheek, the way her nipple puckered when he brought one arm around her to cup a breast.

When he finally came, it wasn't in one tidal wave of pleasure, but, rather, in little bursts of ecstasy, like waves lapping against the shore, dancing over his flesh and tingling in his balls and shivering through him in an endless, full-body rush. Huh. Exhausted sex apparently had its perks.

"Can't move," he mumbled when the bliss finally ebbed. "Sleepy."

He scraped up enough energy to pull out and peel off the condom, then slung his arm over Miranda's waist and snuggled close to her warm, lithe body.

He didn't know how long he slept, but he'd never felt more rested when he finally opened his eyes a while later. Pleasure tugged at his heart when he realized Miranda was still in bed with him. No longer tucked into his chest, but lying on her side, her hazel eyes fixed on his face.

"What time is it?" he asked, reaching up to wipe the sleep from his eyes.

"One thirty."

"Damn, woman, you let me sleep past one?"

"You needed it." She touched his jaw, running her fingers over the thick stubble.

He groaned. "Oh, right there, scratch right there."

With a laugh, she scratched the itchy spot on his chin, summoning a contented sigh from his lips.

"I should really shave," he conceded.

Miranda gave a mock gasp. "Wait, you actually own a razor?"

"Yes, I own a razor." He grinned. "I just don't use it very often."

"I can't picture you clean-shaven." Her fingertips skimmed the stubble above his upper lip, then trailed over the beard growth along the line of his jaw. "I don't think I'd like it."

"You like your men scruffy, huh?"

She offered a self-deprecating look. "I've always been attracted to scruffy, tattooed bad boys. It's a problem of mine." Then she gave his jaw another scratch and it felt so good he nearly purred like a fucking kitten.

"Are you hungry?" she asked, sitting up.

She'd gotten dressed at some point when he'd been asleep, and he enjoyed the way the fabric of her black tank top was pulled taut over her breasts. The bra she wore must have been thinner than toilet paper, because he could see her nipples poking through, and his lower body stirred at the sight.

"I'm starving." He wiggled his eyebrows suggestively, but his attempt at flirting was betrayed by the loud rumble of his stomach.

She laughed again. "Uh-huh. There's my answer."

Much to his unhappiness, she scooted off the bed and headed for the bedroom door. "Omelet or regular eggs?"

His mouth immediately watered. "Omelet."

"Ham, cheese, mushrooms, green peppers, onions?"

Oh fuck. Now he was liable to drool all over her damn sheets. "All of those sound great."

"Good. I'll be in the kitchen."

Seth dragged himself out of bed and ducked into the hall bathroom to use the john and wash up. His gaze was drawn to the toothbrush holder on the edge of the porcelain sink. Three toothbrushes—an adult-sized one and two kiddie brushes with Disney characters on them. It was an intrusive reminder that Miranda didn't live in this apartment alone, but luckily he hadn't spent much time with the rugrats since they'd left his house. He'd either come by here when the kids were in school, or Miranda stopped by his place for a quickie if she managed to leave the club early.

When he entered the kitchen five minutes later, she already had an omelet sizzling in a pan. She nudged it with a wooden spatula and the most incredible aroma floated in his direction.

"You need any help?" he offered.

"I've got the omelets and toast covered, but you could pour us some coffee. Mugs are in the cupboard to your left."

Seth grabbed the coffeepot and poured the hot liquid into two ceramic mugs, then headed for the fridge to get the milk. He splashed a bit into Miranda's cup, dumped in two sugars, and carried both mugs to the small kitchen table. He sipped his coffee, his gaze following Miranda's movements and admiring the way her boxer shorts clung to her perfect ass.

"Oh, and by the way," she announced, perching one hip against the counter, "I'm still *horrified* by what you said the other day."

He chuckled. "I say a lot of scandalous things, baby. You've gotta be more specific."

"About Gomez being technically better than Carvo?" she prompted.

"Oh, that."

"'Oh, that'?" She raised her spatula in the air as if she planned to whack him with it. "Manny Gomez is clearly the superior fighter, Seth. He won *two* of the three matches between him and Carvo—"

"It was a split decision—"

"It's still a win!" She harrumphed. "Jeez, next thing you'll be telling me is that Ali wasn't the greatest boxer of all time."

"He wasn't. Sugar Ray Robinson, hands down."

Miranda's mouth fell open. And stayed open. She just stared at him in shock for a good minute.

He stifled a laugh and gestured to the stove. "You gonna deal with our breakfast before it burns?"

After a beat, she snapped out of whatever mental lecture she'd been giving him and shut off the burner.

"I can't believe you said that about Ali," she muttered after she'd served their food and joined him at the table. "I think that might have been blasphemy."

"Hey, everyone's entitled to their own opinion," he chastised.

"Not when it's *wrong*."

The stubborn look in her eyes made him grin. He liked that she had no qualms about arguing with him. Or challenging him. Or sassing him. Miranda always spoke her mind, which he appreciated. A lot of females expected you to be a damn psychic. They wanted you to anticipate their moods, to know when they were pissed off without them having to tell you, and then they got even angrier when you didn't. It was refreshing being with a woman who didn't expect him to do any unreasonable guesswork.

Being with her? the little voice in his head echoed, wary as hell.

Sleeping with her, he amended. Hanging out with her. Flinging with her. Whatever.

There was a lull in the conversation as they ate, but the silence was comfortable. After they finished eating, they carried their plates to the sink and cleaned up together. He washed, she dried, and as detergent soap bubbles floated over the sink, Miranda sneezed so many times Seth actually got a stitch in his side from laughing so hard.

It wasn't until they refilled their coffees and headed for the backyard so he could have a smoke that he realized how this entire morning just smacked of domesticity. He'd never had breakfast with a woman before. Never washed dishes with a woman. Never had coffee in a woman's backyard, or chatted about bird feeders with a woman.

Shit.

What was he doing?

"Sophie is convinced one of those sparrows is after her." Miranda's laughter broke through his thoughts.

He followed her gaze to the birds pecking at the seeds in the red wooden feeder hanging off the fence that bordered the yard. "She could be right," he mused. "That one on the right looks a tad aggressive."

"She claims it sits in front of the window and pecks at the glass, looking at her with, and I quote, 'bad-people eyes'."

He laughed, then reprimanded himself for it. Shit. Again, what was he *doing*? This thing with him and Miranda...it was about sex. About satisfying the hot, primal urges she unleashed in him. Nothing wrong with enjoying her company at the same time, but there needed to be a balance between, say, talking about boxing like friends and washing dishes together like an old married couple.

Except...doing those dishes had been fun, damn it.

Everything he did with Miranda was fun.

"Fuck," he mumbled.

She glanced over in confusion. "What?"

"Nothing," he lied. "Just thinking about how the rugrat might be right—that bird really does look like a shithead."

Miranda threw her head back and laughed, and it was the sweetest sound he'd ever heard.

It was also another sign that he was treading into some very dangerous territory.

He thought doing chores as a couple was *fun*?

He thought the sound of her laughter was *sweet*?

Fuck.

Chapter Thirteen

Two weeks later

"Jeez, someone call the smile police," Andre announced with a laugh. "You've smiled so many times in the last ten minutes it ought to be illegal."

"Seriously," Ginny agreed. "What kind of happy drug are you on and where can I get some?"

"Can't a girl be in a good mood?" Miranda lifted one leg and rested her ankle on the sleek barre spanning the studio wall. She curled her spine and reached to grasp her toes with her hands, and as she stretched, she tilted her head at the two instructors sprawled on the blue mats. "You're acting as if I usually walk around here like the Grinch. I smile all the time."

"Not this much," Andre countered.

"Not this much," Ginny echoed.

With a laugh, she switched legs and began a new series of stretches. Truth was, she knew exactly what they were talking about. She'd noticed it herself these past couple of weeks. Her spirits were at an all-time high, and she was smiling so often her facial muscles were beginning to hurt. She couldn't help it, though. Life was good. Her apartment showed no signs of the damage caused by the flood, seven new students had enrolled at the school, and the preparations for the summer recital were coming along well.

Oh, and she was having mind-shattering orgasms on a daily basis.

What was there to complain about?

"So," Andre said, catching Miranda's eye in the floor-to-ceiling mirrors that took up one entire wall of the studio, "what's his name and why don't you ever bring him by the school?"

She finished her stretch and walked across the shiny floor toward the two teachers. They'd all come in early this afternoon to go over some details about the recital, but now that they'd squared everything away they had some time to kill before students started showing up.

Plopping down on one of the mats, she grinned at Andre. "His name is Seth, and he doesn't come by because there's no such thing as Bring-Your-Fling-To-Work Day."

Ginny, a slight blonde with big gray eyes and an endless supply of energy, snickered loudly. "Well, there should be because that sounds awesome."

"So it's really just a fling?" Andre's brows drew together in a frown. "Doesn't seem like your style, boss."

She was about to say "it isn't", until she remembered that her only other sexual relationship had been nothing but a fling too. At the time, she'd thought she loved Trent, but it wasn't until after he'd deposited her back in Vegas and told her to "get rid of the kid" that she'd realized how naïve she'd been. Trent hadn't loved her, and now, seven years later, she understood that she hadn't loved him either. It had been nothing more than girlish infatuation.

With Seth, it wasn't much different. She was an adult now, and she was well aware that sex and love didn't necessarily go hand in hand. She was sleeping with Seth, yes. She enjoyed spending time with him, of course. But to call this anything other than a fling? Maybe if she was still a naïve girl, sure, but the eighteen-year-old Miranda had bid good-bye to her naiveté in that delivery room giving birth to twins.

"I'm just having a little fun," she answered, her tone noncommittal. "It's not serious at all."

Ginny leaned back on her elbows, her elfin features filling with curiosity. "What's he like?"

"He's…" She sighed. "The consummate bad boy. Smokes, hardly ever shaves, says what's on his mind, rough around the edges."

"Great in bed?" Ginny teased.

"What do you think?" she said dryly.

Andre's expression remained grave. "And you don't think it could lead to anything serious? There are no emotions involved at all?"

She didn't miss the irony that the female teacher was trying to score the sex details while her male counterpart was more concerned about the emotional nature of Miranda's relationship.

"Of course there are," she told him. "There's bound to be some emotions whenever you're sleeping with someone. But this won't become serious."

"You sound very sure of that."

"I am." Confidence rang from those two words. "Seth is fun to be with, and he's unarguably amazing in bed, but he's not someone I can see myself with in the long-term. When or if I make a commitment to someone, it has to be with a man who's willing to be there for my kids."

Now Ginny was frowning, her silvery eyes losing that gleam of humor. "Wait—are you saying he doesn't like Soph and Jase? How could *anyone* not like those two?"

Miranda exhaled slowly. "It's not that he doesn't like them per se. I think kids make him uncomfortable. Not just mine, but all children. With Sophie and Jason, he just sort of...*tolerates* them, know what I mean? But I'm pretty sure that if he had the choice, he wouldn't want them around."

The thought brought a sting of pain to her heart, along with a jolt of disenchantment. It really did bother her that Seth still hadn't warmed up to her kids, even after nearly a month of being in their lives.

"Has he spent much time with them?" Andre asked.

"Not really. I mean, we stayed at his house when our place was being renovated, but his schedule is kind of messed up, so either he wouldn't be home when the twins were awake, or he'd be sleeping during the day after being gone all night. He's a SEAL," she said hastily, when her explanation earned her two suspicious looks.

Ginny's distrust instantly transformed into delight. "A SEAL? Oh, hell yes, Miranda. That's *so* hot and I'm *so* jealous."

She rolled her eyes. "Just because he's a SEAL doesn't mean I should marry the man. Actually, I have a feeling if I even brought up the word *marriage* he'd run screaming in the other direction."

"Commitment-phobe," Andre said knowingly.

"Kid-phobe," she reminded them. "Seth doesn't want to be a dad. He didn't explicitly say it, but it's fairly obvious he has no intention of ever having children."

"Maybe that's because he hasn't spent a lot of time with them," Ginny pointed out. "It's easy for people like us to shake our heads and say 'what the hell is *wrong* with that guy?' but we hang out with children of all ages every day. Not everyone has the same opportunity. Is he an only child?"

Miranda nodded.

"Okay, so he didn't have any younger siblings running underfoot. And he's in the military, surrounded by men and women his own age or older." Ginny shrugged. "He probably has no idea how to talk to kids. They make him uncomfortable because he can't relate to them."

Andre joined in, his tone grudging. "She has a point, boss. A lot of people can't interact with children. If you don't have any of your own, or aren't in a kid-friendly environment, then chances are you don't know how to handle being around them."

They raised a good point, and Miranda grew quiet for a moment as she let it all sink in. Heck, maybe Ginny and Andre were right. Maybe it wasn't that Seth didn't *like* children. Maybe he simply didn't know how to relate to them. She remembered a time when she hadn't known the first thing about kids—but she'd had to learn pretty damn fast once motherhood had been prematurely forced upon her.

"So, what, you think I shouldn't write him off just yet?" she asked uneasily.

Ginny's head tilted pensively. "I don't know. I'm just saying that if it's the kid thing that's holding you back, maybe you should get him to spend some more time with Soph and Jase and see if he starts feeling more at ease with them."

She supposed that wasn't a bad suggestion. *If* she wanted something more serious with Seth. But did she? She'd sworn to herself that she wouldn't settle for anything less than a reliable partner who was willing to give their relationship 100 percent. She needed someone who would always be there, someone who wouldn't let her down, who wouldn't let her *children* down. Because she wouldn't be the only one getting attached to the man she brought into their lives. Sophie and Jason would get attached too.

But maybe it wouldn't hurt to be more open about this thing with Seth. They'd spent a lot of time together over the past two weeks, in and out of bed, and she truly did enjoy his company. She loved arguing with him, loved curling up against his broad chest, loved how when she talked about people or places in Vegas, he knew exactly what she meant because he'd grown up there too.

Would it really be so terrible to lower the shield around her heart? Just a little bit?

Battling a mix of uncertainty and trepidation, she finally put an end to her troubling inner debate by making a decision. From now on when it came to Seth, she was officially keeping an open mind.

LOUD LAUGHTER AND LEWD CATCALLS WERE THE TWO MOST COMMON side effects of poker night, and Friday was absolutely no exception. The men had only been gathered at Carson Scott's place for twenty minutes and the good-natured heckling was already occurring in full force.

Carson, who'd just been taunted about the hickey on his neck, remained impervious in the face of it all. "What can I say? My wife can't keep her mouth off me. I'm a walking turn-on and I ain't gonna apologize for it. In fact, I embrace it."

Dylan groaned right along with everyone else in the living room. He was suddenly happy he hadn't bailed tonight the way he'd been tempted to do. Normally he loved hanging out with the boys, and poker night was always a blast, but for the last couple of weeks he'd avoided connecting with any of his teammates outside of the base. Matt, in particular, which made him feel pretty shitty because he loved chilling with O'Connor.

Unfortunately, Matt was BFFs with the one person Dylan didn't want to see at the moment, which was why he'd been making himself scarce.

His insides had been tied in rigid knots the entire drive over here. He'd barely said a word to Seth in the car, too busy envisioning all sorts of awkward scenarios. But all that worrying had been futile because when he'd walked into Carson's living room, Aidan Rhodes was nowhere to be found.

Relief had soared through him. And at the same time? Disappointment. A hefty dose of it. Rather than focus on the latter, he'd clung to that rush of relief, finding solace in Aidan's absence. He'd only seen Aidan once since he'd moved back home, and the encounter had left him feeling even edgier than before.

"And you know what? I'm perfectly happy to give you boys lovemaking lessons if you need to brush up on your skills. Call it a training demo."

Carson's voice snapped Dylan back to the present. Or maybe he'd been zapped into the twilight zone—because had the lieutenant seriously just uttered the word *lovemaking*?

"Lovemaking?" Matt echoed before breaking out in gales of laugher.

Seth shook his head in amazement. "Fuck, he's gone off the deep end."

"I'm serious. I bet you're all lacking when it comes to pleasing your women, so I'm happy to share my knowledge."

From his chair across the table, Ryan Evans rolled his eyes. "Whatever helps you sleep better at night, LT."

Carson feigned puzzlement. "Sleep? What's that?" He broke out in a grin. "I'm too busy rocking my wife's world."

And Holly Scott's world must have been rocked really fucking nicely last night, because you could always tell how many orgasms the lieutenant's wife had experienced by the amount of food she served. Tonight, Holly had laid out an entire feast. Six different kinds of salad, homemade bread, a cheese tray, mini-sandwiches, pigs in a blanket. And who could overlook the drool-inducing chocolate cake sitting in the glass dish on the kitchen counter. The woman was a damn saint. Of course, she had to be for putting up with Mr. Cocky over there.

That last thought gave Dylan pause when he remembered Cash mentioning that Carson and Holly had been having problems a while back, around the time Cash had gotten together with Carson's sister, Jen. But as far as he knew, the couple had worked everything out, and judging by the happy vibes Carson was radiating, their reconciliation had stuck.

Dylan sipped his beer, then snuck a peek at the two cards Ryan had just dealt him. A six and a queen, off-suit. Man, Lady Luck was not on his side tonight. He'd received nothing but shitty hands so far. When the flop revealed three completely unhelpful cards, he folded instantly and leaned back in his chair, watching the game develop. They were missing a few of the usual players, namely former SEAL John Garrett and the team's CO, Thomas Becker, who were both at home dealing with sick kids.

As always, Cash's crappy poker face divulged the awesomeness of his hand, which resulted in Carson, Matt, Ryan and Seth folding. Jackson, who was possibly the *worst* card player on the planet, stayed in for much longer than he should have and ended up losing his entire buy-in.

Cue: another round of heckling.

Hearing Jackson explain away his terrible poker decisions in his southern drawl was highly entertaining. For a man who hailed from Texas, Jackson sucked ass at Texas Hold 'Em, and Dylan was doubled over in laughter as he listened to the other man's reasoning for sucking.

He was so absorbed, in fact, that he was caught completely off-guard when Aidan Rhodes strode into the living room.

"Sorry I'm late," Aidan said in that deep, easygoing voice of his. "I had a dinner date and it ran late."

Uh-huh. *Of course* he'd had a date. There was no shortage of women in Aidan's life, or at least that's what Dylan had witnessed the week he'd stayed at the guy's condo. Aidan seemed to have a date every damn night. And every damn night, he'd take the chick into his bedroom and fuck her. Hard. So hard that all Dylan could hear was the goddamn *thump-thump-thump* of the headboard banging into the wall.

Not that he was jealous or anything.

"Beer's in the fridge," Carson said as he tossed a few green chips into the growing pile. "Help yourself, Rhodes."

Dylan noticed that Aidan didn't even spare him a look as he headed for the kitchen. Just as well. God knew they'd exchanged enough looks during the week they'd roomed together. They'd completely exceeded their look quota, actually.

All the tension that had slowly been draining away seeped right back into Dylan's body, congealing into an uneasy pretzel in his gut. For the next hour, he put on a good act, trash-talking, joking, laughing, but the entire time, he was wholly aware of Aidan on the other side of the table.

At one point, their eyes met and he could swear Aidan's mouth took on a hint of a smirk.

After losing his second buy-in, he threw down his cards with a groan. "I'm sitting out the next round. I need to regroup."

Cash grinned at him. "Why don't you regroup your way to the kitchen and get me a beer?"

He flipped his buddy the bird, but headed to the kitchen anyway because he could use a refill himself. Sticking his head inside the fridge, he welcomed the rush of cold air, hoping it would douse the flames licking his lower body. He didn't have a hard-on, but his dick was aching. A dull, continuous ache, his cock's way of expressing its unhappiness over Dylan's refusal to give it what it wanted.

"So how long are you going to keep avoiding me?" Aidan's amused voice sounded from the doorway.

He closed his eyes briefly, steeling his resolve, then ducked out of the fridge with two Coors bottles. He kept his tone light. "I'm not avoiding you."

A chuckle. "Bull. You've been blowing me off for weeks."

Damned if his dick didn't throb at the word *blowing*.

Shrugging, Dylan leaned against the granite counter. "Things have been hectic. I saw you texted a few times after the night we played pool, but I've been hanging out with that blonde from the club so I didn't have a chance to message you back."

Total lie. He'd seen Rachel Carver a whopping one time. They'd had sex at her place, it had been vaguely satisfying, and they hadn't spoken since.

But Aidan didn't need to know that.

"Speaking of the night we played pool…" Aidan cocked a brow.

"What about it?"

"You barely said two words to me, man. After you left, O'Connor asked me what I'd done to piss you off so bad."

Shit. Matt had noticed that he'd gone out of his way not to be overly chummy with Aidan?

Of course he did, you moron. You weren't exactly in stealth mode about it.

"So I'm thinking we cut the bullshit and address the *real* issue here." Aidan crossed the room with purposeful strides, stopping when they were two feet apart.

Dylan gulped. The dude looked good tonight. Black trousers, snug gray V-neck, dark hair artfully rumpled. And he smelled good too. Lemon-scented aftershave and a hint of soap.

"You wanna know what that real issue is?" Aidan prompted.

Their gazes met and held. Dylan's pulse sped up.

With a tiny smirk, Aidan leaned closer, his lips inches from Dylan's ear. "You want to fuck me."

The crude observation drove a spike of lust straight into his cock.

Jerking his gaze away, he grabbed the beers from the counter and sidestepped the other man. "Cash is waiting for his beer."

An annoyed breath sounded from behind him.

"So yeah, I've been busy. Training, hanging out with Rachel, that kind of stuff." Christ, why was he still talking? *Just get out of the kitchen, man.*

"Dylan."

He took another step to the door.

"Dylan." A commanding note entered Aidan's voice.

Drawing a deep breath, he slowly turned around. "What?"

"I want the same damn thing."

Shock slammed into him like an eighteen-wheeler. For a moment he thought he'd misheard the guy, but the heat glimmering in those dark brown eyes said otherwise.

They watched each other for a moment. The tension in the air intensified, hot and thick, liable to choke him.

"Where the hell is my beer?" Cash yelled from the living room.

Dylan was so grateful for the interruption he nearly wept with joy. "Uh…can't keep the man waiting," he mumbled.

He hurried out of the kitchen before Aidan could say another word.

Chapter Fourteen

MIRANDA HAD JUST PICKED UP HER SON FROM HIS BASEBALL COACH'S house when her cell phone rang. The words *Private Caller* flashed on the screen. Since her car was an older model that didn't have a Bluetooth system, she had to settle for clicking the speakerphone button.

"Hush, guys," she told the twins, who were giggling in the backseat. Then she raised her voice and said, "Hello?"

"Miranda? It's Eric Porter, Catherine's dad."

Fucking hell.

She stifled a sigh, wishing she'd let the call go to voice mail. She and Porter had been playing phone tag for the past few weeks. The man was determined to arrange a meeting with her—and only her—but their schedules never seemed to line up.

"Mr. Porter, hi," she answered. "How was Miami?"

"Please call me Eric. And as for Miami, I'm still here, and it's wonderful." He chuckled. "The conference I'm attending, not so much."

"I'm sorry to hear that." Actually, she wasn't. She didn't care about this man's business dealings in any way, shape or form, but he was the father of a student, so she was forced to feign interest.

"I tried to call you last night," he said. "I couldn't get through."

She stopped at a red light and checked the rearview mirror to make sure the twins weren't causing trouble, but Sophie was quietly playing with her doll and Jason was flipping through a stack of baseball cards.

She returned her attention to the aggravating phone call. "I was bartending last night. As I mentioned before, I have another job, so I'm usually out of touch four nights a week."

"I understand."

His voice was so warm and genuine she felt bad about all those times she'd cursed the man. "I assume you're calling so we can figure out another time to meet." She injected some warmth into her own voice.

He chuckled again. "I'm hoping we can actually make it happen this time. I'd like to discuss Cat's future with the school and hear your thoughts about whether she has what it takes to pursue dance as a career."

If you overlooked the borderline-annoying persistence, Miranda had to admit that his eagerness to be involved in his kid's life was admirable.

"What's your schedule like next week?" he asked. "Next Sunday maybe?"

She thought about it. "I teach two morning classes on Sunday, and then I have plans with my children for the afternoon. I'm back at the school at five to teach another class, and that usually runs until about seven."

"Can I interest you in dinner then?"

Dinner? She'd been hoping for a quick chat in the studio after the lesson wrapped up.

"Um…"

"There's a little bistro right down the street from the school. I imagine you'll be hungry after class, so we can grab a quick bite."

She hesitated again. The twins would be at home with Kim, so she supposed she could ask the babysitter to stay for an extra hour, hour and a half. She didn't particularly want to have dinner with the man, but it could potentially be good for business. According to Elsa, Porter was incredibly wealthy, and that meant he had wealthy friends who could afford to pay for dance lessons for their kids.

"Sure, that sounds great," she relented. "But just a quick bite. I'm not sure what my babysitter's schedule is."

"No problem. I won't keep you too long," he promised.

After they arranged to meet at the school the following Sunday, Miranda hung up and glanced over at the twins.

"You guys okay back there?"

"Yup," Jason said.

"We're counting how many times the car thumps," Sophie chimed in.

She frowned. "What are you talking abo—"

Thump. Thump.

Her words died as she heard it loud and clear. Oh shit.

"Shit, shit, *shit*," she mumbled.

"Mo-om, that's a *bad* word!" Jason said accusingly.

She ignored the reprimand and focused on gradually reducing her speed. The phone call had distracted her from the fact that the steering wheel was pulling to the right, and that her front tire was so flat it was a miracle the car didn't tip right over.

Miranda winced when the wheel began making a loud noise, metal scraping over concrete. Shit. She hoped the rim hadn't been damaged.

Damn Eric Porter.

"Why are we stopping?" Sophie demanded as Miranda turned onto a side street and pulled over at the first available opportunity.

"We have a flat tire, guys." With a sigh, she unbuckled her seatbelt and flicked on the emergency blinkers. "Stay in the car. Mommy's going to investigate."

She hopped out of the sedan and walked around it to inspect the front passenger-side wheel. Her spirits instantly sank. Crap. What on *earth* had she run over? The tire was completely punctured, and it didn't take long to find the culprit—a two-inch nail wedged in the jagged flap of rubber that had come loose. On the bright side, the rim seemed to be in good shape.

Opening the passenger door, she leaned in to shut off the engine and yank the keys out of the ignition. "Guess what," she told the twins.

"What?" they said in unison.

"Your mom is about to change a tire for the first time in her life."

She expected cheers and high fives and maybe some encouragement. Instead, she got two dubious looks.

"That sounds hard," Sophie said frankly.

Jason offered a thoughtful look. "You can call Sef. Sef can help."

Miranda bristled. She was *not* calling Seth to come to her rescue. She was perfectly capable of rescuing herself, the way she'd done her entire life. She'd never needed a man to save her before, and she didn't need one now.

She'd definitely call him later, though. They hadn't had much of a chance to connect this week—she'd been busy at work and with the twins, and Seth had been away for two days on a training mission in the desert. The timing had actually worked out well because she had her period and she wasn't one of those women who enjoyed sex during her time of the month. But now that her lady parts were functioning at full capacity again, she was suffering from some serious Seth withdrawal.

But there was still no way she was calling him to bail her out.

"Don't get out of the car. I mean it, guys." She shot them a warning look, then closed the door and rounded the sedan.

She unlocked the trunk and lifted the floormat, peering into the compartment to inventory its contents. Spare tire, jack, wrench thingie.

Tire iron, dummy.

Right, tire iron.

She wished she could remember the lesson that the guy at the used car dealership had given her, but the details of How to Change a Tire 101 were a bit foggy.

But it couldn't be too hard, right?

Of course not. I'm a modern, independent woman and I can change a fucking tire if I put my mind to it.

Setting her jaw in fortitude, she heaved the spare tire out of the trunk and set it on the grass next to the curb, then went back for the tools. She stared at the flat tire and pursed her lips. First things first, she needed to loosen those screws. Or were they called lugs? Lugs, she decided.

She crouched down and placed the tire iron on the first wheel lug. She turned. It didn't budge. At all.

"Son of a bitch," she mumbled under her breath.

Take two. This time she used brute force.

Zero movement.

Holy Mother of God. Who had tightened those things? The Hulk?

She was by no means a weak woman. She was a dancer. She had solid muscle definition in her arms. But for the life of her, she couldn't loosen a single one of those wheel lugs.

"Hi, Mom!" Jason called, poking his head out the open window.

A hysterical laugh bubbled in her throat. "Hey, sweetie."

"Can I help?"

"No, it's okay. I've got it under control."

Ha. Yeah right.

She wiggled her arm, shook it around, trying to get herself jacked up. A deep breath, and then she tried again.

"Lefty loosey, righty tighty," she muttered as she attempted to loosen a lug with all the strength she possessed.

No movement. Not even a freaking millimeter. And now her arm hurt. It actually hurt. Frustration sliced into her and she nearly whipped the stupid tool into the speed limit sign three yards away. She reined in the impulse at the last second, let out a strangled breath and decided it was time to come to grips with her own pathetic inadequacy.

"Jason, can you please pass me my phone?" Her voice was calmer than a fucking blue ocean.

Her son's little hand popped out of the window.

Clenching her teeth, Miranda stood up and brushed pebbles off her leggings. She took the phone from her son's outstretched hand. After one very long moment of reluctance, she called Seth's number.

"You're still a modern, independent woman," she assured herself.

But sometimes even modern, independent women were forced to admit defeat and call for help.

SETH WAS CHUCKLING TO HIMSELF DURING THE ENTIRE DRIVE INTO SAN Diego. He knew Miranda was probably stewing up a storm over the fact that she'd been forced to call him. He'd heard the irritation in her voice when she'd tersely explained the situation and asked him for help. Hell, he was surprised the words "help me" actually existed in that stubborn woman's vocabulary.

He couldn't wait to see her, though. He'd been busy this week, spending a couple of days in Nevada training with the team, and then last night he'd gone to Carson's rather than the club. He'd promised Miranda that he wouldn't hover over her at work anymore. Besides, he knew that if he'd gone there last night, he wouldn't have been able to stop himself from nailing her in the employee break room.

Hopefully they could find some alone time later tonight. Maybe she'd sneak him into her place after the rugrats went to bed.

He turned onto the street she'd indicated, immediately spotting her blue Ford on the side of the road. He pulled up behind it and hopped out of the Jeep, finding Miranda and the twins sitting on the curb.

"Somebody call roadside assistance?" he said mockingly.

Miranda scowled at him. "Wipe that grin off your face, Masterson. I'm not in the mood."

"Mom has crazy eyes," Sophie spoke up.

He laughed despite himself.

Both kids' eyes widened in surprise.

Ignoring the resulting wave of discomfort, he focused on Miranda, who had crazy eyes indeed.

"I hate this," she said dully. "If I could just manage to get those lugs off, I could totally change that tire."

"Of course you could." He wasn't being sarcastic. He had absolute faith that Miranda Breslin could accomplish anything she set her sights on.

Seth rolled up the sleeves of his black button-down and appraised the tire. "No fixing that, I'm afraid. You'll need to spring for a new one."

"I know," she said glumly.

"Tire iron?"

She handed it to him. He squatted down and tackled the first wheel lug. The amount of resistance he encountered made him grunt, but he managed to loosen the lug.

"Jesus, these *are* tight," he admitted as he went to work on the next one.

Miranda's voice rang with triumph. "Ha! I knew it wasn't just me. They're insanely tight, right?"

"Or maybe you're insanely weak," he teased.

"My mom's not weak!" Jason fiercely protested.

Seth rolled his eyes. "That was a joke, kid."

"Oh."

He finished up and reached for the jack, but Miranda gave him that stubborn head shake he'd grown accustomed to. "I want to do it," she announced. "That way I'll be prepared if I ever get another flat. Talk me through it?"

When she looked at him with those earnest eyes, he couldn't deny her a damn thing.

He spent the next fifteen minutes talking her through the rest of the process, enjoying the way she bit her lip in concentration, and the little fist pumps she did every time she successfully completed a task. When the spare tire successfully made it on the car, Seth and the twins broke out in applause.

Miranda took a bow before wagging a finger at her children. "I told you I could do it. Now get in the car and buckle up. We still have a pizza place to go to."

"Is Sef gonna come?" Jason's jubilant expression revealed precisely how he felt about *that* possibility

"He's not gonna come," Sophie told her brother. "You know he won't."

Maybe it was the alpha male in him, but Seth didn't take kindly to challenges, and that little girl's eyes? Chock full of challenge.

"I could go for some pizza," he said smugly. "That is, if it's all right with your mom."

Miranda looked as shocked as her children. "Uh, sure, you're welcome to join us."

"Great." He picked up the punctured tire. "Let me just throw this in the trunk. Like I said, I don't think you'll be able to patch it up, but your mechanic might say something different."

She helped her kids into the backseat, then followed him to the trunk. With the trunk door up, neither child could see them through the back windshield, and Seth took full advantage of that.

His mouth was on hers before she could blink. Tongue sliding into her mouth, hands cupping her firm ass, pelvis rocking into hers. Oh sweet Jesus. He rubbed his aching erection in the cradle of her thighs, desperate to be inside her.

She whimpered. Clutched the front of his shirt with both hands as she hungrily kissed him back. His head was spinning by the time their mouths broke free.

There was a smudge of motor oil on her cheek, which made him smile. "You've got oil on your face," he said gruffly.

Moistening the pad of his thumb with his tongue, he wiped the dark spot away, then ran his fingers over the tiny freckles that looked so out of place against the backdrop of her olive-tinted skin.

"Thanks," she murmured when his hand dropped from her face.

"You're welcome." His mouth tingled with the urge to kiss her again. So he did. Pressing his lips to the hollow of her throat, enjoying the way she shivered. "I missed you, babe."

"I missed you too." Her tone was a tad reluctant, as if making the admission was difficult.

He kissed her again, the sweet minty taste of her setting his blood on fire. He wanted to fuck her right here, right now, against the back of the car. He was seriously debating whether they could pull it off when a loud "Mo-om!" wafted from the open window.

Miranda flew out of his embrace, nearly banging her head against the trunk. Her cheeks were flushed, her eyes glazed as she looked at him. "Pizza," she said firmly. "We're going for pizza."

"And later?"

Wicked promise flashed across her face. "Later I put the kids to bed and you and I have ourselves some dessert."

TEN MINUTES LATER, SETH WANTED TO KICK HIMSELF FOR RISING TO Sophie's bait and agreeing to have dinner with the Breslin clan.

The restaurant was one of those family-type joints with red-and-white checkered tablecloths and huge vinyl booths. It was jam-packed with families. So many families that the noise level was on par with that wave of machine guns the team had encountered in the desert last year.

But he ordered himself to make the best of it. If he could survive a crazy Middle Eastern gunfight, surely he could survive dinner in the restaurant equivalent of hell.

"We usually get a large pepperoni for the three of us," Miranda said after the waitress came by with their drinks. "But we'll definitely need to order two today. What do you like on your pizza?"

Seth reached for his plastic cup of Coke. "I usually load up on the veggies."

"Veggies?" Jason gawked at him. "Gross!"

"See, I told you vegetables are yummy," Miranda said. "Even Seth agrees with me."

Suspicion flickered in the little boy's eyes. "You really think they're yummy?"

Seth nodded and tried not to smile.

Jason didn't respond after that, but he grew very quiet, as if Seth's revelation had completely blown his mind. When the waitress returned to take their orders, Jason was the first to speak.

"Two pizzas with *veggies*," he announced.

The waitress laughed. "What kind of veggies, little man?"

Perplexed, Jason turned to Miranda, who seemed to be fighting back laughter. "How about green peppers, mushrooms and tomatoes?" she said graciously.

Jason mulled it over, then turned to his sister, who nodded. "'Kay," the boy told the waitress. "What my mom said."

After the waitress left, Miranda offered Seth a wry look. "Clearly I need to bring you along more often. I've never seen either of them so enthusiastic about vegetables before."

His chest tightened in discomfort. Christ. Miranda's son wouldn't quit staring at him. He felt like a specimen under a microscope, even more so when Sophie also turned her brown-eyed gaze on him. With him and Miranda sitting on one side of the booth, and the twins on the other, there was at least some distance between him and the kidlets. But those stares were burning a hole in him. And the restaurant only seemed to get louder. Childish shrieks and giggles mingled with scolding parents and "stop that!" and shrill wails.

A throb was actually beginning to form in his temples. Which spoke volumes about the noise levels, because he'd grown up in *Vegas*, the noisiest place on earth.

For the next ten minutes, he did his best to make small talk with Miranda and the kids. When the waitress finally slid two pizza dishes on the table, Seth was overcome with relief, eagerly shoveling food in his mouth so he wouldn't have to talk anymore.

This was *not* his scene. He wasn't cut out for all this domestic stuff.

To make matters worse, the quieter and more aloof he became, the more eager Miranda's son was to engage him. There was no denying that Jason was a cute kid. Smart, funny, sweet. But Seth didn't want to bond with him. He'd only end up hurting the boy in the end, and that was the last thing he wanted.

So better to keep his distance. Draw a clear line in the sand and pray that Jason didn't cross it. At least he didn't have to worry about Sophie.

The pigtailed imp had decided ages ago that she didn't like him, and she seemed content to stick with her original impression of him.

"You okay?"

He lifted his head and found Miranda's concerned eyes on him. "Yeah, I'm fine."

"You got really quiet all of a sudden."

"Just thinking, that's all."

"Mom," Sophie piped up. "Can me and Jase have quarters for the gumball machine?"

Miranda glanced at their empty plates and gave a pleased nod. "Sure, but only one gumball each, okay?" She reached into her purse and pulled out her wallet.

After the kids dashed off toward the bright red candy machine across the room, she turned back to Seth. "You didn't have to come, you know," she said quietly.

His voice was gruff. "I know."

"So why did you?"

"Honestly? I have no idea."

Evidently that wasn't the answer she'd hoped for, because a wrinkle appeared in her forehead and she seemed to be chewing on the inside of her cheek.

The waitress approached to collect their plates, sparing Seth from having to elaborate.

"You folks need anything else?" the curly-haired server asked with a smile.

"Just the bill, please," Miranda replied.

"No problem." The young woman took a step away, then stopped and looked from Seth to Miranda. "By the way, you have lovely children." Her voice lowered to a conspiratorial pitch. "Much better behaved than a lot of the other kids that come in here."

Miranda grinned. "You know, the twins have only ever thrown one tantrum in public."

"I find that surprising."

"It's true. We were at McDonald's when they had their meltdown. I threatened to throw their Happy Meal toys in the garbage, they kept screaming, and I proved that I don't make idle threats. To this day, they haven't acted out in public again."

The waitress burst out laughing. "Good for you." With another smile, she glanced at Seth. "That's one tough broad you've got there. And your kids are adorable."

Seth felt all the color drain from his face.

"Oh," Miranda said quickly, "They're not—"

"They're not my kids," he blurted out.

An embarrassed look washed over their server's face. "Oh gosh. I'm sorry. I just assumed…"

"They're not my kids," he repeated, his tone much sharper than he'd intended.

Next to him, he felt Miranda stiffen.

"My mistake. Sorry about that," the waitress said before flouncing off, red-faced.

Silence descended over the booth.

Seth cleared his throat. "Miranda…"

"Wow. Twice." Bitterness lined her tone. "Did you really need to deny it *twice*, Seth?"

Fucking hell. That second round of "they're not my kids" had definitely been unnecessary. He'd just gotten caught off-guard.

"I'm sorry," he mumbled. "I was just trying to make it clear that—"

"Oh, you made things very clear."

"I'm sorry for saying it twice, okay? I shouldn't have done that."

"Is it so awful that we were mistaken for a family?"

He faltered. "No. It's just…"

"It's just what?"

Shit, he needed a cigarette. And his head was killing him—why was this restaurant so fucking *loud*?

She shook her head, wearing an expression he couldn't for the life of him make out. "This was a bad idea," she said softly.

"Miranda…"

"You know I'm right. It was a bad idea. We're not a family, Seth. You're not my children's father. You're the man I'm—" her voice became a whisper, "—fucking."

If he weren't already battling confusion, unease and a strange jolt of terror, he would've been offended by the tiny twinge of scorn that accompanied the last word.

"So let's not fool ourselves into thinking this is anything more than what it is," she said with a weary sigh. "Let's just stick to what we're good at. Sex, and nothing more."

Before he could respond, Jason and Sophie raced back to the booth, holding up the gumballs they'd gotten.

"Mom, look, I got a *pink* one!" Sophie gushed.

"And mine was blue." Jason's bottom lip dropped out. "I wanted red but blue's okay, I guess."

Neither child picked up on the tension between Seth and their mother.

But it was there.

Chapter Fifteen

One week later

"GOD. THAT WAS NICE. I NEEDED THAT." WITH A CONTENTED SIGH, Miranda slipped out of bed and stalked naked toward the chair on which she'd left her clothes.

Seth watched from the bed, struggling with a wave of disappointment. She was getting dressed? Already? Well, maybe it wasn't *that* fast, he amended when he saw the time on the clock. They'd been in his bedroom for nearly an hour.

But still.

She was the most graceful woman he'd ever met. She even made the act of putting on a bra and panties look like a sensual dance. Another disappointed burst went off in his chest. He didn't want her to go. He never wanted her to go.

He just didn't fucking know how to ask her to stay.

If he hadn't blown it that evening at the pizza place, things wouldn't have had to change. They'd still be doing the whole morning-sex-and-breakfast thing instead of these super-hurried quickies. Still be lying tangled in each other's arms after recovering from their orgasms instead of Miranda jumping out of bed to find her clothes.

Her eagerness to hurry off after he'd made her come brought a pang of unhappiness. He hated this new wham-bam-thank-you-Seth mentality of hers. He felt...used.

Aw, poor baby Seth bitching about how a woman wants no-strings sex from him.

"So this is really happening," he said, feeling edgy as hell and unable to hide it.

Miranda pulled her tank top over her head. "What is?"

"You're leaving."

She shot him a *duh* look. "Yes, because I have to go to work."

"Not for another hour."

"I told you, I want to grab something to eat before I head over to the club."

"And I offered to cook you dinner here."

"And I said I appreciated it, but it's not part of the deal." She rolled her eyes. "Should we recap the conversation again, or is it going to stick this time?"

Swallowing the strange lump of misery that rose in his throat, Seth hopped off the bed and slipped into his boxers. "No, it's fine. I forgot that dinner isn't part of the, you know, *deal*." He put on pants and a T-shirt. "Come on, I'll walk you out."

Her voice stopped him before he could leave the room. "Seth."

Turning around, he met her eyes. "Yeah."

With a faint smile, she eliminated the distance between them and looped her arms around his neck. Her expression softened as she stood on her tiptoes and kissed him. "I had fun tonight."

"Did you?" he murmured.

She brushed her sexy lips over his in another fleeting kiss. "I did." Her lips peppered kisses down the column of his neck. "I had a lot of fun."

"I'm glad." He shivered when she nibbled his earlobe, and his hands slid down to cup her ass.

"So please stop treating the word *deal* like it's an expletive." She skimmed her fingertips over his bottom lip. "This is a good deal. We're making each other come almost every other night. No promises, no hassles, just a lot of awesome sex. How are you unsatisfied?"

"I'm not. I am satisfied." He forced a nonchalant shrug. "No promises, no hassles. That's exactly how I like it, babe."

To his displeasure, she nodded in agreement. "Me too. Well, in this case at least." She planted a quick kiss on his cheek. "I've gotta go."

Seth walked her to the front door, doing his best not to dwell on that last zinger she'd left him with. *Well, in this case at least.* What did that mean? Did she mean that if she were fucking some other man, she would *want* the promises? So it was just *his* promises she wasn't interested in?

So many conflicting emotions raged in his gut that he didn't even know which to focus on.

"Miranda, wait, before you go." Dylan suddenly appeared in the hallway, his hair damp from the shower, a white towel draped around his trim hips.

"What's up?" she asked as she slipped into her sneakers.

"Are the twins in school tomorrow?"

"Yes, until three. Why?"

Dylan's expression turned sheepish. "What do you think about me hanging out with them tomorrow? Maybe going out for ice cream or something? I could pick them up from kindergarten if you want."

Miranda looked incredibly confused by the request, and when she glanced at Seth, he gave her a fucked-if-I-know look. He had no idea what to make of it either. He studied his roommate's face for signs of concussion or intoxication, and found none. But he couldn't rule it out, either.

"You want to take my kids out for ice cream?" Miranda finally said.

"Yeah, if it's cool with you."

"Um. Well. Why?"

"What can I say? I miss the little dudes," Dylan said, offering the boyish smile that Seth had seen him use to seduce countless of women.

Sure enough, some of Miranda's hesitation melted in the face of that smile. "You miss my kids?" she echoed.

Dylan nodded. "I had a lot of fun with them when you guys stayed here. And I saw on the news today that the weather is supposed to be beautiful tomorrow, so I thought, hey, maybe the twins would enjoy hanging out."

Seth didn't bother masking his mistrust. He had no idea what his roommate was up to, but this was fucking strange. In fact, lately *strange* seemed to be the norm with Dylan. Dude was bitchier than usual, hardly ever left the house, and now he wanted to spend an afternoon with a couple of six-year-olds he wasn't even *related* to?

If Seth didn't have complete confidence that Dylan would never harm a hair on a child's head, he might've given Miranda a slight shake of the head, as in, *Say no. Now.* But Seth trusted Dylan with his life. Whatever this was about, he knew it wouldn't result in Miranda's kids getting hurt.

"Well, I guess that would be okay," Miranda said, still looking baffled. "I can call the school tomorrow and let them know you'll be picking them up instead of me. Unless you want me to come along...?" She let the question hang.

Dylan flashed his pearly whites again. "Up to you, honey. I figured you'd enjoy having the afternoon off to go shopping or take a nap or do whatever. You know, treat yourself. But if you don't trust me with your children's safety, I understand."

Miranda snorted. "My children are probably safer with you than they are with me. You're a SEAL, for Pete's sake. And look at you."

Seth did not enjoy the way her eyes roamed the broad expanse of Dylan's smooth chest. He glared at his roommate in an unspoken order to go put on a fucking shirt—and pants, damn it—but the guy remained completely unfazed.

"What time are they done school?" Dylan asked.

"Three. I'll text you the address. You'll have to show your ID to the school secretary and sign the twins out. It's the school policy when someone other than a parent picks up a child."

"No problem. Can't wait to see them."

"They'll be thrilled to see you too," Miranda said with a warm smile.

Seth found himself bristling again. If Dylan's plan had been to come out here and present himself as the sweetest, most thoughtful dude on the planet while reducing Seth to antichild, pond-scum level in Miranda's eyes, then he'd totally succeeded.

"And if you decide not to join us, I'm sure Masterson here would appreciate the company," Dylan said, proving that he always had a fellow soldier's back. "Poor Seth gets really lonely sometimes."

Oh Jesus. Why did Dylan make it so difficult to think bad thoughts about him?

Asshole.

"Oh no. I might have to come over and hold his hand for a bit, then." Miranda's expression made it clear that she'd be holding a lot more than his hand.

She gave Seth a kiss on the cheek and then she was gone, leaving him free to interrogate his roommate.

"You want to *hang out* with her *kids*?"

"Yeah. What's wrong with that? Those little dudes are tons of fun."

Seth crossed his arms. "Should I be worried about websites putting a little green dot over our house to indicate there's a sexual predator living here?" he cracked.

"Fuck you."

"Says the man who just arranged a date with two children while wearing a towel. Seriously, what the hell was that about?"

After a beat, Dylan released a breath. "I have an idea for the birthday present, all right?"

"No clue what you're talking about, man."

"Miranda's birthday is on Saturday."

"It is?"

His roommate raised his eyebrows. "Do you know anything about the woman you're screwing, bro?"

Now it was his turn to say, "Fuck you." He trailed after Dylan, whose bare feet slapped the hardwood floor on the way to the master bedroom.

Dylan dropped the towel the moment he entered his bedroom, but Seth was too unsettled by this entire discussion to pay much attention to his roommate's bare ass.

"Anyway, remember when they were crashing here after the flood and the kids kept bursting into tears every other second?"

"Yeah," he said warily.

"Well, turns out they weren't just crying for the hell of it. They were working on a birthday present for Miranda—they drew all these pictures for her, and they were organizing them into a book. I think their teacher was supposed to help them bind it."

Seth's brows dipped in a frown. "How do you know all this?"

"They told me." Dylan put on a pair of sweatpants and strode to his closet to find a shirt.

"They told you," Seth echoed.

"Yep. Those kids love me, bro. Maybe because, unlike you, I don't treat them like I'd rather have my back waxed than spend time with them." A shrug. "They were pretty devastated, especially Jason. He was hiding the pictures under his bed and everything got destroyed in the flood."

"So you're taking them out for ice cream to cheer them up?"

"No. See, that's the thing." Dylan was practically beaming now. "I was telling Jen about what a bummer it was that the present got ruined, and she came up with an idea. Sophie and Jason won't have time to redo all the drawings, but Jen offered to take their picture. You've seen her photographs, right? They're fucking amazing. She said she'll take a whole bunch of photos of the kids and they could use them to make a new book. Good idea, right?"

Seth stared at his buddy.

"What?" Dylan said defensively.

"You like those kids so much that you actually spent time thinking about the birthday present they were making for their mother?" he said in a dull voice.

"So? What's wrong with that? I happen to be a nice guy."

Translation: *I'm not an asshole like you are.*

Seth raked a hand through his hair, wishing he could make heads or tails of the eddy of emotion that swirled inside his chest. Shit, what was happening to him? Why did it matter whether Dylan liked Miranda's kids? Why should he care that Sophie and Jason had confided in his roommate—and not him—about their stupid picture book? Whatever. Let Dylan spend tomorrow afternoon with the rugrats. That just meant Seth got more time with their mother.

An entire afternoon with Miranda. Just him and Miranda.

Yeah. Miranda. Whose birthday is on Saturday.

His stomach clenched. Why hadn't she told him when her birthday was?

Why hadn't he asked?

Holy shit. If one more *why* so much as entered his brain, he was going to punch something.

Curling his hands into fists, he left his roommate to get dressed and marched back to his bedroom.

His sheets still smelled like Miranda. His pillow still bore the indentation of her head. And his heart? Well, his heart was having a very tough time remembering that it played no part in their *deal*.

"OH MY GOSH, THEY ARE JUST THE CUTEST," JEN SCOTT DECLARED. SHE peered at the screen of her camera and giggled. "Look at this one. Sophie looks adorable."

Dylan leaned in for a peek. "Adorable indeed."

"I love how she kept insisting on changing her hairstyle at each location." Jen started clicking through the insane amount of photos she'd snapped today. "Pigtails, pigtails…ponytail…hair loose…oh wait, here's my favorite, the ballerina bun."

The two of them were sitting side by side on Jen's couch, trying to pick which shots to send for printing. At Jen's suggestion, the twins had decided to create a calendar for their mom, each month featuring a different picture of them. Dylan and Jen were footing the cost, unbeknownst to the twins, who just assumed professional calendars got made for free. But the kids were so excited about the project that Dylan was willing to pay for the whole damn thing if need be.

"This was a really fun day," Jen said happily. "Being around such cuteness kinda makes you want to have kids of your own, doesn't it?"

"A little," he admitted. "But first I need a woman, don't you think?"

Jen smiled, and his breath actually caught. She was so beautiful that sometimes it hurt to look at her. Vivid blue eyes, tousled waves of golden hair, centerfold body—every inch of her was pure perfection, making Cash McCoy one very lucky man.

"You and Cash talking about having kids yet?" he asked, sipping his iced tea.

"Hardly. It's only been six months. I think the next step is living together. Then marriage. *Then* kids. So talk to me in a couple of years."

"You guys are good, though? Still madly in love?"

"Of course." Her blue eyes softened. "Cash is amazing. I've never known anyone like him."

"And the new job's going well?" Jen worked as a freelance photographer for several magazines, one of which happened to be very prestigious.

"You know, the fact that you have to ask me all these questions just proves that we haven't hung out nearly enough these past couple of months." Her cupid's-bow mouth puckered unhappily. "What's going on with you, Dylan? Are you pissed at me or something?"

"What? Of course not."

"Are you pissed at Cash?"

He took the camera from her hand and gently set it on the table, then slung an arm over her shoulder. "I'm not angry with you, honey. Or Cash. Or anyone, for that matter."

Except maybe himself, but she didn't need to know that.

"Then what's wrong?" Her features grew pained. "You hardly ever hang out with us anymore, and Matt says you haven't been responding to his texts."

Damn it. Sometimes it sucked that Cash and O'Connor lived together. Those two gossiped more than the trio of white-haired ladies Dylan flirted with at Starbucks every morning.

"I just haven't felt like going out," he said with a shrug. "I've been staying at home lately, working out, watching TV, shooting the shit with Seth. You know, just maxin' and relaxin', chillin' like a villain."

Jen looked like she was torn between laughing and groaning. She settled on the former, but the amusement on her face faded fast. "I call bullshit, by the way."

He arched a brow. "On which part?"

"The you-haven't-felt-like-going-out part. What are you avoiding? Or should I say, *who* are you avoiding?"

Strands of discomfort climbed up his spine.

"Ha! So you *are* avoiding someone. I swear, Dylan, if you don't confide in me, I'll sic Cash on you. Actually, no, I'll sic every single one of your teammates on you, my brother included. You know, your *lieutenant*."

He sighed. "We both know if I confide in you, it's the same as confiding in Cash. Anyway, I don't want to talk about it."

She looked hurt. "You think I'll go running to Cash with whatever you tell me? You don't trust me?"

Another sigh shuddered out. "I trust you, Jen. Okay? I just don't feel like talking."

"Why not? You *like* to talk. That's the best thing about you—how open and honest you are about what you're feeling. You're not one of those men who bottles everything up and pretends the hurt and pain and all that crap doesn't exist."

"Maybe I am one of those men," he shot back.

"No, you're not. And this? You getting all flustered and bitchy? Clearly proves something is wrong. So what is it?"

"Nothing is wrong," he ground out.

"Bull. What's wrong?"

"Nothing."

"Quit lying and tell me what's wrong."

"Jen, I swear to God…"

"What's wrong, Dylan?"

"I want to fuck Aidan Rhodes!"

The words flew out before he could stop them, stunning both himself and Jen into silence. Her mouth fell open, blue eyes widening.

As heat burned his cheeks, he averted his eyes, wishing he'd kept his mouth shut.

"Wow. Okay, so…wow." Jen shook her head once, twice, three times, as if trying to clear it of cobwebs. "You want to…um, have sex…with Aidan."

"Yes." Pure misery shot through him, and yet with it came a feeling of liberation. This was the first time he'd said it out loud.

"Does he…want to have sex with *you*?"

I want the same damn thing.

Dylan swallowed. "Yeah. Yeah, I think so."

Jen went quiet again. Then she shrugged. "So have sex with him."

"Are you kidding?"

"No. Are you?" She frowned. "Wait, do you *not* want to sleep with Aidan? Are you punking me?"

"I'm not punking you," he said in sheer aggravation. "But I'm frickin' confused—you think I should have, um, have…"

"Sex," she filled in, her voice dry.

"Sex…with Aidan."

"You just said you wanted to. And if he wants the same thing, then why not go for it?"

"Because…because it's another man," he burst out. "I'd be having sex with another man, Jen."

A laugh popped out of her mouth. "Are you kidding me? Dylan, the very first night I met you, you gave Cash a *blowjob*." Her voice softened. "And I don't think it was your first time, either. Was it?"

He slowly shook his head.

"So clearly you have no problem fooling around with another man."

"No, but…"

"But what?"

"Every time I've been with…" he felt himself blushing again, "…with another guy, there's always been a girl there too. It's never one-on-one."

"And one-on-one is bad?"

"I don't know. Maybe." He shrugged helplessly.

"You don't want to think of yourself as gay, is that it?" Jen's tone was so gentle, and so thick with understanding, that his throat clogged.

"I'm not gay," he answered honestly. "I love women way too much to be considered gay."

"Yeah, I noticed." She paused. "But you're into men too."

"Yes."

"So then you're bi."

Amusement trickled through him. "I love how everything always has to be defined. Why can't people just fuck whoever they want without feeling the need to label it or explain it away?"

Jen pointed her finger at him. "Ha! Exactly!"

Shit. He'd totally walked into that one.

"Now change the word *people* to *you*, and *whoever they want* to *Aidan*." When he didn't respond right away, her blue eyes turned shrewd. "Wait a minute—are you freaking out about having sex with him because this is about more than just sex? Do you have *feelings* for Aidan?"

That uncharacteristic rush of helplessness returned with full force. "I don't know," he admitted. "I like hanging out with him, I know that much. When I stayed at his place last month, we got along really well. We have a shit-ton in common, he's easy to talk to. So yeah, we're buddies. I can't fuck one of my buddies. That'd be like me hooking up with Matt or Ryan or Texas."

"Except you don't want to hook up with Matt or Ryan or Texas. You want *Aidan*." Jen got a dreamy look in her eyes. "And good choice, by the way. Aidan is gorgeous. And those dimples…Lord."

She pretended to fan herself, and Dylan had to laugh. "Dude's not hard on the eyes," he agreed.

She smiled. "I'll give you the same advice Annabelle gave me when I was hesitating about going after Cash—life's too short. Go after what you want."

Uncertainty seized his chest. "I don't know."

"Yes you do. You know exactly what you want. And you're putting way too much pressure on yourself. You're acting like sex will lead to a relationship and a commitment ceremony and marching in the Pride parade—maybe it will, maybe it won't. But maybe you should talk to Aidan and find out what *he's* looking for before you make assumptions."

She raised a good point. "I guess I should, huh?"

Really? You've only now *figured out that avoiding him like the plague is a bad idea?*

He ignored the internal taunt. Yeah, maybe actually taking Aidan's calls, instead of acting like the conversation they'd had on poker night hadn't happened, would've been the more mature course of action.

"You're right. I need to talk to him." He cleared his suddenly dry throat. "Thanks, Jen."

She rewarded him with that beautiful smile that never failed to take his breath away. "No problem." The smile widened, curving into smirk territory. "And by the way? If you end up doing the deed with Aidan? I expect details. Like, a lot of details. Oooh, I can lend you my camera! And I'd expect a lot of pictures. Maybe one of you and Aidan making out, and one where he's on his knees…"

She was too busy verbalizing her fantasies—which she'd clearly put *a lot* of thought into—to notice that he was flipping her the bird.

Chapter Sixteen

WORKING ON YOUR BIRTHDAY ABSOLUTELY *SUCKED*. MIRANDA HADN'T minded teaching at the studio today, which hardly counted as work because it was something she loved to do, but spending her birthday night at the club? Sucked.

At least Alex was here. She could always count on him to make her shift entertaining, and he didn't disappoint. For the past ten minutes, he'd been mixing drinks to the music à la Tom Cruise in *Cocktail*, cracking Miranda up and eliciting a wave of oohs and aahs from the crowd of females gathered at the bar.

"Miranda! You can go on break now!"

She slid two Corona bottles in front of a customer, then turned to her manager. She had to shout over the hip-hop remix pounding out of the speakers. "I just took one an hour ago!"

It was hard to tell in the strobe lights, but was that a secretive smile on Wendy's face?

"Take another one! Chill out in the break room for a while."

Uh-oh. Miranda got a very bad feeling as she untied her apron and tucked it beneath the cash register. She supposed she could've insisted she wanted to keep working, but who the heck turned down a *break*? Still, she had the sneaking suspicion that she wasn't going to like what she found in the break room.

Oh God, had Wendy somehow managed to organize a party? Maybe called in the other bartenders and bouncers who weren't on duty tonight? Would there be a cake?

Her stomach churned with anxiety. Aside from Alex, she wasn't buddy-buddy with her colleagues at OMG. And she hated parties. With a passion. The only time she enjoyed being the center of attention was when she was on stage, but even then it didn't exactly count as "attention".

When she danced, she blocked out everything and everyone, focusing only on the music, the rhythm, the sense of peace that washed over her and carried her away to another realm where life just made sense.

Offstage, having people fawn over her made her self-conscious. She'd dealt with it earlier tonight at the pizza place, when Sophie and Jason announced to everyone in the restaurant that it was their mom's birthday. But for her kids, she'd suffer through the embarrassment of wearing a paper crown and having a bunch of strangers sing to her.

At the thought of the twins, her heart absolutely melted. She couldn't believe what a thoughtful present they'd given her today. When she'd flipped through all the incredible professional photos in the calendar they'd created for her, she'd literally burst into tears. She definitely had the best kids on the planet. Like, superior to all other kids, and she didn't care if thinking that was politically incorrect.

"Excuse me," she said as she made her way to the back of the club. Several people refused to move, forcing her to elbow a path through the Saturday-night mob.

When she reached the door of the break room, she hesitated, fearful of what she'd find on the other side of it.

Saying a quick prayer, she turned the knob and stepped into the room. Her jaw dropped. "Seth?"

Okay, well, she hadn't been expecting *this*. The room was empty, save for the sexy SEAL sitting on the couch, his long legs stretched out, his gray eyes burning hot when she entered the room. As usual, he wore all black, his dark T-shirt a stark contrast to the pink cupcake in his hands.

Her lips twitched. "Is that for me?"

"Sure is." He stood up, pulling out a lighter as he walked toward her. He lit the pink-and-white-striped candle poking out of the pink icing. "Happy birthday, Miranda. Make a wish."

Equal doses of joy and apprehension soared through her.

No, she couldn't get all soft and gooey about this man again. She'd already tried that. She'd kept an open mind about potentially letting their arrangement become something more, but by freaking out at the restaurant last week, Seth had shown her what a bad idea that was.

He'd been mistaken for her children's father—and he'd been horrified.

Horrified. As if the mere idea was on the same level as being butchered by a serial killer who wanted to make a skin suit out of your carcass.

She leaned close to the iridescent flame, determined to wish for a successful summer recital, or for the school to start making a profit, or maybe for world peace. But she couldn't control the unrealistic wish that popped into her head at the last second.

I wish this could be something more.

Aw crap. Total waste of a birthday wish.

She blew out the candle, then pulled it out of the cupcake and licked the icing off the bottom. Seth focused on her mouth, the heat in his gaze unmistakable.

"Thanks for the cupcake," she said as they headed to the couch and sat down. She devoured the yummy treat, polishing it off in no more than three bites. "God, this is delicious. Which bakery did you get it from?"

He looked incredibly insulted. "Bakery? I baked this motherfucker myself, Miranda."

An amazed laugh flew out. "No way."

"Yes way."

Okay. Wow. She knew Seth could cook, but now she suddenly had an image of him in a frilly apron mixing cake batter in a bowl, razor-sharp stubble coating his sexy jaw and a lit cigarette dangling from the corner of his mouth. The fact that her pussy actually clenched confirmed that, no matter what this guy did, he would always be the ultimate specimen of masculine hotness. To her, anyway.

"Then I'm officially demanding you bake me an entire batch of these," she announced.

"Already did. They're in my fridge. I'll drop them off tomorrow at your place, if you want." He slid closer and swept his thumb over her cheek, his gaze smoldering. "Want the rest of your present?"

"Are you about to say that it's in your pants?"

He gave a rogue grin. "Yup."

"Wait—my manager let you back here?" When he nodded, Miranda shook her head. "Wow, you must have really cranked up the charm. Wendy lectures us at least once every shift about how this room is off-limits to non-employees. Who did you say you were?"

He shrugged. "Your boyfriend."

"And she accepted it, just like that?"

"She did look a bit upset that you'd never mentioned me to her before. She was under the impression that you two were friends. But I assured her that the relationship is still very new and you're kinda embarrassed to talk about it, you know, since I'm so much better-looking than you and you're afraid people won't believe we're a couple."

Miranda gasped. "You ass."

His husky laughter sent a shiver up her spine. "I'm kidding. I didn't say any of that, except for the boyfriend part. Anyway, she said you've got the room all to yourself for the next thirty minutes. I suggest we quit wasting time, don't you agree?"

Even if she'd wanted to disagree, her body wouldn't have let her. Her panties were already wet with arousal and her pulse had been off-kilter from the moment she'd laid eyes on Seth.

"What are your thoughts about birthday oral?" he asked in a conversational tone.

She pretended to think it over. "Better than any old regular-day oral, but not as good as holiday oral, I think."

"Interesting." His big body left the couch and he crouched on the floor in front of her, those calloused hands resting on her bare knees. Goose bumps promptly rose on her flesh. "What's the next holiday we've got coming up?"

She scanned her brain. "Fourth of July?"

He shoved her black miniskirt all the way up to her waist and parted her thighs. She knew he'd noticed the damp spot on her bikini panties because he groaned softly, his gaze fixed on her crotch.

"Fourth of July," he echoed hoarsely. "Okay, so I'll go down on you on the Fourth of July, and then we can compare which is better, birthday or holiday oral."

"Sounds good."

Her laughter died midbreath as Seth shoved his hands under her butt and brought her body forward. Anticipation coiled in her belly. When he slowly peeled her underwear down her legs, her breath hitched, core tingling as she awaited his next move.

And boy was it worth the wait. The kiss he planted on her clit was so gentle, so warm and sweet, that it sent a full-body shiver rolling through her. Her head lolled to the side. Seth continued to kiss her most intimate place, using only his lips, depriving her of a tongue she knew to be oh so talented.

"You're teasing," she whispered. "And we don't have a lot of time."

"We've got twenty more minutes at least." His hot breath tickled her.

"Yeah, but…" A moan slipped out when he rubbed his lips over her clit in another delicate kiss.

It wasn't long before she realized he intended to use their allotted half hour to focus entirely on *her* pleasure. He worshipped her pussy like it was the single greatest treasure on earth. He kissed, licked, swirled, spreading her lips so he could tend to her clit and drive her closer and closer to the edge.

His stubble teased her inner thighs, deliciously scraping her sensitive skin, each raspy scratch heightening her rising excitement. She was so wet she could feel herself dripping, but Seth lapped her up with his tongue, groaning with approval.

The tension grew. Miranda looked down, mesmerized by the sight of his dark head between her legs. She threaded her fingers through his hair, bumping her groin into his face, losing herself in the pleasure he offered so sweetly.

"I want you to come." His voice was low, strangled, vibrating in her core. "Come on my tongue, baby. Let me taste you."

"Oh *God.*" Dirty talk was always guaranteed to send her teetering over the edge, and Seth was so damn good at it.

"Come on, baby," he urged, then flicked his tongue over her clit. Quickly, precisely, knowing exactly what it would take to make her explode.

But the orgasm remained elusive, rippling beneath the surface, skipping across her skin in teasing little sparks, refusing to catch fire. She was gasping for air, clutching Seth's hair so tightly she was surprised he didn't protest.

So close. She was so close. All she needed was—*that.* Seth pushing two fingers inside her and wrapping his lips solidly around her clit. He sucked, and she climaxed, soaring into a spectacular plane where nothing but sheer ecstasy existed.

"Well?"

She emerged from the blissful daze to find him eyeing her expectantly. "Well what?" she wheezed, still catching her breath.

"You think the Fourth of July has any chance of topping that?"

"Not at all," she confessed.

He gave her one last lick, and her pussy was so sensitized she squirmed out of reach. Chuckling, Seth put her panties back on, tugged her skirt down and wiped his face with the back of his hand.

Miranda moaned when she noticed that his facial hair was glistening. God, that was hot.

"You okay?" he asked gruffly.

"Not really. I can't move my legs and I totally don't want to go back to work."

"I don't blame you. Hey, if you want, I can stick around until closing time." Something that resembled vulnerability crossed his face. "There was something I wanted to talk to you about, anyway."

"I won't have time to talk tonight. I have to wake up early tomorrow. Morning classes, remember?"

"Ah. Right."

"Talk to me now. We've still got some time."

That odd expression fluttered in his eyes again. "Um. Okay, sure."

She flopped on the couch and waited. And waited. And waited some more. But he was just standing there, fidgeting, running a hand over his stubble, through his hair, behind his neck.

She started to get up. "Well, this has been thought-provoking, but—"

"I want to date you."

Her ass plopped right back down. "What?"

"I want to date you." His chest rose as he inhaled a deep breath.

"Seth..."

She had no clue what to say to that. No clue what to make of the little burst of joy that tickled her heart. Why was she happy, for Pete's sake? Last time she'd considered letting the fling evolve into more, Seth had burst that bubble with four little words—*they're not my kids.*

"No, just hear me out." Misery clung to his voice, and it took her a second to grasp that the weird flicker in his eyes? It really *was* vulnerability. Wow. Who would have thought?

Seth sat beside her, resting his elbows on his knees and looking completely ill at ease. "I'm sorry for the way I reacted at the pizza place. Your children are great, Miranda. They're smart, thoughtful, cute as hell. I'm just not fully comfortable with them."

He was echoing the same words Ginny and Andre had said in the studio, and Miranda didn't hear a trace of insincerity.

"I also have this thing…about disappointing people, I guess." His voice was so thick and gravelly he sounded like he'd just smoked thirty cigarettes in a row. "I don't like letting people down. I've disappointed a lot of people, especially my mom, and a part of me shuts down whenever I get too close to someone, because I know that in the end, I'll end up disappointing them."

Her heart squeezed painfully. The ravaged look on his face stole her breath, made her reach for his hand and grip it tightly.

"Hey, I'm sure that's not true," she murmured. "And whatever you think you did, you could never let Missy down. That woman adores you."

His Adam's apple bobbed as he swallowed. "I guess." He didn't sound too convinced of that. "So yeah, those are just my bullshit insecurities. But see, with you, I don't shut down. With you, I always feel like I'm stripped bare. I hate it, but at the same time I'm okay with it. I want you to know me. I want you to be with me."

Her breath caught. "Seth…" She trailed off. Didn't know how to finish, how to formulate a response.

"I don't like seeing you walk out the door right after we sleep together. I miss everything we were doing last month. Eating breakfast, washing dishes, cuddling in bed. I miss it and I want it back. So I'm making you a promise, right here and now. Give me a chance, and I swear I'll make an effort. I'll be nicer to the rugr—to Jason and Sophie. I'll be patient, I'll be attentive and I'll be accepting of the fact that if I'm going to be a part of your life, then I need to be a part of theirs."

He finished with the most endearing little shrug she'd ever seen.

Miranda was at a total loss for words. If someone had told her Seth would be reciting a speech like that, vowing to accept her children, she would've laughed them right out of San Diego. But here he was, nothing but honesty shining in his eyes. He meant it. He actually meant every word he said.

But meaning something, and following through on it, were two very different things.

"So what do you say?" he asked roughly.

"I…don't know what to say."

"Let me prove that I'm serious." Determination streaked across his face. "I can come over tomorrow when you're done at the studio. We'll have dinner with the kids, hang out at your place, maybe play a board game or something?"

"That sounds…" *Nice*, she almost said, until she remembered it wasn't possible. "Wait, I can't tomorrow. Kim's coming over to babysit while I have dinner with the father of Elsa's student."

"Since when do you have dinner with a student's parents?"

"I don't usually, but he insisted."

Seth narrowed his eyes. "This dude…he's the one who suggested dinner?"

"Yeah." She shot him a questioning look. "Is there something wrong with that?"

"Nope." His lips tightened. "But you *are* aware that this is a date, right?"

Surprise jolted through her. "No, it's not. We're just meeting to discuss his daughter's progress."

Seth looked unconvinced. "Didn't you say she's Elsa's student?"

"Yes, but—"

"Then shouldn't he be meeting with Elsa?"

"Yes, but—"

Seth smirked. "But what? Let me guess, he refuses to discuss this with anyone but you. You, the smoking-hot, highly desirable former showgirl who runs the school."

She couldn't help but gape at him. "Are you suggesting he wants in my pants?"

"It isn't a suggestion, babe. It's a stone-cold fact."

"Oh come on. That's just silly. I'm not going on a date with this man."

"Does *he* know that?"

There was no mistaking the hard note in his voice, or the cloud of jealousy that turned his eyes from gray to turbulent silver. Was that it? Was he jealous? The notion was pretty damn gratifying—it was so rare to see Seth get rattled about anything. But it was also annoying as hell, because tomorrow's dinner with Eric Porter was *not* a date.

"Yes, he knows it," she replied firmly. "We're seeing each other in a professional capacity."

Seth's jaw was tense and inflexible. "It's a date, Miranda."

"Jeez! Stop saying that." Yet even in her annoyance, she found herself laughing.

"Fine, I'll stop—if you say yes to the other thing we were talking about."

Her laughter faded. "Say yes to dating *you*, you mean."

"Yup."

"Seth...I don't know." When she glimpsed the disappointment in his eyes, she released a sigh. "This isn't the kind of decision I can make without giving it some serious thought. I have to consider how dating you will affect my children, how it will affect the life I'm trying to build for them. I know you say you'll make an effort, but what if you do and you discover that you actually just hate kids? I don't want Sophie and Jason getting attached to you, only for you to disappear from their lives."

"I understand. I really do." He hesitated. "What if we start with something small? A way for me to dip my toes in the water, for lack of a better way to phrase it."

"Meaning what?"

"Instead of Kim babysitting tomorrow, why don't I do it?"

Her brows lifted in surprise. "Are you serious?"

"Yes. How long do you think the date will last? An hour, two?"

"Probably, and it's not a date."

"So let me watch the kids. And I promise, I won't hold back this time. I won't keep my distance or try to pretend they're not there."

"And if you do all that and decide you really don't want to be around them?"

"I don't think that will happen."

"But if it does?"

"If it does, then we end this." Unhappiness underlined each word. "I can't do a fling anymore, babe. For some baffling reason, I actually want more than sex from you. Trust me, that's never fucking happened before."

She offered a faint smile. "I imagine."

"But you can't have a relationship with a man who doesn't love your kids." A resigned light entered his eyes. "I know myself. If by the time you get home I'm not convinced I can be what you want me to be for those kids, then we say good-bye. And you don't have to worry about the twins getting hurt. I'll just be babysitting them for a couple of hours, and they're not overly attached to me at the moment, anyway. Besides, if we do end this, Sophie will probably organize a parade. She hates me."

Miranda's lips twitched. "She doesn't hate you."

"Liar. You know she does." He searched her face. "Well?"

Indecision skipped through her, but the genuine hope softening Seth's rugged features made the decision for her. "All right. You can watch the twins tomorrow."

"Are you sure?"

She nodded, then reached for his hand and pulled him off the couch. Wrapping her arms around his waist, she rested her cheek on his chest and murmured, "Thank you for my birthday presents. The cupcake *and* the orgasm."

His fingers threaded through her hair, stroking gently. "You're welcome. And thank *you*. For listening. And for not laughing me right out of the room when I asked you to give this a shot." He brought his lips close to her ear. "And most of all, thank you for agreeing to let me babysit your children while you're out on your date."

She huffed out an irritated breath. "It's *not* a date!"

Chapter Seventeen

THE NEXT MORNING, MIRANDA HAD A BITCH OF A TIME GETTING BOTH her kids in the same room together. Jason was running around the apartment throwing a baseball in the air, and when she finally got his butt settled on the living room couch, Sophie darted off to find her doll, only to get distracted by one of the sparrows out in the backyard, the one that was supposedly out to get her. So while Miranda was calming down her daughter and assuring her that sparrows were harmless, Jason took off again, this time ducking under the kitchen table to play with his little green army men.

Needless to say, by the time she finally had both kids in front of her, she was exhausted, flustered and kind of sweaty.

"Okay, guys, this is serious. I really need you to listen," she said, sinking into the small armchair next to the couch. "Sophie, put Emily down. Jason, I know you have one of those soldiers in your mouth. Spit it out. Now."

Emily and a green soldier landed on the coffee table with a thud.

"All right. Are you listening?"

They nodded.

"Mommy's going out for dinner tonight, so—"

"I wanna go to dinner too," Jason interrupted.

"Me too!" Sophie piped up.

"I'm sorry, guys, but you can't. It's a business meeting, so it's going to be super boring. Trust me, you'll have a lot more fun at home." Remaining casual, she added, "With Seth."

Sophie gasped in pure horror. "Sef's coming?"

Jason beamed with pure delight. "Sef's coming?"

"Yep. He's coming over to hang out with you while I have my business meeting."

"I don't want Sef! I want Dylan," Sophie retorted.

"Dylan is busy tonight," Miranda lied. "But Seth was free, and guess what, he's so excited about coming over. He said he really wants to watch a movie with you guys, and make popcorn, and maybe even play in the yard for a bit."

Sophie looked so dubious that Miranda almost laughed.

"Is Sef gonna get me from Ricky's house?" Jason's jaw dropped as another thought occurred to him. "Is Sef gonna come to my *game*?"

"I'm afraid he won't be at the game, kiddo. Coach Diaz will drop you off at home afterwards." She glanced at Sophie. "And you get to drive in Ginny's cool convertible. She'll bring you home while I wrap up my last class. You and Seth will hang out until your brother gets home."

Now Sophie was the one gaping. "I hafta be *alone* with Sef?"

"She gets to be alone with Sef? No fair!"

Miranda sighed. "Enough, guys. Close your mouths before bugs start flying in there." She gave each of them a strict look. "I expect you to be on your best behavior tonight. You're going to treat Seth with the same respect you give to me and Kim, understand?"

They nodded, Sophie albeit reluctantly.

"And no running in the house." She glanced at Jason. "No indoor baseball, Jase. And you—" she pointed at Sophie, "—don't you dare throw things at the bird feeder again."

Fine, so maybe she was stacking the deck in Seth's favor a little, but the man was making an effort, so why shouldn't her kids do the same?

"Are we good?" She looked from one child to the other.

"Yup," they said in unison.

But there was no mistaking the tiny glimmer of mischief in her daughter's eyes.

Uh-oh.

With a sigh, she got to her feet. "All right, let's get you two dressed. We've got a busy day ahead of us."

SETH'S PALMS WERE UNUSUALLY DAMP AS HE WAITED IN MIRANDA'S LIVING room for the kids to come home. He'd let himself in with the spare key she'd given him last night at the club, and it felt weird being in Miranda's apartment when she wasn't there.

He couldn't believe he'd agreed to watch her kids this evening.

Agreed?

Right. Try *offered.*

And Miranda was actually trusting him with her kids. The woman had a lot more faith in him than he had in himself.

The irony didn't escape him—he was a Navy SEAL, for fuck's sake. He could carry out a hazardous black-ops mission in his sleep, infiltrate a terrorist cell's lair without batting an eye, throw himself in the line of fire without hesitation. He'd saved lives before. Many, many lives. His government specifically *entrusted* him with the task of saving lives.

And yet he was terrified that he wouldn't be able to protect a pair of six-year-olds.

He gulped when he heard the front door open. Footsteps thudded, a female voice wafting from the hall. A moment later, a petite blonde with pale gray eyes entered the living room, holding hands with a frowning Sophie.

"You must be Seth," she said. Her eyes gleamed appreciatively. "I'm Ginny, one of the instructors at the school. Miranda says you're babysitting tonight."

"Yep." He rose from the couch and walked over to shake her hand. "Nice to meet you, Ginny. Hey, Sophie."

The little girl stared at him in surprise. He suddenly realized this was the first time he'd ever addressed her by name.

"Hi," she said suspiciously.

"Well, I'll leave you to it then." Ginny smiled again. "Oh, and Miranda wanted me to remind you that she left money for pizza in the jar next to the fridge."

Seth resisted a snort. They'd argued over the phone this morning about how he wasn't going to let her pay for dinner, and as far as he was concerned, he'd won the argument already.

"I'll walk you out," he told Ginny.

They headed for the door, the blonde tossing out a light "have fun" before she left.

When Seth returned to the living room, Sophie was standing exactly where he'd left her. She had a little pink duffel bag slung over one shoulder, and she wore red cotton shorts, a black T-shirt with yellow stars on it and black ballet flats. Her hair was up in a ponytail, brown eyes flickering with mistrust.

"So." He cleared his throat. "What do you want to do until your brother gets home?"

"I dunno." Her lack of enthusiasm was hardly promising.

Smothering a sigh, he took her duffel bag and set it aside. "Come on, I'm sure there's *something* you want to do. We can watch a movie or go out in the backyard or draw a picture—pick anything you want."

"Anything?"

He could've sworn he saw a devilish gleam in her eyes.

"Anything," he echoed.

"Fine. I wanna play with my dolls and make their hair pretty so they can dance at the recital."

God help him.

From the smirk she gave him, he knew Sophie expected him to recoil in horror. Maybe revert back to the Seth she'd called mean, and tell her to get lost.

When he didn't answer right away, she crossed her skinny arms over her chest and said, "I *knew* you wouldn't wanna." She scowled. "You wouldna be good at it anyway."

Seth raised a defiant brow, then squatted down so they were at eye level. "Sophie, I'm a United States Navy SEAL. Know what that means?"

She shifted uneasily, then shook her head.

"It means I can do whatever I set my mind to, so if you think I can't give your dolls some awesome hairstyles, I'm ready to prove you wrong."

She giggled, then clapped a hand over her mouth as if she couldn't believe she'd dropped her guard around him.

"So you ready to do this, or what?" he challenged.

As Sophie dashed off to get her dolls, he gave a brisk nod, declaring himself the winner of round one. In fact, he planned on winning every damn round tonight, if only to prove to Miranda that he had what it took to be her boyfriend.

Boyfriend. Christ, he couldn't believe he even wanted to be someone's boyfriend.

Well, not just *anyone's* boyfriend. *Miranda's.*

He was falling for the woman.

He was actually fucking falling for her, and wasn't that another dose of irony right there. He'd always believed love was a choice, that you had to be open to it in order to feel it, but his feelings for Miranda had crept up on him. One day he was thinking about how much he wanted to fuck her, the next he was fantasizing about holding her hand and making her laugh and seeing her eyes light up with joy.

She was the strongest woman he'd ever met, not to mention stubborn, resilient, compassionate, generous. He'd never been in a serious relationship before, but he wasn't averse to the idea either, and if there was anyone he could picture himself with for the long haul, it was Miranda. And if *she* could penetrate the shield he always threw up, then why couldn't her kids? All he had to do was lower his guard and give himself a chance to care about those children.

And it wasn't difficult to care about a kid like Sophie. For the next thirty minutes, Seth had a blast with the girl. They were sprawled on the living room floor on the brand-new hardwood that sparkled from the sunlight streaming in through the window. Sophie had brought out half a dozen dolls, along with tiny doll accessories—hair elastics, little pink hairbrushes, barrettes and clips of all shapes and colors.

If any of the guys had asked, he would've said it was the lamest thing he'd ever done in his life.

The truth?

It was pretty fuckin' fun.

As his huge fingers tried to grip a teeny hairbrush to brush the silky hair of an anatomically-incorrect Barbie, Sophie was laughing at him so hard her face had turned beet red.

"You have giant fingers!" Pure glee radiated from her little body.

"I can't help it," he said defensively. "Okay, new plan. You do the hair brushing, I'll braid this foxy mama's hair." He reached for the voluptuous Latina doll in the hot-pink minidress.

"Deal," Sophie said.

They were so absorbed in their respective tasks that their heads jerked up in surprise when they heard the front door fly open.

"I'm home!"

A second later, Jason skidded into the living room, halting when he noticed what Seth and his sister were up to. "You're playing with *dolls*?"

Seth couldn't have answered the question if his life depended on it. The second he laid eyes on Jason, his throat closed up to the point that he couldn't suck in a single breath, and he felt like he'd just gotten knocked in the gut with an iron beam.

Holy fucking shit. He was going to have a panic attack. His heart raced, and his palms were tingling. Black dots appeared in his vision—he actually welcomed them, because that meant he didn't have to focus on the little boy standing in the doorway. The white-and-blue-striped uniform and blue baseball cap and little black sneakers.

The hat was the wrong color, though. It was supposed to be red.

"—fun and you don't hafta." Sophie's haughty voice broke through Seth's anxiety attack, but it sounded tinny and incredibly far away. "Me and Sef are making Emily and her friends pretty. You can play with Sef after."

"Can we? Can we play after?"

He felt a pair of eager brown eyes boring into him. He couldn't do it, though. He couldn't look at Adam again or else he might pass out.

Jason.

Shit. That wasn't Adam. It was Jason.

He bit hard on the insides of both cheeks, doing his best to breathe, to control his dangerously fast heartbeat.

"Can we play catch outside when you finish playing dolls?" Jason asked.

Seth abruptly shot to his feet, the doll in his hand falling to the floor with a thump.

"Hey!" Sophie protested, lunging for the doll.

"I...I'm going out for a smoke," he blurted out.

He felt both children watching him in confusion, but he ignored them as he hurried to the kitchen.

One foot in front of the other. Keep walking. Don't think about that fucking baseball uniform.

Yeah, maybe he would've stood a chance, if Jason hadn't scampered after him like a dog nipping at his owner's heels.

"Please, Sef?" Jason pleaded. "I wanna show you how good I pitch!"

He swallowed. His throat was so clogged it burned. Memories he'd banished years ago came out of exile. Adam used to beg him to play catch too. Sometimes he'd say yes. Most times he'd scoff and tell him to quit being a whiny brat.

Agony constricted his heart. He'd been a total shit back then too, hadn't he?

Should've been you, man. Should've been you.

Seth's eyes started to sting, his hands shaking so badly it was a miracle he managed to dig his cigarette pack from the front pocket of his button-down. It took two tries to open the sliding door that led to the backyard. Five tries to get his fingers to work the lighter. And then he inhaled a lungful of smoke in a pull so long and so deep he got a head rush.

He exhaled in shaky puffs. It was still light out, but the sun was beginning to dip toward the horizon.

"And I wanna show you my new mitt," Jason was babbling. "Mom got me a new one because my old one got wet from the storm but the old one still works great so now I have *two* gloves."

Seth's heart continued to pound. He kept his gaze focused straight ahead, his jaw tense, teeth grinding together. He couldn't look at the kid. He couldn't do it, otherwise he'd break the fuck down.

"Mom says smoking is bad for you," Jason said matter-of-factly. "You should play sports instead of smoking."

He took another desperate drag of his cigarette. Fixed his gaze on the bird feeder hanging across the yard.

But Jason wasn't having it. The kid was determined to be paid attention to, come hell or high water. He moved in front of Seth and started bouncing around, a bundle of energy and smiles. The baseball uniform was all Seth could register, and a rush of pure helpless agony seized his chest again.

"You wanna play now? Can we play now?"

"For the love of God, I don't want to play baseball with you!"

Silence crashed over them.

Jason was stricken for a second. Then his entire face collapsed, his bottom lip beginning to tremble.

Seth sucked in an unsteady breath. Exhaustion settled, making him feel like he'd just run a marathon.

"Just…go inside, Jason," he muttered. "Please…go inside."

Eyes shining with tears, the little boy hurried away without a word.

The weight on his shoulders was so heavy he couldn't stay upright anymore. He sagged to the ground, crushing his cigarette on the grass and bringing his knees up. He rested an elbow on his knee and dropped his forehead in his hand. He blinked rapidly but the tears came anyway. Burning his eyes, choking him up.

He had to go inside. He knew that. He couldn't leave Miranda's children alone for too long.

But goddammit, how the hell was he supposed to face that boy?

Pain streaked through him. He couldn't do it. He needed to call Miranda and ask her to come home. He shouldn't be responsible for the safety of her children. Any children. He shouldn't—

Seth jumped when he felt a warm hand on his arm.

"Don't cry, Sef."

Sophie's voice was so gentle and so sweet that his throat clogged right back up.

He swiped a hand over his wet eyes. For the life of him, he couldn't shrug off Sophie's hand, and when she placed it over his, he was floored by how small her fingers were. All five of them barely covered two of his knuckles. She was innocent and tiny and fragile and she shouldn't be around him, damn it. The thought brought a fresh wave of moisture to his eyes.

Fuck, he couldn't sit here crying like a fucking pansy. He had to call Miranda and tell her to come home.

Sophie flopped down on the grass beside him, then wiggled her way beneath his arm so that he had no choice but to sling it around her slender shoulders. She peered up at him, her brown eyes shining with encouragement.

"'S'okay, Sef. I cry when I'm sad too."

His shoulders sagged in defeat, his arm tightening around her, bringing the little girl close to his side. "I lost him," he croaked.

"No, you didn't. I'm right here."

A somber Jason appeared in front of them, his face red and tear-streaked. He still had the uniform on, but for the first time since the kid had come home, Seth's vision was seeing everything clearly. He saw Jason's brown eyes, not Adam's gray ones. Jason's short brown hair, not Adam's unruly black curls.

As guilt swelled in his gut, he met the boy's gaze. "I'm sorry," he said quietly. "I shouldn't have yelled at you."

Jason sniffled. Took a step closer.

"I was…upset. When you came home, you reminded me of someone else. I looked at you and I saw someone else." He wiped his eyes, grateful that none of his teammates were bearing witness to this show of pure and utter weakness. "I'm so sorry, Jason."

"Who did you see?" the boy asked, taking another curious step forward.

"My little brother. He was about your age. He's…he's in heaven now."

Another explosion of guilt hit him square in the chest. Breathing through it, he held out his hand, beckoning Jason.

Without hesitation, Miranda's son plopped down on Seth's other side. Sophie was still holding his hand, and now Jason held his other one. The warmth radiating from their little fingers seeped into his body.

"Did you cry when your brother went to heaven?" Sophie asked.

Seth slowly shook his head. "No. I never did."

"You shoulda. Mommy says it's okay to cry when you get sad."

"You can keep crying now if you want," Jason offered. "We won't laugh at you, right, Soph?"

"Right," she confirmed.

Damned if that didn't get him all fucking teary-eyed again.

"Thanks, guys. But I think I'm all cried out. I'm kinda hungry, though. What do you say we order that pizza now?"

He stood up, heaving the twins up with him. Before he could question himself, he lifted them both into his arms, eliciting a pair of delighted gasps. Two sets of arms wrapped around his neck, clinging tight, but he didn't feel smothered. As he breathed in the scent of sweet kiddie shampoo, something shifted in his chest. Heart might've cracked a little bit too.

He glanced down at Jason, then Sophie. "I'm sorry. I really am sorry I was such a big jerk to you guys all those times."

"'S'okay," Jason said with a shrug.

"'S'okay," Sophie chimed in.

Was it, though? He tried to keep his spirits up as he carried the kids into the house, but in the back of his mind, he knew that it *wasn't* okay. And soon Miranda would know it too.

Chapter Eighteen

As Dylan waited outside Aidan's door he was suddenly reminded of why he'd been so eager to get the hell out of Marin County ten years ago.

He loved the house he'd grown up in, loved his mom and his brother and his dad, God bless his soul, but living in that bubble of normalcy had been so fucking oppressive at times. Everyone at his high school had been preppy and conservative to the core. He could only imagine what his old friends would say if they knew that at this very moment, he was standing on the doorstep of a man he desperately wanted to have sex with.

Aidan opened the door looking as appealing as always. Dark hair messy, tall frame clad in basketball shorts and a black sleeveless tee. "Hey. Come in. Keep your boots on, though. I was sitting outside."

Dylan entered the apartment and followed Aidan out to the stone terrace. Aidan reached into the cooler on the ground and fished out two beers.

"Thanks," Dylan said, sitting down. He took a quick sip before shooting the other man a sheepish grin. "I'm sorry I've been such a dick."

Aidan shrugged. "Sorry if I freaked you out at Carson's last week."

"I wasn't freaked out. I was…surprised." He slugged back some beer for liquid courage, then said, "I didn't expect it. What you said. You know, about wanting…"

"You?" Aidan supplied. Those dimples appeared. "I don't normally advertise it, but yeah, I swing both ways."

"Me too."

"I figured, what with the way you were undressing me with your eyes the night of the club fight."

"Hey, you were undressing me right back."

"Damn right."

"So what do we do now?"

Aidan tipped his bottle and took a long swig. "What do you think we do?" Then he paused. "Wait, don't tell me you're a virgin."

Dylan rolled his eyes. "I'm not a virgin."

"You been with another man before?"

"Yes. But…but I've never been with *just* a man. Always had a woman there." He studied Aidan's face. "What about you?"

"I've been with just girls. I've been with just guys. I've been with both."

"I see."

There was a beat of silence, and then Aidan chuckled. "Is that why you've been acting all jumpy around me? It freaks you out because there's no chick around to serve as a buffer?"

"Kind of," he admitted. He promptly chugged more beer.

"Let me ask you something." Aidan put down his bottle and casually rested his hands on his knees. "You ever sucked a dick and gotten sucked off?"

The dirty images triggered by that question sent a bolt of lust to his groin.

He managed a quick nod.

Aidan looked intrigued by that. "Okay. You ever fucked a guy's ass and gotten fucked?"

Another nod.

Now Aidan laughed, a deep rumble that came from deep in his chest.

Dylan's skin prickled with offense. "Something funny?"

"Yeah, a little. I mean, you've had a cock in your ass, but hey, it's fine because there was a woman around. You've had your dick in another man's mouth, but gee, no biggie, there was a chick there to keep it all aboveboard and hetero."

It did sound pretty absurd when you put it like that.

Aidan chuckled again. "If you and I do this—"

"If?" Dylan couldn't curb the note of challenge that entered into his voice.

Those dark eyes flashed with sinful promise. "I guess there's no *if* about it, huh?" Aidan's tone went from dry to regretful. "But it won't be happening tonight."

Damned if that didn't elicit a rush of disappointment.

"I'm catching a flight to D.C. in a couple of hours."

Dylan furrowed his brows. "Why didn't you tell me that when I called? Shouldn't you be packing or something?"

"I'm all packed." Aidan checked the watch on his left wrist. "And I don't have to leave for the airport for another hour, so I had time to meet up."

"Why are you going to D.C.?"

"I'm being sent as a liaison for my CO and the ONI. We've got this new joint task force we're setting up to discuss some potential new approaches to maritime intelligence."

"Sounds pretty cool. How long will you be gone?"

"A month." Dylan saw his own frustration reflected back at him in Aidan's eyes. "That's why I don't want to start anything I can't finish right now."

"Makes sense." Too bad his cock didn't operate on logic and schedules—the little soldier was a hedonistic motherfucker, and at the moment, it was demanding gratification.

Ignoring the relentless throbbing in his body's southern hemisphere, Dylan finished his beer and stood up. "I think I'll bounce then. You need to leave for the airport soon, and I—"

"Will be too tempted to do me if you stick around," Aidan finished.

"Something like that."

"Fair enough. I'll walk you out."

They fell into step with each other. Neither said a word, at least not until they reached the front hall.

"Fuck it," Aidan burst out, at the same time Dylan mumbled, "Fuck."

And then he found himself being slammed into the wall and a hot, male mouth was capturing his in a harsh kiss.

It was the kind of kiss that set your entire body on fire, and nothing short of dying could have compelled Dylan to break free. They both groaned when their tongues met, and again when Aidan ground his pelvis into Dylan's, leaving no question as to whether or not he was turned on.

Feeling the hard ridge of Aidan's erection rubbing against his thigh was the hottest fucking thing on the planet.

With a growl, he dug his fingers into the nape of Aidan's neck and deepened the kiss. He tasted the alcohol on Aidan's tongue, breathed in the man's lemony aftershave, and the lust whipping through his body intensified from the sensory overload. A five o'clock shadow scraped his jaw, a thrilling reminder that it was just the two of them. Just him and another guy.

"Son of a bitch," Aidan hissed when they finally pulled apart.

They were both breathing hard, resting their foreheads together as they caught their breath.

When Dylan noticed the hunger flaring in Aidan's heavy-lidded eyes, he chuckled, knowing he was probably broadcasting the same damn impatience.

"A month, huh?"

"A month," Aidan said grimly.

He let his hand drop from its perch on Aidan's shoulder and took a step away. "I think it's even more crucial that I go now."

"Probably."

"Let me know when you're back in town."

"You'll be the first person I call."

Their gazes locked. The temperature in the hall spiked at least ten degrees. Oh yeah. This was going to be interesting, Dylan decided.

Really, really interesting.

OKAY, THIS WAS *TOTALLY* A DATE.

Miranda had no choice but to accept the unwelcome truth as Eric Porter once again steered the conversation away from his daughter, the school and his daughter's future at the school.

Stupid Seth had been right. She'd laughed off his suspicions, even joked about them with Andre at the studio today, but clearly Seth's bullshit radar was more technologically advanced than hers. Or maybe he was simply naturally suspicious, while she tried to see the good in people.

But it was getting harder and harder to find anything good about the man across the table from her. Vain, self-absorbed, no sense of humor whatsoever. And the kicker? The douchebag seemed like a *terrible* father.

"All right. Eric. I'm going to stop you right there," she said after he'd just invited her to go "yachting" with him next weekend. "I'm actually seeing someone at the moment. And even if I wasn't, there could still be nothing between us. I don't date students' fathers."

Porter's lips curled in displeasure. He wasn't an unattractive man, but he wasn't her type either. Midthirties, nondescript features. Great hair, though—brown, thick and wavy. And he was obviously in good shape, judging by the way he filled out his expensive black suit. Nevertheless, he was too polished, too bland and too fucking slimy.

"I thought we were connecting." He gestured to their half-eaten pasta dishes and glasses of red wine.

"And I thought we were here to discuss Catherine," she said coolly.

Clearly we were both wrong, asshole.

"We did." Porter cast a grin she suspected was supposed to look boyish, but came off as sleazy and made her skin crawl. "And now we're discussing other subjects. I'll be honest, Miranda, I was taken with you from the moment we met."

Seth's voice cackled a continuous loop of *I told you so* in her head.

"I mean, you're an attractive woman, and you—well, I'll just come out and say it, you've got an amazing body."

Ew, gross. Had he really just said that?

"*Amazing*," he emphasized, then eyed her expectantly, as if he was waiting for her to thank him.

What she did was drop her napkin on the table and rise to her feet.

"I'm sorry, I should get going," she said, though she wasn't sorry at all and they both knew it. "I need to get home to my kids." Oh, screw it, why even lie? "And if I'm being honest, I'm not entirely comfortable with where the conversation has headed. If I led you on in any way, Mr. Porter, then I apologize, but like I said before, I won't be getting involved with you, now or in the future."

There was a brief silence. Porter's features darkened with contempt. He swiftly yanked a leather wallet from the inside pocket of his suit jacket. "Well, I can't say I'm not disappointed," he muttered.

And then he officially graduated from the class of douchebag and proved he belonged in the league of *nasty son of a bitch.*

"Not just in you, but your school," Porter said snidely. "I wonder if it might be more beneficial for Cat if she worked with an instructor who had more than just 'Las Vegas showgirl' on her resume."

Miranda decided not to mention that Catherine wasn't even her student. She also decided slapping this man in public wasn't the brightest of ideas.

"I'll have to discuss it with Cat's mother," Porter added. "See how she feels about the situation."

"You do that," Miranda said coldly.

A gust of anger, annoyance and disbelief followed her outside like a black cloud over her head. Un-fucking-believable. She couldn't believe she'd wasted an entire hour with that jerk.

Curling her hands into fists, she marched down the sidewalk toward the end of the block and headed for the parking lot behind the dance school. She didn't bother going inside to tell Elsa about the unpleasant encounter with Porter, but she did send a quick text saying she'd fill her in tomorrow.

All she wanted to do at the moment was go home and see how Seth was faring with the kids. She hadn't received any SOS texts this past hour, so she assumed he was holding his own, but she was still incredibly curious about what she'd find when she walked through the door.

Just as she started the car, her phone rang. A Nevada area code flashed on the screen, bringing a wry smile to her lips. It wasn't quite a call from Seth, but close enough.

"Hey, Missy," she said after she switched the call to speakerphone.

"Hey, sugar pie! How's my favorite birthday girl doing?" With the way Missy Masterson chain-smoked, you'd think she'd sound perpetually hoarse, but Seth's mother had one of those breathy, Marilyn Monroe voices that only added to her sexpot status.

"I'm doing good. I got the voice mail you left yesterday. I wanted to call you back during my break—" *but I spent it with your son's tongue between my legs,* "—but I didn't get a chance. Thanks for the birthday message. It was sweet of you."

"I can't believe you worked on your birthday. Shame on you."

"Hey, as I recall, you were at the theater until three in the morning last year on *your* birthday."

"I'm the choreographer. Where else would I be? Now, tell me everything you've been up to. We haven't spoken in ages. How's business?"

"Pretty good. Enrollment has doubled, and we're expecting a full house for the recital at the end of July. All the parents are super excited." She rolled her eyes to herself. "Except for maybe one. Actually, I wouldn't be surprised if his daughter doesn't end up dancing in the recital at all."

She quickly told Missy about the awful "date" with Porter, and when she finished, the older woman sounded utterly disgusted. "What a prick! Send my son to beat him up, pronto."

Laughing, Miranda set the phone in the cup holder and drove away from the studio. "I totally should. Seth would be happy to do it—he already kicked the ass of one man who had the audacity to bother me."

Seth's mother was not perturbed in the slightest. "My boy's always been a hothead. And too big and strong for his own good." Missy sounded suspicious. "Is he giving you any trouble? Because he definitely has the tendency to bulldoze people in order to get his way. He gets his bossy, overbearing side from his father."

"Seth has a father?"

The second she asked it, she felt like a total moron, and Missy made it worse by snorting. "No, Miranda, my son was born via immaculate conception."

Okay, she deserved that. "I mean, neither of you talk about Seth's father. I didn't realize he was ever in the picture."

"Oh, he was. Not for long, though. He bailed when Seth was five. But good riddance, because that man was nothing but trouble. Anyway, I wanted to make sure Seth isn't being his usual jackass self and causing you any grief. Is he hitting on you left and right?"

For a second she almost confessed that she and Seth were kind of dating, but she wasn't sure if he wanted his mother to know about them. And depending on what happened tonight, dating might not even be in the cards.

So she opted for a casual response. "No, he isn't causing me grief. Why would he?"

"Because he's been panting over you for more than a year."

"What?" Astonishment shot through her.

"Don't you remember when he came to visit that time? He just got back from wherever the hell they sent him and he showed up at the theater?"

With flowers for his mother. Right. She *did* remember.

Seth had lusted over her from way back then?

That baffling piece of information was still on her mind long after she'd hung up with Missy. She made a mental note to tease Seth about it when she saw him, but teasing was the last thing she wanted to do when she walked into her living room a half hour later.

Her eyes nearly bugged out of her head. Seth was sprawled on the couch, his gaze focused on the Pixar movie playing on the TV, but it wasn't his willingness to watch a bunch of animated toys dance around that stunned her.

It was the two children tucked on either side of his chest, fast asleep. *Her* children.

Seth was actually cuddling on the couch with her kids.

His gaze sought hers, one finger coming up to his lips. She was surprised the twins had already conked out—it was only eight o'clock, and normally they didn't go to bed for another hour or so.

"Let me take them to their room," she whispered.

In the end, Seth was the one who carried them, and he even tucked Sophie in while Miranda tended to Jason. She was floored when she noticed him brush a lock of hair off her daughter's forehead with infinite tenderness.

What the heck had happened here tonight?

She couldn't wait for some answers, but the mom in her needed to get the basics out of the way first. "Did they eat their dinner?" she asked Seth in the hallway.

"Every last bite." He fished his smoke pack from his pocket. "Can we do this interrogation outside?"

Nodding, she followed him out to the backyard. "Did they give you any trouble?"

"None." His movements were oddly ungainly as he lit a cigarette and sank into one of the chairs near the door. "Miranda..."

It suddenly occurred to her that he hadn't so much as touched her since she'd walked into the house. No kiss. No hug. Not even a hand squeeze. Wariness promptly rose inside her, making her stomach churn.

"What's going on?" And then just like that, she knew. He hated her kids. He didn't want to make a real, solid go of this after all.

Her heart dropped, but at the same time, annoyance and indignation rustled through her.

"So that's it, huh? You were with them for two hours and you've decided that you can't—"

"I yelled at Jason and made him cry."

Miranda's jaw snapped shut. Then fell open. Her body went colder than a block of ice. "Excuse me?"

The despair on Seth's face did nothing to dim the anger that entered her bloodstream. "It was a moment of panic. Jason came home, and he was bugging me to play baseball with him and—"

"And the idea was so terrifying you decided to *yell* at him?" she interrupted, her mouth tightening in outrage.

"It was the uniform. I..." A ragged breath escaped. "It caught me off-guard."

Now she was just confused. "What, you've never seen a Little League uniform before, Seth?"

He took a quick drag and then extinguished his cigarette in the small plastic bowl she'd placed on the table earlier for that exact purpose. Her confusion grew as she watched him reach into his pocket for his wallet. He opened the leather flaps, dug something out of one of the card slots and handed it over.

Miranda stared at the square of newsprint. "What's this?"

"Just read it," he said roughly.

The paper was folded about fifteen times, so it took a few moments to unfold it and smooth it out. She'd figured it was a newspaper article, and she was right, except she wasn't prepared for the headline that glared up at her. It was written in huge block letters, the lettering a faded gray when it had once been crisp black, but there was no mistaking what it said.

MISSING BOY'S BODY FOUND IN DESERT.

Her breath caught. The picture beneath the headline showed an adorable little boy in a white baseball uniform, a red cap on his head, and a big grin on his face. He was missing his two front teeth and giving a thumbs-up to the camera. The caption read: *Adam Jonathan Masterson, age 7.*

"Is this..." She searched Seth's veiled eyes.

"My younger brother."

"Oh. Oh God, Seth." Shock and horror spun inside her, along with a rush of sympathy. She stared at the date on the top of the page, and understanding suddenly dawned.

She stumbled to her feet and went to him, sinking into his lap and slowly lifting up his shirt. She traced her fingers over the row of dates inked below his rib cage.

"The day you became a SEAL," she murmured, touching the third date on the list. Her fingers moved to the last date. "First time you saved a life." She touched the first row of numbers, exactly one day before the date on the article. "The day they found your brother's body." Her fingers hovered over the second row and she looked up at him, questioning.

"The day we buried him," he said hoarsely.

"Oh, Seth. I'm sorry."

He sighed. "Read the article."

She ended up reading it twice, her heart breaking the entire time. Seth had been eleven years old when his brother was abducted. A man in a pickup truck had snatched little Adam Masterson right out of his front yard, where he'd been tossing a baseball around. According to the article, Seth was supposed to watch his brother, but he'd turned away for a minute, giving Adam's killer just enough time to grab the boy and haul him into his truck.

Seth had seen it from the doorway and run after the pickup for two blocks before giving up the chase.

"Oh my God."

She ran her finger over the third paragraph, which detailed the search for the abducted boy and the police detective's suspicions that the abduction was connected to a string of child murders he'd been investigating for the past couple of months. Three boys had been abducted and killed, under similar circumstances. And those three bodies had also been found in the desert, all within a mile or two of Adam Masterson's body.

"Did they catch him?" Miranda asked, her voice cracking.

Seth nodded. "Jarvis Henderson. He was apprehended trying to kidnap another boy. Son of a bitch opted for suicide by cop. He refused to lay down his weapon during the standoff and the officers had no choice but to shoot. Back then I remember being happy he was dead. Now I feel cheated. Death was too good for that sick fuck."

Miranda placed the article on the table and rubbed her forehead. "I can't believe Missy never told me about this. I had no idea you had a brother. That she'd had another child."

"She doesn't talk about it." Seth's voice grew dull. "Ever. Not to me, not to anyone. She pretends Adam never existed." Now he sounded angry. "And that part in the article about me turning away for a minute? It's bullshit, Miranda. I left him in the yard. I left him alone in the yard."

Her breath hitched. "Seth—"

"I was bored of playing catch so I went inside to watch TV, and I left Adam out there. I was supposed to be watching him, but I was a selfish little bastard and I couldn't be bothered to play ball with my brother." He hissed out a savage curse. "It's my fault that psycho got him."

The guilt swimming in his eyes had her placing her hands on his broad shoulders to give them a firm shake. "It's not your fault."

"I heard the truck door slam and when I went to the window, I saw him grabbing Adam." Seth's expression was flat, empty. "I ran outside just as the pickup was pulling away from the curb. I couldn't catch up to it."

"You were eleven years old. Of course you couldn't keep up with a truck," she said gently.

"Adam wouldn't have been in the truck to begin with if it weren't for me." Bitterness dripped from each word. "So yeah, it was my fault. I knew it. The cops knew it. Mom knew it. It was a long time before she was able to look at me again. She couldn't look me in the eye for about three years after he died. I think she didn't want me to see the blame in her eyes."

Miranda cupped his cheeks and swept her thumbs over his stubble. "I don't believe Missy blamed you for what happened. She worships you."

He shrugged. "We moved past it."

"By pretending your brother, her son, never existed."

"Pretty much, yeah."

She wanted to point out how unhealthy that was, but who was she to judge how other families dealt with their grief and heartache? Yet it ripped her apart that Missy Masterson hadn't comforted her son, that she might've even led him to believe he was to blame for his brother's abduction.

"Do you understand now?" he said in a rough voice. "I don't trust myself around children, and I know that's ironic because I'm supposed to be this big, bad soldier who fights for the innocent and saves lives and all that. And I do save lives." His rugged features hardened with determination. "I enlisted for the sole purpose of doing good. To make up for what I did that day."

"What you *did* that day…" she echoed, shaking her head in disbelief.

He didn't seem to hear her. "But I always made an effort to stay away from kids. Because what if I fucked up again? What if I turned away for even a second and then…then…" He swallowed. "I didn't want to like your kids. I didn't want to love them. Because the last kid I loved *died*. He fucking died, Miranda, and I'm the reason."

"You were *eleven years old*," she burst out, unable to control the fierce wave of protectiveness that swept through her. She gripped his chin and forced him to look at her. "You were a kid yourself and you shouldn't have been alone with Adam in the first place! Isn't twelve years old the legal age to leave a child home alone in Nevada? I'm not assigning blame here—because sometimes fucked-up, horrible things happen and it's nobody's fault—but if anyone *is* to blame? It's Missy. She should have known better than to leave two young boys to fend for themselves."

Seth looked slightly stunned. "She…was working. To support us. And…"

"And nothing. Adam's death is not on your head, Seth. It's not on your mom's head. It's on Jarvis Henderson. He's the monster who…" She couldn't even finish.

Next thing she knew, Seth's strong arms came around her. Miranda couldn't control the big gulping sobs that slipped out. She cried for Seth and Missy and Adam, for the pain and suffering each of them must have experienced, for all those years Seth had closed his heart off because he was terrified of losing someone else he loved.

When her tears finally subsided, Seth was watching her with a sad expression.

She sniffled and wiped her eyes. "What?"

"Let's just get it over with," he said grimly.

"Get what over with?"

"The good-bye."

She nearly fell off his lap. "What are you talking about?"

"I yelled at your son. I made him *cry*."

She couldn't deny that the thought of someone reducing her son to tears unleashed her maternal claws, but she forced herself to retract the mom talons and look at the situation through a different lens. Her gaze shifted to the article on the table, focusing on the smiling boy in the baseball uniform. Then she imagined Jason bounding up to Seth in such a similar outfit, and she couldn't help but empathize with Seth, couldn't help but understand where his irrational response had stemmed from.

"Did you apologize to Jason?" she asked.

He nodded. "We worked everything out. All three of us."

Remembering the adorable scene she'd come home to, Miranda had to smile. "I noticed."

"The rugrats and I are good. I think…" He looked a touch amazed. "I think we might actually be friends now. But I understand if you don't want me to be around them again."

She eyed him sternly. "Do you plan on yelling at either of my children again?"

"Never," he swore.

"Will you ever make them cry?"

"Never. Well, unless I'm ripping a Band-Aid off real fast or something, but you can't hold tears like that against me."

Her heart squeezed. "I think the most important question I should ask is, now that you've spent some time with them, do you want them in your life?"

"Yes," he said simply.

"Then there's no reason to say good-bye, now is there?"

Hope flickered in his eyes. "You mean that?"

"I mean it." A smile tickled her lips. "So here's another question for you—Seth Masterson, will you be my boyfriend?"

Chapter Nineteen

July

THE MONTH OF JULY FLEW BY SO FAST MIRANDA WONDERED IF MAYBE she'd blacked out for a portion of it. Somehow, it was now the night before the summer recital, and of course, disaster had to strike the second she patted herself on the back in the belief that everything would go smoothly tomorrow.

"What do you mean you ripped your costume?" she demanded, unable to comprehend why her daughter sounded so calm. Normally Sophie would be freaking out. "How bad is it?"

There was a pause on the other end of the line. Miranda had left the twins at the apartment with Seth while she'd driven back to the school to meet with the other instructors and finalize the details for tomorrow night's big event. Now she was heading home, where a torn costume apparently awaited her.

"It's very bad," Sophie said in a frank tone.

"It's not bad at all," Seth's muffled voice called.

Miranda released an annoyed breath. "Wait—is it bad or not? Put Seth on the phone."

He came on the line a second later. "Don't worry, babe, it's just a minor tear and some sequins popped off. I'm handling it."

Her eyebrows rose. "You're handling it?" The unmistakable whir of her sewing machine filled the extension. "Are you *sewing* Sophie's costume?"

"Duh. How the fu—how else do you expect me to patch it up? Using duct tape?"

"You're sewing," she repeated, dumbfounded.

"Miranda, I grew up in a Las Vegas dressing room. I know my way around sewing machines. And a needle and thread—I'll definitely have to stitch those sequins back on by hand. I'm hanging up the phone now. You're distracting me."

A click sounded in her ear.

Wow. Just wow.

Then again, it probably shouldn't surprise her that Seth had entered into this relationship with the same gung-ho attitude and intensity he committed to all his other endeavors. The man never ceased to amaze her, though. This past month, he'd completely debunked her conviction that bad boys made terrible boyfriends. He'd been attentive, sweet, quick to offer his assistance, and more than willing to hang out with the twins while she was at work.

She wasn't sure if he'd finally let go of the guilt and blame, or if maybe the simple act of sharing his grief with her had lightened some of the load, but since the night he'd told her about his brother, Seth had become a different person around her kids. He played catch with Jason, attended Sophie's tea parties, took them out for ice cream. Sometimes he picked them up from school if he finished early at the base, other times he'd surprise them in the evening by showing up with dinner.

No doubt about it, Miranda was enjoying this new lighthearted Seth. But that didn't mean the old Seth had up and disappeared—her mocking, arrogant badass still simmered beneath the surface, usually making an appearance at night, when the twins were asleep and he could have his wicked way with her.

Come to think of it, that sounded very appealing at the moment. Maybe after she dragged him away from the sewing machine they could find some time to be wicked to each other.

When she got home, her daughter greeted her at the door, beaming like a Christmas tree. "Look, Mom, Sef fixed it!"

Sophie did a little spin. The sequins on the top half of her leotard winked in the hall light, while the filmy blue skirt swirled around her knobby knees.

"Let me see." She stilled her daughter's twirling body and squatted to search for the damaged part of the fabric. But for the life of her, she couldn't find it.

"That good, huh?"

She lifted her head to see Seth smirking at her. His black hair had grown out over the past month, curling under his ears in a scruffy way, and he wore his trademark black T-shirt and cargo pants. With his feet bare and his jaw prickly with beard growth, he made a seriously sexy picture.

"I can't find a single flaw," she admitted. "The stitching is impeccable."

"That's because I'm awesome." He shot her a cocky grin.

Rolling her eyes, she stood up and reached for her daughter's hand. "You should be in bed," she said. "It's past nine. Where's Jase?"

"Already in bed," Seth replied. "I tucked him in a while ago. But Soph was too excited to sleep."

"I get to dance tomorrow!" Sophie said happily.

Miranda smiled. "Yes, you do. And you know what you get to do now?"

"What?"

"Sleep," she said sternly. She glanced at Seth. "I'll be back. Thanks for taking care of the costume."

"My pleasure." His eyes smoldered the second the word *pleasure* left his mouth.

Their gazes collided. Miranda's entire body got warm and tingly as anticipation began to form.

"Come on, Soph, time for bed."

She practically dragged her daughter away, while Seth's soft chuckle wafted from behind.

When she and Sophie reached the twins' bedroom, Miranda's phone buzzed in the back pocket of her jeans. She pulled it out and checked the display, grinning when she saw who it was from.

When she read the message, she nearly choked on her own tongue.

Taking a quick shower. Wait for me in bed. Be naked.

Her cheeks heated up when a follow-up text popped up.

And don't even think about getting yourself off before I get there.

Oh my.

MIRANDA HAD LEFT THE BEDROOM DOOR AJAR WHEN SETH SKULKED up to it wearing nothing but a towel. His footsteps made no sound on the hardwood, his breathing so quiet he himself couldn't hear it. One of the many benefits of being a SEAL—he could transform into a ghost when he wanted to.

He peered through the crack in the door, hot lust clamping over his groin like an iron fist when he saw what his woman was up to.

She was naked just as he'd ordered, her long limbs sprawled on the puffy white comforter. She lay in the ultimate pinup girl pose, with one arm crooked behind her head, her legs parted and a knee propped up, providing him with a candid view of her delectable pussy. Her eyes were closed, her perfect breasts rising and falling with each breath she took. She was stroking herself, but he could tell it wasn't a race to the finish. More of an idle exploration, fingers lightly brushing her clit and gliding up and down her slit.

As his cock thickened beneath his towel, he stepped into the bedroom without making a sound. Miranda didn't stir and her eyes remained shut. He would've loved to announce his presence by latching his mouth on her clit, but the bedroom door decided to betray his presence—it creaked the second he started to close it.

Miranda's eyes snapped open and her fingers quit stroking as she gasped.

He grinned. "Don't stop on my account."

"Holy shit, Seth. I didn't even hear the water stop. How long have you been standing there?"

"Long enough."

She looked more impressed than upset. "That's a mighty useful skill to have, Masterson. Maybe I should become a SEAL so I can learn to sneak up on people like that."

He flipped the lock and closed in on the bed, pausing at the foot of it. "Did you get all the recital details squared away?"

"Sure did."

"What about the asshole's daughter? Is she going to dance in the show?"

"She is, but Catherine's mother said her ex-husband is out of town, so he won't make it." Miranda snorted. "I think Porter's just too much of a wuss to face me."

"After you dumped him on your first date, you mean?"

"Funny."

"I thought so." He toyed with the edge of his towel. "You know, I never got to hear you say it."

"Say what?"

"That I was right. I told you that slimebag wanted you." He lifted his brows, daring her to defy him. "So let's hear you say it, babe."

After a long pause, she yielded to him. "You were right, Seth."

As much as he liked hearing those words come out of her mouth, he hated the thought of some sleazebag lusting over Miranda. A streak of possessiveness shot through him, followed by a rush of anger that sizzled in his bloodstream. His gaze gravitated to the luscious female body stretched out on the bed before him, and suddenly the only thought that registered in his head was *mine*. This woman was *his*.

His fingers trembled as he reached for his towel again. He let the soft terry cloth drop to the floor, enjoying the lust that flared in Miranda's eyes.

"I want your mouth on my cock," he said roughly.

She was off the bed and scrambling to her knees in a nanosecond.

Smiling, he twined a strand of her hair around his finger and said, "Eager much?"

"Very much," she murmured. And then she opened her mouth, and his blood burned hot. Fuck, that was sexy.

Without a word, he guided his erection to her waiting mouth. She wrapped her lips around his shaft and made a soft humming noise that vibrated along his flesh and made his balls tingle.

"That's nice," he muttered when she delicately licked a circle around the crown. "Keep teasing me, baby."

She kept teasing. Tongue darting out only to quickly retreat. Lips closing over his tip only to flit away before he could thrust deep.

Her fingers stroked his aching balls, her loose brown hair brushing his thighs and tickling his knees. He tangled his hands in her silky hair, but he didn't take control of the encounter, no matter how badly he wanted to push all the way to the back of her throat and fuck her mouth until he came.

"I love your cock." Her breathy whisper heated his shaft, which was slick with saliva and precome.

"That's good, because my cock loves you," he rasped.

She laughed before getting to her feet. She gently stroked his erection, laying her other palm directly over his left pec. "Your heart's racing," she noted.

"Are you surprised? You're getting me kinda excited here."

She squeezed the tip of his cock, and another clear drop of fluid seeped out. She rubbed her thumb over it and smiled. "Hmmm. You *are* excited."

His hands, which had been idle until now, cupped her bare tits and did some squeezing of their own. When he toyed with her nipples, getting them nice and stiff, Miranda responded with a sharp intake of breath. Then he pinched those distended buds, eliciting another gasp.

"You like a little bit of pain?" He studied her passion-glazed eyes.

She nodded wordlessly.

Intrigued, he bent to capture one nipple with his mouth. He flicked his tongue over the tip, then grazed it with his teeth, taking a gentle bite. Miranda jerked in surprise, then moaned when he soothed the sting by rubbing his lips over the pretty pink pearl.

"Do that again," she begged.

Pure male satisfaction coursed through his blood. Chuckling, he repeated the process on her other nipple, summoning the same excited response. He moved a hand between her legs and discovered that she was wetter than ever. Oh yeah.

As he teased her with the tip of his finger, Miranda kept jacking his dick, her strokes lazy, tender.

Bringing his hand between them, he wrapped his fist around hers and squeezed hard. "I'm in the mood for rough tonight, babe. Jerk me harder."

Her movements became faster, forceful enough that he groaned. He pushed his finger into her pussy, curving the tip and stroking that sweet spot deep inside, the one guaranteed to make her moan. His other hand played with a breast, pinching and toying with her nipple.

When Miranda began grinding into his hand, Seth couldn't handle a second more of foreplay. "I need to be in you. Now," he ordered.

"God. Yes." She shifted around and grabbed for something on the comforter, a position that put her perfect ass on display and made his mouth water.

She turned back with a condom in her hand. Seth tore it open and had the latex on in a nanosecond, but rather than throw Miranda on the bed, he gripped her waist and spun her around.

"I'm going to fuck you from behind." He pressed his erection against her ass and rolled his hips.

She responded with a moan and wiggled her cute butt, straining to get closer.

Bending her over the bedframe, he admired the arc of her spine, the flexibility of her dancer's body. One day they'd have to explore all the delicious positions those flexible limbs of hers had to offer, but tonight he was too impatient for experimentation.

He slid into her in one fast stroke, filling her to the hilt. Her wet heat surrounded him, her inner muscles clutching him so tightly he realized there was no chance in hell of taking this slow.

"Tell me if I hurt you," he mumbled, and then he pulled out and slammed right back in, so hard she cried out.

"We have to be quiet, baby." He ran a soothing hand over the curve of her ass. "You okay? Did that hurt?"

"No. It felt amazing."

He wished he could see her face. She must have sensed he needed reassurance because she twisted her head and shot him a faint smile. "I'm serious. I want it hard and rough tonight." Her face blazed with scorching, needy desire. "Now make me come."

He narrowed his eyes. "You getting sassy with me, woman?"

"Yep. You got a problem with that?"

"Not in the slightest. Sass turns me on."

He started to move, gripping her ass as he rammed into her with absolutely no mercy. Each stroke went deep, sending him closer and closer to the edge. The slap of their bodies echoed in the air, accompanied by erratic breathing and Miranda's soft moans, which grew more and more agitated by the second.

When he saw her hand dart between her legs to rub her clit, he growled and quickened his pace, desperate to feel her pussy clench from her orgasm.

His own release gathered in his balls, but he held off, waiting, fucking her harder, urging her with husky commands to let go. When she came, he felt it in his cock, her muscles clenching and unclenching, milking him so hard he came without warning. His vision blurred, heart thudding uncontrollably as he lost himself in the mind-shattering sensations.

Eventually he collapsed on her, his sweat-soaked chest sticking to her sweat-soaked back. Groaning, he flung one arm around her chest and climbed up on the bed, then rolled them over so they were spooning.

He was so blissfully content, so utterly sated that his blood was humming and his heartbeat had slowed to a lazy tempo. And maybe that body-numbing release had shorted out his brain and messed with the wiring up there, because that was the only explanation he had for the words that slipped out of his mouth.

"I love you."

Miranda shifted around in surprise, and when her entire face lit up, he realized a fried brain was *not* the reason he'd said those words. Not by a long shot.

"I love you," he repeated.

The light in her eyes shone brighter. She brought a hand to his cheek and gave it a gentle stroke. "I love you too."

Chapter Twenty

August

"I can't believe what I'm seeing."

Dylan glanced over at Jen and rolled his eyes. "Would you stop saying that? You sound like a broken record."

"I'll stop only when you provide me with a logical explanation for *that*." Jen pointed a dainty finger at the frolic fest happening in front of them.

He followed her gaze, and yeah, even he had to admit that seeing Seth horsing around in the pool with Miranda's children was pretty frickin' surreal. But unlike Jen and the rest of their friends, Dylan lived with the guy, so he'd had more time to come to terms with Seth's transformation. If you could even call it that. Truth was, Seth was the same cocky, sarcastic smartass he'd always been. He wisely toned that side of himself down when he was around the twins, but as far as Dylan was concerned, the only differences in Masterson were that he now seemed to like kids, and that he was madly in love with Miranda Breslin.

"She's right," Jackson drawled, overhearing Jen's last remark. "This is weird and unnatural."

The tall Texan sat on the edge of Jen's lounge chair, the beer bottle in his hand dripping with condensation. It was sweltering hot, so Dylan had suggested they hang out at the pool over at Cash and O'Connor's building. It was only supposed to be him, Seth, Miranda and the kids, but somehow the little soiree had ended up tripling in size.

Cash, Jen and Matt had appeared in their swimsuits, and Jackson had decided to stop by too. Then Ryan Evans and his girlfriend Annabelle had come down from their third-floor apartment to join the group, and, not long after, Carson and Holly Scott made an appearance, carrying huge platters of food.

The concrete deck ringing the rectangular pool offered white lounge chairs and a handful of tables with umbrellas that provided some shade, and the area was now teeming with SEALs and their wives and girlfriends. Oh, and two highly energized six-year-olds who were currently being tossed around like beach balls by Cash and Ryan, leaving Seth free to swim away and corner the children's mother in the deep end.

"Cut Seth a break," Dylan said with a grin. "He's in love. Which is perfectly *un*weird and very natural. Even smartasses are allowed to be happy."

Jackson sighed enviously. "Who wouldn't be happy with a woman as fine-looking as that warming your bed?" His whiskey-colored eyes rested on Miranda, who was treading water with Seth at the edge of the pool, laughing at something he'd said.

Dylan followed Jackson's gaze. He had to admit, Miranda did look mighty fine in that black string bikini. Shit, so did Annabelle, he realized, when his gaze shifted to the curvy brunette whose full breasts were practically pouring out of a low-cut, red one-piece. He shifted his gaze and noted that Holly's perky ass looked incredible in her boy-short bottoms. And Jen, in her skimpy yellow two-piece, made for a tantalizing sight too.

Son of a bitch. He was in need of sex in a dire way.

Jen caught him staring and raised one delicate eyebrow. "Is there a reason why you're checking out every woman in this pool?"

"Other than the fact that he's a man?" Jackson answered for him.

"I don't see *you* doing any ogling. Does that mean you're not a man, Texas?" she asked sweetly.

"Oh, I've been ogling, sugar. I'm just not as obvious as Wade over here." Jackson's tone grew distracted, his gaze elsewhere. "Oh nice, there's still some ribs left." The big man got up and absently ambled off to the table where Holly had left all the food.

The second they were alone, Jen snapped into interrogation mode. "So?"

Dylan feigned innocence. "What?"

"Are you really going to play dumb?"

"Are you really going to make me talk about it *here*?" He shot a discreet look in the direction of the pool.

She waved her hand. "No one's paying us any attention. So spill."

"There's nothing to spill." He reached for the beer he'd set on the deck and brought it to his lips.

"But isn't he—" she lowered her voice, "—isn't he supposed to come home this weekend?"

Frustration lodged in Dylan's throat. "Nope. He has to stay in D.C. for another month."

"Aw, really? That sucks!"

No kidding. He'd been trying not to dwell on it ever since he'd read Aidan's disappointing email last night. For the past month, he'd been distracting himself by training, hanging out with the boys, and hitting the clubs, but he hadn't gotten laid since Aidan left town, and hadn't intended to. Now, with the grim knowledge that relief was still another month away, he might have to rectify his celibate status and give one of his regular hook-ups a call.

"But when he gets back, you're going to…?" She grinned, letting the question hang.

"I don't know. We'll see what happens."

"Don't forget what I said about taking pictures."

"Don't forget what I said about 'fuck off, Jen'." He punctuated that by flashing his middle finger.

She threw her head back and laughed. "Fine. But I still expect details."

Fortunately, his phone rang before he had to give her the finger again. But then he saw his brother's number and stifled a sigh. If Chris was calling to announce that Claire was pregnant or some shit, Dylan was going to flip.

"My brother," he told Jen as he rose from his chair. "I'll be back."

He walked to a quieter location on the manicured lawn away from the pool, the grass warm and soft beneath his bare feet. "Hey, man, what's up?"

"Nothing much. Did I catch you at a bad time?"

"Not really. I'm just hanging out at my buddy's pool. I've got a minute to talk, though."

"Oh, good. I wanted to let you know that Claire and I will be in town at the beginning of September. It's only for one night—I've got a meeting with one of the senior partners at our firm's San Diego location." Chris paused. "I was hoping we could stay with you."

"Of course," he said, making an effort to hide his lack of enthusiasm.

Last time Chris and Claire stayed at the house, the woman hadn't uttered more than five words to him. He was so not in the mood to deal with Little Miss Ice Queen again, but what was the alternative? Force his only brother to stay in a hotel?

"Great," Chris said, sounding excited. "We're coming in on September first. We'll take a cab from the airport, so don't worry about picking us up."

"Okay, but if you end up needing a ride, let me know."

"Will do."

After he hung up, Dylan stood there for a moment, his gaze taking in the flurry of activity happening across the lawn. In the pool, Sophie was shrieking with delight as Cash and Seth played a game of human catch with her, while Jason splashed around in the shallow end with Ryan and Annabelle. Carson had stolen Dylan's lounge chair and was chatting with his sister. Over by the tables, Holly's green eyes were animated as she spoke with Miranda and Matt, who were both laughing their asses off.

At times like these, he was so incredibly grateful for the life he'd built for himself here in San Diego. Joining the navy, undergoing SEAL training, forging a bond with his teammates…best decisions he'd ever made.

He suddenly had to wonder if getting involved with Aidan was a decision that would fall under that same category, or if it'd end up being a huge mistake. Screwing around with a random guy, sure, probably wouldn't result in much. But what if he embarked on a sexual relationship with Aidan only for it to blow up in his face? For it to end in a messy, catastrophic way that ensured everyone he knew found out?

Chewing the inside of his cheek, he tried to quell the troubling questions. No point in overthinking any of this. He and Aidan had already opened that door. The explosive kiss they'd shared last month made it impossible to turn back now.

Anticipation coiled tight, tormenting his cock. Definitely no turning back. He might have to wait another month, but he still had every intention of walking right through that door and seeing where it led him.

Miranda couldn't believe the number of calls she was getting. Ever since the summer recital, her phone was ringing off the hook with parents wanting to enroll their kids at All That Dance, and nearly all of them had been referred by existing clients. The parents who'd attended the recital had been thrilled with their children's progress, and several of them had brought Miranda and the other teachers flowers after the show. She was thrilled about how well the show had gone, not just because it had led to an influx of business, but because she was genuinely proud of all the kids who'd participated.

When she'd left Vegas, this was exactly what she'd hoped for. She truly had loved dancing on that big stage at the Paradise Theater. Contrary to what a lot of people believed, the theater's performances had been more *A Chorus Line* than *Showgirls*, and sometimes Miranda still missed the bright lights and deafening applause and elaborate costumes. But she'd gotten tired of working six nights a week and constantly leaving the twins with babysitters. If they were at school during the day and she was at work during the night, how were they ever supposed to spend time together? Now that they were getting older, it was even more important for her to be a strong presence in their lives. Unfortunately, that hadn't been possible in Vegas.

But now it *was* possible. Hell, nothing seemed impossible anymore.

Smiling to herself, she listened to the latest message in her voice mail and jotted down the details, adding to the growing list of calls she had to return. Through the glass sliding door, she saw Seth and Sophie in the backyard, putting seeds in the bird feeder. Her smile widened, taking on a dreamy quality as she fixed her gaze on Seth's sexy ass, which looked exceptionally yummy in his snug gray board shorts. It was Sunday evening and they'd already eaten dinner, courtesy of Seth, who'd offered to cook because she'd come home from the dance school sore and exhausted.

A loud shriek jolted her back to the present. Sophie was sprinting toward the sliding door, and either Miranda was hearing things, or Seth was actually shouting, "I'll cover you!"

Both of them were breathing heavily as they burst into the kitchen. Sophie made a beeline for her mother and threw herself into her arms. "It tried to kill me, Mom!"

She smoothed the top of Sophie's head in a reassuring caress. "What are you talking about? What happened?"

Seth approached the counter, shaking his head in amazement. "She's right, babe. That fricking bird has a vendetta against her. I saw it with my own eyes."

"It just flied into my head and tried to steal my barrette!" Sophie said, her eyes filling with tears.

"*Flew* into your head," she corrected, then knelt down to wipe her daughter's tears. "Are you okay? Did it peck you?" Wow. What a question to be asking your child.

"I'm okay. Sef saved me." Now dry-eyed, Sophie walked over to the table to get her doll, then wandered out of the kitchen chattering away to herself.

Once Sophie was gone, Seth headed for the fridge to grab a beer. "Miranda, this isn't a joke. We need to burn that bird feeder. That psycho sparrow could've really hurt her."

The genuine concern in his voice floored her. Sometimes she still couldn't wrap her head around the fact that Seth actually cared about her kids. She suspected he was even starting to love them. The way he loved her.

Warmth circled her heart. It had taken a while, but the apprehension she'd felt about dating Seth had finally withered away. After she'd told him she loved him, she'd instantly wished she could take the words back—not because she didn't mean them, but because saying them out loud made everything feel so...real. She hadn't wanted to love Seth. She hadn't wanted to love any man. For the past seven years, she'd been on her own, and she'd been doing just fine. So why rock the boat? Why open her heart to a man and risk being let down?

But Seth had proved time and again these past couple of months that she could count on him. He was there for her. He was there for her kids. Nowadays, she couldn't imagine not having him in her life. Not seeing his mocking grin anymore, or hearing his raspy voice, or feeling his powerful arms around her.

Seth twisted off the bottle cap and sipped his beer. She'd started stocking the fridge with beer for the nights he stayed over, which were starting to be a lot. So often, in fact, that he had his own toothbrush in her bathroom now.

"Does one of us need to pick up the rugrat?" he asked. He'd taken to calling the kids that again, but now he said it with affection rather than scorn.

"No, Coach Diaz is dropping him off."

She knew Jason was disappointed that she and Seth hadn't made it to his Little League game. She usually managed to show up halfway into the game, sometimes earlier if she broke a few traffic laws, but her afternoon ballet class had run late today. And Seth had gone to the beach to work out with a few other SEALs, so he'd been MIA too.

"Oh, I forgot to tell you. I'm going to be scarce for the next few days." Seth's expression displayed a hint of regret.

"How come?"

"We're going to the desert again. Doing some mock extractions, I think." He set the beer on the counter. "We go wheels-up at oh-dark-hundred hours, so I don't think I should crash here tonight."

"Yeah, probably not," she agreed. "Tomorrow is the one day we all get to sleep in."

Ironically, that day was Monday, which most of the world dreaded. But the twins' school didn't open until noon on Mondays, and she didn't teach any classes at the studio, so that meant none of them had to get up early. Still, she'd miss waking up in Seth's arms.

"You know, we could solve all our problems with one easy move."

She raised her eyebrows. "We have problems? Plural?"

"Well, just one." He yanked her into his arms and rested his hands on her lower back, seductively stroking the strip of exposed skin where her tank top had ridden up. "I want you around all the time."

Miranda was momentarily distracted by the delicious way his rough-skinned fingers traveled over her flesh. "You're saying that's a problem? Wanting me around?"

"The problem is that you're *not* around. And the solution is simple." He met her eyes. "Maybe we should all get a place together."

Shock slammed into her. "Are you serious?"

He nodded. "I'd suggest I move in here with you guys, but this place is too tiny, and I need enough space for all my workout equipment and my gear."

She was still trying to absorb it all. "What about Dylan? You're just going to abandon him?"

"Our lease is up in November, so we just wouldn't renew it. Or he could renew and find a new roommate. Or Dylan could move out and you guys could move in. There're a lot of options."

Wow. Living together. The notion was scary as hell, but it also sent a thrill soaring through her.

"I...would have to give it some thought," she finally said. "A lot of thought."

He grinned. "That's exactly what I knew you would say. But I figured I'd bring it up anyway." He dipped his head and brushed his lips over hers, the prickly stubble on his jaw scratching her chin. "You've got until November to mull it over. No rush. Just know that the option is there."

Chapter Twenty-One

September

CLAIRE MCKINLEY WAS INFURIATINGLY ATTRACTIVE. GORGEOUS, EVEN, which only pissed Dylan off further as he took the overnight bag she handed him, and lugged it to the spare bedroom. She'd only been in his presence for five minutes, and he already wanted her to leave.

Though in the woman's defense, his brother *was* being a bit of a dick.

"I don't have a choice. He had a last-minute emergency so the meeting was cancelled." Chris's soothing voice drifted out of the living room. "And the senior partner invited me to join him at the country club for a round of golf. Was I just supposed to say no?"

"Yes," Claire shot back. "It's one thing to dump me off on your brother while you have a legitimate business meeting to attend, but you're blowing me off for golf? Can't you see how that might be a tad annoying, Chris?"

His brother didn't have the decency to sound remorseful. "When the senior partner invites you to his club, you say yes, end of story."

After taking a calming breath, Dylan pasted on a happy face and strode back into the living room. "Your bags are in your room." AKA *fuck you, big brother, for turning me into your damn bellhop.*

"Thanks," Chris said absently.

Claire didn't say anything.

Dylan studied her discreetly, wondering what his brother saw in the woman yet at the same time knowing *exactly* what Chris saw in her. The woman was sex on stilettos. She had reddish-brown hair that cascaded down her back in long waves, enormous amber-colored eyes, a cupid's-bow mouth that was made to be wrapped around a man's cock. And she was packing a lotta sweet, sweet curves beneath her sleek black business suit.

"Did I hear something about your meeting being cancelled?" Dylan said casually.

Chris nodded. "The partner I was supposed to meet bailed. So I'm playing golf instead."

"Should we go out for dinner later?" He made sure to include Claire in the offer by sparing her a pithy glance.

"I'm having dinner at the club with the senior partner, and then he mentioned something about a cigar lounge. I'm not sure when I'll be back tonight."

As much as he hated feeling even an ounce of sympathy for the Ice Queen, Dylan understood why she looked so pissed off. Chris really *was* abandoning her.

"So you'll be spending the entire day and night hanging out at a country club?" Dylan eyed his brother warily.

"Such is the life of a corporate lawyer," Claire spoke up. Her voice was tighter than a drum. "Just think, Chris, you wouldn't get to experience these luxuries if you'd taken that job at the public defender's office."

Dylan picked up on a note of displeasure in her voice—directed at *him*. And just when he thought he'd imagined it, Claire actually scowled at him.

WTF? What did *he* have to do with Chris turning down a public service job and choosing to suck on the corporate teat?

"As you can see, my fiancée isn't very happy with me at the moment," Chris said wryly. He wrapped his arm around Claire's shoulders and offered that puppy-dog grin Dylan had seen him flash to get out of trouble during their entire childhood. "Don't be mad at me, dear."

Dear? Had they moved into an old folks' home without telling him?

"You know what a great opportunity this is," Chris went on. "And it's not like you'll be alone. You can spend some time with Dylan, get to know your future brother-in-law."

Both Dylan and Claire cringed, but Chris didn't seem to notice.

"I have that carnival thing tonight, remember?" Dylan said, not bothering to hide the relief on his face. No way would Claire want to spend her evening at such a lowbrow event.

"Hey, that's great. You love carnivals," Chris said to the redhead. He glanced back at Dylan. "She's always trying to get me to go to the carnival near the pier, the one you used to drag me to when we were kids? But you know how I feel about those places. So tacky and boring—" Something buzzed and Chris removed his phone from the pocket of his blazer. "Shoot, gotta take this. You two hammer out the details."

As Chris waltzed off, Dylan sized up his future sister-in-law the way he assessed a mission's potential threat level.

"You don't have to come," he said graciously.

"You don't want me to come," she corrected.

Their eyes met in a Wild West standoff.

She drew first blood. "Look. I don't like you, but Chris wants us to get along, so you know what? Fine. Let's just go to this stupid carnival, win him a big stuffed panda, and come home raving about what a super-awesome-fantastic time we had, okay?"

"I don't like you either."

"You just had to get that in there, didn't you?"

"Thought it was only fair that you knew the feeling was completely mutual, honey."

"Don't call me honey."

"Would you rather I called you *dear*?" He snorted. "What are you, an eighty-two-year-old woman?"

Her cheeks flushed with anger, almost matching the color of her hair. "You know what? Maybe I'll stay here and we can just pretend I went to the carnival."

"Scared that you might fall in love with me?" he mocked.

"Worried I might strangle you," she shot back.

"Then we're in the same boat, honey."

"*Don't* call me that."

"Right, I forgot. Sorry, cupcake."

She looked ready to murder him. Fortunately, Chris slid back into the living room before any dead bodies hit the floor.

Immediately, Dylan and Claire pasted on some smiles.

"Everything okay here?" Chris looked from one to the other.

"We're great," he said cheerfully.

"Super," she agreed. Her happy mask shifted for a second to reveal a flicker of extreme reluctance. "We're going to a carnival tonight. It's going to be so much fun."

"So much fun," Dylan echoed. "We're excited to get to know each other better. Isn't that right, honey?"

Her jaw clenched for a second before relaxing. "Uh-huh. I can't wait."

SETH ACCEPTED THE PIECE OF COTTON CANDY JASON HELD UP TO HIM and popped it in his mouth. The sugary sweetness melted on his tongue and brought forth an image of the dentist's chair he and the twins would be sitting on in the near future.

He wished Miranda were here. She was much better at saying no to her children. He, on the other hand, let those imps walk all over him. He'd already bought them cotton candy, popcorn and snow cones, but he was determined to say no to the next sweet treat they begged for, because at that point, he'd be worrying less about cavities and more about vomit.

"Can we ride the ferry wheel again?" Sophie tugged on his hand to get his attention.

"Ferris wheel," he corrected. "And the answer to that is *heck yes*."

She giggled.

"Jase, you want to ride the Ferris wheel?"

The boy shook his head. "I wanna win a goldfish."

"All right." He searched the crowd for Dylan, finally spotting the blond SEAL near the railing of a nearby ride. "Wade! You two mind taking Jason over to games while Soph and I go up on the wheel one more time?"

"No prob. Get over here, squirt."

Jason dashed off toward Dylan, who'd come in Miranda's place and ended up bringing a smoking-hot redhead along. Seth had been ready to high-five his buddy for a job well done—until Dylan introduced the chick as his brother's fiancée. The two of them had been bickering like cats and dogs since the moment they'd shown up, making him long for Miranda even more.

"I wish Mom was here," Sophie said as he scooped her into the ride car and slung an arm around her.

The safety bar locked into place, and then the car began its slow ascent, each rise providing a better view of the busy carnival grounds. The scent of deep-fried food, popcorn and sugar permeated the evening air. The sun had just set, and the bright neon lights on the rides down below twinkled in the dusky night.

"I wish she was here too," he agreed. "But she had to work."

Miranda had been bummed about it. Normally she didn't start work until seven or eight, but the club was hosting a private party that had begun at five o'clock, so she'd headed over there right after she finished up at the school. Since this was the last night the carnival was in town, Seth had offered to take the twins himself, and now he was glad he had. The kids were having a great time. And honestly? So was he.

It still amazed him, how different things were. How different he *felt*. Telling Miranda about Adam had been the most liberating thing he'd ever done. The second he'd given her that article, voiced his fears and insecurities, it was like a weight was lifted off his chest. Miranda had said it wasn't his fault. A tiny part of him even believed her. But a bigger part knew she was wrong—he *was* responsible for Adam's abduction. That certainty hadn't changed.

But Miranda had made him feel like there was hope for him after all. Her trust in him made him want to trust himself.

"Soooo pretty," Sophie gushed as she peered down at the lights.

Her small hand slipped into his, and his chest tightened with emotion. Shit, he was starting to care something fierce for these rugrats. Sophie was the smartest, sassiest girl he'd ever met, and Jason was so damn energetic, so eager to please and quick to smile.

Five months ago, he wouldn't have dreamed that he'd be atop a Ferris wheel with a six-year-old nestled against him, yet here he was, doing exactly that—and actually enjoying himself.

When the ride came to an end, he lifted Sophie into his arms and made his way to the games area. Didn't take long to find the rest of their party. Jason had abandoned his quest for a goldfish—he and Dylan were at the shooting gallery now, whooping up a storm and shooting BBs at a slew of metal chickens that rapidly popped up as they flew along a motorized loop.

"Where's Claire?" Seth asked, looking around.

"Restroom," Dylan replied without taking his eyes off the targets. "Even bee-otches need to pee."

Jason looked curious. "What's a bee-otch?"

"It's a word you're going to forget and never mention again," Dylan said cheerfully.

"Sef, come shoot!" Jason begged, promptly forgetting about his pursuit of the definition of bee-otch.

"But I wanna see the pony," Sophie whined, pulling on the collar of his T-shirt.

He set her down on the ground. "We're going to the petting zoo when we're ready to leave," he reminded her. "Because it's all the way on the other side of the carnival near where we came in, remember?"

She pouted. "But I wanna go now."

"Soon," he promised, playfully pulling on her ponytail. "Right now, why don't we shoot some chickens with your brother? It'll be fun."

"But I don't wanna shoot chickens."

He stifled a groan. "Then you can watch us for a bit."

"But I don't wanna—"

"Jase didn't want to ride the Ferris wheel but I took you anyway, remember?" Seth said gruffly. "So now it's your turn to let your brother do something *he* wants, and then we'll all go to see the ponies together. Cool beans?"

After a beat, Sophie grudgingly said, "Cool beans."

He lifted her up on the counter right next to the shooting station and handed her the bag of cotton candy. "You can witness firsthand what awesome aim I have," he told her.

Seth gave the kid manning the booth a five-dollar bill and reached for a rifle. For the next ten minutes, he and Dylan showed Jason how it was done. The air was alive with metallic *ping* noises as BBs spat out of the weapons and collided with the targets. Jason was cheering loudly, having declared himself on Team Seth, while Sophie took pity on Dylan and rooted for him.

The two SEALs didn't miss a single shot, so the contest eventually became about which spot on the chicken they could hit.

"Now hit the beak!" Jason ordered.

Seth pulled the trigger with ease. *Ping.* Perfect beak shot.

Dylan nailed it too.

"The feet!"

Ping. Ping.

After every shot, he'd glance at Sophie from the corner of his eye to make sure she wasn't up to any funny business. Every quick look revealed a flash of pink—her T-shirt and the cotton candy she was stuffing in her mouth.

"Sef, show me how to aim better," Jason demanded.

He knelt down. "First thing, you have to hold the rifle properly. We take this hand—" he reached for Jason's right hand, "—and put it here, and your other hand here on the undergrip of the weapon. And we want the butt—"

Jason giggled.

"The butt of the rifle," Seth said, rolling his eyes. "We want to rest it here, on your shoulder, and not in your armpit like you were doing before. Now…"

He gave Jason a few more tips about how to better aim, then stood up and watched as the little boy took a shot. *Ping.* Jason hit a chicken dead center.

"Sweet!" Dylan raved.

"Very nice," Seth agreed. "Did you see that, Soph? Your brother just—"

Sophie was gone.

He had to blink a couple of times to be sure. But no. She wasn't there. Only the bag of cotton candy remained.

His heart stopped.

"Sophie!" Panic clawed up his throat. "Dylan, Sophie's gone."

The other man instantly went on the alert. "Are you fucking kidding me?"

"No, I'm not fucking kidding you," he spat out.

As his pulse shrieked like a whistle in his head, he scooped Jason into his arms, ignoring the kid's startled yelp.

Holding the boy tight, Seth scanned the crowd for Sophie. Miranda had dressed both kids in the brightest colors known to man—a neon pink tee for Sophie, a neon green one for Jason. She insisted that as dorky as they were, the T-shirts would ensure the kids stood out like billboards in a crowd.

"Look for a pink shirt," Seth ordered, finding it difficult to hear himself speak over the pounding of his heart.

He searched the mob of people cluttering the carnival grounds. Blue shirts, white shirts, black, red, pink—nope, different kid. He continued scanning and dismissing, his panic intensifying each time he struck out.

Holy Mother of God. He'd lost Miranda's daughter.

Sophie was *gone*.

Everything got very, very quiet. The chatter of the families around them. The bells and whistles and clangs and dings in the game area. The happy shrieks and whoops echoing from the rides area. It all faded into a dull, muffled hiss.

And every single person in the crowd turned into Jarvis Henderson.

"Seth. Yo, dude, it's fine, we'll find her."

Dylan's voice found a way into Seth's nightmare. He blinked, saw the visible concern on his friend's face.

"Sophie's gone," he mumbled.

"It's okay. We'll find her." Dylan's brother's fiancée stepped into his line of vision, her voice gentle, her hand even gentler as she touched his arm.

Jason was clinging tight to his shoulders, his face streaked with tears as he looked at Seth. "Where's Sophie?"

"I don't know, buddy." His voice cracked. The panic spiked. "But we're going to look for her. Okay?"

He glanced at the other two adults. "We split up. Dylan, check rides. Claire, keep looking here. Jase and I will head to the food area and the pett—" He stopped abruptly.

The petting zoo.

Could she have wandered off in search of the ponies she'd so desperately wanted to see?

"I might know where she is," he blurted out. "Keep your phones on. Call if you find her."

Seth took off with Jason in his arms. Dodging people left and right, he muscled his way through the crowd, wishing everyone would just drop dead. Each frantic beat of his heart bruised his ribs, ravaged his chest.

He'd lost Sophie.

He'd turned away from her for thirty seconds and now she was gone. *Should've been you, man.*

The guilt he'd harbored all these years came flooding to the surface. Goddammit. *He* should've been the one playing in the fucking yard when that sick fuck Jarvis Henderson drove up in his pickup. Adam should've been inside, watching TV. It should've been Seth's beaten and mutilated body those hikers found in the fucking desert.

He kept his eyes open for the color pink, but Sophie was nowhere to be found as he raced through the carnival. In the distance he saw the big wooden sign advertising the petting zoo.

Please let her be here. Please let her be here.

He wasn't a religious man, but he was praying to God as he neared the enclosure that housed the ponies. Praying that he didn't have to call Miranda and tell her that her daughter was gone.

"There she is!" Jason's delighted voice broke through his terrifying thoughts.

Seth nearly keeled over when he spotted her neon-pink T-shirt by the wooden fence closing off the petting zoo. Sophie stood on her tiptoes, her brown ponytail swishing back and forth as she tried to get a better look at the two black-maned horses.

A wave of relief slammed into him. "Sophie!"

She turned around and happily waved him over. "Sef! Come see the pony!"

Lingering adrenaline coursed through his blood, making his hands shake and his vision waver. He managed to pull out his phone to call Dylan, telling him and Claire to meet them here.

Sophie must have noticed the wild look in his eyes, because the joy in her eyes faded into guilt. "Uh-oh," she said.

He sucked in an unsteady breath. "Uh-oh is right."

"Your friend looked…wrecked." Claire dropped her purse on the floor in the front hall and bent down to unlace her tennis shoes.

"Sophie taking off like that really shook him up. Shook me up too," Dylan confessed.

"Yeah, me too." For the first time all evening, the antagonistic glint left her golden brown eyes, and suddenly she looked very young and very pretty. "I keep thinking about what would've happened if we hadn't found her…" Claire shuddered. "Oh God. Imagine losing a child."

Silence settled between them, not quite comfortable, but not quite hostile either.

Finally she cleared her throat. "Anyway, I'm going to bed."

"At nine o'clock? Gee, *dear*, did all the excitement get to you?"

Her lips tightened. "And he's back."

Dylan had to grin. "You know you missed me."

"Missed the smartass remarks and not-so-veiled barbs about my character? Sorry, can't say that I have." She headed for the doorway. "Good night, Dylan."

"'Night, honey."

He thoroughly enjoyed the way her back stiffened. And he couldn't help but check out her ass as she stalked off. She hadn't worn her snooty little suit to the carnival—she'd put on a pair of jeans, a gray v-neck tee, and those cute sneakers.

He had to admit, she'd impressed him earlier. They may have sniped at each other the entire time, but when that little girl had gone missing, Claire had snapped to action, calming Seth down and going to look for Sophie without hesitation.

He shut off the hall light and headed for the living room, wondering when Chris would be back. He'd literally spent a total of ten minutes with his older brother—dude had gotten off the plane, deposited Claire at the house, and raced off to a country club for golf and cigars. Dylan couldn't remember his brother ever being so...pretentious? He wasn't sure if that was the right word, but he did notice that his somewhat-conservative older brother seemed a bit more...*uppity* these days.

A knock on the door had him walking toward the front hall instead. Good. His brother was back. He wondered why Chris hadn't used the key he'd given him, but the answer became clear when Dylan opened the door and found someone else on the other side of it.

Aidan's dimpled grin hit him like a shot of whiskey. Heat traveled through him, settling in his groin.

"What are you doing here?" he asked in surprise. "Your email said you wouldn't be back for two more days."

"They didn't need me anymore so they sent me home. I came straight from the airport. I texted," Aidan added, "but you didn't respond."

"My phone died." He studied the other man's chiseled face. "You came here instead of going home first? Why would you do that?"

"Why the hell do you think?"

A current of electricity moved between them. Aidan ran a hand through his hair and leaned a broad shoulder on the doorframe. "You gonna let me in or what?"

"No."

Surprise registered on Aidan's face. "You serious?"

Dylan let out a rueful sigh. "My brother and his fiancée are here for the night. Sure, I can invite you in and we can watch TV for a while and have a beer, but we haven't seen each other in two months, and honestly, if I'm in the same room as you right now, I don't know if I'll be able to control myself, so…" He offered a shrug.

Aidan chuckled. "So I should go home and we'll see each other tomorrow."

"Glad you understand."

"Oh, I understand. I definitely understand."

Lust tightened Dylan's muscles as he stood there in the face of Aidan's hungry appraisal. The man was looking at him like he wanted to eat him up. Bastard even licked his lips.

Dylan was pretty hungry himself. Despite having just gotten off a plane, Aidan looked better than ever. The top two buttons of his white long-sleeve were unbuttoned, revealing his corded neck. And his trousers did nothing to hide the unmistakable bulge at his crotch.

"Where're your brother and his fiancée now?" Aidan's voice was low, raspy.

"Chris is out. Claire went to bed."

A second later, Aidan pushed his way into the front hall, got Dylan against the wall, and kissed the crap out of him.

It was another one of those greedy, unforgiving kisses. Aidan's tongue filled his mouth, exploring in seductive thrusts that left him breathless.

"You sleep with anyone else this summer?" The question came out of left field, but Dylan didn't see any anger in the man's eyes, only interest.

"Yes."

"Who?"

"This chick I hook up with every now and then. You?"

"Yes. A woman I know in D.C."

He found it interesting that they'd both slept with women, yet here they were, pressed up against the wall, rubbing up against each other like contented cats.

Aidan's tone held a note of contemplation. "I can't decide if I'm jealous." Those warm male lips found Dylan's again in a soft, fleeting kiss that was sexier and more potent than any tongue-tangling make-out.

"Neither of us promised to live like monks," he murmured.

Aidan nodded his agreement. "No, we didn't."

They kissed again. Aidan's hands stayed above the waist, one flat on Dylan's chest, the other at the nape of his neck.

"So this regular hook-up," Aidan mused. "Was she good?"

"Mmm-hmmm." He nipped at Aidan's bottom lip, his cock aching so bad he was surprised he could be this playful. Truth was, he wanted to rip this man's clothes off, rip his own clothes off, and stay in bed for three days straight.

Clearly Aidan wanted the same thing, because Dylan suddenly found himself being spun around. He braced his palms on the wall, swallowing a moan when he felt the hard length of Aidan's erection pressing against his ass.

A hot puff of breath tickled his neck as Aidan leaned in close. "That hook-up of yours…I wonder if her pussy was as tight as your ass will be."

With a chuckle, Dylan ducked away and reversed the position, getting *Aidan* against the wall and rubbing *his* aching erection all over the man's ass. "Funny, I was just wondering the same thing."

As his cock throbbed uncontrollably, Dylan caught Aidan by the waist and brought him back around. This kiss was all tongue, all domination, and they were both breathing hard when it ended.

Laughing, Aidan took a step back and smoothed his rumpled hair. "I should definitely go."

"Fuck yeah."

They grinned at each other.

"You wanna come by my place tomorrow night?" Aidan asked.

"Yep." He didn't even hesitate.

He was still grinning to himself as he let Aidan out and locked the door behind him, but the grin faded the moment he turned around and saw Claire standing in the shadows of the hallway.

Her wide amber eyes and the shocked O of her lips told him she'd witnessed most—if not all—of that very private, very intimate moment.

Between him and another man.

Shit.

As his stomach churned with uneasiness, Dylan waited for her to speak.

"I…" Her voice was hoarse, and she was staring at her feet now, avoiding his gaze. "I…"

He waited.

Claire lifted her head and met his eyes. "I won't say anything to Chris." And then she hurried away.

Dylan watched her go, feeling queasier by the second.

Shit.

When Miranda got home at two thirty in the morning and found Seth wide awake and smoking a cigarette in the backyard, she immediately knew something was wrong. He'd been cutting down this past month, so it was rare for him to have a smoke before bed anymore. Unless he was upset.

Which he clearly was now.

"Hey," she said.

He glanced over. "Hey."

Her forehead creased in concern. Closing the door, she stepped outside and sat in the chair opposite his. "What's going on?"

He didn't answer. The orange tip of his cigarette glowed as he inhaled.

"How was the carnival?"

No response.

"Okay, you're scaring me. What the fuck is going on, Seth?" The color drained from her face, propelling her to her feet. "Are the kids all right? I didn't check on them when I came in. Are—"

"They're fine. Sound asleep in their beds."

Miranda relaxed. Slightly. "Something's still wrong," she insisted. "Talk to me, babe."

His lips quirked at the endearment. Sort of like the way *rugrats* had turned into a term of affection, so had *babe*. She'd started saying it to taunt him, but it had kind of stuck.

The smile he offered faded fast, though. "I almost lost Sophie today," he said quietly.

Her stomach dropped. "What?"

"The little devil took off on her own. She wanted to see the ponies and refused to wait for us to finish up at the shooting game. I had my eye on her the entire time, except when I turned away for half a minute to help Jason with something. That's when she snuck off."

"Shit. It's not the first time she's done that," Miranda admitted. "She gets so impatient sometimes, which is weird because Jason is the one with all the jittery energy. Last time she got away from me in the mall, I threatened to make her wear one of those kiddie leashes. I guess the threat didn't work. Don't worry, I'll talk to her."

It took her a second to realize that Seth was gaping at her.

"That's it?" he demanded. "I told you that I lost your daughter and you're not pissed off at me?"

"But you didn't lose her. She's safe and sound in her bed. You said so yourself, you turned away for less than a minute."

"Exactly. I turned away from her."

"We can't be expected to have our eyes on our kids every second of the day. It's impossible. But we can expect our children to listen to us when we tell them not to run off after they'd been asked to stay put." She released another breath. "Like I said, I'll talk to Soph. Or we can talk to her together if you want, so she sees how upset you are that she disobeyed you."

"I can't do it," he said flatly.

Her stomach clenched. "You can't talk to her with me?"

"I can't do it. *This*."

"This?"

"Us."

Her entire body went rigid. Cold. "Because Sophie didn't listen to you and ran off?"

"Because I don't deserve you. I don't deserve them."

"Seth, that's just insane."

"No, it's not." He stabbed his cigarette out in the ashtray. "I was starting to let myself off the hook for Adam's death, and look what happened, Sophie almost gets abducted."

"She didn't almost get abduc—"

But he was past listening. "I'm not supposed to have this. Any of this." He waved his hand around the backyard. "My whole fucking life has been about atonement. I enlisted, I signed up for the most elite training there was, and now I spend my life helping people."

Bitterness hardened her tone. "You're not helping me or the twins by leaving us."

He stubbornly shook his head. "You'll be better off. I'm not meant to have any of this. Love, children, a family. I don't deserve it."

Agony seized her heart, bringing tears to her eyes. Lord, she didn't know what to say to him. Didn't know how to change his mind, how to show him how irrational he was being, how completely *wrong* he was.

But Seth didn't even give her a chance to formulate a response. He stood up, his shoulders stiffer than boards. "If I stay, I'll end up hurting you. So I have to go."

The tears spilled over. "I can't believe this."

"I love you, Miranda, but I don't deserve you, and I can't take the risk that one day I might end up hurting you or the twins."

He paused only to plant a soft kiss on her forehead, to gently touch her cheek with his calloused hand, and then he left the backyard.

A minute later, she heard the sound of a car engine rumbling to life. And then silence.

Chapter Twenty-Two

"Mom, wake up! Mom! Wake up, wake up, wake up! Mo-om!"

Miranda opened her eyes to find Sophie standing at the foot of the bed, bouncing around like a pogo stick. She still wore her pink cotton PJ's, her hair was mussed up from sleep and she was packing a scary amount of energy in that little body of hers.

"What is it?" Miranda asked sleepily.

"We hafta go dancing. Ginny called and said it's late and why aren't we there."

It took a moment to notice her phone in Sophie's hand.

Rubbing her tired eyes, she slid up into a sitting position. "You answered Mommy's phone?"

"Mmm-hmmm. 'Cause it was ringing and ringing and ringing—"

"I told her not to but she didn't listen." Jason barreled into the room in his Spiderman pajamas.

Glancing at the clock, Miranda realized that not only had she slept through the alarm, she'd overslept by *three hours*. It was ten o'clock. Holy shit. Her first lesson of the day started in a half hour.

She flew out of bed, ready to do the impossible by getting her and the kids out the door in ten minutes flat, but then she froze in the middle of the room, the heartbreaking events of last night rushing to the forefront of her brain.

Seth had broken up with her.

He'd actually broken up with her.

Suddenly the last thing she felt like doing today was *dancing*.

With a sigh, she lowered herself to the edge of the bed. "Actually, guys, I'm not feeling too well today. I think I'm going to call Ginny and tell her to cancel today's lessons. At least for my students."

Sophie's bottom lip dropped out. "But I wanna dance."

"But I have a game," Jason reminded her.

"You can still go. Coach Diaz is picking you up at noon for the game." Normally she brought Jason to the school with her and Sophie, and the coach picked him up from there, but she'd have to call and ask Diaz to come here instead.

As for her daughter, she offered a remorseful look. "Mommy's not feeling well at all. Neither of us will be dancing today, sweetie. But we can still have fun. We'll stay home and watch movies and then we'll go to the field and cheer for your brother."

Jason pumped his fist with excitement. "You *never* get to see a whole game! Will Sef come too?"

An arrow of sorrow pierced her heart. "I don't think so."

"Why not?"

"Will he take us for ice cream after, like last week?" Sophie asked.

"No, I don't think he'll do that either." Her throat closed up and she had to swallow several times before she could talk again. "Come sit with me, guys."

The twins bounded over, flopping down on either side of her. She looked from her daughter to her son, and let out a shaky breath. "Seth might not be coming around that much anymore." *If ever*, but she didn't say that.

"Why not?" Jason asked in confusion.

Sophie, on the other hand, didn't look confused at all. Her lip began to tremble. "Mommy?"

"What is it?" The tears clinging to Sophie's lashes triggered a rush of concern. "What's wrong, sweetie?"

"It's my fault Sef's not coming! I made him mad at the carnival 'cause I wanted to see the ponies and I ran away!" Sophie gulped for air. "And now he *hates* us again!"

"Oh, baby, he doesn't hate you. He *never* hated you. Seth told me all about what happened yesterday." She injected a stern note into her voice. "I'm not happy that you ran away from Seth, but I promise you, that's not what this is about."

"Yes it is," Sophie insisted.

"No, it isn't. I promise."

"Is it my fault?" Jason demanded.

A sigh slipped out. "Guys. Neither of you did *anything wrong.* Seth cares about you, he cares about you a lot. This is between your mom and Seth. It's a whole bunch of boring grown-up stuff that you don't need to worry about, understand?"

They nodded.

"I don't know what's going to happen, or when we'll see him again, but even if we don't, it doesn't matter. Want to know why?"

Both kids looked at her with curious eyes.

"Because we have each other." She kissed the top of Jason's head, then Sophie's. "We're the three musketeers, remember? The three amigos. The three stooges."

"The three little pigs!" Sophie piped up.

"The three zombies!" Jason chimed in.

Miranda chose not to point out that his contribution wasn't a real thing. Instead, she smiled and said, "So what's the magic word?"

"Three," the twins said in unison.

"Three," she confirmed. "And the three of us are going to be just fine."

Her kids beamed at her, proving that she'd succeeded in allaying their fears and convincing them everything was all right.

Too bad she couldn't convince herself.

"Put the fucking bottle down."

Seth cranked open one eye, glimpsed Dylan in the living room doorway, and promptly let his eyelid flutter closed. He'd been lying on the couch for the past hour, one cheek plastered on the cushion, one arm flung out, still holding the tequila bottle he'd been nursing all night.

"I'm serious. Drop the bottle."

Seth did the opposite. He tucked the bottle to his side and held it with the protective grip you'd use on a baby.

Footsteps thudded against the hardwood.

"You're really going to make me wrestle you for it? This is actually happening?"

"Fuck off," he mumbled, his voice rusty from lack of use. He didn't think he'd said a single word since he'd left Miranda's house last night. Jesus. And his breath reeked of booze.

"Give me the bottle, asshole."

"Go away."

The footsteps got closer. "Motherfucking fuck. I do not have time for this," he heard Dylan mutter.

And then chaos erupted. The bottle was yanked out of Seth's possession and suddenly he was no longer on the couch but sailing through the air. His ass landed on the floor with a heavy thump, head bouncing off the hardwood.

Pain shot through his temples, not just from the hit, but from the ridiculous amount of alcohol he'd been consuming since last night. His stomach roiled, nausea scampering up his throat, but he managed to choke it down before he hurled all over the place.

"That's it," Dylan said in disgust. "I'm calling Miranda. She can come and deal with this."

He tried to sit up and groaned when the room started to spin. "You can't call Miranda. I dumped her."

Silence.

And then, "Are you *insane?*"

He continued to struggle, but eventually staggered to his feet. "It's done. We're done. So let me get drunk in peace, okay?"

"No, not okay. Why the hell did you break up with her? That woman is—"

"Amazing? A goddess? The best thing that ever happened to me? Yeah, I know." He made it all the way to the door before his vision got all blurry again and he needed to regroup.

Dylan marched over, shaking his head in disbelief. "If you know all that, why would you end it?"

"Because I don't deserve her."

More silence.

"Did you cheat on her or something?"

"No."

"Then I don't get it. I mean, yeah, you're a total dick sometimes, and your smart mouth has gotten us all into trouble, but you're not a horrible monster or anything." Dylan shrugged. "Miranda's lucky to have you."

"Aw, isn't that sweet of you to say," Seth said snidely. He took a breath and made it out of the living room. "Leave me alone, man. I really don't want company right now."

He managed to walk in a straight line all the way to his bedroom. As he collapsed on his bed, he heard Dylan's low murmur from the hallway and made out some of what his roommate was saying. "Can't come over tonight…I know…fuck, yeah, me too. But things are…weird over here. Yeah, I'll…later maybe…"

"Hey, Dylan! Don't cancel your plans on my account!" Seth yelled at the closed door.

"Hey, Seth! Go fuck yourself!"

Footsteps receded, and then the house grew blessedly quiet. Unfortunately, the silence offered too many opportunities for thinking, and before he knew it, his thoughts were running rampant again and doubts were resurfacing.

He'd done the right thing, hadn't he? Cutting Miranda loose. Ending things now, before they got even more serious, before the twins started looking to him as a father figure. He'd let Adam down all those years ago, but he refused to let Miranda and those kids down. Better to hurt them a tiny bit by walking away now than hurt them even worse in the future. Which he would. He'd eventually hurt them. He knew it.

Christ, he was such a screwup. It was a miracle his mom hadn't disowned him years ago.

At the thought of his mother, his chest clenched. How could that woman even love him after what he'd done? She was a fucking saint. And he'd never even apologized to her, he realized. He'd never once told her he was sorry for what he did to Adam.

He fumbled for the phone on the bed table, fighting another wave of vertigo. He had to squint to find his mom's number on his contact list, but eventually he managed to click on her name.

Missy answered on the fifth ring, sounding harried but delighted. "Hey, sugar pie! I was hoping you'd call."

"You at the theater?" He made an effort not to slur his words.

"Yeah, but we're in between performances so I have some time. I want to know all about this new relationship of yours." She sounded incredulous. "I couldn't believe it when Miranda told me you were dating. And you, of course, haven't given me any details! But I've been good, haven't I? I've been waiting for you to call *me* to talk about it. And you say I *pry* too much. Proved you wrong, huh? Anyway, I want to know all—"

"I'm sorry I got Adam killed."

There was a shocked gasp, followed by total silence.

It lasted so long that he had to check the display to make sure his phone hadn't dropped the call.

"Mom?" he said gruffly. "Did you hear what I said?"

"I heard." Her voice was barely a whisper.

"Okay. Well, that's it. That's why I called. I'll talk to you la—"

"Don't you dare hang up on me!" Missy roared.

"Oh. All right. Are we gonna talk about it then?"

"Are you fucking kidding me, Seth? You just apologized to me for *killing your brother*, and you think we're not going to talk about it?"

He'd never heard his mother sound so livid. Her breathy little-girl voice was sharper than the blade of his Bowie knife, each word oozing with red-hot fury.

He gulped. "I figured you wouldn't want to. You never want to talk about him."

A heavy breath echoed in his ear. "You're right. Dammit. You're right, I never talk about him."

"'S'okay. I get why you can't. It's hard for me too." A lump rose in his throat. "Look, I know you forgave me for what happened, but I needed to say it out loud. Just once. I needed to apologize because I never apologized all those years ago. I never told you how sorry I was for—"

"Shut up, Seth."

He frowned, annoyed by the interruption. "I'm not finished. I need you to know that I accept full responsibility for—"

"Shut the fuck up, Seth!"

His temples began to throb, the room doing another dizzying spin.

"You are *not* to blame for what happened to your brother," his mother announced. "It is *not* your fault that sick son of a bitch got his hands on Adam."

Shock spiraled through him. "But—"

"But nothing." Another gasp came over the line. "Oh Jesus. Oh Seth. Have you been blaming yourself all these years?" It sounded like she was crying. "Oh baby, it wasn't your fault."

"But...but you..."

"I made you believe that it was?" Horror reverberated from her voice.

"No, but...you couldn't look at me after it happened. And at the funeral, you wouldn't meet my eyes when I..." He trailed off, confused.

"I couldn't look at you because I didn't want to see the accusation in your eyes."

"What are you talking about?"

"It wasn't your fault Adam died. It was *mine*."

Her declaration left him speechless.

"I'm the one who left the two of you home alone instead of shelling out ten bucks for a fucking babysitter. I shouldn't have put you in charge, for God's sake. You were too young." She was crying openly now, each sob bringing a painful squeeze to his heart. "I felt so guilty afterwards. I could barely look at you without thinking of your brother, without thinking about what a terrible mother I was. I'm going to go to my grave knowing I'm the reason my son is dead, Seth."

He was absolutely dumbfounded. He hadn't known what to expect from this phone call—he wouldn't have even called if it weren't for the tequila buzzing in his veins—but hearing his mom take the blame for the one thing he'd been agonizing over for the past nineteen years? Never would've guessed it.

"It's not your fault," he told her. "How could you think it was your fault? *I* was supposed to be watching him."

"*I* was supposed to be watching both of you."

"I couldn't catch up to the truck."

"I shouldn't have left my kids home alone."

They both went quiet for a moment.

A wave of sadness washed over him as he was struck by a very depressing thought. "We've each suffered with this for almost two decades. And we suffered alone. Jesus, Mom, why didn't we talk about this before now?"

"Because you never called me up drunk before and raised the subject." She sniffled. "And vice versa."

"We shouldn't have to be drunk to talk about Adam."

"No, we shouldn't." His mom sighed. "You know, baby, I'm starting to think we've suffered enough. Maybe it's time we..."

"Time we did what?" he asked when she didn't continue.

"Time we accepted that a twisted man by the name of Jarvis Henderson was responsible for Adam's death."

His eyes began to sting. "Yeah, maybe you're right. Maybe it is time for that."

"Seth...I love you. You know that, right?"

"I love you too, Mom."

A muffled female voice interrupted. "Missy! We need you back here!"

"Five minutes," his mom called.

"Go," he said gruffly. "They need you. We can finish this conversation tomorrow."

"You sure?"

"Yeah. Go. I love you."

"Love you too, sugar pie."

The phone fell out of his hand, which began to shake again. He couldn't believe his mother had blamed *herself* all these years.

He couldn't believe they'd both been too guilt-ridden and grief-stricken to have this conversation a long time ago.

The phone call was like an injection of potassium to his bloodstream—he didn't feel drunk anymore. His head cleared, stomach settled, vision stabilized. He was desperate to hear Miranda's voice, but he couldn't bring himself to call her. He'd broken up with her, for chrissake. And suddenly all his prior reasoning, all the things he'd said to her, sounded like nothing but a bunch of crappy excuses.

When his phone buzzed, he assumed it was his mother calling him back, so he answered without checking the screen.

"Hey, I told you, we can talk tomo—"

"Sef?" a small voice asked.

He stiffened. "Sophie? Is that you?"

"Uh-huh."

"What's going on? Where's your mom?"

"She fell and now there's lots of bruises."

"*What?*"

Panic slammed into him. He dove off the bed and hurried to the door, ignoring the wave of wooziness that hit him. Shit, so much for not being drunk anymore. He swayed on his feet, struggling to listen to what Sophie was saying.

"And there's blue bruises and green ones and—"

"Put your mom on the phone!" he ordered.

"I can't. She's sleeping."

Sleeping…or unconscious? Oh shit. An icy rush of fear made him feel even more light-headed.

Should he call 911? Sophie's tone was too damn cheerful—he couldn't imagine her sounding like that if Miranda was passed out at the bottom of the stairs, every limb in her body broken.

But he couldn't ignore it either.

"I'm on my way," he told Miranda's daughter. "I want you to—"

She hung up.

"Damn it!" he roared.

In the hallway, he collided with Dylan, who took one look at his face and said, "What's wrong?"

"I don't know." The floor beneath his feet dipped and he suddenly felt helpless. "Sophie called. Miranda may or may not have fallen. She might be hurt or she might be sleeping or who the fuck knows. I need to get over there right now."

He bounded into the kitchen to look for his keys.

"There's no way in hell I'm letting you get behind the wheel of a car," Dylan spoke up from the doorway.

Frustration seized his throat. "Don't even think about stopping me."

His roommate sauntered over and snatched the keys from his hands. "I wouldn't dream of it. But I'm driving."

MIRANDA OPENED THE DOOR TO FIND SETH AND DYLAN STANDING there. And while Dylan looked handsome in a polo shirt and khaki cargo pants, Seth looked a little worse for wear. His hair was sticking up in all directions and his wifebeater was wrinkled. Not to mention his unshaven face and wild gray eyes.

And yet her heart still skipped a beat at the sight of him.

"Hey, guys," she said warily. "What's going—"

She didn't have time to finish because Seth pulled her into his arms and hugged her so tightly she couldn't draw a breath. Gasping for air, she batted at his powerful shoulders and tried to wiggle away.

He instantly released her, relief radiating from his body. "Thank God. I thought…"

She sucked some oxygen into her lungs before frowning at him. "You thought what?"

"And that's my cue to leave," Dylan announced. "I'm taking the Jeep, bro."

Seth glanced at his friend. "But—"

"You can call a cab to take you home. Though I don't imagine you'll be coming home tonight. The groveling might take all night."

Her frown deepened when she noticed the twinkle in Dylan's eyes. What the hell was he talking about?

His green-eyed gaze focused on her. "I'm glad to see you're not bruised and/or unconscious. Sorry to ring the doorbell and run, but I've got somewhere to be, and trust me, it's been a long time coming."

Miranda had never been more confused in her entire life. She watched Dylan hurry off with a spring to his step, then stared at Seth, who seemed to be…swaying?

"Are you drunk?"

"A little," he said sheepishly.

"And you decided to come over because…?" Maybe her tone was sharper than necessary, but this man had dumped her, for Pete's sake. And now he was on her doorstep, drunk?

"Because Sophie called and said you fell."

Miranda's jaw dropped. *"What?"*

Without waiting for an answer, she scurried inside and yelled for her daughter, who didn't come running.

She marched into the living room, where she found both her kids sitting on the couch, wearing identical sheepish expressions.

She addressed her daughter first. "You used my phone to call Seth?"

Sophie at least had the courtesy to look guilty. "Yes."

She turned to Jason. "And you were in on this?"

That got her another guilty *yes*.

"Ah, don't be mad at them."

She spun around to see Seth leaning against the doorframe. After a second, he stumbled into the room and collapsed on the armchair as if he could no longer support his own weight.

Lord, how much had he had to drink?

"They were just trying to get us back together." Seth glanced at the twins. "Weren't you?"

Sophie nodded.

Miranda released a sigh and joined them on the couch. "It doesn't matter what your intentions were. You can't do things like this, guys. You can't take Mommy's phone and call someone and tell them there's been an emergency. Remember the story I told you about the boy who cried wolf? Remember what happened to the boy?" She shook her head. "I'm very disappointed in you two."

Jason looked stricken. "I'm sorry, Mom. But we did it 'cause you were wrong."

She raised her eyebrows. "Excuse me?"

"You were wrong," Sophie piped up.

"Because it's four," Jason explained.

She was utterly lost. "What are you talking about?"

"The magic number isn't three. It's *four*." Jason's expression conveyed impatience. "You and me and Sophie and Sef."

He pointed at Seth, as if Miranda needed the visual reference.

Her heart jammed in her throat. She drew in a breath, battling the rising wave of sorrow. "Guys, I already told you, Seth is—"

"An idiot," Seth finished.

Her head swiveled in his direction.

"An idiot," he repeated. "I should've never walked out on you. I was just so shaken up after what happened at the carnival and—"

Sophie jumped off the couch and threw herself into his lap. "It was my fault! I shouldna run away and now you don't wanna be with us anymore."

His muscular arms wrapped around the distraught girl, and Miranda's heart cracked in two as she watched him stroke her daughter's hair.

"You shouldn't have run away," he agreed. His eyes met Miranda's over Sophie's head. "But I shouldn't have run away either."

She forced herself to ignore the little pang of hope. It didn't matter what he said. He'd left. He'd ended it. He'd proven that she couldn't count on him.

"Guys, would you mind if I spoke to your mother alone?" Seth asked gruffly.

Sophie slid off his lap and hurried over to her brother, practically dragging him away from the couch. "C'mon, Jase."

Miranda had to smile as she watched them run off, but the smile faded when Seth rose from the armchair and advanced on her.

"I screwed up," he said in a voice thick with remorse. "I let my fears drive me away. But I'm not afraid anymore."

She refused to meet his eyes. "Really."

"I spoke to my mom today."

"Yeah, about what?" She kept her voice casual.

"About Adam." He shrugged. "And we both realized something."

Curiosity had her turning her head. She needed to see his expression, and what she found surprised her. He looked…peaceful.

"What did you realize?"

"That we'd suffered enough. Adam's gone. Mistakes were made, by me, by my mom, but there's really only one person to blame in the end—and that's the person who took Adam's life." Seth swallowed. "But all that isn't important right now. *You're* what's important. I love you, Miranda, and I'm sorry for freaking out last night."

"You left." She bit the inside of her cheek. "The only thing I've ever wanted is someone who will be there for me. Someone I could count on. And you left."

"I screwed up," he said again. "But I promise you, I will never leave again. You can count on me to be there for you."

"Why should I believe you?" she whispered.

"Because you love me. Because you have faith in me. Because you can look in my eyes and see that I mean every word I'm saying."

There was no mistaking the sincerity glimmering in those silver-gray depths. She felt her resolve crumbling with his every word, and when he leaned in to brush his lips over hers, she was a goner. Seth's lips were warm and firm. He tasted like alcohol, but when she pulled back to search his face, he looked stone-cold sober.

"I love you." His husky voice tickled her senses. "Please give us another chance."

"Okay," she murmured.

"Okay?"

She nodded.

In the blink of an eye, he was kissing her again, so deeply that her lungs screamed for oxygen and her brain became foggy. By the time his tongue retreated and his lips left hers, she'd forgotten her own name.

"So…" She gulped. "What now?"

"Now…" He tilted his head thoughtfully. "Now we hang out with the rugrats for a bit, and then we put them to bed."

"And then what?"

"And then I take you to your bedroom, help you out of those pesky clothes, and…" He trailed off suggestively.

"And make sweet, sweet love to me all night long?" she filled in.

"Definitely." He brought his lips to her ear, his mocking voice sending a shiver through her. "But first I'm going to fuck you."

Miranda couldn't have suppressed her laughter even if she'd tried. Here he was, the bad boy she'd tried so desperately not to fall in love with. Rough and crude and dangerous, with a smart tongue and a chip on his shoulder and a whole lot of swagger that he didn't bother apologizing for.

And what do you know—he was exactly what she'd needed.

The End

About the Author

A *New York Times*, *USA Today* and *Wall Street Journal* bestselling author, Elle Kennedy grew up in the suburbs of Toronto, Ontario, and holds a BA in English from York University. From an early age, she knew she wanted to be a writer and actively began pursuing that dream when she was a teenager. She loves strong heroines and sexy alpha heroes, and just enough heat and danger to keep things interesting!

Elle loves to hear from her readers. Visit her website www.ellekennedy.com or sign up for her newsletter to receive updates about upcoming books and exclusive excerpts. You can also find her on Facebook (ElleKennedyAuthor), Twitter (@ElleKennedy), or Instagram (@ElleKennedy33).

Are you ready for the hottest installment yet? Check out Dylan's story, **Hotter Than Ever**, *the next book in the* Out of Uniform *series.*

CLAIRE TURNED TO DYLAN IN CONFUSION AS THEIR TAXI CAME TO A stop in front of a modern high-rise with an endless amount of windows sparkling in the afternoon sunlight.

"Where are we?" she asked suspiciously. "I thought we were going to your place."

He leaned forward and handed the driver some cash, then reached for the door handle. "This is my place."

"Since when?" Claire wrinkled her brow. The last time she and Chris came to visit, Dylan had been living in a house in Coronado with his teammate Seth, a scruffy badass SEAL with a chip on his shoulder.

"Since about a month ago," he answered.

They got out of the cab and Dylan rounded the vehicle to grab their bags from the trunk. It was just past three o'clock, and the sun was so bright Claire squinted to avoid being blinded and wished she hadn't shoved her sunglasses into her carry-on. She couldn't believe how warm it was, especially for December. On the plus side, she happened to be wearing a sundress so thin she may as well be naked.

On the minus side, the barely-there dress had resulted in an hour-and-a-half-long helicopter ride in which Dylan's green eyes had been glued to her breasts.

Which was perplexing, because...he was gay, right? She still couldn't figure it out, but the memory of Dylan's tongue in another man's mouth was completely incongruous to the way he'd been ogling her on the chopper.

And speaking of perplexing, what the hell had compelled her to come back to San Diego with this man? Clearly she'd suffered a mental breakdown after hearing that Chris was leaving town, but by the time common sense decided to make a return, they'd already been landing on the helipad of San Diego's Coast Guard base.

After the taxi sped off, Dylan lugged their bags toward the glass doors at the building's entrance. He didn't turn around to see if she was following, but he did call out a mocking, "You coming?"

She trailed after him, still mystified by their surroundings. How on earth could Dylan afford to live here? This building was way too luxurious for a SEAL's salary. They stepped into a beautiful lobby with dark oak furniture, cream-colored carpeting, and tasteful artwork on the walls, and were immediately greeted by the uniformed security guard sitting behind a spacious counter.

Dylan smiled and nodded at the bulky African-American man, then introduced Claire as his houseguest. The fact that the guard wrote down her name told Claire that security was taken seriously in this building.

Her flip-flops snapped against the lush carpet as she and Dylan headed toward a corridor to their left. She winced at each snap snap, feeling way too underdressed. It didn't help that Dylan still wore the crisp black suit he'd donned for the wedding, which made her skimpy dress and plastic shoes look even more out of place.

"This place is so fancy," she whispered. "How can you afford to live here alone?"

"Always so concerned with finances, aren't you?"

The contempt in his voice raised her hackles. "What's that supposed to mean?"

Dylan pressed the elevator button. "Nothing at all," he said vaguely. "And to answer your question, I don't live alone."

Ding. The elevator opened with a chime and he strode into it without elaborating.

Claire hurried in after him. "You're still living with Seth then?"

"Nope."

His response was casual, but the shuttered look on his handsome face answered her next question. He lived with the dark-haired man. The man he'd been kissing that night.

Heat flooded her cheeks, and to her extreme embarrassment, she experienced a spark of arousal. Damn it! She wasn't allowed to get turned on by it anymore. She'd been trying so hard to stifle that reaction these last couple of months.

But now that the proverbial door had more or less been opened, she found herself walking right through it.

"So. Um." She swallowed. "Are we ever going to talk about what happened back in September?"

Dylan shrugged. "There's nothing to talk about. You walked in on a private moment between me and Aidan. No biggie."

"Aidan? Is that his name?"

"Yep."

The elevator continued its ascent, the numbers on the electronic panel rapidly flashing before stopping on the number 15.

The doors dinged open.

"Listen," Dylan said as they stepped into a wide hallway, "I really do appreciate that you didn't say anything to Chris or my mom about what you saw that night."

She arched a brow. "And yet you insist the whole thing was no biggie."

"It's not. To me, anyway." His eyes went somber. "But it would be a big deal for them. Chris, especially. My brother is very…conservative."

"I know." Claire swallowed again. "My best friend is a lesbian, and, well, Chris has never been openly negative, but I don't think he likes her very much."

"Yeah, he's a bit of a homophobe," Dylan admitted in a pained voice. "There's a whole thing behind it, but I don't want to get into that. Just know I'm grateful that you kept quiet."

They lingered in the middle of the hall, eyeing each other carefully. Claire realized this was the first time in a year and a half that she and Dylan had had a conversation that lacked any hostile undertones.

Might be pushing her luck, but she figured she should capitalize on the cease-fire. "So you and Aidan…you're…together?" she asked curiously.

He sighed. "It's complicated."

She could only imagine. Dylan didn't just have his family's prejudice to worry about—he was also a navy officer, and no matter how progressive the military claimed to be these days, Claire knew his sexual orientation would probably never be fully accepted. And who knew what circumstances the dark-haired stranger—Aidan, she amended—had to contend with.

Sympathy tugged at her heart, an emotion she didn't normally feel in Dylan's presence. Usually she couldn't look past his arrogant, selfish exterior, but she had to admit, he'd been pretty sweet today. Whisking her out of the country club, bringing her home with him so she could lick her wounds in peace. She hadn't asked him to do any of that, and she still couldn't figure out why he hadn't sided with his brother in all this.

"Anyway, my mom and Chris know that Aidan is my roommate, but not that—"

"—you share a room," she finished wryly.

Dylan shrugged again. "Actually, we don't."

She furrowed her brows. "Why not?"

"Like I said, it's complicated."

A hundred more questions bit at her tongue, but he didn't give her the chance to voice them. He was walking off again, leaving her to stare at his retreating back—and his butt. Because really, she couldn't not stare at his butt, so taut and delicious in those snug trousers. And his body was so damn big he made her feel miniature in comparison. Broad shoulders, arms that rippled with power, long legs, a lean yet muscular torso, and of course, that amazing butt.

No doubt about it, Dylan Wade was sexy. And he banked on that sexiness, using it to get whatever he wanted—well, at least according to Chris.

Then again, Chris's credibility was on shaky ground considering he was on his way to Aruba to cash in on the honeymoon her parents had paid for.

Choking down the bitterness coating her throat, Claire followed Dylan to a door at the very end of the hall, then waited as he pulled out a set of keys and stuck one in the lock.

A moment later, they walked into the apartment, Claire feeling slightly apprehensive as she examined the surprisingly large front hall. Actually, nothing surprising about it. Of course the apartments in this fancy-pants building would be huge.

Since Dylan kicked off his shoes, she did too, and beautiful dark hardwood spanned beneath her bare feet as they ventured deeper into the apartment. The front hall widened and spilled into an enormous open-concept space with floor-to-ceiling windows that provided a view of the city skyline.

"Wow," she blurted out. "This place is incredible."

"Yeah, it's pretty sweet." Dylan dropped her suitcases and his small black duffel on the floor, then swept an arm out and gave her a quick verbal tour. "Living room, dining room. Kitchen's over there, and the bedrooms are down that hall."

Claire's gaze took everything in—the masculine furnishings in the living room and heavy-duty entertainment system, the sleek electric fireplace, the French doors leading out to a sprawling stone terrace. She shifted her gaze and studied the low wall that separated the living and dining area from a big, modern kitchen with gleaming stainless-steel appliances and a black granite counter.

And just like Dylan's old place, this one was also neat as a pin, which only supported her belief that military men were the cleanest on the planet.

She opened her mouth to rave about the apartment a bit more, but the sound of footsteps interrupted. Claire turned her head in time to see Dylan's roommate step out of the corridor.

A pair of unbelievably sexy dimples appeared in his cheeks as he swept his dark eyes over the new arrivals. "Fastest wedding ever, huh?"

Claire was at a loss for words over his sheer hotness, and far too fascinated by the man walking toward them. She'd only caught shadowy glimpses of him back in September, and now she was kind of grateful for that, because if she'd known what this man looked like?

He would have haunted her fantasies.